THE SILENCE
OF THE CHOIR

ALSO BY

MOHAMED MBOUGAR SARR

Brotherhood

Mohamed Mbougar Sarr

THE SILENCE
OF THE CHOIR

*Translated from the French
by Alison Anderson*

Europa
editions

Europa Editions
27 Union Square West, Suite 302
New York NY 10003
www.europaeditions.com
info@europaeditions.com

Translation by Alison Anderson
Original title: *Silence du chœur*
Translation copyright 2024 by Europa Editions

Library of Congress Cataloging in Publication Data is available
ISBN 979-8-88966-020-0

Sarr, Mohamed Mbougar
The Silence of the Choir

Cover design by Ginevra Rapisardi

Cover photo © Lev Fazio

Prepress by Grafica Punto Print – Rome

Printed in the USA

CONTENTS

I would like to thank the Centre National du Livre, which supported me in the writing of this novel by awarding me a creative writing grant in 2016.

M. M. S.

For the great Men: Ali, Bandiougou, Séni, and Yves

Nulli est certa domus, lucis habitamus opacis.
"None hath a fixed dwelling; we live in the shady woodlands."

—Virgil, *The Aeneid*, Book 6
Translation J.H. Mackail

THE SILENCE
OF THE CHOIR

He had just woken from a state that was neither sleep nor fainting, nor even reverie; he was under the impression, rather, of something empty, like a great absence, so vague he could find no words to describe it. He tried hard, several times over, to concentrate, to reach a place of recall, but all his efforts were borne away on the huge black lake that his memory had become. He sat up, saw only then that he was naked, and had no idea what he'd done with his clothes. He ventured another step into his memory in search of the beginning of an answer. Like those dreams that gradually fade as one tries to seize them on waking, his memories slid further away on the dark surface. He gave up. He sat up straight and looked more closely at his surroundings. He was in a little thicket, among tall trees whose foliage formed a broad canopy above his head. A deep silence reigned, its density palpable. He thought that perhaps he was dreaming after all, but no sooner had this thought occurred to him than he realized how absurd it was: he knew, with such intuitive certainty that it required no proof, that he was not dreaming. No dream, even the oddest, could seem so devoid of reality; only reality knew how to be so strange.

He was about to stand up when a voice suddenly began to resonate inside him. He couldn't actually hear it: he was remembering. Discouraged by his previous attempts, he hadn't tried to dive back into his memory. But the voice was there. It was a woman's voice. "You will wake up, crazed and alone: that is the condition of the last man, and the first. You are the end of one story, and the opening of the one to come. The epilogue for one, the prologue for the other. Now it's up to you to speak. I have passed everything on to you."

That's what the voice said. When it fell silent, the man felt something very strange happen in his mind. A profusion of precise memories re-inhabited him: sentences, images, faces, sounds assailed him and flooded back en masse, so many that his memory, completely barred to him only a few seconds earlier, soon opened onto a familiar past.

He left the little scene at the heart of the thicket. His nakedness did not bother him: crazed and alone, he no longer owed anything to others, neither decency nor modesty; no, he owed them nothing now, except this tale the voice had bequeathed him, and of which he was the final guardian.

THE LONG ARRIVAL

The seventy-two men were still trying to sleep, having arrived in the little town only a few hours earlier. They needed to sleep. And nothing, neither their fear nor the thin strip of light that was beginning to relieve the gloom in the warehouse that served as their shelter could deter them from that desire: to go back to sleep. By their side since the previous night, Jogoy now watched as they struggled with their obsession, but he knew their effort would prove futile because, for the time being, no true rest was possible. What most of these men really needed wasn't sleep itself, but only the mental and psychological disposition of sleep: the idea that they could abandon themselves to sleep without fear.

Jogoy gave a sigh and rubbed his eyes. His body, too, had known the long assault of insomnia. The first pricklings of deep fatigue ran down his neck like a colony of ants hard at work. A dog barked somewhere nearby, and it was like the sudden clangor of an alarm clock in the ears of the sleeping town, which now began to stretch and yawn and crack its cobblestones, while all the faint sounds of a country dawn besieged it. Dr. Pessoto walked into the warehouse just then with his young assistants, Gianni and Lucia, right behind him. But unlike them, Salvatore Pessoto was not wearing a lab coat. He had long salt-and-pepper hair that he tied back in a classy ponytail, in honor of his idol, "the greatest football player of all time: *il Divin Codino, l'ultimo fuoriclasse*, Roberto Baggio." He headed over to Jogoy as soon as he saw him. The two men had become acquainted thanks to football: the first time they'd met, Jogoy had been wearing the jersey of their favorite team, Juventus, from Turin. That had been enough to place the seal on one of those great friendships that are founded and consolidated by shared passions.

"Ciao, Leone, how'd the night go?" the doctor said, shaking his friend's hand.

"Restless sleep, Totò," Jogoy replied. "Some of them woke up screaming."

"Nightmares. As usual. That shouldn't surprise you anymore."

"No, it doesn't surprise me anymore."

They fell silent. A loud noise of snoring, or something that wanted to sound like snoring, rose in the room but immediately burst and fell, a bird stripped of its wings in full flight.

"Did you watch the match last night?" Dr. Pessoto continued, his eyes still on the frustrated sleepers. "No? Roma-Inter, 2-2. That should make Milan happy. But just wait, they'll see! Just as soon as Juventus makes it back into Serie A."

The two friends had been trying to speak quietly, on the verge of a whisper, although the doctor got somewhat carried away talking about Juventus. But both of them knew that their words, even muted, had nevertheless reached the anxious ears of the men lying before them. The men might not be moving, but every one of them was thinking that if he opened his eyes before his comrades did, it would be proof that he was in less pain than they were.

"I hope their situation will get sorted out quickly," said Salvatore Pessoto.

"Juventus's situation?"

"No, theirs," said the doctor, tilting his nose at the sleeping men.

"Oh, theirs . . . you know how it goes."

Pessoto didn't answer. Jogoy was right: he knew only too

well how it went. Basically, his hope was rhetorical, the way
a question can be. And he knew what it meant, and had only
spoken as a matter of form, to say something vaguely optimis-
tic, something, therefore, that didn't represent reality, but was
a mask behind which his mind sought to hide that reality, so he
wouldn't have to face it head-on. But on closer inspection, however, it wasn't so much reality as his own face that Pessoto was
covering with a mask—a strange mask, an opaque mask with
no holes for the eyes—and it was of less importance to hide
behind it than to disappear altogether while murmuring, "It's
not that I want to avoid recognition; I just want to avoid recognizing anything in this world. I don't want to see any of it."
Pessoto had been deliberately trying to stab himself in the eyes,
so as not to see what was stirring pitifully there before him: a
portrait of human misery. But he had failed. He could still see,
he could still hear. Jogoy's words were echoing in his mind, but
they had departed from his friend's kindly, familiar voice, had
been stripped of that voice to move on to another voice that
was toneless and anonymous, and which gave the words a more
implacable weight and resonance: "You know how it goes."

"Let's hope, rather, that there will be ten good players among
the lot," said Jogoy, tearing the doctor away from the terrible
toneless voice. "Our team has to win this year. I feel like it's our
year."

"We'll see," said Pessoto. "Right, well, Leone, you should
get some rest before the medical checkups. We'll need you then.
The women from the association will join us shortly. Gianni,
Lucia, and I are going to check a few little things before they
get here. Ciao."

He headed down an aisle between two rows of bunks. His
assistants, who'd been standing to one side, stepped in behind
him after greeting Jogoy, each in their own fashion: lovely Lucia
gave him a big smile accompanied by a little wave of her hand,
and Gianni, more timid, gave a brief nod of his head. Jogoy

looked one last time at those recumbent figures as the little medical team moved among them, as if through a labyrinth of tombs. Then he left the warehouse.

A harsh light dazzled him the moment he stepped outside. A meticulous barber, the sun was grazing its glinting blade against the mountaintops. A few housewives with the constitution of caryatids filled the window frames, where they were hanging out their laundry, humming a folk song or the latest romantic ballad by the now-graying sex symbol of their youth. The men, their voices ringing loudly, were on their way to La Tavola di Luca, the best-known café in town, and the only one that opened early. A gentle breeze blew through the streets with the tragic grace of things that don't last; in an hour or less, it would be vanquished until evening by the crushing heat of summer. Jogoy took one of the little cobblestoned streets that wound toward the historic center like so many veins toward a great heart. In the beating of this heart, regular and sonorous, he thought he could hear an echo from the past. It was the voice of this beautiful ancient place. Sicily. Altino lay inland, in the middle of a landscape that looked as if it might have sprung from a verse in the *Georgics*. The little town had been built not far from a major archaeological site that was still yielding up the traces of all the civilizations that had passed through there. Altino's little museum was the pride of its inhabitants. Its showpiece was a statue of Athena from the third century B.C., which was held to be the allegory of the town's memory. Buried in the earth of Altino for centuries, the statue was proof of a long history.

Jogoy loved the town; however, what he liked best was to look at the surrounding landscape of hills. He paused for a moment on the Villa, a vista point, according to the inhabitants of Altino, that offered the finest views in all the region. It was true: the panorama spoke its own language—beauty—and the elation of heights was its only possible grammar. On the horizon, the thin blade of a large imaginary dagger sketched the fine lines of mountain crests, like laundry lines stretched above the valleys, waiting to be hung with groves of olive, pine, beech, and orange trees and assorted prickly pears, which the sun of Sicily drenched daily to their roots. Villages and hamlets spilled down the hillsides, quivering in the light. And at the very limit of what could be seen, emerging from the morning mist like Aphrodite from the foam of the sea, Jogoy saw her, half-naked, wrapped in folds of rumpled clouds: Mount Etna. The volcano, a female figure for Sicilians, was exhaling a fine white vapor.

"*A mossa*," murmured Jogoy. "How beautiful," in Serer, his native language. He set off again, and before long he reached the center of town, crossed the large piazza, past La Tavola di Luca where twenty or more men were drinking their coffee, commenting half-heartedly in a falsely disdainful manner on the morning gossip, straight out of the oven, or the slightly stale and reheated stories (the best kind, actually) from the day before. The soul of an entire nation could be found there. Jogoy gazed at the place for a moment, then continued on his way to his rented room.

Vera and Vincenzo, his landlords, were still sleeping. Jogoy knew that after a night spent in their art studio on the top floor, they wouldn't be up before early afternoon. A few days ago, they'd informed him that they were about to begin a new cycle of work. They were painters. Jogoy went into his little room. Its only furniture was a tall wardrobe, a bed that was too short for him, and an old writing desk that Vera had inherited from a great-great-aunt who'd been as senile as she was racist. Fearful of invoking the ghost of that terrible ancestor, Jogoy almost never put anything on the desk. The only thing that resided there now, firmly closed, was an old black notebook in which he'd started telling his story, but he hadn't written a single word for a long time. This frustrated him. Moreover, an urge to fling the notebook from the top of the Villa was becoming more and more insistent.

To avoid the diary, his gaze landed on the poster above the desk, where the emblem of Sicily, the *Trinacria*, stood challenging him. It depicted the head of a Gorgon, its serpent hair swarming about it, surrounded by a halo of wheat ears and three human legs. Jogoy could just about bear the sight of it, preferred it to that of the notebook. The effect of his sleepless night suddenly crushed him like the repeated blows of a pestle. On his neck, the colony of ants began to bite. The vipers stirred in Medusa's tangle of black hair, threatening to spring out of the poster and into his face; the torn-off legs spun more and more quickly, like a propeller of flesh gone mad; Medusa's gaze yawned like an abyss before him, and Jogoy fell into it as heavily as a boulder. He collapsed on the bed and felt ashamed for falling asleep so easily when he'd spent the night watching over men for whom sleep was impossible. This impression of betraying their brotherhood of insomniacs did not leave him, even in his deepest sleep.

I don't know how those two find the strength to stay in there."

Dr. Pessoto had rushed outside as soon as he and his assistants had finished their rounds. The thought of waiting inside, facing the seventy-two men, was unbearable. He knew the protocol of these waking scenes by heart, and he always thought he could hear the opening strains of the music to a predictable drama in two acts. First, the ragazzi would open their eyes and lie there, incredulous, somewhat skeptical: hope had played them so often, tossing them around like vulgar dice on a table of misfortune, that they suspected every one of hope's manifestations was loaded. Then, in the second act, after these long minutes of incredulity, they would realize that all of this was indeed real. Suspicion would vanish; a great clamor of cheer would arise and remain suspended in the air. Despite God's efforts at scrambling them, several languages would meet in the warehouse, transforming it into a strange tower of Babel that actually reached the sky. Hope would be reborn, alas. That's how it always went. Pessoto knew it well.

He felt more and more like a hostage caught up in a situation for which he was not personally responsible, but which he was obliged to assume, day after day, on his own. Despite all the generous souls—and he was one of them—who labored *together* to make things less dramatic or, at least, to make them seem less dramatic, Pessoto was no fool: what all these people of goodwill shared was not the sentiment that their collective effort was gradually bearing fruit, but a desperate solitude faced with a task that was equally desperate.

He waited outside for breakfast to come, taking deep breaths, relishing the last of the cool, early-morning air. First cigarette. The morning would be long; he couldn't expect to get home before mid-afternoon at the earliest. When he had left at dawn, he'd told Angela he would most certainly not be back for lunch. His wife's face clouded over, but she didn't refuse the kiss he placed on her forehead before leaving. She was finding it harder and harder to accept the fact that he was so busy, and on several occasions she'd asked him to be there more often for their two children, Riccardo and Erica.

He untied his ponytail and ran his fingers through his loose hair. A few minutes later, somewhat blinded by the sun, he saw several figures coming up the street that led to the warehouse. It wasn't until they were a few yards away that he recognized Sabrina, Sister Maria, and Carla. They were walking ahead of a group of four men, each of whom was pushing a little cart.

"The Three Graces . . . *Buongiorno*! You're right on time; I was getting hungry," Pessoto said slowly.

"Good morning, Totò!" exclaimed Sabrina, a tall woman with dark hair. "Look at that, I've never seen you with your hair down. It suits you much better! Don't you think so, ladies? You look a bit like Beethoven, like a sort of crazy, determined genius, no?"

"Also a little deaf into the bargain? *Basta*! Compare me to the *Divin Codino*, Sabrina. 'You look like Roberto Baggio,' that's the only compliment I'll accept."

"It doesn't even flatter you if we say you're the best doctor in town?" said the youngest of the three women, who had short blond hair.

"No, Carla, because I'm the only doctor in Altino. Get a move on, then," said Dr. Pessoto, pointing to the warehouse, not leaving the three women the time to smile. "I think some of them are very hungry. Gianni and Lucia are waiting inside. Jogoy left just half an hour ago," said the doctor, tying his hair back again.

"He'd better get back here soon," said Sabrina. "We'll need him. No major problems, otherwise?" she continued, motioning to the men with the carts to go on ahead into the warehouse.

"The same," said Dr. Pessoto, as the men pushed their carts into the dormitory. "The problem, the only major problem, Sabrina, is the fact that they're here."

"Salvatore!" The third woman, a nun wearing a veil, scolded him. "You have no right to say that. Put yourself in their shoes! What would you have done?"

"That's a terrible trick question, one of morality. I don't know what I would have done. You can't put yourself in their shoes. No one can. No one is capable of—"

"You're talking as if empathy didn't exist!" Sister Maria said, beside herself. "You—"

"Ah, empathy . . . "

Interrupting the nun in turn, his tone one of exhaustion mingled with sarcasm, Pessoto repeated the word "empathy," as if he had long been expecting its inevitable appearance in their discussion, even before they'd begun talking. He gave a bitter, ironic snort, then continued, "Empathy . . . something we came up with to ease our own consciences . . . Yes. To put up with the fact—or hide from it, it's all the same—that you can never leave your own body and truly put yourself in someone else's place . . . That's the oldest human illusion. Tell me, how could we hope to understand another person when most of the time we can't even make sense of our own feelings, not even the simplest ones? And on top of that, how can we possibly understand one of the most complex things that exists in a person—sorrow? What sort of arrogance is supposed to allow that? These men are in their place, and we're in ours. We know nothing about their suffering. And even less how to ease it . . . They shouldn't be here. It's that simple."

He fell silent and took a long, nervous drag on his cigarette. He'd gotten somewhat irritated, and his voice, which he'd raised a level or two, was trembling by the end. He was breathing loudly, almost panting, as if he'd just finished some intense physical workout or made a major confession. Sister Maria was already opening her mouth to reply—in no uncertain terms, judging by the crimson hue of her face, normally so serene. He didn't leave her the time. Making a great effort, keeping his voice somewhat less irritable and therefore more hopeless, Pessoto continued, "Yes, I know. It's terrible. What I just said may disgust you, Sister Maria. The sort of thing a nihilist would say. Or worse yet, a xenophobe or a fascist, I know. But. I wonder if there isn't some truth to their assessment. Their explanations and the consequences they draw from all this are wrong, of course, but—the assessment . . . the clear and simple facts, irrespective of ideology and hatred . . . These men are here, and it's terrible. In this state, into the bargain: immense physical fatigue, with gashes and injuries; they haven't slept, they're dehydrated, stressed, hungry, and mentally totally exhausted. But the worst part . . . ."

Dr. Pessoto tossed his butt to the ground and immediately brought another cigarette to his lips, lighting it with a mechanical gesture polished by habit.

"The worst part," he continued, blowing smoke into the air, and it was impossible to tell whether this was for himself or for the women listening, "the worst part, my Three Graces, is that they still believe. A very strong belief. You can see it in their eyes. But that's something we're used to. We know how it will all end, don't we?"

Initially, the three women didn't reply. And their silence might have meant, "Yes, we know," if Carla, the young blonde woman, had not eventually spoken.

"No, nobody knows, Totò. Nobody knows how it will end. Not even you. And thank God for that."

"Boh!" said Pessoto, making the characteristic movement of hands and shoulders that invariably accompanied this interjection.

Only true Sicilians know the veritable (and variable) meaning of this little word. Depending on the context and tone of voice, it could signify: "yes," "no," "of course," "maybe," "maybe not," "I don't know," "impossible to decide," "we'll see," "only God knows," "it's probable," "it's unlikely," or all of the above at the same time.

In common accord about the meaning of the "Boh!" that had just been uttered, Pessoto, Carla, Sabrina, and Sister Maria lingered a few moments in a strange silence. The three women eventually went into the dormitory, and nothing more was said.

Left on his own, Salvatore "Totò" Pessoto, pensive and rather sad, cast a tired glance toward the mountains. A few minutes later, cries rang out: the Babel of joy, as he'd predicted, was rising amid a clamor of excitement. He made up his mind to go back into the warehouse. "No, Carla, we're not here because we don't know how it's going to end. No. We're here because we know what will happen, but we don't want to become resigned to the fact that there's nothing we can do. I can't do anything for them. I know that. It fills me with shame. A shame that's killing me. We won't die from their distress; we'll die from our own inability to truly put an end to it. We could leave them to their fate, but that would be an even more shameful choice, more mortal, and more unbearable for us, great humanists that we are, with our impeccable ethics, no? Between two types of shame, we choose the one that kills more slowly. That's the honor of people we consider good. That's all they've got left. All *we've* got left. And there you have it: the truth."

When he went inside, the euphoria in the dormitory had not yet subsided. As he watched the jubilant mass, his gaze progressively hardened. He caught himself feeling pity mixed with hatred toward these men as they rejoiced at the welcome they'd found. The feeling lasted for a few minutes, and he didn't try to elucidate or put an end to it, and, when it finally faded, Salvatore Pessoto felt nothing inside, only a great emptiness.

The Three Graces, with the help of the men who'd pushed the carts, were busy getting ready to serve breakfast.

Old Giuseppe Fantini had been at his window for hours. He'd been patiently watching the night make way for the dawn. It was one of his favorite times: the rising of the day, not just of the sun. His rheumatism disappeared during those few enchanted instants, as if it were granting him a truce. Bandino was dozing by his side on a little rug. A few clouds passed overhead with the innocence of a procession of vestal virgins; the hours went by, but not time; in the distance, Mount Etna was brazenly yawning, like a child failing to cover its mouth with the back of its hand. Fantini was happy in that place, at that moment. He could have stayed there. *Otium.*

He knew that no one would come to disturb him. No one dared. The townspeople knew very well that he loved his proud, intransigent solitude. But they had too much respect and admiration for the old man to hold it against him. Because Giuseppe Fantini—although he denied it and actually could not care less now—knew he was a source of great pride to them. A Sicilian, national, global pride. Everyone knew him, and even if for many years he had been living in ever greater seclusion, no one ever forgot that he was a poet, the greatest living poet in Italy. His lines had been translated into countless languages; his poems had been read; they had been taught to generations of schoolchildren and students. Everyone had seen him on TV, receiving prestigious international prizes; everyone had heard him on the radio, his clear voice delivering speeches full of a humble and sensitive beauty, to august auditoriums. He hadn't always been such an antisocial poet, even though he'd always shown a great deal of reserve. Throughout most of his career, he'd been sociable and available, responding to the hundreds of requests that poured in from all over. For several decades his name had regularly appeared on the list of potential recipients for the Nobel Prize in Literature. At the height of his glory, only a handful of football players, one or two *belle donne*, the great Godfather of the Sicilian Mafia, the Pope, and of course, Dante, preceded Giuseppe Fantini in the pantheon of the most popular figures in Italy, over the ages.

There had been a time when, as he strolled tall and elegant through the streets of the town, with Bandino in the lead, joyful swarms of children would cluster around him, or trot and skip in his footsteps, accompanying him with their angelic delight. Men would greet him, doffing their hats or their worn berets, loudly crying, *"Baciamo le mani, Maestro!"*; and women would come up to him, smiling warmly, taking his hand and offering him dried fruit, baskets of vegetables, or a bouquet of flowers. He would be a bit surprised but unassuming and charming, and to each of them he would offer his thanks, a smile, a kind word, a piece of candy, some advice, or a moment of attention.

He had been hospitable, too, at his big house in the north of the town. He had bought it at the beginning of his career, forty-five years earlier, with the money from his first collection, one of the best known, *Blood on Stone*. At the age of thirty, as a promising young poet, he'd instantly fallen in love with Altino and the spacious, distinguished house which an eccentric old aristocrat had let him have for a song; she had decided to leave central Sicily to be with her lover, a Tunisian man a third her age who sold narghiles at a souk in Monastir. The house had three floors, each of them with several large windows that Fantini nearly always left open, except in winter. The moment winter was over, all of spring and summer poured in through the windows, electing the big house as their synecdoche, their small theater. Fantini lived there now on his own. He'd had at least a dozen love affairs, but had never wanted any descendants other than his poems. He'd constantly reminded his mistresses that he only really lived through and for his work. Not a single one wanted such a life. They always ended up leaving him.

His study was on the second floor. It was there that he had composed the works that had brought him success and glory; it was there that he had welcomed both his most illustrious peers and the humblest people. Back in the day, people went to visit Fantini the way one goes on a pilgrimage.

But all of that had changed roughly fifteen years earlier. Now the poet's house was often closed. The shuttered windows were like great wounds on the surface of the walls. Gone the abundance of odors. The light slipped in with difficulty, through tiny interstices, without splendor. Fantini often stayed shut away for weeks on end, without seeing a soul, and no one even knew whether he was there or not. On the rare occasion when he did go down to walk around the town, no one came up to him anymore, and the children no longer played by his side. It wasn't that they disliked him, you don't hate a great poet; simply, they understood him. They understood that he wanted to live in the silence for which he'd been nostalgic all his life. Fifteen years earlier, when everyone was waiting for his Opus to be enriched with new jewels, he had stopped writing abruptly, without explanation. Initially, everyone thought it was a passing crisis, the kind all great artists go through, bringing back an absolute masterpiece when they emerge from their inner hell. But as time went by, Fantini's waiting audience had to face the facts: this was no temporary crisis; indeed, four, five, six years went by, and the poet did not publish. The silence was accompanied by a shift in attitude that was equally abrupt: Fantini became solitary, agoraphobic, taciturn. He no longer welcomed visitors, no journalists or students or publishers, not even his peers. Those who hurried to his door were as anxious as they were curious. But he never answered, and locked himself up in fierce silence.

His reclusion began to look like a renunciation of poetry, a farewell to literature, with all the parade of fascination and mythology that such a move always trails in its wake. Society could not tolerate the mystery in which he sought to shroud himself, refusing to accept the fact that someone might actually want to avoid its gaze. Paparazzi camped outside the house for weeks, eager to uncover the secret of his inexplicable reclusion. They dug through his trash for clues, to reconstitute his secret life. One day in one of the trash cans they found a crumpled old sheet of paper. It was auctioned for tens of thousands of euros: a shopping list which the poet, no doubt to have some fun, had written in the form of a rondeau. The buyer received requests from several museums that wanted to exhibit this first known piece of writing from Fantini in years. The most extraordinary theories circulated about the reasons for his sudden refusal to create. No one could understand how an artist, perhaps the greatest of his generation, could leave behind everything he'd devoted his life to. They imagined that behind the renunciation there must be some terrible, mysterious tragedy. Sometimes it was the price the poet had had to pay the devil in some Faustian pact; at other times, it was his way of expiating some unspeakable crime committed in his youth that had come back to haunt him; unless, of course, it was the perfectly banal explanation that he'd lost his inspiration for good. But this last theory was held to be the most far-fetched: a great poet—what's more, an Italian—could not reasonably lose his inspiration. One day, people claimed the Maestro had sunk into depression, then madness, suddenly, just like that, like Nietzsche; another day, he was gravely ill, on his deathbed. More than once, naturally, he'd been killed. Carried away on the momentum that fed them, these rumors bordered on the extravagant, flirted with legend, even suggested mystery of a religious nature; before long they occupied a pure space of fantasy, utopia, and narrative invention, which the most inspired theorists turned to their advantage. Everyone became a great novelist or brilliant screenwriter, given the incredible material provided by Fantini's reclusion. Fantastic tales continued, proliferated, became ever more complex. Fantini did nothing to try to stop them. He seemed to care as much about the rumors as God does about his people—to the delight of public opinion, which could therefore go on feeding the rumor mill to its heart's content. However, as the years went by, people eventually moved on to other things. Perhaps the truth about the Fantini affair was not as interesting as all that. The poet remained so stubbornly silent that, in the end, he accomplished the feat of exhausting the rumors.

When he happened to show his face in town, no one dared go up to speak to him anymore. Bandino still went on ahead, but he walked slowly and solemnly now. When they went by, hats were still raised, but no one knew whether he took any notice; there were still a few calls of "Maestro," but did he hear them? His face was hard and inscrutable, and all he did (and only sometimes) was give a brief, imperceptible nod, which the townspeople now took for the sole reply to their greetings and tributes. Most of the time, however, if he didn't downright scorn them, he didn't even bother to react to their shows of respect, which he seemed to view as superficial obsequiousness. He walked through town looking stubborn and proud, with an aura of self-satisfied arrogance that discouraged, even forbade, any attempt to approach him, as if his entire being were fearful that he might be soiled by the impurity of other humans and was warning them: "*Noli me tangere.*" He looked like a wild animal, majestic and solitary, both loved and feared by the subjects that populated his territory, whose company he disdained. If anyone other than Giuseppe Fantini had displayed such an attitude, Sicilian public opinion, the most ferocious on earth, would have instantly scorned, execrated, and burned him in effigy on the public square. But this was Giuseppe Fantini. This was the great Poet.

The sun promised brilliant, torrid hours ahead. Along the little pathways that steamed in the sunshine, the dark, lazy masses of old dry stone gave off heat. Every foot, every paw, every hoof that touched the ground, even gently, was enough to raise a fine cloud of dust that then refused to settle, swirling like a warm, transparent veil. No sooner was it born than the day was already stifling from its own energy, which it could no longer contain. The countryside, yellowed in places, blackened in others, was dotted everywhere with the hats of peasants in the fields, the figures of scarecrows in clothes swollen by the wind, the smell of freshly mown stubble, and heat mirages, and threatened to ignite at any moment. The sky had been a pure blue before but was changing now to a chalky white, and if you chanced to look up, the glare was so strong that you could no longer see any clouds or birds or the sun, only a uniform expanse, radiant with light and suffocating with heat, that dazzled faces and forced brows to humility. The uninterrupted chirring of invisible cicadas, the heavy odors of overripe fruit, hot leather, and turned earth, the dusting of intense light that caused the horizon to quiver, the ardent breath of the sirocco, that desert wind so dry it could drive you mad, the provocative nudity of the sky, the hard-working hum of the craftsmen: it all emerged from the town, fermenting in the heat, mingling together to saturate the air with a sensuality that made men's heads spin, like a beautiful woman in the street or an old and pure alcohol. The poet drank it all in, straight from the bottle, manners be damned, great gulps of it, so avidly that it ran from his lips and was lost in the tangle of his beard. He felt a generous intoxication welling up inside him. The great verse of everyday life was unfolding, seeking its rhythm and precision. A few more minutes. A few seconds. Eternity. Then he closed the window. Bandino got up, stretched his large form and followed his master up the stairs to the bedroom. It was time to get back to business. *Negotium.*

The truce was nearly over: his knees and back were beginning to torture him again. He would have liked to go for a walk in town that morning, but the heat dripping from the sky compelled him to postpone his outing until later, until early evening, when the temperature would prove kinder.

S lowly emerging from an exhausting sleep, Fousseyni Traoré needed a few minutes to remember where he was. It was the same thing every time he woke up: he had to distinguish between his dreams, his nightmares, his memories, and reality. This daily operation of bringing his mind up to date was beginning to look like a ritual. He performed it. Bit by bit, events grew clear, and he knew where he was. Adama wasn't there. He knew he wouldn't be there, but he glanced over all the same, instinctively, in the insane hope that a miracle might have occurred and he would see his friend there next to him. But there were no miracles for people like him: there was only reality. He missed Adama.

He suddenly heard the creaking of the door opening and quickly shut his eyes. Several people came into their space and immediately started talking. Two men. But they were whispering so quietly that Fousseyni, even if he heard them, could not understand a thing they were saying. Loud snoring rose in the silence of the room. The two men continued their discussion. One of them seemed to be very excited by what he was saying. He raised his voice for a few seconds. Fousseyni caught the word Juventus in passing. The two men were silent for a moment, spoke again briefly, then Fousseyni heard the door creak again.

For a few seconds there wasn't a sound; then there were footsteps, coming closer. He closed his eyes and went more deeply into himself. The footsteps were still coming. Fousseyni held his breath: they were there next to him, right there, just behind him. The footsteps were regular, very light, not pounding the floor. There was a scent along with the footsteps, the scent of oranges, sweet and intoxicating. It engulfed him for a few seconds, then the footsteps moved on.

A voice—the same excited voice he'd heard before—said something, then the door opened again and closed quickly. He could tell that the others, his comrades, were getting impatient: on their bunks, they were showing more signs of anxiety. Like him, they wanted to know what awaited them, what would become of them. The door to the big room opened again. He glanced over discreetly and saw four men come in. Each of them had a sort of pushcart that looked like Maiga's, Maiga who sold sandwiches and curd and couscous, who went around the neighborhood loudly hawking his wares. Suddenly some lights came on. The white glare hurt his eyes. All around him, the men were sitting up. A gradual hubbub arose in the room. The door to the dormitory opened again. Three women came in. Fousseyni immediately recognized them: the one who wore a nun's veil, the one with short hair, and the one with long black hair, who was the tallest. All three of them had been there the day before when they arrived. The tall dark woman clapped her hands to get their attention. Everybody was awake. She spread her arms wide then said, in English that sounded all the more cheerful for her strong accent:

"*Welcoma to Italia, welcoma to Altino! You will be safe here! Don' be afrai-de anymore!*"

On hearing these words, the men who knew a little English began shouting for joy and clapping their hands. The others, on seeing their comrades' reaction, understood that the news was good, and they began to clap and cheer, too. Fousseyni, however, kept quiet. One of his neighbors, a pot-bellied man with a mustache and powerful shoulders, rushed over to his bed and hugged him with surprising force, kissed his cheek, then let him go and went on to hug someone else, shouting, "At last! At last! We made it, we're in paradise! We're in paradise!" Drunk with joy, he kept saying, "We're in paradise! We'll have money!" It was a great cry of liberation, a violent outburst of joy.

Fousseyni looked at the woman who'd made the announcement: she was shouting and waving her arms, but no one was listening now. Next to her, the other two women seemed moved, and very happy. He also noticed a young woman and a young man who were wearing white doctors' coats. Every so often, he caught another glimpse of the man with the big head, still shouting about paradise. He heard exclamations in English, prayers in Bambara, thanks in Arabic, but also other languages, all of which expressed the same feeling: relief. The woman had said they didn't have to be afraid. The four men began placing the contents of their pushcarts on a big table that Fousseyni hadn't seen until now. Just then, he was probably the only one among all his companions to have noticed an older man with his hair tied back who'd come into the warehouse. The man watched them while they were jumping and shouting for joy there before him. Fousseyni got the impression that this man was not all that happy to see them there. He reminded him of the men he'd seen yesterday . . .

They began handing out the food. The girl in the lab coat walked down his row, smiling. Fousseyni immediately recognized the strong scent of oranges. So it was her . . .

They were on their way to paradise, yes, and the first smell, the first light in this paradise, was the scent of oranges.

The symphony of mastication, the conversations in several languages, the rustling of paper bags being opened, the smell of the sandwiches: there was something of a caravanserai about it all. Dr. Pessoto's two assistants were preparing the equipment for the medical checkups. As for Pessoto himself, he left the warehouse every fifteen minutes for a smoke. Standing next to the doctors, Sabrina, Carla, and Sister Maria watched as the ragazzi regained their strength.

* * *

Sister Maria couldn't stop fiddling with the little gold cross that hung from a chain around her neck. The gesture relaxed and troubled her at the same time. Yesterday, so as not to give way to fear and anger, she'd resorted to it with more anxiety than usual. She hadn't been prepared for a reception like that. How could she have been? She wasn't Sabrina; she didn't have her childhood friend's energy or her fighting spirit. Ever since they were little, she'd admired Sabrina for it, that intransigent refusal to let life dictate to her. After their final exams at secondary school, they hadn't seen each other for a long time. Sabrina had left the little town where they'd grown up to go study law. But although Sister Maria knew back then that they would meet again, she had never imagined it would be in circumstances like these.

Sabrina had specialized in migrant protection law. And

when, a few years ago, she had called Sister Maria and asked her to join the association she headed, Sister Maria had immediately said yes. She dreaded the task that awaited, but was even more fearful of the gaze of Christ on his cross if she did not try to fulfill this task. Sister Maria was prepared to concede that these three years spent in close contact with the ragazzi may well, on a human level, have been the richest but also the most trying in her entire life. The reception they'd been given the day before had not helped matters. Thinking back on it, she clung to her little cross with infinite devotion.

* * *

Standing next to Sister Maria, Carla felt tired. Her eyes, usually such a vivid color, seemed to have lost some of their blueness. As if the electricity of her gaze had been unplugged. For two nights, she hadn't slept because they'd been getting ready for the reception.

All the things she'd had to do: channel Sabrina's eager but over-effusive bursts of enthusiasm. Prevent Sister Maria from lapsing into apocalyptic visions larded with Latin about the Hell that awaited those who did not agree to accept these men: "*maledictis flammis acribus addictis.*" Drag her fiancé Roberto now and again away from his interesting theories about the use of palatal consonants in Kru funeral rites. Cheer up the ever-timid Gianni. Reassure over-sensitive Lucia. Guide Pietro, the psychologist, who was as sharp in his analyses as he was awkward outside his office. Prevent Rosa and Veronica, the two sisters from the association (one in charge of Italian lessons, the other communication), from tearing each other's hair out. And finally, thank the inhabitants of Altino for having volunteered to help. All of this had worn her out, but she would probably have been even more tired if she hadn't been able, all this time, to rely on the precious help of her deputy, Jogoy.

Carla had been the association's first recruit. Her CV had immediately impressed Sabrina. After talking it over with her partner Roberto, who was preparing a thesis in ethnomusicology at the University of Catania, Carla had agreed to join Sabrina in Altino. She'd quickly grasped the nature of her work and had grown accustomed to the receptions. However, in ten years of mediation, she'd never experienced anything as tense as what had happened the night before.

Her gaze met one of the ragazzi's. He looked very young, and his eyes were full of deep melancholy. The adolescent turned away as soon as he realized she was watching him, and with timorous gestures he went back to eating. Carla sensed he had no appetite for anything, neither his meal nor life. The young woman stood up straight. She mustn't let this boy fall into the precipice that sadness was carving out inside him. Someone flipped the switch again, and Carla's eyes regained their powerful blue brilliance.

* * *

Sabrina had always thought that their initial contact with the ragazzi was the most decisive thing, when it came to what would follow during the reception, so she never stopped smiling at them. But she couldn't kid herself; she could feel a lurking concern spreading through her. Convincing the Altino town council to take them in, not even two years since the last time, had been a struggle. To be sure, she'd always had the support of the town's mayor, Francesco Montero. He would soon be coming to the end of his third successive term as mayor, and when it came to taking in the ragazzi, he'd been a militant from the beginning. Deep down, Sabrina sometimes doubted the sincerity of his engagement: she got the impression the mayor was using this cause to enhance his political image. But the main thing, she thought, is that, sincere or not, he's agreed to taking them in and convinced the local authorities to come on board. Francesco Montero had often achieved this with ease, by wielding his influence. This time, however, the council vote had been so close that she'd actually been afraid it wouldn't pass. In the end, Montero won, after an unruly council meeting and a close vote.

She didn't hold it against the officials who'd cast a dissenting vote. In the end, they were only expressing a sentiment that was popular, and Sabrina could tell it was on the rise among many of Altino's inhabitants. It was no longer just reticence or hostility; it was something else, something deeper and harder, a more personal thing. It was out of the question, however, for her to let Maurizio win. Because she knew very well that it was Maurizio who was responsible for this something else that had taken hold in certain hearts. Breakfast was nearly over. Sabrina smiled even more, trying, with every expression of her round, determined face, to emit signals of hospitality and kindness. It was out of the question to let Maurizio win.

* * *

Jogoy had managed no more than two hours' sleep, but it was enough; he'd gotten used to recovering quickly. He had a bite to eat, then headed back to the warehouse, where he arrived just as breakfast was coming to an end. Everyone was on hand for the medical checkups: Dr. Pessoto and his two assistants, of course, but also the fire fighters and a few carabinieri, who were there to make sure everything went smoothly. Sabrina and Sister Maria had arrived. So had Carla, who did not fail, as usual, to tease Jogoy gently about the state of his hair when he was fresh from a nap, as rumpled as a badly folded shirt. He'd met her five years earlier, a few weeks after his arrival in Sicily. She was the one who'd offered him this position as a mediator. She told him that because he spoke so many languages, his translation skills would be invaluable. Jogoy had accepted the offer. He'd already learned Italian, so he set to work at once. And of all the tasks his position as cultural mediator involved, it was his role as translator that he valued the most.

He saw translation as a metaphor for the human condition, something that perhaps best symbolized two contrary movements whose tension was at the heart of their lives: on the one hand, the impossibility of communicating a part of what was essential—in other words, the failure of language faced with the human enigma—and on the other hand, in spite of everything, the desperate attempt through language if not to name that enigma, at least to get closer to it. Failure and hope. Translation was no more than that. It always implies a failure, a catastrophe foretold, that of incomprehension, because if a translator is needed, it's because at least two individuals do not understand each other, or have failed to understand each other, and this incomprehension, which has been made official and can never be put right, is a disaster, the symbol of a community that has been irremediably lost, a primal misunderstanding. But if it is the sign that something has been lost, translation is also the promise that something else will be re-created. To translate is, with one and the same gesture, to mourn the primary language, and to wager one can build another one on its ashes. What would be better for mankind: to have a single language that everyone could speak, or several languages that could be mutually translated? Were people richer before or after the loss of their single language of Babel? The God of the Old Testament believed he had destroyed Babel by taking away that ancient language; in reality, He merely contributed to the construction of another tower. People always understand one another. Babel has never stopped being built, but it has changed its *direction*. It is no longer vertical, but horizontal; it is no longer trying to reach the sky, it is trying to connect humanity. Whether it has succeeded remains open to debate.

Jogoy spoke ten languages, some better than others: six African ones (Serer, Malinké, Fula, Wolof, Soninke, Bambara), to which he added French, English, Arabic (learned at school), and finally, Italian, which he'd learned here. This enabled him to communicate with nearly all the ragazzi who ended up in Altino. He'd had the good fortune of spending most of his Senegalese childhood in a region where all the African languages he had mastered were spoken, given the mixed population. The good fortune, also, thanks to his parents, of having received an education.

For some time now Jogoy had been asking for other interpreters to help him out. He had quickly realized that it was an exhausting task to have to translate for everyone. Learning Italian took time, and until the ragazzi acquired a working knowledge that would allow them to carry on a discussion, Jogoy was a slave to his task. Everybody wanted him. His telephone never stopped ringing. There were days when he was in such demand that, dog-tired, he ended up switching it off. The association had promised him they would find more translators "soon." A word which, in Sicily, as Jogoy had come to realize, often meant "at some indeterminate and indeterminable time." In spite of that, however, he still managed to find some free time to catch a few matches with his friend Salvatore "Totò" Pessoto. They watched the Juventus matches together, which were often held on a Sunday, Jogoy's only day off. And often in the evening, after a long day at work, he would write. But that was a long time ago. For months, the notebook had stayed hopelessly unopened.

One Way
Tale of a Voyage, by Jogoy Sèn

Chapter I

I arrived on a stormy night. The tempest
hit a few minutes after the lights on the
coast appeared. We didn't know what city they
shone from, but those dots of light in the
distance were our lifebuoys, the only proof
that, somewhere, there was still land, and
life. Could this be Italy at last? Or the
Libyan coast all over again? Nobody could
tell. We'd been lost for four days. Our navigator had told us he was familiar with the
crossing. That he'd done it several times.
When the men on the boat began to have their
doubts, after we'd been lost for three days
(everyone knew that two days without seeing
the coast meant you were adrift), and they
threatened to throw him into the water, he
confessed it was the first time he'd sailed
"this far." "I'm a simple fisherman from the
port of Tripoli, but Atab was my master; he
showed me what to do to get to Italy. And my
uncle gave me some good maps, too. I'll get
you to Italy, inshallah," he said.

I'll say more about this "Atab" later on.
As for the uncle in question, that was Hamid,
the smuggler who'd put us all in this situation. I'll get to him, too, later.

On the fourth day of the trip, in the middle of the afternoon, a few influential men on

the boat (three of them, to be exact) decided to get rid of the navigator. "He won't save us. He deceived us. He's useless." In three sentences, his fate was sealed. I think the navigator sensed the coming danger when he saw the three men talking together on their own. He must have guessed they were deciding his fate. I saw him take a little gun from his bag. Once the three men had easily convinced a few other passengers that the navigator had to go, they turned to him, and he aimed his gun at them and fired. All we heard was a little mechanical click. The weapon was jammed. The men were enraged that he'd wanted to kill them. Four guys grabbed hold of him. He was screaming, but his cries were lost to the vastness of the sea and horizon. He pleaded with them in Arabic, he wept, humiliated himself, soiled his clothing. He struggled until he had no strength left. "That will teach you to make fools of us; it serves you right, after what you made us go through in Libya." The waves, the sea, the unmoving sun in the sky. Not even a bird. The earth's primitive décor. The thirst for revenge became visible on several faces. They threw the navigator overboard, abandoned him. I'll never forget the look in his eyes. I didn't do anything to try and save him. Maybe I hated him, too. I don't know anymore. The group of men took control of the boat. One of them, who said he was a Bozo—from an ethnic group of fishermen—took over the sailing. He started the engine. For a long time, I watched the navigator where he was, cast into the waves. Only his head floated above the water; it was as if the great blade of the sea had beheaded him. I watched that head until it was just a tiny thing far away on the horizon. And finally it disappeared. I think the navigator died when the image of his head vanished from my sight.

We drifted for three more days like that. We saw nothing: no ships from the Italian Navy, no fishing boats, no rescue helicopters.

Then came the storm. The waves picked up, towering things, and crashed furiously against the hull of the boat. It wasn't a blind fury: they seemed to have singled us out for their anger. They saw us. The sea wanted to kill us. It methodically aimed its thirst for murder at our vessel. Suddenly we were being driven toward the coast, incredibly quickly. The Bozo fisherman fell overboard with the first onslaught of the storm. That's when the lights appeared in the distance. But between those lights and us was this raging sea, in such a rage that it suddenly rose straight up, like a porcupine raising its spines when threatened, and there were great rocks just ahead of us that we only saw at the last minute. They seemed to have been planted there by the angry god of the sea. I had time to jump before the boat shattered against the lethal rock-face and broke in two. The current was too strong. I tried to swim toward the shore. But I was so exhausted that I passed out before I could reach it, and I sank unconscious into the icy waves.

I came to on the beach; I'd landed there like useless debris. It was still dark. I was soaked through. The storm had abated. The sea was nothing more than a huge, polished black stain beneath a sky rinsed clean by the storm, all its clouds wrung dry. I tried to get up, but the minute I was on my feet, I felt dizzy. I hadn't regained my strength. I lay back down. There was no sign of the others. There had been sixty of us leaving Tripoli; now I was alone. On the beach behind me, tall rocks formed a circle. With difficulty, I crawled toward that makeshift shelter, then sleep came over me.

6

Everyone—doctors, firefighters, carabinieri, ragazzi—was waiting for the medical exams to start, filled with irritable impatience that was only made worse by the stifling heat in the warehouse. Finally, Sabrina motioned to Jogoy. It was time to speak. He came forward and began to address the room in a loud voice. He started in Serer, his mother tongue, the language of all beginnings. But he didn't seem to have any Serer listeners among the ragazzi. And so he switched to Bambara, a language that might be more easily understood.

"Hello everyone, may peace be with you. My name is Jogoy Sèn. Maybe you saw me yesterday; I was in Catania. You've come here after a difficult journey. We're here to help you. The people you see behind me are from an association called Santa Marta. It's an association that welcomes refugees and helps them obtain their documents."

He could feel a shiver go through the ranks; already, a low, wretched murmur could be heard: "Documents . . . Residence permits . . . We've been saved . . . Real documents . . . " He went on: "Now you're in a little town called Altino, in Sicily. You're going to stay here, and the Santa Marta Association will try to help you. You have to be patient and trust the association; it's here for you. You also have to be disciplined and make an effort. The association is going to teach you Italian. Here, we will find you homes, we'll make sure you have enough to eat—"

"And work? And money?" a voice interrupted, in Bambara, that of a man standing in the first row.

He must have been in his forties. It was the stocky, pot-bellied man with a mustache who'd been shouting that they'd made it to paradise. He had a keen, dark gaze, which gave his face a determined, aggressive look.

"Regarding work and money," Jogoy said, "we'll get to that later."

"When, later?" grumbled the man.

"Tomorrow."

The man didn't answer. "Here," Jogoy continued, "we'll give you clothes, food, and a roof. You'll have everything you need. But you have to be patient and disciplined and responsible. You have to attend the Italian classes. That will help you get your papers."

Before he continued, he saw several men nod their heads. "Now there will be a medical checkup. You'll go through one by one so that the doctors can make sure you're healthy. Then you'll be resettled in your new homes."

Jogoy repeated roughly the same speech in all the languages he spoke. No one interrupted him after that, but he thought that, each time he mentioned documents, he could see that same vital and pitiful tremor going through his audience. The ragazzi gathered in rows to start the medical exam.

Just then, the warehouse door flew open, and, ushering in a train of sulfur and sirocco, a man in a black cassock came in. In the silence that presided over the medical exams, his unexpected appearance was like a bolt of lightning. Stunned, everyone watched as he strode vigorously toward the group. Dark glasses concealed his eyes; his nervous hand, heavy with rings, waved a long cane before him.

"No one gives me an ounce of respect in this damned association!" shouted the blind man as he came in, his voice hoarse, yet powerful.

"Padre! Let me explain," said Sabrina, the first to react.

"There's nothing to explain, my girl! You've left me out yet again, and for who knows what stupid reason! Why was I not told yesterday that they'd be coming? After I made it perfectly clear to you, Sister Maria, that I wanted to be kept informed! And it was in a café, while I was listening to the gossip all around me—can you imagine!—that I heard about the scandalous way some people in this godforsaken town greeted them yesterday! I hope you, at least, managed to stand up to them, since you decided an old blind man was incapable of doing so!"

As he said this, he drew a large circle with his cane, narrowly missing Sabrina.

"Padre, Padre Bonianno, calm down!" she said, rushing to the defense of poor Sister Maria, whom the priest, once he'd removed his dark glasses, was crucifying with his dead but terrible gaze. "It's my fault," Sabrina said, finding it difficult to withstand the fixed gaze the man was now casting in her direction, "I was the one who asked Sister Maria not to tell you."

"Ah! And may I ask why?"

His expression had turned ferocious. The contrast between his huge staring eyes and the animation in his face—all the deep wrinkles coming together, almost giving an impression of scar tissue—was striking. He still had thick white hair, carefully combed back. His marked, angular face emanated the harsh beauty of old age.

"Padre Bonianno, please . . . " stammered Sabrina. "At your age . . . "

"At my age! At my age! I'll have you know, my girl, that I could still climb to the top of Mount Etna if I wanted to! The top! Not just the first hectometers of the slopes, like you lot— you're a generation of idle weaklings and flabby namby-pambies, you've got no calf muscles, you get out of breath, all you're good for is picnicking in the lowlands. The top, I tell you. With a pack on my back. And not just for a picnic! Right to the summit. Real climbing. With the strength of my calves. So, at my age, my age, what a joke . . . a bad joke, to boot. Women are lucky I'm a little quieter these days, otherwise, I can tell you—the Lord is watching me, and He's not blind—not a single one would be talking to me about my age; we'd be having one hell of a pleasurable romp!"

"Padre!"

"She asked for it!" replied the man in black, while Sister Maria, who had interrupted him, shook her head, resigned. "And good morning, everyone," he continued, turning to the doctors and firefighters who were there behind the table. "Forgive me for this rather untidy and theatrical entrance, but I had to make these young women understand that I'm not yet totally burned to a cinder."

Like everyone else in the warehouse, with the exception of the ragazzi, who were still somewhat dazed by the priest's entrance, Sabrina was smiling. She was a bit surprised that Padre Bonianno's fury had not been greater and his words more incendiary. He'd accustomed them to all of that. He was a man who was not ashamed of his emotions, or, rather, of the only emotion that seemed to inhabit him: rage. A sort of physical and spiritual incandescence that drove him to refuse any show of mildness in the presence of others.

However, the old man had now turned to the ragazzi. He appeared to consider them for a while, then addressed Jogoy in French, his voice booming just as loudly. "How many are there, my boy? Fifty, like they told me?"

"There ended up being seventy-two, Padre."

"And when were they going to tell me that there were twenty-two more?" he roared, his face still turned to the men lined up in front of him.

"I was going to come and see you tomorrow, Father," said Carla.

"Ah yes, my girl, ah yes! Tomorrow! Oh! And what if I died during the night, eh? It's quite possible; we *have* been talking about my age. Don't go thinking that, at the age of eighty, the only risk is getting tired; you can also die in your sleep, maybe even while dreaming of beautiful women. Seventy-two men, seventy-two stories. Do you think that Christ comes down off his cross at night to whisper scenarios to me? No, alas! Our Savior, well, he was nailed very precisely to his cross, with a certain craftsman-like talent; he won't come down! The Roman nail was the most reliable on earth back then!"

And in a low voice, but loud enough for Jogoy to hear him, he let out a swear word in dialect. Then he began greeting the ragazzi, one after the other. He walked slowly now, without his cane, which he'd put to one side. He went up to each man with his right hand lifted slightly, but it was impossible to tell whether it was because he was feeling his way, or because he intended to shake their hands. Either way, the men, initially astonished, ended up taking his hand. From time to time, he paused for a few seconds with one of them and exchanged a few words, both hands squeezing the hand of his surprised interlocutor. When that happened, Jogoy knew that the man he was talking to was Senegalese, because the priest spoke several of the country's languages. Jogoy recalled the first time he'd met Padre Bonianno, and his own astonishment when the priest had greeted him in Serer. He had initially spoken to him in French:

"Do you speak French?"

"Yes, I do," Jogoy replied.

"Ah, you're from Senegal. I can hear it. And I'll bet you speak Serer. You've got that strong singsong accent Serers have when they speak French, I think I can hear it. Let's see if I'm right."

And there, without leaving him the time to reply, with a sudden flash of light in his unmoving pupils, Padre Bonianno had greeted him in his mother tongue, in Serer: "*Na fiyo, Koor u maak*?"

Jogoy had been so moved on hearing those few words that he was momentarily speechless. Coming from Padre

Bonianno, in this place, Serer was no longer a familiar, familial language but a rare one, so unexpected that at first it had seemed foreign to him. On hearing it so unexpectedly, a sort of lethal tremor went through him, and perhaps it was just then, because the sound of his own language—which he was supposed to know, after all—had come to him as a mortal surprise; perhaps it was just then, indeed, that he'd received the ultimate proof he was no longer at home. Fortunately, he survived that mortal attack, and it even restored to him the mental universe of his origins. The entire Serer language began flowing in his veins once again, with the sweet vigor of his mother's milk. Initially hesitant, he replied in Serer, as if he were unearthing it from deep, silted-up memory, but he felt more and more at ease as he spoke. Words he thought he'd forgotten returned to his lips, accompanied by the savor of childhood meals. He emerged exhausted but happy from that exchange.

* * *

The old blind priest went on greeting the men. When he'd finished, he slowly returned to stand by the big table, and he told Sabrina he hoped to be able to work with the ragazzi soon. Then he made a gesture toward the place where he'd left his cane. The young man who was closest picked it up and brought it over.

"*Grazie*," said the priest before continuing in French, "Do you speak French?"

"A little," said the young man who'd brought the cane.

"You're from Mali . . . What's your name?"

"Fousseyni. Fousseyni Traoré."

"Well, Fousseyni Traoré, thank you. We'll talk again soon."

He put his dark glasses back on, told the others he could see their idiotic smiles, and then smiled himself, a hard smile. As his lips spread wide, his wrinkles wove a complex spider's web; then he left.

That was the eighty-year-old blind priest from the little town of Altino.

7

By early evening, the medical exams were over at last. Francesco Montero, the mayor of Altino, came then to welcome the ragazzi. Jogoy found it difficult to translate his hollow and bombastic speech. Then they had a quick supper—the carts were back—and, at around seven o'clock, the members of the association set off with the ragazzi into town to show them to their new accommodations. They didn't form lines: Sabrina thought they mustn't give them the impression that they were, as she put it, "cattle being led to the slaughter." So they'd simply asked the men to come out of the warehouse and follow Jogoy. Dr. Pessoto chose to go home to his family. "I've no particular desire to go with them. You'll manage fine on your own, Leone," he said. He called him Leone because he'd found out that the name Jogoy meant "lion" in Serer.

The lion led the way; because he was tall, it was easy for everyone to see him. Behind him, Sabrina chatted absent-mindedly with the mayor, who was sorry he hadn't worn his official sash. Behind them came the ragazzi and the members of the association. Carabinieri, faces tense and weapons hanging from their shoulders, escorted the whole group. Even though night was falling, the heat of the day still hung over Altino, a thick smog of concentrated humidity.

* * *

As the procession made its way through the little town,

inhabitants came out of their houses, leaned on their window-sills, paused in the entrance of a café, turned their gazes to stare, stopped in the street, approached them. All of a sudden, the rag-azzi were no longer the vague subject of a verb conjugated in the conditional or future tense. They were no longer the ones who "would arrive" or "will probably be here soon." They were no longer objects of fantasy or rumor: they were there, walking past them, among them, toward them, up to them. Once again, fate, with a drunken hand, was tossing the ragazzi like so many dice onto the huge baize mat of the world, that wild table where there were no rules, where they would have to struggle to survive the cruelty of chance that the throw of the dice, yet again, had not managed to abolish. They were walking slowly. Their long hu-miliated shadows slid fearfully over the old dry stone, as if they wanted to cling to it. The last rays of the sun struck their faces, which were drawn with fatigue, but now and again a spark of faith in the promise of a new life would slip in between the shad-ows of fading relief and resurgent bad memories. They say every-one has the right to a second chance in life. The truth is that most people never experience the visceral anxiety of someone who's cornered, someone who, by choice or lack of it, is close to death, uncertain if they'll be able to take the second chance life has had the grace—or cruelty—to offer them. Few people, basically, have *seen* their second life being offered. The ragazzi, in these mo-ments as they traversed the town that had taken them in only last night, were seeing their second chance, were touching it. They were perfectly conscious of belonging to that accursed or privi-leged sector of humanity whose first life was about to die like an old star and whose second one was flashing intermittently in the distance, glowing with promise. Young star. But what light would it give? What if that light was dark? Life's second chance can be better than the first go-round, but it can also turn out worse. For the ragazzi, there could be no doubt: it would be better. It could be nothing but better. It had to be. They believed in it.

They went on walking. At the same time as it seemed to be replacing the world, the town of Altino also seemed to shrink, to become a tiny stage. Ragazzi and inhabitants were all caught there: so close, like two people about to meet in a narrow street, they could neither ignore nor avoid one another. The moment that had given rise to all the beauty—but also all the woe—of history was being re-enacted: one group of human beings was meeting another.

Ragazzi and Sicilians were not the same. At first it was only the differences between them—gaping—that stood out glaringly in the light. The differences in their bodies and in what those bodies showed, their faces and what they expressed, their expectations and what they hid, their past lives and what they concealed. What could they have had in common at that point? A shared space, a shared feeling of foreignness to each other, the prospect of a shared future, whatever it might be. They were all human, and they wanted to live. It wasn't a lot, but it might already be everything.

They went into the town, toward the center of Altino; they went deep into its very bowels, like the bony fingers of a haruspex trying to read the city's future in its viscera. They made their way slowly, ever more heavily, ever closer together, as if they could sense the imperious need to comfort one another, to grow closer, to become a single Man.

They were the Man who has arrived. Who is loved, feared, hated, to be welcomed or driven out—but here.

There were places where they were met with applause, and the inhabitants shouted, joyful and sincere, "*Benvenuti*!", words from the heart, warming their hearts. There were other places where people looked at them with a mixture of commiseration and charitable empathy, and several locals crossed themselves as the men went by, and murmured, "Poor souls!" with an expression of affected gravity. In other streets, they were greeted with unfathomable, funereal silence, a silence that was suddenly

torn, like a shroud, by brutal verbal blades: "Pickpockets!
We'll pick your pocket! *Negri*! I'll run you out of here! This is
our home! Thugs! This is our home! Monkeys! Galley slaves!
We live here! Spongers! Our home! Layabouts! This is our
town! Thieves! This is our home!" Words from a window, a
wretched alleyway, a balcony, a mouth with pursed lips. There
were times when, abruptly, like blood from a deep wound, a
laugh would violently spatter the streets as they went by, an
ugly, coarse laugh, long and hard, as if expelled from the lungs
of the very universe. It was horrible, yes, the rage in that laugh,
which drowned out all the rest, horrible like the single-mind-
edness of a vengeful djinn or Fury, horrible and frightening, as
well, the mystery of its provenance: who was laughing? But the
most horrible thing about that laugh, the most intimidating, as
it rang out, was its endurance: only a brief pause, the time for
a voice still trembling with mirth, in which one could hear the
frisson of a vulgar pleasure, to shout: "Here they are at last,
our famous guests, look at them! Go on, have a look, get out
the red carpet!" And that was it. The words were lost in that
roar of laughter as again it poured out, ever louder, torrential,
cavernous, a flood, leaving the impression that it could carry on
with its convulsions for all eternity.

A victory parade, applauded; a religious procession, pitied; a
convoy of shame, insulted; a caravan, mocked; a cabinet of cu-
riosities, inspected: the group went through the town and was
all of these.

From time to time, with the thrust and grip of the crowd
growing ever larger, or simply because the street suddenly
narrowed and there was no alternative, the parade slowed its
pace, searching for a gap, an escape, air, a way through. But the
convoy never stopped altogether: it stamped its feet, nervously,
with a dull rumble, rolling on itself, reversing, hesitant, leaning
to the left, heading off to the right, refusing paralysis, struggling to contain all contrary motion, as if these were powerful

undercurrents working against the depths of an unquiet ocean. Once or twice, there were passages so narrow that the ragazzi had to go through in single file, between hedges of stone and human bodies. At such moments, they resembled a column of defeated Romans in the Caudine Forks. The group broke apart; for a time there was no more reassuring protection, and every man was on his own again, vulnerable, left to his own resources and to the fury of the moment. And every man was free again, but it was a vertiginous, frightening freedom combined with absolute solitude.

Night was knocking impatiently at day's door. At the head of the procession, pushing aside the crowd that had massed in the streets, Jogoy made his way, his expression inscrutable. A few yards behind him, Sabrina followed with a heavy step, her head held high. Francesco Montero, next to her, had put on his most official smile, his mayor-who-is-there-for-you smile, raising his hand now and again in a wave, or giving a casual nod. Carla could not stop turning around to look at the ragazzi, to reassure them and try to intuit, from their manner, what they were feeling. Sister Maria was smiling; she still clung to her gold cross, but her face was serene, no longer distorted by anxiety and the perpetual fear of Sin. She thought of the road to Calvary, and was sure she was in the parade of glory. Lucia, Dr. Pessoto's assistant, wore a mask of fear, however; her lovely pale face had grown somber. A few yards behind her, her colleague Gianni was silent and impenetrable.

And the parade continued to make its way to the heart of the town, cleaving through the crowd.

8

F eeling a little lost, Fousseyni walked with his head down. Whenever he looked up, his gaze sought the tall form of Jogoy Sèn, at the head of the group. He was the only beacon Fousseyni had, and when he saw Jogoy's head emerge from the tide of all the others around him, he felt a little better. Then he lowered his gaze again to the tips of his shoes and let himself be carried along on the tide. He didn't dare look out at the town, or at the men and women who filled the streets where they filed past. This walk, instead of reassuring him, reminded him brutally that he was in an unfamiliar, perhaps hostile place. The intense sweet scent of oranges suddenly enveloped him and disrupted his troubled thoughts. It surprised him, filling his heart, his mind, his entire body. The person who wore that scent was next to him.

It was the girl in the lab coat who'd walked by his bunk that morning. She was smiling at him. Fousseyni took in her brown hair. And the scented zest of her skin. And her eyes. It was the first time he'd seen eyes like that, of a color he couldn't define. Was it green? Yellow, like a cat's? Brown? This strange and sudden apparition permeated with the scent of oranges was still looking at him and smiling, and not saying a word. He hesitated to go through the ritual of mental updating again. Was this real? Fousseyni, showing exceptional courage, finally spoke to the orange-girl.

"Huh . . . Hello," he stammered, making a great effort.

The girl didn't answer, but her smile grew wider. Fousseyni, whose greeting was still hanging in the air, thought that oranges generally don't reply. Sheepish, he looked down. The girl very gently touched his arm, and when Fousseyni again looked up at her, she gestured to him. At once he understood. She was mute.

Surprised, still heady with the sweetness of oranges, Fousseyni remained stupidly silent. The girl took a piece of paper from her pocket and quickly scribbled a few words. Then she handed it to him.

"Hello, my name's Lucia. I can't speak anymore, but I understand when you speak to me. I know a little French. I studied it in school. What's your name?"

Lucia could tell he felt awkward. She was annoyed with herself for having embarrassed him, dragging him out of the carapace where he seemed to have withdrawn. Ever since the group had left the warehouse, she hadn't stopped looking at the young man: in his eyes there was a deep shadow, old and buried inside him like a thousand-year-old root in the earth, and it seemed to clash with his fragile, youthful look. It was only his gaze that was old. That was what had intrigued her.

"My name's Fousseyni. Fousseyni Traoré," he said, after reading her message.

"I'm glad to meet you."

"Me, too," he replied, after the next piece of paper.

They walked for a few seconds side-by-side, awkward, barely glancing at each other. Fousseyni was about to say something when Lucia heard someone shout her name. Gianni, her colleague, walking a few yards behind her, was calling to her. He asked if everything was all right. Surprised (Gianni so rarely spoke to her), the young woman slowed her step and looked back to reassure him with a nod: everything was fine. *"We're just getting acquainted. His name is Fousseyni,"* she wrote to Gianni. It took only a few seconds, but when Lucia went to resume her dialogue with Fousseyni, he was no longer where she'd left him. He'd gone deep into the heart of the procession, although until then he'd been walking along the edge. He was looking down. The carapace had closed back around him. She tried in vain to wave to him, to get his attention, but his gaze, his sad, handsome gaze, remained hopelessly focused on the blackened cobblestones of the Via Rolando Ettorini where they were walking. Afraid she might have bothered him, Lucia no longer tried to wave to him, even though, from time to time, she furtively turned her head in his direction. But Fousseyni didn't go back toward her for the rest of the walk.

* * *

By roughly 9 P.M., all the ragazzi were settled in. The association—Carla, in fact—had made sure that for their first days they wouldn't have to worry about a thing; every accommodation had already been provided with everything they might need so that the occupants could manage for a few days, long enough to get their bearings and begin to get by, in Altino.

9

At the same time, a large gathering had assembled in another huge warehouse at the entrance to town. The men and women who made up this crowd, as they settled onto their chairs, conversed in low voices, with an air of gravity.

"Did you see them on your way here?"

"I crossed the street."

"I don't want them here, and I told them so."

"Did you see their prying eyes? They've only just got here, and already they want to rob us."

"We're not safe here anymore, that's for sure."

"And what about our kids? Especially the girls . . . "

"Did you see what happened in Germany? There were mass rapes! And guess who did it!"

"And their white teeth . . . "

"Their red gums . . . "

"Their big lips . . .

"Black . . . "

"Dry . . . "

"Chapped . . . "

"Fleshy . . . "

"Thick-lipped . . . "

"And those traitors from Santa Marta . . . To think they give them apartments! I put in a request to social services two years ago for subsidized housing, and I'm still waiting. The slum I live in is in ruins. My family is suffering. Every winter, I pray that none of the kids will die from the cold. And these migrants come here, and right away they get one of those apartments. It's intolerable! Their lives are worth more than my family's, is that it?"

"You're so right."

"But even worse, I think, is those locals who support them. There were a lot of them, did you see? We're a real minority in this town. My own neighbors—can you imagine, my own neighbors, and I thought I knew them!—were out there welcoming them. You really don't know who to trust anymore."

"They have to go."

"Yes, but try telling that to the government without getting accused of being racist or xenophobic. We're not the Northern League! We just want our kids to be safe and have a future."

"This is our country. They're invading us."

"They're chasing us away."

"They're replacing us."

"We have to go on like we did yesterday, and show them we won't let them in."

"Enough blackmailing us with human misery."

"They're dirty, they'll stink up our—"

When Maurizio Mangialepre came into the big room, the hubbub died down; a heavy, almost mystical silence fell. Maurizio was used to having that effect on people, but he didn't brag about it. The cause was greater than a single, insignificant person. He gave a humble, noble wave of his hand to greet the many faces that had turned to him; then, without haste, he walked through the room toward the podium, between two rows of the faithful friends who made up his retinue. Behind him, two giants dressed in black from head to toe marched in with powerful strides. Their shirts looked as if they were about to burst open from the pressure of their muscles. They were twins: the same smooth-shaven skull, the same massive shoulders, the same ferocity in their gaze. They even carried their twinship right to the cut of their beards. Their heavy footsteps, six feet behind Maurizio, caused the hardwood floor to creak and the windows in the room to shudder.

But everyone's attention was focused on Maurizio. The two hundred or more attendees couldn't take their eyes off him. Yet his physique was hardly impressive: you might even qualify him as ordinary, any more so and he could even have been ugly. His entire face seemed crushed by the laws of both physical and moral gravity: he was shriveling, shrinking. A fairly advanced bald spot and discreet stoutness rounded out his physical portrait. Add to that the asthma that Maurizio had suffered from since childhood: he was out of breath in no time and often had to break off in the middle of a sentence to gasp for air, *puff, puff*.

In spite of all that, nature had seen fit, and thought it fair, to endow him with a magnetic aura, although it must be said that his studied elegance and impeccable attire owed very little to nature. The truth was that Maurizio, in every regard, made an effort to be meticulous. This filled his every movement with an alluring confidence; moreover, his serene assurance was confirmed and became contagious the moment he opened his mouth. His ease in speaking was both pleasing and persuasive. His eloquence had even earned him, among his friends, the nickname Caecilius.[1]

He came at last to the end of the guard of honor his partisans had formed for him and stepped up onto the podium. The discreet little platform that allowed him to reach the microphone had already been put in place. The two Titans stood on either side of the tribune, staring out at the room as they crossed their arms simultaneously. Maurizio took a deep breath; then, after clearing his throat, he spoke, in a thin voice.

"My friends. I must start by telling you that since yesterday I've been feeling two things. One is pride, but the other is a

---

[1] Caecilius of Calacte (late 1st century B.C.-early 1st century A.D.) was a brilliant orator and literary critic from Sicily, during the era of Augustus.

persistent bitterness. On the one hand, yes, I am proud of you. The way you mobilized yesterday was not simply a mark of the trust and friendship you have shown me yet again; it was also the sign of your tragic awareness of what we are being forced to endure. This awareness is my great reason for hope. As long as you are here, keeping a watchful eye on our future and that of our children, there will always be a reason not to give in to the despair that threatens us in the monstrous guise of immigration. We are the ones who will defend our land or abandon it; its destiny depends entirely on us. On what we want. On the strength of our convictions. On the truth of our struggle. The continued expression of our concern and our anger will be the best way to kill that bitterness which, I am sure, inhabits every one of us when we see our land being invaded, becoming unrecognizable. It is not so much—*puff, puff*—the invasion that worries me. Because Sicily has always been invaded. Many nations have occupied it amid the bloody turmoil of conquest or the ephemeral illusion of political alliances. Centuries have gone by, impervious to the greed, strategies, intrigues, and betrayals of the thousands of men who have dreamt of possessing our island, as fascinated with it as they are with the three-legged Gorgon that adorns our flag. But Sicily is as fierce as a woman who has seduced you but will not give herself to you; Sicily has, by turns, belonged to and rejected every civilization that has desired her. Our land carries numerous legacies inside her; traces of the cultures that have formed her are still alive on her radiant face. Yes, Sicily is a land that many have passed through. But she has never been stolen from her sons. Before, the populations that arrived here shared their brilliance with us; together, we put it to good use; we offered them our land, and they gave us their science and labor. We enriched each other. But what is left of this mutual assistance? What do these people bring us in this day and age? They come, and their hands are empty; they reach out and wait for us to lift them out of poverty, when we ourselves are impoverished. The work we give them is our work, the work of our children, who are losing all hope of being able to earn a decent living. The housing we give them is our housing, that of all the Sicilian families who live crammed together in old family houses because they cannot afford anything else. It is simple, my friends: whether they want to or not, whether it was their goal or not, the fact of the matter is that the migrants are taking our work, our dignity, our pride, and our life. And they are being helped by people you now know well. We will not let Sicily be ruined, drained to the last drop of her blood by these waves of men who know nothing of the identity of this land. To indignation, we must add shame, when you think that those who are welcoming them, who are organizing this pillage that will bleed Sicily dry if it continues, those people, for the most part, are Sicilians themselves. Or used to be. Because they have betrayed their land, their family, and their history. They have betrayed us. I swear to you that for—*puff, puff*—for as long as I—*puff, puff*—as long as I live, I will fight by your side to make sure that these people, who have come to Sicily without knowing the tiniest fragment of its greatness, who have come to Sicily to steal its gold—those people will not stay here. They must go, so that we can live. Let them go back where they came from! Let them go further north! Let them go to other European countries! Anywhere! It doesn't matter: let them be gone! Let them be gone, my friends! Why did they come here? What are their countries doing? Why do they let their sons leave? What is this lack of political responsibility for which *we* have to pay the price? Those who are truly at fault are the Africans themselves. It's the truth; all it takes is a little clear-headedness to see this. It's too easy for them to accuse Europe without accepting their own responsibility. But we are ready and waiting. Yesterday, the new arrivals got just a quick preview of what we are capable of. It was nothing at all compared to what we'll do in the weeks ahead. This is only the beginning. We have to go on telling them what we alone can tell them: this is not their country, this is our country! Our land!"

The audience rose to its feet as one man, and the mystical silence was transformed into a thundering triumph. Maurizio, somewhat flushed, had trouble catching his breath; maybe he'd taken the passionate register at the end of his speech a little too far. But he had to. The cause was greater than he was; it deserved to be fought for, and Maurizio would fight with all his strength. He was proud he'd been able to organize yesterday's gathering; he had the feeling that from now on everyone would take him seriously. It was now that the real struggle would begin. He had no intention of losing: all the ragazzi had to leave Altino, leave Sicily. The future of all the people who supported him was at stake. His word was at stake. His honor.

Caecilius raised his fist in a sign of determination, a rhetorical gesture he usually never made, but the headiness of the moment called for it, and it seemed perfectly natural. By his side, the two mastodons, electrified by the speech, some of which they had understood, flexed their muscles, ready to take on the enemy. The cheers grew louder, warmer, and stretched on for many minutes. Maurizio, finding it hard to speak again, said he would soon be issuing directives for their next action, and he adjourned the meeting.

The room only emptied much later, after he'd exchanged a word with every one of the many friends who'd stormed the podium at the end of his speech to talk with him, to tell him how much hope he'd given them, to share their fears, or simply to shake his hand.

When at last everyone had left, Maurizio called the two colossuses over.

"Sergio! Fabio!"

The two giants immediately hurried over. Maurizio thanked them for their devotion.

"Your speech was great, cousin," one of them said.

"Thank you, Sergio."

"It was strong, and virile."

"Thank you, Fabio. You've been doing a great job these last few days, my friends, and you were real heroes yesterday at the reception. I'm pleased with you."

Maurizio's compliment made the twins puff up with pride. One and then the other renewed their pledge of friendship and loyalty. Maurizio told them he'd make his own way home, clasped his hands behind his back, and headed out, after wishing them a good night.

Once outside, he breathed long and deep. It was getting cool again. The air was filling with the sweetness of those rare summer evenings that people hoped would never end. The locals had come out to enjoy themselves; feeling flirtatious, night was wearing its loveliest stars. The little town did not seem to be paying much attention to the dramatic events unfolding around it. Not for a moment did its inhabitants seem to realize that seventy-two men from another world, completely foreign to their identity, had just begun, yet again, to mix with them, to add to their poverty. With the exception of the two hundred people who had come to support him yesterday and to listen to him a few hours ago, the townspeople were completely indifferent. They were being deceived by illusions, illusions the migrants created in the shadows. Yes, they were in the shadows, hiding away in the beautiful apartments they'd been given and that they didn't deserve. But Maurizio knew they wouldn't stay in those shadows forever: sooner or later, they would come out and try to take over the town. Maurizio swore, out loud, that he would fight them until his death. He would not let Sabrina and her association win.

CHAPTER II

The bright bulb of the sun roused me from
my dreams and my bed of warm sand. I left my
shelter and walked along the beach. The sea.
Only yesterday, it was the most evil place on
earth: the place where I might die. And the
following day, it was resplendent with seem-
ingly endless beauty.

It was as hot on that beach as on the day
we'd left Libya. That had been before sun-
rise. There were sixty of us, sixty shadows hidden behind a huge container, and we
were waiting for the signal. Absolute silence reigned because Hamid, the smuggler,
had told us that the signal would be a sound:
two short blows of a whistle. So everyone
listened. Everyone searched the quivering
air, hoping to hear the slightest sound of
a whistle. It was the third time that week
we'd tried to leave.

The first time, after we'd run six kilometers to reach the boat, our departure was
canceled; just as we began climbing on board,
a watchman (one of Hamid's henchmen) had
cried out, "Police!" We all had to run for it
in absolute chaos: we knew that if the police caught us, as Black refugees, we could
kiss our voyage goodbye. And our lives. That
day, seventy-one of us had planned to leave.

Eleven got arrested. That was the last we saw of them.

The second time, we had to start running toward the boat, anchored ten kilometers away, at 6 A.M. sharp. Hamid had told us that the boat would set off at 6:45. So we had to run ten kilometers in three quarters of an hour. Too bad for you if you ran out of breath. So right at six o'clock, frantic, we set off for the boat. We were racing against a nightmare, Libya; we were racing toward a dream, Europe; we were racing against ourselves, against our physical weakness, our fatigue, our lack of determination. I wonder what we looked like. A herd of animals? A human herd? What's the difference? We all managed to get there on time that day. But once again, we couldn't leave, this time due to unfavorable weather conditions. Too much wind. Hamid's nephew (at the time, we didn't know he was an imposter) refused to set sail.

We had to go back to the sordid outskirts of Tripoli and wait for further instructions from Hamid. We got them soon enough. That same day, he came to see us and announced that the surveillance along the coast had been stepped up: if we wanted to leave, every one of us would have to give him a certain extra sum of money. It was that or stay on for months in his service, to pay for the next attempt to depart. Yes, we were all working for Hamid as day laborers or dockers. In exchange, he provided housing in sordid apartments in Tripoli and took care of finding a boat for us. We had no choice. It was that or be out on the street at the mercy of armed gangs, racism, scorn, humiliation, and war.

Hamid was a rich businessman. A fat little man with plump hands and stubby fingers covered in huge rings. You could tell he liked his food from his round cheeks, the swelling of his vulgar, fleshy lips, and the way folds of skin were piled higgledy-piggledy into three or four tiers cascading from his little bearded chin. But when his tiny eyes narrowed and three creases formed at the corners of his lips, his rather comical physique disappeared and he became the nastiest man on earth. Everything about him was pure intoxication, greed, coarseness, and cruelty. He was a jailer. So that day, he set out his conditions. Pay and leave soon, or stay on in his employ and leave later—if you survived until then.

We complained: no way could we come up with that amount. The only response Hamid gave to our protest was to stroke his beard, narrow his eyes, and make his inhuman grimace. Then we all knew that we were fucked: to leave, we had to pay. We had two days to come up with the money. A lot of the men, filled with shame, were obliged to call their families back in their country for the umpteenth time to ask for help. Others pawned the only items of value they still had. Still others, with glum faces, went off in the night and came back with enough cash (and then some), and we never knew what they'd done to get it. And as for the remainder who had no solution, they were helped by those who'd managed to gather more than they needed. As for me, I had to go to one of Tripoli's black markets and sell the gold bracelet my mother had had made just for

me, which I'd promised to keep on me always.
Two days later, when Hamid came back, we all
had the money. And the following day at dawn,
we huddled anxiously behind the container in
a heavy silence, waiting for the two blows of
the whistle.

Suddenly we heard it, two short blows. Then
a few seconds went by while each of us hesitated, or made a sudden movement, or wondered
if we'd really heard it and looked at our
neighbors for a sign or a word of confirmation.
One man, more decisively, set off at a run.
The herd followed. And the race continued,
the mechanical but deeply human motion: we
had to run to survive, run or die. That day,
when at last we were able to leave, we kept
silent, fearful of tempting the evil eye if
we rejoiced too soon. It was hot. As hot as
on that beach where I landed and found myself
walking, alone.

10

Matteo Falconi

Glad to be home again. These last two days have been tense, oh yes, very tense; I, Matteo Falconi, would even say that in all the time I've been head of the carabinieri in Altino—twelve years, after all, and I've had my share of tense moments—this was the first time I've felt that level of stress. I was all right, even so, but you should've seen my men! Same thing today, during the housing distribution: all my men were tense, stiff, fingers dangerously tight on the trigger, stroking it. First-class morning erections. If even one of the ragazzi put a foot wrong, I'm sure my guys would've fired and filled him with holes like a piece of good Swiss cheese. Take my word for it. I was born here, my father was a carabiniere; I rose through the ranks, did grunt work, toiled away to earn my stripes, all here—and I've never seen the carabinieri this nervous.

I have to admit that the events the night before left everyone traumatized. Even me. I've been present at four receptions of ragazzi in Altino in ten years, two of them as station chief. Well, the one yesterday . . . There was no problem on our way out there, of course. We received the order to escort the two Pullmans, the coaches that went to get the ragazzi in Catania. Standard procedure. I'm used to working with Santa Marta. They're good people, fine individuals. A lot of women with big hearts. Real Sicilian women, generous, like Sabrina and Carla. Strong and maternal. We talked a little before we set out. We just had to make sure everything was done in the proper order. The usual procedure, in other words. We get to Catania. The ragazzi are there, they've only just arrived, accompanied by Caritas and colleagues from the Navy. We take over. They get into the coaches. Their faces are tired. They only reached Italy yesterday, after an incredible adventure; they still smell of the sea. So they get into the coaches. In one of them, the one in front, there's Carla and the nun who never lets go of her cross. In the other one, there's Sabrina and the translator from Santa Marta, Jogoy; I know him well by now, even if he isn't too talkative. He's very serious. A good guy. I put two of my men in each of the coaches. I get into one of our cars with two other young officers, and we lead the convoy. There's a second car at the rear, also with three men: my immediate deputy, Lieutenant Federico, and two recruits. Routine. We drive to Altino. No problem. The road over the mountain is still just as winding; I was afraid for the coaches, but the drivers were good. Driving through the hills has never been easy. Finally, we were just two kilometers from town. And then, after we came out of a series of hairpin turns, just as we reached the huge open area that marks the entrance to town, we saw them. They were waiting for us.

* * *

Maurizio Mangialepre

I'm glad to be home. My lungs have been bothering me more than usual—all the emotion from yesterday and today has taken its toll. But I can tell I'm alive, and that I'm happy. Everything went fine today. Yesterday, too. But it wasn't a done deal: I didn't know if I had reason to hope, and except for Sergio and Fabio, who are loyal and have absolute faith in the cause, I was sure of nothing. We'd already had several meetings at the warehouse, to discuss possible concrete actions, but from making plans to actually carrying them out . . . I wasn't sure everybody would be on board. Until yesterday morning, I thought a lot of them would back down; I thought the prospect of ending up demonized, of being called fascists and xenophobes, would prove too much for a lot of them. I was wrong to doubt those men and women. It wasn't their hatred of immigration I'd underestimated, but the deep distress it was causing them. The situation has ruined more than a few lives. They all came, determined.

Fabio and Sergio were vital, even though we had to calm their enthusiasm. They wanted to take on the migrants physically. I told them there were other ways we could terrorize them, resorting not to physical violence but to verbal and symbolic violence, the kind that troubles their minds and eats away at them. We just had to get organized to make sure we had plenty of disciplined partisans. Sergio and Fabio understood this very well. They're smarter than they look. They did a perfect job preparing the intimidation. It's not for nothing they used to lead the ultras for the Catania football team.

I saw them get out of their vehicles: Matteo Falconi and his men, Carla—Sabrina's right-hand woman—then Sabrina herself. In person. The same as every time I see her, I felt a tightness in my chest, then a rush, all at once. I saw myself slowing down, saw her again, that selfless attitude of hers, going over to her group and taking charge, totally ignoring Captain Falconi. She shot me a dark look, full of scorn. I made an effort to remain impassive, even though I think I've never hated her more. She said, her tone passionate, that I was unworthy, incapable of grandeur, a pathetic disgrace. She also said she'd never thought I'd end up like this someday. So base. And then that I'd live to regret it, that I was wasting my time trying to oppose the arrival of refugees, because it was inevitable, and as long as she lived she would go on welcoming them, and she'd always fight racists like me.

My chest was about to burst. But in spite of that, I answered Sabrina, told her she was wrong, that I was sure I was right, and that I was every bit as determined to fight against the presence of these men in Altino as she was to have them come here.

Just then, as arranged, my friends put our plan into action: a huge effigy representing a Black man suddenly burst from the crowd. Someone poured gasoline all over it; someone else set it alight. The huge black effigy burned there before Sabrina and her friends and the carabinieri and the migrants, who were still in the coaches. It burned and burned and burned, like an offering made to Sicily . . . And I could see the fear and helplessness on their faces. We had won. They were speechless before the flames and the symbol of their future destruction.

My supporters, however, let out a howl of anger and suffering. Sabrina opened her eyes wide, unable to react. Captain Falconi was the first to regain his wits, but the effigy was already nothing more than a heap of ash, blowing away on the sirocco. Falconi ordered me to put an end to the demonstration if I didn't want him to call for reinforcements. Sabrina renewed her assault just then and said, in sum, that my pettiness was nothing new and that I deserved everything that had happened to me, that this was no surprise . . . That was the only moment yesterday when I faltered. When she got to me. She knew she'd scored a point. I saw a cruel smile appear on her face. But it didn't matter. We'd pulled it off.

11

Fousseyni Traoré

I can't sleep. Everything about this house frightens me. We didn't say the necessary prayers when we came in. There are djinns hiding in corners or on the ceiling ... I'm afraid to close my eyes. They'll steal my sleep. Yet I'm tired, like all the others. It was a long day. They put us in a little house. It's very pretty, but it's little. The rooms are cramped. There are two bedrooms, plus a living room and a little kitchen. There are five of us. Three in the bigger room. And the other two in the smaller one, including me. At least we'll sleep in real beds. We don't all know each other. A short while ago, before going to bed, we talked a little. We all speak Bambara. That's why they put us together. There are two who already knew each other a little, because they made the trip together from Mali. Their names are Mamady Kanté and Ismaïla Camara. They're in the other room; they say they're both twenty years old, but I think they're older. I'm twenty, too, but I don't have a long beard like them. The third one who's with them is called Fallaye Touré. He's Malian, too. He says he's thirty-five and has two wives and three children. He left them back there in Mali, in the Kayes Region. We're all from the Kayes Region. Fallaye told us he was a "coxeur"[2] at the bus station in Kayes.

I'm with Bemba in the other room. He's not from Mali, but

[2] Tout

he lived there a long time. He said he had a business between Bamako, Kayes, and Douala. He said he's from Cameroon. He also told me he sold cars, and art objects, and clothing. But if he was selling all that, why did he come here? I don't know. Bemba says he doesn't know how old he is, but I think he's the oldest of us all. I recognize him. This morning, he was the one who hugged me and shouted, "We've made it to paradise." I recognize his big belly and his muscular shoulders. I recognize his mustache. I also recognize him because a while ago, when Jogoy Sèn was telling us in Bambara where we were and what was going to happen, it was Bemba who stopped him to ask about money and work. For sure, that is what a lot of us want, but nobody dared say it. He said it. It was harsh the way he said it, but at least he was honest. A little while ago, he told us he couldn't wait for tomorrow, to have work and money. Now he's snoring like the old motor of a Jakarta, those vehicles they use for urban transport back home. That's another reason I can't sleep.

I miss Adama, too. If he were here, he'd be in Bemba's place. He'd have said the prayers, he'd have spoken to the djinns. Adama was Kouyaté. The son and descendant of a griot. Dyâli[3] of kings. He was a master of language, a speaker and spinner of yarns, a storyteller of legends, a musician, the memory of the world, a creator of words, a prince of poets, a speech healer. He would have said to me, "You are not Traoré, it's the pink ears who called you that. You are Tarawele! You're a proud prince, friend of Keïta, friend of the great lion and a lion yourself! Tame your fear! Listen to your praise, Tarawele Fousseyni! The noble Turamakan is your ancestor; you cannot be afraid, you must not."

If he'd been here yesterday, I wouldn't have been afraid. But in the coach, I was. We'd been in there for two hours after

[3] A sort of traveling poet, musician, and storyteller

leaving Catania. In our coach, there were also two carabinieri with their guns, the Catholic sister, and the girl with short yellow hair. We were moving slowly, and then suddenly the coach came to a halt. I was in a row toward the front. I looked out ahead to see what was going on, and I saw a lot of people blocking the road. Really a lot. There were three men in front of them. Two of them were wrestlers. The third was much smaller. He was wearing a fancy suit. There was a police car in front of us. The policemen got out. The woman with the short yellow hair got out, too; she ran to catch up with the policemen. I saw the nun, who was in front of me, go down on her knees between the two rows of seats. I heard her say, "Jesus." A few seconds later, the people blocking the road began to shout and say things in their language. We didn't understand a thing. But I knew that what they were saying wasn't nice. I think they were possessed by evil djinns. They shouted and shouted; they were waving signs with things written on them. They shouted and shouted. In the coach, my companions were getting more and more nervous. There were insults coming from their lips: *Bilakoron! Kat leen ndeyam! Niamorodé! Batara den! Domu xaraam!* It was as if everyone understood that those people outside didn't want us there. We didn't speak their language, but we understood everything they meant to say. After that, all at once, I saw there was fire: they were burning something, it looked just like a man . . . Then they left. I was really scared.

When the coach set off again, it was already getting late. We reached the town, and they took us to the warehouse. I was really tired. I fell asleep after I'd eaten the sandwich they gave us when we got off the bus. Today, they took us away again. When we were walking through the town toward our new lodgings, I met Lucia. She's the one who smelled of oranges. Everything about her reminded me of oranges. Even the two little bits of paper she wrote to me on. I kept them. I smelled them again a little while ago. Her scent is still on them. Lucia can't speak.

But when she was writing, I got the impression I could hear her voice. I had to go away, to avoid showing her that I was a little intimidated by her . . . Then there was that old man in the black caftan this afternoon in the warehouse. He was blind! But I've never seen a blind man like him. He came to say hello to us. He was looking at us so intently . . . He said to me, "We'll talk again soon." A really strange old guy! On my first day here I meet an old blind guy who really looks at you, and a mute girl who speaks with the scent of oranges . . . Now I'm here, it's nighttime, Mali is far away, and I can't sleep because Bemba is snoring. I miss Adama. I miss Kouyaté, prince of poets.

What the—I just heard a huge noise outside. As if something had exploded. Boom! Boom! Boom! Like big cannons. Or a huge tam-tam, that someone with enormous hands is beating. I don't know what it is. I'm scared. Yes, I'm scared—me, Tarawele, I'm scared. Descendant of the lion or not, *walay* I'm scared.

12

I t wasn't night that fell over Altino, but Altino that fell into night. The town had melted into it without transition, without twilight, as if night were a trap that suddenly sprang open at the end of day, and day, inattentive after its adventures, intoxicated and blinded by its own light, fell into it. This night revealed the truth about Altino: it didn't cloak it in black, the way a hackneyed cliché would have it, but rather undressed it lovingly. One realized, contemplating Altino by night, that it was a small town nestling in the vast countryside like a slender, loving woman in the middle of a huge bed.

During the day, a host of ordinary sounds cheerfully filled the streets of the town, but after 10 P.M., those sounds surrendered to silence. Not a sad or frightening silence but a meditative one, the kind observed by a town grappling with its memory.

The places we have lived retain everything about us—our voices, faces, words, and gestures—and we don't remember them as well as they, more faithful, remember us. Perhaps, even, it's because they remember us first that we recall them. They take the initiative of memory. Isn't it strange that in a town where we can turn a corner and come upon an impression of something *familiar*, we'll murmur, when referring to that town, that it "evokes" or "says" something to us, as if it were the town or the street speaking to us? Our memory is like a sentence where several words are missing, a sentence whose meaning could not surface if the place, which was the page where it was written, did not complete it by retrieving from beneath its apparent blankness all the missing words and images it once absorbed—thus participating in a story that seeks to bring a shared past to light.

The space of the world, however, is more than just an aide-mémoire for mankind; it's more than just a surface receiving the dim, uncertain light of our memories, a light it then goes on to reflect, to make it clear and sharp for us. No, it's also memory in and of itself, autonomous, the great archive of time and things, of human passing. Banal or brilliant, forgotten by humans or retained by history, ordinary or exceptional, tragic or happy: every event is recorded somewhere, in a space that will have been its arena, its belly, its sex, and which will forever be its guardian. A great revolution. An epidemic of the plague. An ordinary fight between nameless brothers. A massive genocide. A tender kiss between two lovers. An eruption. A rape. The first cry of a newborn baby. A murder. A declaration of war. A peace treaty. A suicide. A gesture of friendship. The hanging of a Black man. Everything leaves a trace. The place forgets nothing; that is its misfortune. But that is also its greatness: it cannot develop amnesia in the constant presence of history and its tragedies. Unlike mankind.

All around us, something is working, thinking, retaining, re-cording. This keen memory is the inner experience of places. Their metaphysics. In most major cities, this metaphysics is dying out. As noisy at night as during the day, the memory of major metropolises is saturated, constantly solicited, hyperac-tive, and overworked, like the lives and memory of its inhabi-tants. Nothing immaterial happens there anymore. The archive is filled to overflowing. There's no mystery hovering over it now. Everything has been discovered, explored, photographed, un-earthed; almost everything has been spoiled by the common gaze, the gaze that looks but fails to see. One can no longer stay in such cities; we merely pass through, armed with a device that sees no more than our eyes do—for all that they are open wide, it's as though they've been gouged out. These cities no longer know how to remain at peace with themselves. Their citizens would like to remember, but they no longer know how. This makes them tragic. Their immediate reality has engulfed them, is crushing them. In ever-tightening spirals, they revolve around the only thing they still know how to explore inside themselves: their own navel. They suffer, work, seek pleasure, despair, forget, live at full speed, run on empty. And then they start all over again. They are bored. Sometimes they try suicide. They fail. They end up washed away, like faces drawn in the sand by the sea. In these soulless cities, one can no longer even die; one simply disappears.

This was not the case in Altino. Not yet, at least.

Giuseppe Fantini was about to go deeper into his thoughts, for he could tell both their doubts and nuances deserved a more thorough examination, but he'd lost the thread. He had difficulty sustaining his train of thought. Something was bothering him. Sitting on a large sofa, with Bandino's big head resting on his thigh, ever hopeful of a caress, the poet tried to regain some serenity. Bandino lifted his head and looked at his master, as if to remind him not to neglect him. The poet, slightly ashamed for having forgotten his friend, gently placed his hand on the dog's head and stroked him tenderly. The old dog knew his master well, and he could tell he'd been preoccupied ever since they'd come back from their walk. Bandino wedged himself more comfortably against the poet's thigh and waited for the confession. And indeed, soon enough, the poet began to speak.

"Do you feel the same thing I do? A true violence, a true force, maybe something real. Did you sense it, too? Did you feel it? So odd . . ."

The old dog, in the pose of close confidant, looked at his master. The poet seemed to be absorbed once again in the whirlwind of his thoughts. When Bandino saw that his master had fallen silent, he jumped down from the sofa and slowly padded over to the window. His master joined him a moment later. And they stood there looking outside, waiting for a secret they knew nothing about.

"You're right, we have to look outside. It's the world that's the true poet. It's the world that—"

A huge noise suddenly interrupted him. It came from Mount Etna. It was less of a true eruption than a series of short but powerful explosions, as if the volcano had suddenly been overcome by a violent fit of coughing. A column of smoke soon began to rise, high into the sky, black as India ink at night. Trails of lava escaped in thin threads from the crater and flowed very slowly like incandescent tears down Etna's cheeks. This happened sometimes. But it was of no consequence: the lava turned cold before it reached the ground, and the surrounding towns were in no danger, except from a rain of ash that Altino, despite its distance from the volcano, would probably not be spared. The clouds of smoke gradually thinned as they headed east in a long train that resembled a widow's headpiece. Tiny cloud-borne particles of ash would leave a grimy soot-like film on the streets. A fine dust would remain in the air and partially cloud the view. Local airports would be closed.

The poet enjoyed the volcano's sudden manifestation. He loved Mount Etna. At the end of the day, this was the only woman who'd stood by him, and he never loved her more than in moments like this, when, proudly, in a rush of gentle anger or, more rarely, vengeful fury, she reminded humankind of her existence. It was true that people had been neglecting her more and more, even shamelessly betraying her with false idols they'd consecrated since any awareness of the myth had collapsed. For many, Mount Etna was no more than an old woman they pimped out for tourists, photographs, guidebooks, businesses, and the ugly appeal of kitsch. She'd lost all the sacred terror she once inspired.

For a very long time, a popular, animist worship had been devoted to her, with rites, dances, and sacrifices. That was in the era when Mount Etna was still an integral part of life in Sicily; a time when her presence was felt by everyone, even in the most private moments of their existence; a time when human beings did not have the arrogance or desperation to believe they were alone, when they still knew how to live as one with their environment.

Tears of gold were still flowing from the volcano's huge eye. The old poet recalled the eruptions he'd seen close up. When he was younger, he was in the habit of walking alone for hours upon the slopes of the volcano. Three times, he'd been caught out by an eruption when he was near the summit. On two of those occasions, the eruption had been mild, like the one he was now witnessing. The third time, however, had been spectacular and dangerous. It could have cost him his life. He'd only been saved thanks to a cool head, his reflexes, and a bit of luck. On that day, as soon as he heard the first explosions, he sought shelter against a steep rockface where a ledge above his head offered protection. He moistened a piece of cloth with some water, then used it as a mask to attenuate the effect of the ash and the risk of asphyxiation. Finally, he wrapped himself in the large sheet he normally spread on the ground when he felt like sleeping under the stars. Then he waited, watching the trails of lava and molten rock that went by on either side of his shelter. Fortunately, that day, the eruption did not last, and the cloud of sulfur, driven by a strong wind, had poured out on the opposite slope. And yet he hadn't been afraid: during those long hours while he waited for the eruption to die down, he'd felt like a privileged guest, invited to see the truth of a place that was inaccessible to man, the wild hidden side of a certain order in the world. He would have liked to stay there forever. To melt into the majestic outpouring of volcanic fire. To abandon himself to

Mount Etna's embrace. And die there, like another poet over two millennia before him: Empedocles.[4]

His tears had dried.

"All this is a signal, Bandino. No! It's more than that: a sign. These sudden blasts, the mild eruption, our walk in town just now, meeting those young men who've left their homes so far away, the discussion with Amedeo after that, and then the sudden, powerful, all-encompassing desire to write a poem, when I haven't written a line in fifteen years . . . It all feels connected. I have a feeling these elements will become an important motif. But which one? Which metaphor about our condition is being shown to us here? Help . . . "

The old dog's sole response was to yawn and clamber back onto the sofa. Giuseppe Fantini turned again to contemplate the volcano, as if voicing a silent prayer. But that night, his old mistress didn't tell him any secrets.

[4] Pre-Socratic Greek philosopher, poet, and doctor who lived in Sicily in the 5th century B.C. It is said he died by deliberately throwing himself into Mount Etna.

13

The "Amedeo" the poet Giuseppe Fantini had referred to was Amedeo Bonianno, Altino's priest. A friendship going back forty years. One might even suggest that each of them was the only true friend the other had ever known. But let us turn our attention for a moment to Padre Amedeo Filippo Bonianno. The life of an eighty-year-old Sicilian priest, a blind, vociferating speaker of French, Wolof, and Serer, deserves, if not to be more widely known, at least to be examined, and certainly to be told.

The story of Amedeo Bonianno began between the wars, in Switzerland. It was to that country that, in 1922, Amedeo's father, Giorgio Maria Bonianno, went into exile because he could not bear Mussolini taking power. On leaving Italy, he gave up a prestigious position as a librarian in Milan. Giorgio Maria Bonianno, a passionate and erudite humanist, had devoted his life to teaching the works of Philippus Theophrastus Aureolus Bombastus von Hohenheim, a renowned sixteenth-century Swiss physician better known as Paracelsus.

Too busy with his love of books and of the mind, Giorgio Bonianno had not found the time to devote himself in any worthy manner to the love of women. He did know a few, but those women, who were overflowing with sexual vitality, ended up leaving him; they went away angry, accusing him of expediting the act of love to get back to his reading ("If only you'd taken the same amount of time making love to me as you did reciting Petrarch afterwards," and so on). Therefore, in Milan, in the apartments of his great library, Giorgio Maria Bonianno often lived alone.

As soon as he arrived in Geneva, however, toward the end of 1922, the rector of the university there, Monsieur Dominique Morand, who had already tried to recruit him when he himself was teaching in Italy, offered Giorgio a position as professor emeritus. So it was there, ten years later, that at the age of fifty-three, he married Sylvie Morand, Dominique's daughter. It was 1932, and Sylvie found Giorgio—a pleasant novelty for him—to be as gentle in bed as the lines by Dante he recited after lovemaking (he'd given up on Petrarch). Giorgio Maria Bonianno drew some elementary conclusions from this. It was perfectly possible to procure women's pleasure through their ears, yes, but not with just any old thing: you had to have the right rhythm, the right music, the right poet. Ergo, in bed, Dante rather than Petrarch. He took note.

Whatever the case may be, a child was born—the only one they would have—of the union between Giorgio Maria Bonianno and Sylvie Morand. Amedeo Filippo Bonianno came into the world in the summer of 1934. Sylvie, a practicing Catholic, made sure the boy was baptized. His father was already fifty-five, his mother forty.

* * *

Amedeo Bonianno had a very happy childhood. During the first years of his life, despite the war that broke out not long after his birth, he was cherished by a loving father and thoughtful mother. Thus he grew up between two protective parents and surrounded by several languages—Italian, English, German, and French—all of which he learned fluently.

In 1945, when Amedeo had just turned twelve, his father died without ever seeing Italy again, but he made his son promise to go there and live for a while in the land of his ancestors, in Sicily. His mother, whose Catholic faith had become more and more fervent, decided to devote herself to religion. It completely took over her life. For the young Amedeo, a new religious education began after his father's death. When he was seventeen and had passed his baccalaureate exam, he went over the border and entered a seminary in Lyon. At the Catholic University there, he studied philosophy and social sciences.

In around 1950, consumed by the sacred fire, Sylvie joined him in France to take up her vocation. She entered the convent of the Visitation Sainte-Marie de Fourvières, where she died in 1961 at the age of sixty-seven, practically a saint. She was buried in Switzerland next to her late husband. A few days before she died, Amedeo had given her the greatest of joys: he had been personally ordained by Cardinal Villot, the Bishop of Lyon. Now a priest, Amedeo Bonianno, at the age of twenty-seven, wanted to travel and see the world. After three years in Lyon, he asked to be sent abroad. In those days, the diocese of Lyon enjoyed numerous fruitful exchanges with certain dioceses in Francophone Africa. So that was how Amedeo Bonianno came to be appointed parish priest in F*, a little town in Senegal.

* * *

The population of F* was predominantly Serer, so Amedeo had to learn the language. His vicar, Raphaël Ndig Juuf, helped him. It took him three long years of intensive daily lessons until he was able to say mass, haltingly, in Serer. Three years with no lack of interesting details, but it would be tedious to go into them here. Suffice it to say that Amedeo Bonianno experienced every ordeal possible for a man who suddenly lands in a foreign country and must, willy-nilly, live with others. He spent eight years there, without going back to Europe in that time, trying patiently—a radical gesture—to understand Serer culture. Which meant living with the fact that Roog Sèn, the

Serer nation's major animist god, received better treatment than Christ, who was unknown in their pantheon. Things were not easy, initially; his attempts to evangelize created tension among the local population. More than once, he was tempted to return to Europe, and just as often, his desire not to fail in his encounter with the Serers won the day. So Amedeo stayed. For the first seven years, he had the impression that everything he saw would forever be strange and incomprehensible.

But gradually, the wariness he aroused evaporated, his ability to listen grew stronger, and he was better integrated into village social life. It was during that extraordinary period, once he was able to communicate with the most important people in F*, that he experienced a sudden leap forward. He was invited to spend a few evenings at the *ngel*, the rudimentary building made of wood and straw where the village elders gathered to speak. At last they welcomed him. The village priest spoke with him. The seer spoke with him. Women no longer fled when they saw him coming. The griottes entertained him with their poems and chants. He was allowed to attend certain initiation rites. Suddenly the austere Catholic priest, always plunged in his Biblical texts, began not only to understand but to feel the ties that bound different people, the solidarity between the human and the sacred, the significance of the world as a *ngel*—a symbolic space where people talked among themselves and with those who came before them, a space where what was said mattered, where the Word carried the sacred density of a creative gesture. All these things moved him greatly. His own Catholic faith, which he had not abandoned, was transformed, as if seen in a new light.

The last year he spent in the village was like a door opened onto paradise. He met Gnilaan Juuf, one of his vicar's cousins, a woman whose beauty was haunting and ecstatic, like the last sip before drunkenness. Her teasing laugh. That vigorous body. An innocent sinner. Amedeo Bonianno heard her confession every

Sunday evening without fail, once Christ, drunk with the wine of His blood, had fallen asleep above them on His cross. And while the Lord, drunk and tired, lowered His guard, the priest lifted his cassock.

Alas, it was in that moment when the stars were burning brightest in his eyes that darkness gradually began to extinguish them. An old disease, which had spared Giorgio Maria Bonianno but had struck his grandfather and great-grandfather, suddenly reappeared. Amedeo, almost blind, had to go back to Europe to seek treatment. And there was nothing for it, despite all the specialists consulted: he was doomed. He never went back to his parish, where Raphaël Ndig Juuf replaced him. The two men corresponded at length, and Amedeo had news of the village. But there came a point when he could no longer continue. In his last letter, he mandated his former vicar to tell the inhabitants of F* that he would never forget them. He asked him to give his regards to Gnilaan Juuf, the Sunday sinner. After that, a few months later, the darkness came.

The Bishop of Lyon, who had been his philosophy professor at the Faculty of Catholic Theology, invited Amedeo to stay with him. Amedeo declined. He asked, rather, that they allow him to officiate in the little village in Italy where his family was originally from. It was not that straightforward. Amedeo had to wait patiently for three years (he used them to adapt to his blindness) until the bishop of the diocese to which Altino belonged agreed to entrust the parish to a blind priest.

Amedeo Bonianno arrived in Altino at the end of 1974. And in this way, he honored the old promise he'd made his father.

* * *

Not long after his arrival, Amedeo met Giuseppe Fantini in extraordinary circumstances that would be too long to relate here. On that famous night, however, and this at least can be revealed, they both got it into their heads to invoke the devil in the little church in Altino. They almost succeeded, so long and loudly did they call him. This forged a solid bond. They became friends and for twenty-five years saw each other regularly. During that time, Fantini published many poetry collections, won awards, and attained world recognition. However, before they were sent to the publisher, every one of his manuscripts was critiqued by Padre Bonianno, his first and most formidable reader. Fantini recited the poems out loud; the priest stopped him angrily the moment a line sounded off.

By the end of the 1990s, however, Amedeo Bonianno saw his friend less and less often. One day, Fantini had told him, with no further explanation, that he was done with writing. With the great discretion that only great friends possess, Bonianno did not ask him why. From then on, after a quarter of a century of friendship, they met less often. It didn't mean that the friendship had waned; their exchanges simply became more sparing. Giuseppe Fantini, shut away in his huge villa, came only rarely into the center of Altino to walk. But whenever he did, the only person he went to see was the priest. And as old friends, they talked about this and that. Fantini learned, for example, several years after his withdrawal from society, that his friend had been approached by a new association that had been founded in Altino and was responsible for receiving the ragazzi. When he asked what sort of work, exactly, he'd be doing for this association, Amedeo Bonianno replied that he'd be helping the ragazzi improve the way they told their stories to the commission in charge of evaluating their cases, even to the point of occasionally tweaking that story a little if it would help.

"A priest who tells lies when it's called for: that's not very moral. What would Christ say?" asked the poet.

"He would tell me that from time to time I have to allow myself to sin, if it means I'm more humane."

"I don't remember that passage in the Bible."

"I added it recently. People have to sin now and again; otherwise Christ and all the loudmouths who trail after him, myself included, would serve no purpose here on earth. But right, enough blasphemy. Enough joking around. Do you want me to tell you honestly about my ragazzi?"

"Absolutely, thank you."

Although the priest tried multiple ways to get him interested in the issue, Fantini was determined to stick to the solitude of his retirement. And so in ten years, he'd met none of the ragazzi. All he knew was that they were there, and that his friend the priest was busy writing and rewriting their stories.

But now, for the first time, Giuseppe Fantini had actually seen those men. When he got to the center of town, he'd been astonished to see so many people out and about, as if there were some spectacle to be seen. Discreetly, with Bandino by his side, he went to the thronged main street and looked at them. He was struck by something in their faces. Once they'd gone by, Giuseppe Fantini hurried to the church. Amedeo Bonianno was there.

"Giuseppe, you old creature, why such an energetic pace?" he said, as the poet came toward him.

"I've come to ask you something."

"Go right ahead."

"Who are these men whose stories you've been writing? Who are they, really?"

"You saw the new arrivals, didn't you?" said the priest, his tone more affirmative than questioning. He looked over at the poet, who did not speak as he waited for an answer to his question. Bandino, who'd been left outside, was scratching at the door to the little church.

"Who are they? . . . I don't really know," Bonianno said finally. "Their crossing is part of who they are. But who they are, deep down, their most secret voice—I'm not sure I've heard that yet. I'm trying. I can hear faint echoes. It's as if I were on the banks of a river and could hear singing, voices from deep in the water. The singing reaches my ears, but the sound of the water stops me from hearing the exact words. To hear them, you'd have to dive into the river with its powerful, raging current. And risk being swept away."

"And why don't you dive in? Are you afraid?"

"No. I simply don't know how to swim."

"What does swimming represent in your metaphor?"

"Last I heard, you were the poet, Giuseppe. You're the one who knows metaphors and how to use them. So you should be telling me. We men of the cloth, we come up with parables, albeit not as beautiful as the those by the world's leading specialist in figures of speech," he replied, pointing to Christ on the cross.

"You started it, with your metaphor about the river—"

"All right, basta! That's all I had to say."

Giuseppe Fantini smiled, then told his friend he had to go home. And Amedeo Bonianno, as he listened to him go, felt certain that something was deeply troubling the poet.

14

Jogoy was exhausted but couldn't resist the urge, before going to bed, to make a detour by the Villa. Of all the things he'd been through since yesterday, what had affected him most was neither the dividing up into groups nor even the hostile reaction some of the inhabitants had given them, no; what had moved him the most was when he'd led the ragazzi to their lodgings. It reminded him of the time when, in F*, his parents' native village, he'd been circumcised and subjected to the initiation rite that made him a man, the *ndût*. That evening, the songs of the *ndût*, the female choir accompanying the procession toward the forest of X*, the loud noise of heels pounding the ground during the dances—all of that, all of the polyphony that described his world, had resurfaced in his memory. Then he had sung quietly to himself, reciting, murmuring. All the voices came together in his voice.

* * *

A circle delimits the space of the free word. Men of the present and men of the past form a living circumference, interspersed with warm gusts of air. Side-by-side, shoulder-to-shoulder, they are there, they are singing. The word circulates among them, from body to body, heart to heart. It brings them together. It creates. In the center: the fire, the initiators, and the young initiates. The décor is minimalist. A clearing in a great, sheltering forest. One night. Few stars. Animals all around. There is no backstage: the stage here is wide enough for everyone to find a place. The beat-ing of a tam-tam. The rolling sound is no more than the amplified echo of all the heartbeats around them: heart of Man, heart of Animal, heart of the Earth, heart of the Forest. It beats for a long time, sets the rhythm to the dances, accompanies the chanting. It is the coryphée in the middle of the stage. Its furious beating min-gles with the Men's words, and it too becomes word. Then, all of a sudden, it falls silent. The chanting stops. It begins.

Initiators, *their sticks brandished, threatening*
Mbay tak!

Young initiates, *in chorus, trembling*
Woor!

Initiators, *more threatening*
Mbay tak . . . !

Initiates, *raising their hands fearfully to protect themselves*
Woor!

Initiators, *about to lower their sticks*
Mbay tak . . . !

Initiates, *pleading for grace, more loudly*
Woor!

The sticks, prickly with thin stems, green and damp, come down hard all the same, despite the pleading, in a great whoosh of air, strik-ing shoulders, ribs, bare legs, arms. And while the flesh of the initi-ates is still subject to the lashing of the green stems, like a balm being rubbed on their wounds, a voice rises from the group of initiators, to speak of the world to them. And thus they enter into it . . .

Initiator

Nan guil wam yo! (Listen to me!)

Initiates, *in chorus*

In wé nan guil wang. (We are listening).

The initiator chants a lesson of life. He repeats it several times. The initiates listen. After a dozen or so repetitions of the poem, the initiator pauses, then asks a question.

Initiator

Nu nana xam? (Have you heard me?)

Initiates

I na nang. (We have heard you.)

Initiators, *brandishing their sticks again*

Mbay tak!

Initiates, *terrified*

Woor!

Initators, *more threatening*

Mbay tak . . . !

Initiates, *screaming as if their lives depended on it*

Wooooooooor!

This time, the initiators refrain from striking; the sticks do not come down on bodies; their threatening arms drop by their sides, and the beating of the tam-tam takes up the story of the thousand hearts speaking to each other . . .

* * *

Still, Altino was not F*. Its inhabitants did not chant as the procession went by. The women did not offer to the twilight their pure choruses of love, which were the seeds of the earth. There was no sheltering forest. Jogoy knew that. However, this march now looked like a rite to him, with everything that was at stake and on stage: the sudden appearance of a group of men in a new world. The entrance of the ragazzi into town was not the *ndût*, but symbolically it represented, once again, what was at stake: a rite of passage was being performed, the passage from one world to another, the passage from one element (seawater) to another (the earth of Altino), the passage from one company to another, one ordeal to another.

Jogoy decided to go home and get some sleep. But no sooner had he turned his back to the volcano than the first explosion resounded, and he froze where he stood. This was the third time since he'd arrived in Sicily that Mount Etna had raised her voice. He stayed there on the Villa and watched.

Chapter III

Atab: that was the name of the man who was supposed to pilot our boat. He was known all over the port of Tripoli. Every refugee who came there and wanted to get to Europe had heard of him. Even the other sailors acknowledged, with a hint of sharpness and bitterness, that he was probably "the luckiest" among them. We all wanted to go with Atab. It has to be said that in addition to his maritime exploits, the man's stature and character fascinated. He was a giant, hardy, provocative, and charismatic; he was a fighter, a lover of women and drink, and he seemed invincible. Hamid had promised us that Atab would be the one to take us over. But a few days before the first of our three attempts to depart, Atab was found dead in one of Tripoli's unsavory neighborhoods. The fact was, he did have a lot of enemies.

When Atab died, his legend died with him. As did the certainty that we'd have a better chance of survival. We threatened Hamid, told him we'd stop work and take our money back. Hamid's response was to inform us he'd already found a replacement. He told us about one of his nephews, trained by Atab, who worked in the merchant navy. Hamid was lying. We were so naïve and impatient that we still believed what he said. I've already told you, in the first chapter of this story, what happened to his impostor of a nephew.

There were exactly sixty of us on the boat, of various nationalities from West Africa, almost all of us young. The oldest was from Guinea. His name was Hamady Diallo. He was a very pious man who never went anywhere without a little copy of the Koran, which he read almost constantly, even at night, in the light of his little flashlight or of the stars alone. Even at the height of our terror, when after four days we knew we were lost, Hamady Diallo went on reading. He was the one who led the prayers on the boat. Throughout the entire crossing, he scrupulously respected the times for prayer, with sublime devotion. I will never forget my last sight of him (not long before the storm), his solitary form tall and devoted, straining toward the sky: the storm was threatening, and he was praying.

The first two days of the crossing had been calm. We were already dreaming about Europe. Right from the first few hours on board, three individuals imposed themselves as the leaders of the group. In Tripoli, they'd already been our spokesmen. They'd tried to cross several times since their arrival in Libya. Two of them had even been to prison and survived, unlike the majority of Black people the local police arrested. All this gave them an aura, a semblance of natural legitimacy. As if they knew what to expect. The first two days, they did their job well. On the third day, we still couldn't see anything on the horizon.

The flame of hope began to flicker. No one can imagine, unless they've been through it, what goes on in the soul of a man lost at sea, who hopes to see lights but finds nothing but impenetrable darkness. No one.

Lights! Lights! Lights refusing to emerge from the endless night, lights refusing to appear on the horizon, lights that had gone out in the world, gone out in our hearts. Lights! We were begging for them . . . Regularly, like seasoned sailors, little teams of five took turns standing watch. Each watch lasted fifteen minutes. Fifteen minutes of a terrible confrontation with the hideous sea; fifteen minutes while our fellow passengers hung on our every word, hoping to hear the liberating cry: "Lights, over there!" A cry which never came.

I don't know what horrified me more: the feeling that the darkness around us was infinite, or that it was just as infinite below us, in that vast world of the depths, where sunken cities, unresolved mysteries, mythical treasures, legendary monsters, human fantasies and corpses and fears were all mingled together. I was afraid of what I could see. I was afraid of what I couldn't see. Hope and terror, combined. Several times over I thought I could see silver shafts standing upright on the sea in the distance, heading toward us, like some sort of creatures made of light. But it was only the distant motion of the waves, white caps deceiving my hallucinating vision . . .

Day was breaking, but we saw nothing resembling a coastline. Despair and horror, mixed. On waking, in the silence of our shared dejection, the three men threatened for the first time to feed the navigator to the fishes. That was the day he confessed that he wasn't a professional smuggler but a young fisherman who'd never sailed far from the Libyan coast. He owed his salvation that day solely to the fear that continued to paralyze the men, and to the mention of Atab, who still gave off his talismanic aura. But it didn't last. On the fourth day, after another night of fruitless watching, we knew that, this time, we were really lost. That was when the three men threw the navigator into the sea. No one raised any objections, no one, except Hamady Diallo. He protested at length, and told the three gurus that they had no right to dispose of a God-given life in that way. They didn't listen. We were lost at sea, and we committed our original murder, the founding crime of our wandering. Which only left punishment.

Fear soon began to wreak havoc in our ranks. Over the three days that followed, it harvested great swathes of our hearts, offered to its blade like ripe corn to a sharpened sickle. Great fear swept some of us into delirium and hallucinations, others into apathy and prostration. Some turned away from God, uttering sublime, terrible, solitary words of apostasy; others invoked God, shouting obscenities that were at the limit of insanity. All of this in three days. A lifetime to bring God into one's life, three days to expel Him from it. Either the heart of man is inhospitable, or faith is a fixed-price service . . .

Only Hamady still seemed to believe in God, right to the very end.

The three gurus lost control of the boat. Madness began to take hold of them, as well. They argued about who should make the decisions, and eventually it became a duel to the death as the others looked on, too weak or concerned with staying alive to intervene. They wounded each other. The Bozo fisherman survived; the other two—the ones who'd been in prison—died. Blood ran along the deck, under our feet.

On the morning of the sixth day, our tub was adrift, with no motor or captain on board, a tiny tomb in a vast ossuary. There were no lights. We no longer expected to see any, other than the lights of death. I didn't even have the energy to think about my family; my memories were all muddled up with visions of the hell that was coming, that was already there.

During the night of that sixth day, however, when I was exhausted and felt like I was emerging from a great black hole, I heard a shout, full of a vigor I never expected to hear again on that boat: "Lights, over there!" The men who hadn't died or fainted found the strength to get up and look into the distance. And there we saw them at last: the lights, the lights . . .

Then the storm came.

* * *

How was I received, after the storm and the shipwreck?

I was still walking along the beach, and I could tell my strength was beginning to abandon me. I was tired and hungry, and it was very hot. But I didn't want to stop before finding someone to help me. I came upon a few people soon enough, by which time I was completely drained. People out for a swim.

It was a woman who first saw me. She let out a shout. What must I have looked like to frighten her so? Was it my face, marked with fatigue and want? Or my whole body, affected by the journey, by fear and the relentless struggle against death, for days on end? I don't know. I simply saw that I'd frightened her. She pointed at me, and the other swimmers turned in my direction. It was then that I saw they were all naked. I stopped abruptly. It was the first time I'd ever seen this. I didn't understand. We looked at each other for a long time. The swimmers, surprised to see me. And me, surprised to see them naked. My first acquaintance with Europe: naked bodies on a beach on the Sicilian coast. I stood there motionless for a few seconds, not sure what to do. The crushing heat added to my exhaustion and hunger. I tried to take a step toward the group of swimmers and collapsed.

One man, still naked, immediately ran over. He was very thin and wore little round glasses. That was all I could see. I was too weak to make out his features in detail. I closed my eyes and sensed that the man was kneeling beside me. He touched my forehead, took my pulse, and opened one of my eyes, which he examined for a few seconds. Then I heard him speaking Italian. His voice was faint and faraway, as if he were being suffocated. I passed out . . . A few seconds (or minutes, or hours) later, the sensation of cool water pouring down my throat revived me. They were giving me something to drink. My eyes still closed, I let them. I had no strength to do otherwise. I was little more than a dead man they were trying to bring back to life . . . I couldn't tell when the water stopped pouring into my mouth, but I heard the man's voice, more clearly this time.

"Do you speak French?"

"Yes," I managed to croak.

"My name is Mario. Mario. You're very weak. Dehydrated. We're going to call an ambulance."

His words had the effect of a sudden electric shock. Forcefully, I grabbed his arm, roughly pulling him closer, and I stared up at him, with a crazed look in my eyes.

"No, no, Monsieur . . . Please, no ambulance, no police. Nothing."

The effort cost me a great deal. I fell back, unconscious. When I opened my eyes again, all the swimmers were leaning over me. Their faces were initially very blurry, then I gradually managed to make them out. They'd gotten dressed. Thank God, I was still on the beach and not in the hospital or at the police station. I sat up. The swimmers moved back. I don't know if it was out of fear, or to give me more air. Mario came closer again and handed me a bottle of water. I drank greedily, with no manners. Then he gave me some fruit and a few cookies. I devoured them in silence, surrounded by a little circle who observed me with a mixture of curiosity, fear,

and amusement. I was hungry. To hell with all
the rest. I soon felt better. Mario came over
again. At last I could see his blue eyes behind his glasses. His teeth were blackened,
ravaged from smoking.

"What's your name?"

"Jogoy. My name is Jogoy Sèn."

"Jo-gay."

"Jo-goy. O. Goy."

"Jo-goy. Jo-goy. Okay. What are you doing
here, Jo-goy Sèn?"

I didn't answer.

"I see," he said. "You can come with us if
you want, Jogoy. We're going to have something to eat."

"Thank you, Monsieur Mario, but I have to
keep going . . . Thank you . . . for the food.
And for not calling anyone."

"Keep going? To where? What are you going
to do?"

"I don't know. Maybe I'll go to the nearest
town and try to find work."

"But where will you live, how will you
eat?"

"I don't know. I'll manage."

Mario went and spoke for a few minutes to
a woman with long white hair. The swimmers
around me began to scatter along the beach.
Mario and the woman came back toward me.

"Jogoy," said Mario, "this is my wife,
Valeria. I don't want to make you feel uncom-
fortable, but I'd like to suggest something.
Around here, there are mostly small towns.
The nearest one is Marzamemi. Valeria and I
live in Noto. It's farther away. It's a little bigger than Marzamemi. We've talked it

over. We thought maybe you could come there. And stay at our place . . . If you want. Long enough to find some work, or to get in touch with a host association. We know of one; our daughter works there. As soon as you feel rested, we can go there. But for now . . . "

I looked at them for a moment, surprised. It was true I had nowhere to go, but that didn't mean I was ready to trust just anyone. But I accepted their offer. What helped me make up my mind was the simplicity with which Mario and Valeria had offered to help. I detected no trace of ill intentions or calculated kindness. They weren't trying to harm me or to make themselves look good. They were perfectly sincere. I told them I would be indebted to them for life.

"Don't worry, Joqoy," said Valeria in English, with a smile. "We're not naked at home."

That was how, with nothing, naked, too, in my own way, I went to Noto, to Mario and Valeria Ferrante's place. Carla's parents. That was how, after surviving a shipwreck in which all my companions perished, I was taken in by these Sicilians who, for all that they were nudists (and that's something I'll never understand), were also generous, simple souls.

WAITING

15

Salvatore Pessoto

They've been here for almost six months. They're beginning to get impatient. Their dreams are not yet broken, but they've got cracks. Babel is trembling. Babel will fall. They're experiencing that moment when a person gets the feeling that something's not right. That's when it starts to turn tragic: it's not the actual event, but what you sense is going to happen. It's like death. Some patients die as soon as they sense death is coming. Before their heart or their brain even stops.

Some of the ragazzi have begun to speak a little Italian. When they see me in the street, when they're not at practice, they always give me a long, respectful greeting. They ask for news of my family. I tell them things are fine. Then they start sharing their moods and emotions with me, even though I didn't ask them anything. They all say roughly the same thing: "We want to leave this place, Dr. Pessoto. There's nothing here." I never know how to answer. I listen. When they stop speaking, a silence settles over us. But their gaze is burning. They're waiting for an answer. And so eventually I say, "Take heart, everything will be okay." Of course that's a lie. I think they know it. And yet I'm a doctor. I should be able to tell them the truth, that nothing will really get better and that they'll have to learn to live with it. But instead, I lie to them. "Take heart," I say. I'm the one who has no heart.

"Take heart, it will be okay." It sounds so nice. But it's never really comforted anyone. Like everyone, or nearly everyone, I've heard those words when things weren't going well. And like everyone, or almost everyone, I know they didn't change anything. But you have to pretend. When you want to comfort someone and you say, "It will be okay," all I see is two people who are suffering. One of them is immersed in their own sadness. And the other is drowning in their inability to address the other person's pain. Now, when I'm confronted with other people's sadness, I opt for silence. Silence is convenient. It can signify unspoken but deep compassion, just as it can hide absolute indifference. No way of knowing. The next time I come upon one of those guys and they share their sadness with me, I'll keep silent. I hope that he'll see empathy in my silence, as Sister Maria would say. If they want to believe it . . . A lot of them play football. I coach them twice a week. I didn't really have much faith in it, but we have a good *squadra* this year. I get the feeling that, on the pitch, with the ball, they're happy. They shouldn't be. It won't last.

16

V era and Vincenzo Rivera were unique in that they always painted together, all four hands, without conferring with each other, without preliminary sketches or plans; they each let their individual talent find their partner's naturally. Their canvases, which were absolutely puzzling, met with considerable success. Vincenzo and Vera were known in the region. They were established in artistic circles, and their artwork featured in prestigious collections. They had begun, moreover, to enjoy a certain renown beyond the island, in the North, ever since a major national daily paper had done a portrait of them in their "Fashion, Culture, and Glamour" pages.

For several months, they'd hardly seen Jogoy. In fact, they saw no one: they were struggling to finish their new cycle, the latest fruit of their twinned genius: *Vanitas Vanitatum*. The children of wealthy families, they'd settled in Altino ten years earlier, back in the days when the town was taking in its first ragazzi. To them, however, that seemed like a minor phenomenon, without any aesthetic potential. They both viewed it as vulgar reality, too sociological and restrictive, unsuited to fostering creativity. All that suffering, all that distress, the stifling administrative aspects, the poverty—such things weren't interesting, were alienating for true artists. So they haughtily ignored the ragazzi and all the activities connected with their integration; they preferred to look elsewhere for inspiration: in sexuality. A subject which was, of course, brand new in the art world.

Their first joint creation in Altino was, therefore, entitled

Post-coitus. It was a series of paintings they'd made immediately after fucking (over a thirty-day period). And as they indulged massively that month (beating their own record), the cycle yielded such a profusion of paintings that they were obliged to classify them according to the quality of the orgasms. They established a typology of three categories (or sub-cycles): major orgasms, neutral orgasms, and insipid orgasms. Each of these three categories was on display. The "neutral orgasm" sub-cycle enjoyed resounding success; apparently their peers found it a faithful reflection of the sexuality of the era. With this cycle, the Riveras had wanted to "*remove sex from the domain of pleasure consumption alone and expand it into a space where Art can be constantly and intelligibly produced, to create a carnally critical hyperawareness of Beauty, and to achieve orgasm on the canvas by continuing to ejaculate into the face of the painting and that of the inane bourgeois viewer: to de-virginize it*" (said Vera in an interview for a local paper).

Post-coitus was, on the whole, a success. The works were exhibited at the museum in Altino, in the main room where the statue of Athena stood. The Riveras made a grand entrance onto the Sicilian art scene. The installation toured several towns. Members of Sicilian high society rushed to see it, and, after enduring the ejaculatory spurts that were meant for them, they voiced hyperbolic praise of the kind that bourgeois philistinism alone can produce. There was only one fly in the ointment: for the opening presentation of the cycle, the "major orgasm" category, Vera and Vincenzo had sent an invitation to the great poet Giuseppe Fantini. They thought that inviting the old Maestro would suit everyone: Fantini would add prestige to their work, and they would offer him the chance to renew his ties with the upper crust. Fantini declined the invitation. In response, he sent them a seriously ironic sonnet. It didn't matter: Vera and Vincenzo indulged the old man, assuming that he suffered from the bitterness of the dried-up, has-been artist.

They went on creating as a duo, for they were the true artists, they were the ones stricken with an intense creative fever. Their reputation grew with each successive work. *Vanitas Vanitatum*, which they were trying to finish, would be their eighth creation.

They'd been working on it for six months. The work was difficult, stubbornly resistant to their dual sensibility. But they would overcome the obstacles soon enough. Vera and Vincenzo Rivera even planned to give themselves a moment's respite, the time to enjoy a dinner with Jogoy. Jogoy would surely tell them everything that had happened since the last convoy of ragazzi had arrived. Because yet again, they had not manifested any interest. But their conscience had long been clear regarding the issue. Ever since they'd agreed to rent Jogoy the little apartment at the far end of their courtyard, they considered that they'd generously fulfilled their role as humanists and that, for now, there was no shame in turning their backs on the adjacent situation. Jogoy was their clear conscience, the blank check handed to them and with which they validated their certificate of kindness to others, to those who suffer, to the developing world.

And so they were content, that evening, as they dined with Jogoy, to hear him speak about the situation. As a matter of form, they asked questions, frowned, put on sad or indignant expressions, showed a great amount of pity. They found it all very restful; they enjoyed the pleasure of talking about prosaic things after their bitter struggles at inhuman heights with Art. They even succeeded, that evening, after drinking two bottles of wine, in making love without being critically hyper-aware of Beauty. An almost-major orgasm. And then, content, they slept the luminous sleep of painters of genius. *Vanitas Vanitatum* was almost finished. It was the only thing that made sense.

17

Fousseyni Traoré

I t's hard to get up. It's getting colder and colder. Today, I felt like staying under my thick blanket. But I wanted to go to class. From the very first day, Jogoy told me I must always go to class, to learn Italian. In six months, I haven't missed a single session. I'm beginning to speak some Italian. Jogoy tells us every day that speaking Italian can help with our documents. So I go. And never mind the documents, I just like being back in school. I stopped studying a long time ago, when I was fourteen. I didn't even finish secondary school. It wasn't because I was stupid or anything, don't go thinking that, but because my uncle didn't want to pay for my studies anymore. I stopped so I could do carpentry.

I had a wash, then performed my ablutions, and then I prayed. The morning prayer is the one I like best. There's not a sound. I think this silence is the voice of God. I prayed for my mother who's back home, and for Adama. And at the end, I prayed for all my companions here: I hope we'll all be granted asylum and find work, inshallah. I'm the only one who's leaving the house this early. The others almost never come to Italian class anymore. There aren't many people around in the morning in Altino. There's one café open. Men are having breakfast. They never put sugar in their coffee. The first time I drank Italian coffee, I had to spit it back out. It's impossible to drink it without sugar. When I see Italians drinking it in one swallow, just like that, I wonder how they do it. Their tongues must be naturally sweet. It's really cold out. Two months or so ago, it was still kind of warm. *Siamo in inverno.* It's winter. In winter, it's cold, and it snows. *L'inverno fa freddo e nevica.* That's the way it is. I've never seen snow. They say it will start soon. Lucia wrote that it's like big grains of salt falling. So snow is the salt that God adds to the dish of the world when it hasn't got any taste.

I'm always the first one outside the room where we have class. It's not far from the Santa Marta office. As soon as I get there, I go and ask Jogoy, the first one at the office, for the key. We greet each other in Bambara; he looks a little tired to me. All my pals know him. He's the one we call when we have problems and don't know what to do. He's on his feet all day long. His phone never stops ringing.

He tells me about the assessment interview, part of the asylum process. I tell him I'm scared. He says the president of our assessment commission is a kind man, and that he goes pretty easy on asylum seekers. That reassures me a little. Jogoy tells me not to worry. The association will help us prepare for the interview. We'll rehearse together with Padre Bonianno so we'll know what to say during the interview. You have to have a good story to get asylum. No one knows yet when the interviews will start, but everyone's apprehensive. Everyone's waiting for them. Jogoy tells me that to have luck on my side I have to go on attending Italian class. He gives me the key, and I go into the classroom. As usual, I sit at the back of the room. All the way at the back, on the left, near the machine that gives off heat. That's my favorite spot. Rosa arrives at eight o'clock on the dot, as always. She's the one teaching us Italian.

I don't know how old she is, but Bemba says she is a "little sister." That means she's younger than he is. But since I don't know how old Bemba is, either, it's complicated. Rosa is a really tall woman, and very thin. The first time we saw her, Bemba said she looked like the stalk of a millet plant, and that her butt was flat like the surface of the Mali River in dry season, and that she had hollow breasts like a cave in the Bandiagara and that someone should make her eat yams and manioc. Fallaye said that was all true, but that she had a lovely face, but Bemba said a lovely face was useless without any flesh on her bones. Bemba likes curvy women. When he talks about women, he says, "What I like is to be able to grab onto a woman so I won't fall *vaap* onto the ground! Look at Sabrina or Veronica: their faces are not the loveliest in the cosmos (I didn't know that word), but just look at their bodies, my young brothers: you climb on, you know you won't fall off, you forget their faces, just grab hold and screw her well! That's what I like." I don't agree with Bemba when he says that a pretty face is useless if the rest of the body has no shape. The face matters. Rosa has a lovely face. Not as lovely as the face of Lucia the orange-girl, but lovely. It's no big deal if she's not curvy; she has a good heart. She has a long neck like a giraffe. One day, she wore a colorful necklace, and she looked like a ritual Dogon statue.

Today, she's giving a class on nostalgia. I didn't know the word. But I know the feeling well. Now I know how to express it in Italian, thanks to Rosa. *Il Mali mi manca. Mi piacerebbe rivedere mia madre.* I repeated it to Lucia the orange-girl when I met her after class. She said it was very sad, and she took my hand. Maybe nostalgia is sad. But Lucia took my hand. For days, it will smell of oranges. I won't wash it. I'll figure something out for my ablutions. God will understand.

18

S ergio and Fabio Calcagno, Maurizio Mangialepre's right-hand men, were feeling somewhat frustrated at having to hide like this to carry out their mission. It was more than frustration, actually; it was a kind of shame. What?! They were the legendary Sergio and Fabio Calcagno, the terror of Catania, the twins from hell, the two heads of the devil, as they'd been called, and now they were stealing like common thieves along the streets of the little town of Altino—just to put up posters? The dishonor of it! The disgrace!

What would the ultras from the Catania football team say if they saw their two former champions creeping through town like timorous shadows? And what, above all, would the ultras from the rival Palermo team say, who took it as a point of honor to have such courageous, virile, remarkable opponents? Their entire legend had been written on their ability to incarnate, in broad daylight for all to see, the spirit of the ultras and their values: strength, courage, manhood, tradition, honor, identity, respect.

The Calcagnos! Their name alone sufficed to strike terror into the hearts of the *tifosi* from the other side. When you stood face-to-face with them, you sensed not only their passion for Catania but also their violence, their male desire to completely annihilate their opponents with the purest brutality. In the ultra milieu, to confront the Calcagnos was a challenge, or better still, an honor. They were the yardstick with which you measured bravery. People said that to confront them, it wasn't enough to just have balls; they must, in addition, be securely attached.

"Remember . . . ?" Sergio began, as his brother spread paste onto the museum wall.

"Yeah," said Fabio. "I remember it well. Very well."

They understood one another, suspected each other's supreme shame—after having once been at the summit of glory—at being reduced to hanging posters around this insignificant town. And both of them, in frustrated silence, went on with what they were doing. They were nostalgic for the atmosphere of the matches: the flares, the chants, the choreography, the fans in their multitudes, the percussion, the grand finale after the winning goal, the insults they hurled at the opponent. They missed the adrenaline rush of the stadium. But even more than the match, it was the post-match atmosphere they were sorry they couldn't experience now—gathering outside the stadium, whether they'd lost or not, to close ranks with the others and lead them against their opponents' ultras in violent urban battles, intense and all too brief (because the police arrived on the scene fairly quickly) but good for building courage and necessary for respect and self-esteem.

"Remember Andrea and Cesare?" Sergio asked.

"How could I forget? *They* were proper rivals. Led the Palermo ultras. Real men. They don't make em like that anymore. I'd like to fight them again."

"Me, too, bro. Hand me a poster; we'll put one here, one last one on the gate to that lily-livered mayor's house, and then we'll go home, basta. If it weren't for Maurizio . . . "

And they continued on their way toward Francesco Montero's house, avoiding the streets that were too well lit, or where a few night owls or drunks might still be hanging around. Because Maurizio had told them to be careful. They obeyed him. Because they knew very well that if it weren't for him, they'd still be in prison for a long time (they'd seriously injured a kid during a free-for-all). The Calcagnos were all the more indebted to Maurizio because he was their first cousin, a member of the numerous Mangialepre-Calcagno clan, prestigious and well-liked, with branches spread all over Sicily.

They didn't know him yet when he'd come to see them for the first time, two years earlier, at the main prison in Catania. He'd been their court-appointed lawyer for the defense. Maurizio had immediately told them that they were related, and he added that this was why he was there. It was this mark of family solidarity, his concern for his blood that had, more than anything, had an emotional impact on the twins. Maurizio promised he'd get them out of it, and out of prison, but in return he asked them to pledge their loyalty to him and help him with a task he wanted to entrust them with once they were out. Fabio and Sergio Calcagno gave their oath. Eleven days later, Maurizio came to set them free, without meeting any opposition. "Stefano Scarpatto, the judge who was going to convict you, is an old acquaintance, and old acquaintances don't forget each other," he explained.

As soon as they were free, Maurizio Mangialepre brought them to Altino. He gave them a big apartment he owned in the center of town and helped them find work at the Altino funeral parlor: the owner, Simone Malamorte, was one of his friends. He hoped in this way to oblige his burdensome cousins to stay out of the limelight in this little town lost in the hills, but, above all, he wanted a devoted workforce who'd help him with his mission: to combat the mass influx of ragazzi, the majority of whom were African. It must be said that Sergio and Fabio Calcagno had been a bit disappointed with the work, which came nowhere close to matching the excitement they'd known with the ultras of the Catania football team. But they'd already given their word. And a Calcagno never goes back on his word. So it was all agreed.

They did a clumsy job of sticking their last poster (*Migrants Make You Poorer!*) on Mayor Montero's gate, then headed, with a half nostalgic, half humiliated step, toward the home of Maurizio Mangialepre, the first cousin to whom they owed their freedom.

19

Maurizio Mangialepre would have liked to join his cousins and help them with their task. He hated to think he might be projecting the image of a boss commanding operations from afar. But the cold weather had dissuaded him. Low temperatures were torture to his lungs. His cousins knew this. Sitting by the fire, his features placid, wearing a black dressing gown with a purple-and-yellow-striped afghan thrown over his lap, Caecilius looked every bit like an old Scandinavian count about to tell a fantastic tale to an invisible guest.

But despite the apparent calm that, at first glance, seemed to prevail, inside his skull Maurizio's thoughts were in a whirlwind. He was trying to define a course of action. Over the last six months, since the seventy-two ragazzi had arrived, he hadn't been able to orchestrate any significant action. The reception he and his friends had reserved for the newcomers at the entrance to town back in June had been their first and, thus far, only demonstration. He'd been sure, at the time—he'd even promised as much to his supporters—that other actions would follow very soon. But perhaps he'd underestimated how hard it would be to instigate any mass protest movements once the ragazzi had settled in. The first time, the element of surprise had worked in their favor, but now that Santa Marta knew what he was up to, it was harder. Sabrina had asked Francesco Montero—and got what she wanted, of course, since Montero was a lump with no personality—to reinforce the means the carabinieri had at their disposal so that Captain Falconi could provide greater protection. This would make it more complicated to maneuver.

Under pressure from his supporters, Maurizio had organized several meetings. The debate was lively, and two tendencies emerged. On the one hand was a radical fringe, led by Gennaro Orso, a local butcher, who wanted to launch a head-on offensive against the enemy, whether the carabinieri were there or not. On the other hand, and far more numerous, were the defenders of a gentle guerilla movement, pressing for a kind of psychological harassment. Sergio and Fabio were, naturally, in favor of the first fringe. Maurizio, however, thought that both approaches were insufficient for the same reason: they wouldn't work. A head-on attack would subject them to the law, and as for the gentle guerilla strategy, it might work now and again, but Maurizio didn't think it could produce an upheaval of the kind that would force the ragazzi to leave Altino. In the meantime, with a majority in favor, they decided that gentle guerilla tactics (for example, substituting pork for beef and selling it to the ragazzi, who were predominantly Muslim, or sabotaging the heating in their apartments in the middle of winter, among other things) would be the preferred strategy, even though Maurizio was far from satisfied with it.

He had to find a more incisive, direct form of action. They must strike at the source of the Evil: minds, morale, and will. How would they do this? By refusing to give the migrants the only thing that—

Fabio and Sergio were so thoughtlessly noisy upon their arrival that it caused Caecilius to lose his train of thought. The two colossuses were tramping up the stairs that led to the room he was in. Maurizio Mangialepre greeted them with mulled wine and questions.

"Well then, cousins, did you manage to hang up all the posters?"

"Yeah," said Sergio. "We stuck them kind of all over the place."

"Really, everywhere?" said Maurizio, his voice unctuous and mean.

"Yeah," said Fabio, as his brother emptied his glass. "At the town hall, on the door to the mayor's house, at the entrance to Santa Marta, outside the school, at the museum, in front of a few cafés, at the bus station, along the Via Rolando Ettorini—"

"At the church?" Maurizio interrupted.

Fabio didn't answer and shot his brother a look, calling for help. It was Sergio who, after a few seconds, tried to speak.

"Well, uh, Maurizio, cousin . . . as for the church, the thing is, I, well, we—"

"I understand, my friends," Maurizio said, putting an end to their discomfort with a mocking, indulgent smile. "I see you're both still fervent Catholics and afraid of . . . of . . . yes . . . blasphemy!"

"It's just that . . . Christ has no business being mixed up in this," Fabio protested.

"This is a matter for men," said Sergio.

"Yes, of course. But don't forget," Maurizio added with an ironic pout, "don't forget—*puff! puff!*—that the church here, and that includes Christ, supports Santa Marta, which means it supports hosting . . . So that's where you should have stuck your posters, before anywhere else."

"Don't you believe in God anymore, cousin?"

"Not even a little?" Fabio added.

Maurizio marked a pause. Outside, the snow that had been forecast for several days had finally begun to fall over Altino, huge flakes of it.

"God, my dear cousins," he eventually said, "is the only old acquaintance who forgot me when I needed his help most. And forgetting calls for forgetting. I'm taking my revenge. God must pay."

And when he'd finished speaking, he gave a diabolical grimace at the sight of the expression of fear distorting their faces. Like so many of his militants, his cousins were incapable of setting aside their fondness for a belief that actually justified the very thing they were claiming to be against. The sight of their inner torment amused Maurizio Mangialepre. A few minutes later, the two colossuses stood up and decided to go home before the snow could stop them.

The fire was crackling. Caecilius could hardly stay awake. Just as he was about to nod off at the last border between waking and sleep, the thoughts Sergio and Fabio had interrupted on opening his front door came clearly to mind. He had time, before nodding off, to finish them. *They must strike at the source of the Evil: minds, morale, and will. How would they do this? By refusing to give the migrants* . . . the only thing that mattered to them, and that was keeping them here: asylum. And he thought he knew how to achieve this. A smile of satisfaction began to spread slowly over his face, but sleep got there first, and he dozed off with his face set in a terrible half-smile. The fire only went out much later, in the middle of the night. But the room was so warm by then that Maurizio, well protected by his afghan, felt none of the intense cold that was now gripping the town.

CHAPTER IV

Two days after Carla's parents took me in, the media announced that wreckage from a boat had been discovered on the beach at Marzamemi. But it wasn't only wreckage: the Coast Guard also found thirty-seven bodies washed up on the shore, disgorged by an ocean so well-fed with humans that it had the luxury to cough a few of them back up. Judging by the state of the corpses, the investigators and rescuers reckoned the shipwreck had occurred two or three days earlier. Mario asked me if I'd been on that boat; I replied that I might well have been, but I couldn't be sure.

The TV and newspapers didn't talk about the event for long. It only filled one insert, a little news item, the space of a paragraph; it got one sentence on a red banner that unfurled along the bottom of the screen, with vague information and a few numbers. Two days later, it was forgotten. Tragedy was becoming ordinary. Dramatic events tied to immigration were playing a macabre game of musical chairs; on a daily basis, each new event eliminated the previous one, taking its place, until the next one came to dislodge it in turn. It was exhausting, but people were getting used to an uninterrupted state of disaster, even if the truth of it remained unbearable. The dramatic event that reveals the horror of the world to us is all too often the one we eventually accept the most readily.

A few days later, Mario informed me that the authorities had put up a monument to the dead. I went there to pay my respects with Mario and Valeria. It was a man's bust, set among the rocks, his face turned out to sea. Next to him, there was a plaque with a fitting in memoriam.

On the way home, we were silent. I could tell that my hosts wanted to speak to me. But they said nothing. It was better that way: I wasn't ready yet.

I'd been able to call my family as soon as I arrived. It had been several days since they'd had news. I could have been dead for all they knew. My mother wept so hard that day that I wanted to go home there and then. What does the pain of those who leave amount to, compared with the suffering of those who cannot make them stay?

Mario and Valeria were people without depth—this is not a criticism. They were cloaked in a light grace. They lived in a big house at the heart of a working-class neighborhood. Their lives beat to a slow rhythm, bubbling like a stew on very low heat. In that big house, where I stayed for two weeks or so, photographs of their younger selves covered an entire wall. They were good-looking. Mario explained to me that they had both taken early retirement, as soon as Carla started university.

One day when we were out for a drive, we saw a group of young Black men emerge from the field next to the road. Valeria slammed on the brakes. The five men stopped, surprised. We stared at each other for a moment, then I climbed out of the car and spoke to them, first in Serer (I got no reaction), then Bambara.

"Greetings to you. How are you?"

"You speak Bambara? Greetings to you."

"What are you doing here? Who are you?"

"We're traveling. We got here yesterday. Do you have some money for us? We want to buy some food and call our families."

I was about to continue the conversation, but an ambulance siren somewhere in the vicinity began to wail. Without pausing to think, the five young men, terrified, set off at a run, deep into the field on the other side of the road. They thought it was the police coming for them. I never saw them again.

Mario and Valeria showed me a large part of the south of the island. Of all the places I saw, my favorite was Noto Antica, a hamlet at the top of a mountain with only a few houses and an abandoned monastery. To get there, you had to take a narrow track, hardly wide enough for a single car. It was the sort of road used mainly by herds. If you were in a hurry, you had to hope you wouldn't run into one, because if you did, the herd had right-of-way. That was the code, on mountain roads. We did meet a herd, and we had to stop for a quarter of an hour. A low wall of white heaped stones was our only protection against the void. The huge flock of sheep went by; you could sense them coming from quite a distance, from the chaotic sound of their hooves, the pungent smell of fleece, and their insistent bleating. The shepherd went by, a rifle over his shoulder, preceded by two huge white dogs. He gave a nod of his head to greet us. His skin was the color of the mountain, as if he were made from the same matter. And from where we'd stopped, next to the void, we gazed out at this scene from a vanishing world, a candle flame lacking for air.

We wound our way through the heart of the mountain toward the summit. The bends in the road were tight, and you had to blow the horn to warn any motorists hidden beyond the bend. On the other side of the abyss, peculiar caves occasionally appeared, and they looked like eyes, staring at us as if keeping watch.

From the high plateau at Noto Antica, I could see the lights of the towns along the coast and beyond. Portopalo down there. Marzamemi a little closer. Those lights—I had seen them from the boat a few days ago. Before the shipwreck. Now I was seeing them again from inland, from the other side of the picture. What had changed in the meantime? Was I happier?

That day in Noto Antica, I felt ready to tell Mario and Valeria about my journey. So they heard the story about the three ringleaders and Hamady Diallo, Atab, and Hamid, the navigator abandoned at sea, and all the others.

At the end of my story, Mario and Valeria observed a pause, then Valeria asked me why I'd left my home.

A long moment went by; then I eventually said the only, banal, thing a man who leaves everyone he loves behind can possibly say:

"Because I had to leave, Valeria."

20

W hy did you leave your home?" That's a tough question for refugees. They'll never be able to avoid it. Everyone will ask them. They'll hear it when they go for their interview. People moved by their presence will ask them. And those who are hostile, too. These three different interlocutors will ask the same question, and while they may all be very different, they do share this desire to know.

Let's take the example of the first two types of interlocutor, in other words, assessment committees and the kindly people who are moved by the plight of refugees. In their presence, a refugee has two types of response at their disposal: the ones that begin with "because" or "due to" on the one hand, and those that begin with "in order to" or "for" on the other. In the presence of a European committee or a kindly person eager to feel for them, the migrant can insist on the *cause* of departure or on its *aim*. On the *grounds* or the *purpose*. On the *reason* or the *goal*. The option they choose will determine the immigrant they become. Those who say "because" or "due to" have a greater chance of affecting their listener and being granted asylum: in the presence of an interviewer or someone who is moved by their situation, their answer will reflect the absolute necessity of departure—war, famine, persecution, discrimination, natural or ecological disaster, and so on. These are the good migrants: they were being threatened by certain death. Those who say "in order to" or "for" are more suspect: their response may still convince or move, but they will have more trouble because, in the eyes of their interlocutor, this response connects their departure to a reason that is not absolutely necessary, or is even superfluous: to earn more money, help their family, find a job, have prospects for the future, improve their life. These are the bad migrants. The death that stalks them is *merely uncertain*. The distinction between good and bad migrants can now be made as much through evaluating their usefulness and adhesion to the host country as through assessing their degree of exposure to death in their country of origin. So good migrants are no longer just honest, decent immigrants who have left their country to continue their studies or put their skills to good use elsewhere, in a land whose values and lifestyle they more or less go along with; no, for all those countries wondering whether all the misery of the world can land just like that on their shores, the good migrants are the ones in the process of becoming almost-dead migrants. Yes, almost: one last gasp of life must remain in order for them to relate the circumstances in which the grim reaper, in one form or another, very nearly wielded his scythe. Becoming a migrant is tantamount to earning a diploma with different honors, the most prestigious of which is, "very nearly died, for real!" With moments of failure, too. In our age, if some refugees fail, it is no longer solely because they didn't make it to a host country; it's also because they got there without almost dying first. If they cannot prove that death was hot on their heels, they are worthless. They will not be taken in.

Over time, and with the help of the host associations, many *ragazzi* have eventually understood that it is always better to begin their story with "because." A good number of them, even if their motivation is strictly economic, exaggerate or invent causes of absolute necessity. Basically, there are those who massage the truth. It's perfectly banal to say so. But this question, "Why did you leave your home?" is so harsh that no one should be surprised if those who are subjected to it end up lying when they give their answer. They even have the right to lie. Or the obligation: to obtain asylum, the most important thing for a refugee is not the truth of their story but its tragic verisimilitude.

Let's take a look at the third case, which concerns those who are hostile to the presence of immigrants. Such people don't give a damn whether refugees left home "because" or "in order to." What bothers them is not the reason for the refugees' departure, but the reason for their arrival. The fact that they are here, now, is the only thing that interests them. They're asking the wrong question. Instead of saying to the migrants, "Why did you leave home?" they should be saying, "Why are you here?"—which is a slightly different question. But by making this mistake, those who are hostile are the only ones who have actually put their finger on what may be the truth of the matter. Yes, they are the only ones who view the migrants, even if it is often for unfortunate reasons, as people who are here, who have arrived, who have a life in the present and want to build a future. Where the other two categories try to define refugees on the basis of their past alone, and where the migrants only seem human because they've been forced to leave for dramatic reasons, the anti-migrants, obsessed with their phobia, see immigrants in spite of everything as people who are present, who are there, with them (even if that is the very thing they cannot bear).

From this angle, paradoxically, it is those who are hostile who are right. Without realizing it, due to their unfortunate reasoning, they nevertheless manage to ask the migrants another question, one that's more problematic but perhaps more pertinent where they themselves are concerned: "Now that you're here, what do you want from us?" This question makes more sense. It doesn't reduce a refugee to a walking tragedy. It interrogates their desires, their dreams, their inner life, their deepest aspirations. But who is interested? Who wants to know the deep, complex story of a human soul? Who even wants to tell it? Or, more simply, who thinks they *can*? And who thinks they can listen to it? In the end, the story of "Why did you leave?," despite the difficult issues it raises, is perhaps the question that best suits everyone.

21

Bemba

This can't be what Europe is like! No way! No way did I risk my life in the Sahara and on the sea for this! They're hiding something from us. Why'd they put me here? Even Kayes is better than this damn village! Where's the luxury? Where's the money? Where are the white women, young and old, who love Black men and their big hard veiny *bangalas*? Where's all that? What I say is, they're hiding something from us. They're hiding us in Altino. They're keeping us here to stop us from seeing the real Europe. And why is that? How should I know? The people from the association haven't given us our papers, even though they promised. They haven't given us work, even though they said they would. It's true that a few months ago we did have a little job to do: we went picking fucking olives in the fucking fields. They paid us a little, but not enough. Since then, nothing. The association hasn't found anything. They're there, they do bugger all, whenever we go see them they say our files are being processed. How damn long do they need to get processed? Not forever? Even administration comes to an end somewhere! But no, the files are still being processed, they're tireless, on and on they go, getting processed.

And they want us to go to class to learn Italian. Do they really think that an old guy like me, Bemba, with more hair around my cock than on all the bodies of their fathers put together, that I have time to go to class so some little sister can teach me to speak like a kid? Do they think I have time for stuff like that? And they want me to go out in the cold and snow! Even if that girl *could* give me the appetite and the courage—but nope! Lord, there's not an ounce of flesh on her. *Vaap* and down you fall. Really not encouraging.

I want to get out of Altino; there's nothing for me here. I want to go where there's some business, good business. First I have to get my papers before I leave, but we've been here for six months, and the interviews haven't even started. I've stopped going to school. I stay home sleeping all day long, or I go around the shops to see if they have any work. I'd even clean toilets. So long as there's money afterwards! Real money, okay? Real euros! Bank notes. None of that, what do they call it again, yeah, that "pocket money" the association gives us. It's pretend money, vouchers we exchange with the shopkeepers so we can eat. What are we supposed to do with those vouchers? Nothing. That's not what you need to build a nice house back home, a cute little place wearing heels and makeup. Their pocket money is just for surviving. We're slaves to it. That's how the association keeps us here. They know we have nothing and that if we leave, we leave without papers, empty-handed. We're slaves to these vouchers. Every Friday, when I see the guys lining up for their rations of pocket money, I'm ashamed, I'm really ashamed. I never go and get it for our apartment. It's always Fousseyni who goes. I really like little Fousseyni; he's a good kid, a good little brother. He's polite and helpful. We're in the same room, and we get into conversations. He's had a rough time of it, that kid. I get along well with the guys in the house, Fallaye, Kanté, Ismaïla, and Fousseyni. For sure we're not all the same age, but we're brothers. Almost all of us made the same crossing; that makes us brothers. Ismaïla does the cooking most of the time. He's a really good cook. When we asked him where he learned to cook, he said his mother taught him. Apparently, she's a great chef who has a restaurant back home.

Fallaye and Kanté help him in the kitchen and do the dishes. Fousseyni and I clean the apartment together twice a week.

From time to time, Jogoy Sèn, the mediator from the association, comes to see us. I don't care much for him. I don't think many people do. He comes and acts the sergeant, thinks he can give us advice. Look at that, he wants to give advice to people older than him. He has no respect, and on top of it he dares to tell us we have to be patient, that he's been in the same situation himself, and blah blah blah . . . Leave us alone, man! He's not like us, he works for the association, he's always hanging out with that pretty little blonde woman, Carla, I'm sure it's all *zanga* and *mougou* real good, he gets paid, he lives alone in a little studio apartment, why does he come talking to us? He doesn't have to use pocket money. It's all too easy for him to come and tell us we have to wait: he's got his papers, he's got euros, he hangs out with pretty girls, why does he keep bothering us? The only thing we need him for, sometimes, is to translate, so we can fill in our asylum applications and send some money home when we have some. For all the rest, it's the same as with the other people at the association. All *wawa*. All chatter.

As a rule the whites around here are nice. They smile, they give you supplies, fruit and veg, sometimes clothes. But never any money. I think they're very poor, too. From time to time I've found a little work, but it's getting harder and harder to find. There are some racist white people, too. In the street, I look in their eyes, and I know they don't like me. So I give them a nasty look back. I wait for one of them to say something; I'll show him I ate yams and manioc when I was a kid. The first dog who dares to act too familiar with me, I'll give him one. They'll see this man's bones are heavy, and his mother didn't feed him from a bottle but from her breast! They'll see that my mother didn't carry me on her shoulders wrapped up in toilet paper or an old newspaper, but inside her pagne!

My aim is to go to England or the United States and become a used car dealer. That's where I'd like to be headed. I want work. I'm a strong man. I feel very close to Nigerians and Ghanaians. They're very strong, too; they want to work. They're big guys. We've had a lot of discussions; I manage okay in English. I know they're just like me, ready to do anything to get money. They've also been saying that they're fed up being here and that the association keeps us here to stop us from going anywhere. No, honestly, this can't be all there is; this can't be what Europe is like. I'm not asking for heaven and earth; there are just two things I want: to make money and sleep with white women. As much as I can, in both cases. It's not like I'm trying to salt the Mali River . . .

22

C hristmas was coming and, like every year, the members of Altino's Santa Marta Association were preparing their traditional year-end calendar. It was principally for promotional purposes, not so much a means of time-keeping as a surreptitious campaign in favor of the ragazzi's presence. The ragazzi were featured at their best: smiling, maybe even happy. Or putting on a happy face, in any case—that was what mattered. It meant a lot to Francesco Montero, who financed the calendar's publication: it was an opportunity for him to pose with the ragazzi as their benefactor.

This year, however, they were behind schedule with the calendar for a very simple reason: there weren't enough pictures showing the refugees in a happy light. Out of the seventy-two who'd arrived a few months earlier, only a handful had agreed to pose. The association raised the issue with all the members at a meeting on their premises. That meant Jogoy, Carla, Sister Maria, Lucia, Gianni, and Rosa, but also Veronica (Rosa's sister, who was in charge of communication) and Pietro (the psychologist). Sabrina presided.

"What exactly is going on with this calendar? I thought everything was squared away," she said, annoyed, looking at Veronica, who was usually in charge of the publication.

"Nothing has been squared away. I couldn't take more than a dozen or so photos. And out of the lot, there are only four without the mayor. He's in the way in all the other pictures."

"So what's going on with the ragazzi?" Sabrina insisted.

"I was getting there. A lot of them have refused to have their picture taken. It's as simple as that."

"Why?" asked Carla.

"I'll let Jogoy explain. He's the one they spoke to, and I'm not sure I really understood. Or rather, I understood all too well."

"A lot of them refused on religious grounds," Jogoy explained.

"What sort of religious grounds?" said Sabrina.

"Some of them said they didn't want to be represented, that representation through images is forbidden by their religion. They said it would be an offense to their prophet."

"But a lot of them take pictures of each other, don't they? Sometimes I see them posing for group shots, or on their own, and sending the photos to friends and family back home," said Pietro. "That doesn't exactly add up."

"Yes, but that's what they said."

"Was that the only reason?" asked Pietro.

"No, there's another reason, also on religious grounds. Some of them are Muslim and don't want their picture taken with Christian symbols. They just don't want to be photographed for a calendar published by a Christian association for a Christian holiday."

"I don't see what the problem is," said Sister Maria, her voice somewhat agitated. "We're not exactly proselytizing."

"Particularly since it's this same Christian association that's been looking after them," said Veronica.

"They told me it bothers them," Jogoy replied.

"How? We're not coming after their faith. We're just asking them to pose to show the work the association does, and the effort a lot of locals have made to welcome them here."

"Calm down, Maria," said Sabrina. "I agree with you, but this is the problem we're facing. Let's try to find a solution."

"We've never had this problem before," said Pietro. "What's different this year?"

"The reception," said Carla.

"Our reception?"

"The reception in general, Pietro," said Carla. "It's not just an association that receives the migrants, but an entire city, an entire place. This year, it just so happens that there's been a lot more reticence. You can feel it."

"More reticence from the locals?"

"From more of them, yes. In any case, I can feel it."

"From the ragazzi, too," said Rosa. "I can tell from Italian class. They're showing up less and less. Very few come to class regularly. I think it's not so much reticence as it is a lack of trust."

"The two go hand in hand," said Carla. "It's reticence that creates a lack of trust."

"That's as may be, but can we get back to the issue of the photographs?" said Veronica irritably.

"That's precisely what we're talking about."

"Frankly, I don't see the connection between posing for a simple photograph and the problems of reticence for some or a lack of trust for others."

"But that's just it, Veronica," said Carla. "For the ragazzi, these are *not* simple photographs. They're not neutral; they're significant. And it's their image, after all. They have the right to say no if they want."

"We do so much for them; they could at least make an effort to adapt!"

"You can be so stupid when you think like this, Veronica," said Rosa to her sister.

"And *you're* in denial! You honestly think they're angels we owe *everything* to, without the slightest effort or sense of obligation on their part? When the ragazzi ask the association for more money to celebrate their Muslim holidays, we give it to them gladly, and no one raises any objections. But when the only effort we're asking for in return is that they have their pictures taken, they refuse—and you think that's fine?"

"I'd like to point out that they're not all Muslim. And I think that among those who refused, there were also some Christians. What you're saying is idiotic. And after all, yes, it is their image; they can refuse to let us use it if they want."

"Please calm down," said Sabrina in a loud voice.

"It's a mistake to look at the issue like this," said Jogoy. "It's not our job to discuss who has to adapt to whom. That's a question for politicians."

"But that's precisely what's at stake: adapting," Veronica replied curtly. "What are we supposed to say?"

"We just say, 'How can we live together?'"

"And that's not a political question?"

"It is. The only real, honest political question, actually. Though we're already living together, in spite of all our problems. What we should be asking is, 'How can we live together *better?*'"

"How can we . . . that's naïve, Jogoy. It's not realistic or lucid. Whether you like it or not, despite all our efforts, we've got two opposing outlooks. You ought to know that, Jogoy, you were . . . how to put it? Well, yes . . . one of them. Living together, if that's what you really want, means everyone making compromises. We're in the middle of a—"

"—confrontation?" said Pietro. "Clash of civilizations?"

"Civilizations, I don't know. But a clash of values, definitely. The men who end up here are not empty vessels. They bring the values their cultures have instilled in them. And maybe those values are not the same as ours."

"Oh really? And what are our values?" said Pietro. "Are we sure we agree on this question? And who exactly is 'we'?"

"We won't get anywhere if we start talking about a clash of civilizations, or even values," said Jogoy, interrupting Veronica, who was about to answer Pietro.

"But we're *not* talking about a clash of civilizations; we're living it," she said eventually.

"Then we'll have to create a different reality," said Rosa.

"And deny what's actually happening? Like I said, you're in denial. It's not just stupid; it's suicidal."

"Reality isn't a god. It's not inevitable. Somebody actually creates reality!" said Rosa.

"Well, it's not us, that's for sure. The reality of the situation is something we're being subjected to."

"What is it you want, Veronica? What's your perfect outcome?"

"You're so tiresome," Veronica sighed. "I don't want anything at all. I get the feeling that if we keep talking, you're going to end up thinking I'm attacking the ragazzi. I wish them well, like we all do. I'm just sad to find out that a lot of them see us as Christians trying to impose our faith on them, or attack theirs. This isn't a crusade."

Sister Maria didn't say anything, but nodded her head in approval. Lucia took a little piece of paper and began writing something, very quickly. Everyone waited for what she had to say. She stopped writing, re-read it briefly, then handed the paper to Gianni, and in a timid, low voice that no one would have heard if the silence hadn't been so profound, he read, "*I think we should also avoid just seeing them as Muslims who think their faith's being attacked. Because they're not all Muslims, first, but also because they're something else. For some of them, maybe there's something deeper behind the refusal to have their picture taken.*"

Gianni fell silent and kept his head down, staring at the piece of paper as if he wanted to hide in it.

"What Lucia means maybe is that the source of the problem isn't religious," said Carla.

"In any case, not only religious," Pietro added.

Lucia started writing again. Gianni read it out, still just as unsure of himself, scarcely audible.

"*Exactly. I think the ragazzi are strong men, but they're tired*

of people thinking and acting for them. And that's what we're
doing. Let's help them, but we shouldn't try to force them to be
happy or pretend to be happy just for a calendar. They're not im-
ages, they're not tools of communication, they aren't projects or
proof of what the association is doing. They're human beings.
They're here, and they have other problems. Let's get back to ba-
sics."

"I agree," said Jogoy.

Veronica exploded. "Basics? What do you mean by basics?
Basics for who? I think you're pretending not to know them.
They have other problems? Sure. Money problems. That's all
they talk about when they come to see us."

"That's not true," said Rosa to her sister. "They also talk
about their families, how sad they are, how precarious their situation is, how they're scared they won't get asylum and haunted
by the thought that they might never be able to go home. You've
never experienced anything like that. They talk about money,
too, fine, but the way we all do. The Western world talks about
nothing else."

"So now it's the fault of the Western world? Not only are
you in denial, but you're also *constantly* ashamed; it's moral
self-flagellation. I'd be curious to see you in your Italian class.
Is this what you teach them? That it's the West's fault if they're
here and have no money?"

"I was just trying to tell you that they were talking about
money, but not only that."

"And I've been trying to tell you that it's their main preoccu-
pation. In any case, that's how it seems to me when I talk with
them. We can't allow ourselves to become fascinated by these
men. They come here with problems, yes. They're very brave,
yes. But they find problems here, too. What do they expect
from us? What do we expect from them?"

"And all the while," said Pietro, "here we are, reducing them
to a pronoun. 'They' and 'them' aren't here."

"That's enough," said Sabrina. "Veronica's right about one thing: the calendar isn't the main thing we do. Even if, with these shameful posters, it's pretty clear how important images are in the ideological struggle to host the ragazzi. But the basics, our basic task here, is to welcome them and stand by them until they get their papers. Defend them if need be. That's Santa Marta's purpose for existing. We'll publish the calendar with the few photos we have. We'll do without the other ones."

"The mayor won't be happy," sighed the psychologist.

"We were talking about adaptation before—he'll adapt. Now, everyone back to work. The first interviews will be starting soon. We have to finish putting together all the files and get them to Padre Bonianno so he can work together with Pietro and Jogoy to get them ready. And speaking of Padre Bonianno, don't any of you go telling him we had this meeting without him. He would kill you. And kill me after that."

23

C arla was pensive as she watched the members of the association file out of the meeting room. This was the first time at Santa Marta, in an internal discussion, that the question of values had been raised so radically. She thought of Veronica's question: "What do they expect from us, and what do we expect from them?" And she wondered why she'd never asked herself that question. Maybe because to her it seemed there was no distance between "us" and "them"; maybe she had just believed, until now, that there was only an "us," an entire ensemble where everyone was united by the same humanity, and came together.

Her naïveté overwhelmed her: humanity, humanity alone, the thing that had explained everything to her until now, suddenly seemed incapable of incorporating this sudden diversity that had come into being: a diversity of feelings, of thoughts, desires, hopes, and expectations on the part of all the human beings involved in this situation. It turned out that humanity—a certain definition of humanity—couldn't explain everything. Because despite the humanity that united them, she was different from the ragazzi. And despite their shared humanity, she was nothing like the supporters of Maurizio Mangialepre, who were against taking in the ragazzi. Too cowardly, too paltry and imprecise, "humanity" meant nothing anymore.

She'd always imagined that when you spoke about humanity, that meant identifying what was good and generous in people. That way of looking at things had now turned out to be wrong, or obsolete at best. Because it presupposed that inhumanity existed, too, an accursed aspect situated outside humanity that belonged to barbarity, savagery, wickedness, all those categories of horror, all those rear courtyards of the unspeakable, where human beings—making a grimace of repulsion that reinvigorated and elevated them in their easy conscience—discarded anything that was not morally useful to them. Now Carla suddenly realized something—perhaps it was banal, but it shook the very foundations of her view of the world and of humankind: the most horrible acts were themselves always perpetrated by human beings. There were no "inhumans," she reasoned (and this thought terrified her as it insinuated itself implacably into her mind); there were no inhumans, there were only people. There were only people who were capable of the best and (not "or") the worst. What was an evildoer? In the old days, Carla would immediately, without hesitating, have said, "a monster." Now, however, another answer came to her, simple and painfully banal: an evildoer was a person in spite of everything, a person you could hate, punish, fight, or scorn, but a person who could not be stripped of their humanity. In the name of what? How? Who could be so sure of their own purity that they dared claim to punish those they viewed as less pure? Where did humanity start and where did it end? It had never been clearly defined, but everybody pretended to know, implicitly. As if of a common accord. That was wrong. In the absolute, no one knew. If a huge survey were conducted, where everyone was asked to define the limits of humanity, according to their individual conception of it, there would be some big surprises. Complex, mixed, beautiful and ugly at the same time, sometimes bathed in a heavenly light, sometimes plunged into the abject chasm at the heart of every soul. That was humanity. Nothing else. Carla tried to think of other things. She didn't like dwelling on matters like this. It wasn't in her nature. She was an optimist; she believed in the basic goodness of human nature. She mustn't sink into pessimism or cynicism.

The calendar problem came back to her. In all honesty, she hadn't really been surprised that some of the ragazzi didn't want their picture taken. Their refusal was merely one expression among others of a rising bitterness she'd noticed over the last few weeks. To various degrees, taking varying forms, these ragazzi were voicing a frustration Carla hadn't seen before, or at least not with such intensity.

Along with Sister Maria and Jogoy, she went on their *giro case* three times a week. These were the visits the association mediators made to the ragazzi's apartments to check in: to ask if they had any problems, to see what their living conditions were like, and to talk with them. Then, once they'd taken note of the men's complaints, questions, desires, and needs, she transmitted them to Sabrina. After ten years of cultural mediation, four receptions, and hundreds of *giri case*, Carla had learned to recognize signs of bitterness among the ragazzi. With this last group, however, these signs pointed to something deeper and more vehement. The men's faces were harder, their questions more insistent, their attitude more distant and not as warm. This attitude didn't affect all of them, of course, but she noticed it in a lot of the men. They were as if burned from the inside, gnawed by impatience, by incomprehension.

She thought again of their faces, that atmosphere, and Veronica's question took on its full significance: these men were indeed waiting for something which, manifestly, they were not being given. But what was it? She had no idea. And then Carla remembered the discussion she'd had with Sister Maria, Sabrina, and Pessoto outside the warehouse that first day. Maybe Totò was right, she thought. Maybe she really couldn't understand anything about these men's aspirations.

"Are you okay, Carla?"

Jogoy had come up to her.

She looked at him, surprised. She opened her mouth, hesitated, and for a moment seemed to give up on what she wanted to say, but then she came out with it. "There's something I wanted to ask you, Jogoy. Since you're one of the . . . I mean, since you were . . . "

"You mean, I was one of the ragazzi. And still am."

"Yes. Since, in a way, you were in their place a few years ago, I wonder if you could tell me, I'd like to know: what does it mean to you, being welcomed?"

Jogoy thought for a few seconds. Carla was looking up at him with an eager gaze, as if his reply were about to determine the fate of the world. Jogoy gazed at her lovely face for a long time.

"I think," he said eventually, "it means being given something more than just a roof and some bread. It's being given something beyond hospitality. Maybe it's selfish. Food and shelter are both important things. Vital. But not essential. They're not enough. Human beings, all human beings, need deeper reasons to exist."

24

At the beginning of the afternoon, just as they were getting back to work after lunch, the members of Santa Marta had an unexpected visit. It was Veronica who saw him first, as he entered the premises. She was so surprised that only a single, stifled word made it past her lips.

"Maestro . . . "

Carla, Pietro, Sister Maria, Rosa, and Jogoy looked up and saw the man to whom they needed no introduction: Giuseppe Fantini. They all got to their feet, spontaneously, the way a class of schoolchildren would for their teacher. When they were younger, they had all, except Jogoy, recited his poems, hummed his verses; Fantini was someone they knew by heart.

This was the first time since he'd been in Altino that Jogoy would meet the great poet he'd heard about so often, who was an object of such veneration to Rosa that she'd taped several of his poems to the wall of the classroom where she gave Italian lessons. To be sure, Jogoy remembered seeing him at a distance once, and Carla, who was with Jogoy at the time, had told him that the man over there with the dog walking in front of him, the man strolling slowly, with his stern face and his hands clasped behind his back, that man was the great Italian poet. That had been Jogoy's first sighting of him. There would be others, but always from a distance. For Jogoy, until today, Fantini, had been no more than a solitary figure following his dog. And now, for the first time, he was in his presence, so close. And he was seeing his poet's face and his poet's hands. Hearing his poet's voice, a clear, sharp voice, without flourishes.

"Good morning. I don't make a habit of disturbing people, so I'll be brief. My name is Giuseppe Fantini."

"Maestro . . . Maestro . . . " gasped Rosa, about to swoon.

"This is an honor, Signor Fantini. A great honor," said Pietro.

Fantini's face remained imperturbable. There was even a certain hardness to it, as if he were immune to compliments.

"I won't keep you long; you have important work to do," he said. "Would it be possible for me to meet the person who runs this association?"

Sabrina came out of her office just then and, delighted, went up to the poet. She held out her hand, but Fantini didn't take it. He simply gave a little nod. An impassable distance separated him from other people, and now he seemed to want to make it wider still. Sabrina, embarrassed, eventually let her hand fall to her side.

"I'm Sabrina, the president of the Santa Marta Association. This is a great honor. These are the members of our association."

She introduced them one by one to Fantini, who was clearly as annoyed as could be by such formality. But he controlled himself. As soon as Sabrina had finished, he began speaking again, curtly: "I'd like to meet the young men you look after. Is that possible?"

"Of course, of course, Maestro," said Sabrina. "We'll organize a big lecture; we'll—"

"No," said the poet, harshly. "Anything but that. I just want to meet them."

"Why not ask Maestro Fantini to come with us on our *giro case*, if he'd like?"

Carla's suggestion surprised everyone.

"That would be a bit complicated," Sabrina answered, feeling unsettled by the poet's unpleasant attitude. "Signor Fantini might not be able to—"

"What is the *giro case*?" asked the poet.

"It's a regular visit where we go around and check if the ragazzi need anything," said Carla.

"And you go to their homes?"

"Yes."

"At what time, and when?"

"There's a visit tomorrow evening at eight o'clock. We leave here at half past seven."

"I'd like to take part," said the poet. "There's no need to change your schedule for the visit. We'll do it just as you always do. I'll just tag along. Thank you very much, and enjoy the rest of your day."

Before any member of Santa Marta could reply or even move, the poet was already leaving the room, not looking at anyone. Not once did his face relax, let alone show any emotion. Even Sabrina, who as a rule was unflappable, had felt the impact of the poet's antisocial behavior.

"So it's not a legend," said Jogoy. "He's as tough and aloof as they say."

"And he actually seemed quite courteous today. We even got an 'enjoy the rest of your day,'" said Pietro, imitating the poet's diction.

"Yes, he is peculiar . . . But he's Giuseppe Fantini," said Rosa, her voice full of emotion.

25

The main room of La Tavola di Luca was brimming with life and ambiance, like it was every night, and had to turn customers away. The restaurant had the best location you could imagine: right at the heart of the old town, at the crossroads of all the preoccupations, gossip, intrigues, drama, comedies, tragedies, small-scale epics, harmless lies, great pretenses, and simple truths. Anyone who wanted to get to know Altino, who wanted to seize upon some small part of the Sicilian soul, had to be there. There was always something happening.

But that wasn't all there was to it. The location alone wasn't enough to justify La Tavola's popularity: the service had to be good, too.

And it was.

And that was partly due to Concetta, the restaurant's chef, a local girl, robust and sweet with a loud laugh and round, rather red cheeks, who was an excellent cook. The men who came to eat there were fully aware of what they owed her, and they did not fail, now and again, to let her know quite noisily. Frequently, after last call, a handful of men who were feeling replete and rather drunk would break out into song, a song devoted to her that all the bar's regulars—this was a point of honor—were expected to know by heart:

Concetta ci fa mangiare
Come le altre non sanno fare
Così vorremmo darle in cambio amore
Più che alle altre, con maggior vigore

Ma Concetta è una dea
Fa l'amore come una dea
Cucina come una dea
E noi siamo solo poveri imbecilli
A pancia piena e pure troppo brilli.
Oh, Concetta![5]

When her hymn of glory rang out, Concetta emerged from the kitchen, scolded her admirers in dialect with a humble, tender smile, and told them they'd be better off heading home and to bed. Then she went back into the kitchen and wept, sad that none of these men was actually prepared to marry her. For sweet Concetta was unmarried and had never even experienced the joys of a love affair.

Along with Concetta, Signora Filippi was the other pillar of the restaurant. She was the big boss. Luca, her late husband, had built the place and given it his name. Upon his death, Signora Filippi had taken over the family business with an iron hand. A Sicilian madonna, a giant despite her diminutive stature, barely higher than the bar counter, she vociferated like a ship's captain on the quarter-deck during a tricky maneuver. She took the customers' orders and shouted them into the kitchen, where Rustico, Concetta's apprentice, a thin little man with a mustache, wrote them down. Signora Filippi was an energetic redhead, heavily made up. When the room grew too quiet, she would suddenly start singing, an old Sicilian refrain that everyone knew, and the customers, roused from their torpor, merrily joined in the singing. Sometimes, when she began to sing, she would even perform a few dance steps, to clamorous applause; and her big breasts bounced and bobbed in her blouse like kids on a trampoline.

---

[5] Concetta has fed us / Better than our wives / And we'd like to make love to her / Better than to our wives / But Concetta is a goddess / She makes love like a goddess / She cooks like a goddess / And we are only stupid imbeciles / Drunk and stuffed / Oh, Concetta!

Still, the surest asset of La Tavola was neither its location nor Concetta's talent; nor was it the dancing opulence of the inimitable Signora Filippi's bosom. In truth, it was the presence of her two daughters that Signora Filippi had to thank for most of her clientele. Serena and Francesca. Twins by blood, twins by the insolence of their beauty, each of them equally hypnotic. When they would walk among the tables, serving, the customers ceased to eat, drink, talk, or breathe, subjugated by so much beauty equally divided between two human creatures. Signora Filippi, who was well aware of the attraction her daughters exerted on her customers, oversaw it all with a stern, protective gaze from behind the counter (on tiptoes).

That evening, however, Signora Filippi lacked the few inches she needed to see over her counter to where a man, standing at the back of the room, had his eyes riveted on the derriere of one of her daughters. But who could have suspected the respectable Francesco Montero, Altino's beloved mayor, the husband of a ravishing woman and father to lovely children, of indulging in such unworthy ogling? No one. And so the mayor enjoyed full moral immunity while waiting for his appointment. Signora Filippi, per his request a few hours earlier, had reserved his usual table at the back of the room. Despite her astounding sixth sense, she did not suspect that of all the customers who devoured her daughters with their gaze, Signor *Sindaco* would prove the greediest of the lot. He had ordered a bottle of wine, which he only tasted after he was already inebriated at the sight one of the sisters had just unwittingly offered him, bending over deeply to clean a neighboring table. A good vintage. Round on the palate.

The town was getting too small for Francesco Montero's ambitions. He'd been feeling increasingly cramped after three successive terms in Altino. He'd cut his teeth here; not only had they had time to grow long, but now they were also sharp, ready to tear at any obstacle that could stop him from showing the full measure of his political talents. He dreamt of entering the Italian parliament; he already saw himself in its seats as a magnificent orator, laying out his vision for Italy and his solutions to the crisis the country had been going through for so long.

After all, he was not *that* old: half a century, on the political scene, meant that one was merely mature. He had a good track record. Altino was the only municipality on the entire island where the vote on hosting ragazzi had been yes three times in a row. This gave him the necessary legitimacy to present himself, on a regional level, as the champion of openness and magnanimity. This was all thanks to him, and he was proud of having made his town the only one that had not succumbed to the nauseating appeals from fascism and the Northern League. Proud, too, that he had been the "political artisan of openness," as they called him in the *Corriere della Sera* in a major two-page spread devoted to him. He intended to use this media success and his growing reputation to rise to a higher office— Francesco Montero, the son of a Sicilian peasant, who, through force of will and the skill of his alliances, had prevailed over the destiny his humble birth seemed to designate him for. It was strategy that had induced him to start his career with a modest position as mayor. And he'd been right: many of his colleagues, too impatient, confusing ambition and arrogance, were now floundering in the deepest anonymity, careers broken by the cruelty of the political game. Montero was patient, cautious, far-sighted, clever: he rose through the ranks with the agility of a young monkey. The old sea dogs of the system appreciated his leisurely ambition, his unhurried determination; everyone predicted he would have a fine career if he remained this astute in his rise. And he did. Perhaps for too long. Several times, the opportunity to take up a more prestigious post had arisen. But each time, he'd turned it down. The thing was, he wanted a position closer to the head of state. The opportunity had not yet come, but he wanted it to.

Francesco Montero poured a second glass. A customer who had recognized him greeted him. Montero responded with an official, mechanical, rather silly smile. The customer raised his glass of beer in his direction, took a sip, then disappeared into the crowd at the bar.

Francesco Montero smiled—this time, it was a hard smile. He enjoyed this false naïveté he adopted for his constituents. He knew that many of them thought he was a simple country official, rather soft, familiar with politics but not destined for great things. He laughed at the image he'd constructed for them: the good-natured little mayor, good Christian, humanitarian, favorable to hosting the ragazzi, happy with his little wife, his little house, his cute blonde children, his little car. Everyone thought that he aspired no further than the role of mayor of Altino. That he was only working to see his name, later on, given to a stadium, a library, a park, or a street in town. Nobody suspected him of being some great political animal, cynical and ferocious, soon to be projected into the highest circles of the country. His falsely naïve speeches were mocked, as were his rather ridiculous poses in the Santa Marta calendar, but no one came close to imagining that it was all deliberate. He was keeping his true face for that decisive hour when he would have to fight for a prestigious position. In the meantime, he went on playing the harmless little mayor.

At 9 P.M. on the dot, Maurizio Mangialepre arrived, elegantly dressed, with the little touch of fantasy that only just—but what thing of beauty in this world can be obtained other than "only just"—rescued him from too classical a perfection. They shook hands, coldly, then sat down without saying a word. The mayor of Altino poured the wine for his guest; they raised their glasses and drank in silence.

They were already acquainted. At the two last municipal elections, Maurizio Mangialepre had been Francesco Montero's main opponent. And while Montero easily won their first contest (which was the first time Maurizio had run), the next election, held two years ago, was tougher. Maurizio had been gaining in popularity, and he deployed his eloquence to rally the masses in greater numbers. He became more than Montero's opponent: he was his rival. Montero owed his victory solely to the solid traditional base he had among his supporters. It was a narrow margin. Since then, the two men had occasionally run into each other in the street or at certain local events, and they were bound by a cordial enmity, of the kind that only politics can create and foster.

"A good vintage," said Maurizio. "I didn't know you were into anything other than politics."

"What do you expect, Mangialepre? I'm a busy man."

"No, you're not, Francesco," Maurizio said softly, putting his glass back down. "A busy man doesn't arrive early for an appointment and wait calmly sipping good wine for his guest to arrive. He arrives late and apologizes for having only ten minutes of his time to spare."

"I'll give you five. After that, I have to go."

"That would be a pity, given what I have to tell you. I have a proposal to make."

"Are you trying to corrupt me, Mangialepre?"

"Let's not resort to such big, hackneyed words." Maurizio Mangialepre then shot a bright, terrifying gaze at the mayor, who remained impassive, although his rival's demented expression did unsettle him.

"I'd like to make a deal, Francesco."

"You could go to prison for suggesting it, Mangialepre. You know that."

"I know. But I won't. Unless you're not the man I think you are, deep down. Don't act surprised, Francesco; I know you. I have been and always will be your political opponent. Practically your enemy. You can fool everyone except your enemy. Hatred strips a soul bare."

"Cut the empty rhetoric. I still don't know what you're driving at—"

"Go on putting on your act, if that's—*puff! puff!*—what you want. But I'm speaking to your true nature now. It's to your true nature that I want to offer—*puff!*—"

"Spit it out, wheezer!"

"—a seat in the Italian Senate."

Maurizio Mangialepre fell silent and looked Francesco Montero in the eye. Montero did not flinch, which was the sign, cleverly concealed, of great interest. Maurizio sipped his wine, never taking his gaze off the mayor of Altino. He had just gotten his attention. He could see in his eyes the growing, wild desire—all the wilder for being veiled by his feigned indifference—of the political animal lured by the strong, bloody, obsessive odor of power.

"Not only are you committing a serious crime by trying to corrupt a mayor, but, on top of that, you're doing it on the basis of a lie. You should be ashamed, Mangialepre. You lied during your campaigns, and you're lying now. You don't have the power to offer me anything. And even if you did, you know very well I would refuse anything that smells of corruption. You're lying."

"*You* know very well I'm not. Tell me, honestly, that you want to know more, rather than resorting to your fancy rhetoric to make me speak. I'm not an amateur, Francesco. You know that."

The only response Francesco Montero gave was to set both elbows on the table and interlace his fingers.

"Fine," said Maurizio Mangialepre. "All you have to do is to run in the next legislative elections for the region of Sicily. I'll take care of the rest."

"How will you do that?"

"That's my business. All you have to do is run. Do you agree?"

"You haven't given me all the terms of your contract. I suppose if I accepted, I'd still have to do something in return. What is it?"

"Two months from now, the regional Council of Sicily has to elect a new president for the commission that decides the fate of the refugees—"

"I knew it! So that's your obsession; I should have suspected as much."

"Let me finish—"

"All that hatred. It's not just political or cultural. It's visceral, and we both know why, Mangialepre," said Francesco, with a derisive smile.

"—all you have to do," Maurizio continued, his voice increasingly shrill, "is vote for Sandro Calvino."

Francesco Montero smiled. Maurizio Mangialepre was out of breath. His face, already crushed, collapsed even further. He was literally in the process of decomposing, of melting away, like an ice cream trickling down a child's fingers in the summer heat. All of a sudden, the advantage had turned in the mayor's favor, and he continued his assault.

"So it's the ragazzi that are your big problem. You're not fighting me; you're fighting them. Your struggle isn't for Altino or Sicily; it's for your own self, to appease your hatred. They haunt your nights, don't they?"

"Do you agree?" Maurizio gasped.

"You know that I know what's fueling your hatred . . . I haven't forgotten."

"You don't know a thing. Will you accept my offer, Francesco?" said Maurizio. His anger was suffocating him.

"You know that I know. Pathetic. You are pathetic."

"Francesco, please," he said, and in his voice anger had turned to pleading. "Stop . . . "

"So that's your weak spot; that's your Achilles heel . . . "

"Will you do it?"

Francesco Montero was silent, stunned. Although he'd just seen the rage and pain overwhelming Maurizio, though he'd been hoping he would crack and humiliate himself, the man had suddenly regained his composure, and it was frightening. His voice, trembling only a few seconds earlier, was now under control. His red eyes alone seemed to indicate that a fire had nearly consumed him. The duel was shifting. Once again Francesco Montero saw before him the terrible adversary he'd had so much difficulty defeating during the last municipal elections.

"How would you get me elected if I said yes?"

"That's my business," said Maurizio Mangialepre. "I'll do it. Vote for Sandro Calvino, and you will be a Senator of the Republic. Will you do it?"

"And if I don't? If I refuse? Huh, Mangialepre? If I refuse? If I have you arrested for attempted corruption? I'll die, is that it? Like in the mafia? Like a line from a gangster movie? Go ahead. Tell me, like a good Sicilian padrino, 'If you don't do it, you're dead, Francesco.'"

"No, Francesco. You won't die. You'll simply continue as a little mayor in an insignificant Sicilian town. For someone like you, that's a fate worse than death. If you refuse, I'll make sure you stay here forever."

"That sounds like a threat, Mangialepre."

"It is one. And you can be sure that, unlike you with your political promises, I keep my threats. I carry them out."

"You don't impress me."

"Do you accept my offer, Francesco?"

"No."

The mayor's tone was firm. Maurizio Mangialepre stared at him.

"It's out of the question," Francesco said.

"I'll wait for your call, then," said Maurizio, unctuously. "You have until midnight on New Year's Eve. After that, it will be too late. Thank you for the wine."

He stood up and went out, smiling. Francesco Montero emptied his glass. At the bar counter, five or six drunken men were laboriously trying to articulate the first verses of the hymn to sweet Concetta.

26

Giuseppe Fantini was walking behind Carla and Jogoy. His presence, which he was trying to keep as discreet as possible, nevertheless caused a heavy and unusual silence to weigh upon the *giro case*. As a rule, these visits were moments when Jogoy and Carla felt completely relaxed, their time to get together after work. But this evening, they seemed petrified by the unspeaking shadow of the poet behind them. They'd only exchanged a few words.

The *giro case* was nearly over: they'd been able to visit several apartments and were heading toward the last one on their list. The poet's presence hadn't seemed to trouble the ragazzi they'd seen. A few of them had asked him in Italian who he was. And so Fantini introduced himself and said he was a poet. It had no effect on the ragazzi, even though they'd already heard his name: Rosa had given them a few of his poems to read in Italian class, but they were not in awe before him. They didn't see him as a great poet. This filled Fantini with a secret joy. In the last apartment they'd visited, however, the one they'd just left, Fantini was surprised to hear one of his poems recited to him.

"What's the name of that young man just now who knew my poem?" he suddenly asked the two mediators walking with him.

"Oh! That was Fousseyni Traoré," Carla replied. "He's from Mali. He's the face of the association this year. He's sweet, he's touching, and those eyes of his . . . "

"I see. Thank you." The poet cut her off rather abruptly before falling silent again.

The memory of young Fousseyni Traoré stayed with him for a time. It was true that he had a disarming gaze, the kind you can't meet without a certain sadness filling your soul. He'd recited Fantini's verses in the most natural way imaginable, his diction simple and unadorned. While listening to him, for a few seconds Fantini thought that he could almost feel the original words that had flowed into him forty years earlier, when he'd composed the poem.

They came to the last apartment they had to visit. Jogoy gave three short knocks on the door. It stayed closed. He knocked again, harder. No one came to open.

"I can hear their voices," said Jogoy. "They know it's us. That's why they don't want to open up."

"Three Nigerians and four Ghanaians live here," said Carla, turning around to Fantini. "They can be a bit difficult."

The poet didn't say anything. Jogoy knocked again on the door, louder still, not with his knuckles but with the side of his fist. They could hear shuffling steps approaching.

The door opened, and the large torso of a man filled the doorway. Jogoy spoke directly in English.

"Good evening, Stephen. *Giro case.*"

The man who'd opened didn't bother to give a clear answer—barely a grunt—and went ahead of them toward a large, dimly lit room from which there came bursts of conversation and laughter and a strong smell of alcohol and tobacco. Fantini, Carla, and Jogoy went into this large, untidy living room. On one side, sprawled on a sofa, two men were watching a football match. Stephen joined them and paid no further attention to the visitors. On the other side of the room, a few men were playing cards on a table cluttered with cigarette butts overflowing from ashtrays. Litter and ashes were spilled among bottles and empty beer cans, and plates showed traces of a meal, its color dubious, its smell even more so. Carla recognized Bemba among the seated card players.

In one corner of the room, as if at the heart of the surrounding noise he'd found an atmosphere conducive to reading, or was isolated by an invisible bubble, a man was tranquilly seated with a big book in his hands. He didn't look up when Carla, Jogoy, and Giuseppe Fantini came in. He was not the only one: not one of the eight men in the living room seemed to be paying the slightest attention to their presence. The three ragazzi by the television, with their casual attitude, kept their eyes glued to the screen; the card players were speaking English, laughing, accusing each other of cheating, announcing their winning tricks; and amid this commotion, the only one who stayed silent, his face impenetrable as he leaned over the open pages before him, was the reader at the back of the room.

Carla reached for the remote and turned down the sound on the television, as well as the heating; the excessive temperature made the room feel like a sauna. The men made as if they were just then noticing the visitors. Jogoy headed toward the card table and told them they could maybe clean up the place where they were living.

"Pay someone to do that!" one of the men said.

"You're not at a hotel, Appiah Mohamad. This is your house. Take care of it."

"It's not my house. And don't tell me what to do. Who are you? Who do you think you are to tell me what to do? You don't know anything about our lives or the way we feel!"

He was a bald man with a big jaw. In the middle of his forehead, a little brown spot was visible: this was the mark of those Muslims who so fervently prostrated themselves during prayer that their bodies kept a distinctive, almost elective trace. This man, Appiah Mohamad, had spoken harshly. Silence fell around the room like a winning card slapped on the table. Everyone, with the exception of the solitary reader, was watching Jogoy.

He towered over Appiah Mohamad because he was tall, but the other man didn't seem intimidated.

Jogoy decided it was pointless to respond. He was used to being told—particularly at this house—that he didn't understand anything and wasn't allowed to judge people whose feelings, they said, were alien to him. This was hurtful, but he'd learned not to react. What could he have said, anyway? That he, too, had lived through this situation? That he, too, understood their frustration? That he, too, had had to wait and be patient amid the uncertainty, the bitterness, the anger? No doubt. But Jogoy knew that saying this wouldn't change anything; they would've told him that even if he was a migrant once, he wasn't anymore. He'd gotten his papers; he'd crossed over to the other side of fear. He no longer had the right to say he understood them. He embodied the very thing they wanted to become but also hated, because they were not yet that thing and weren't sure they ever would be. He was a man who'd been granted asylum. Jogoy was the personification of their paradox: the object of both their desire and their jealousy, even their hatred.

"I didn't come here to argue with you," he eventually said.

The man with the big jaw went on staring at Jogoy, his face defiant. Carla came to the rescue and started speaking. Although her English wasn't perfect, she could get by. They could understand her.

"We just want to know if you need anything. The association is doing everything it can to move things alo—"

The man who'd been reading at the back of the room now slammed his book shut. He stood up. He was almost as tall as Jogoy and was wearing a sort of long garment that seemed part caftan, part shroud. He put his book onto a chair—it was the Bible—and began slowly walking toward Carla and Jogoy. Jogoy had always been greatly troubled by the resemblance between this man and Hamady Diallo, his boat's imam. The same dry face, the same hollow cheeks. Only their eyes were different. Hamady's had been large and generous, whereas the eyes of this man before him . . .

"Good evening, Solomon," said Carla unenthusiastically, as if she would have preferred for the man walking toward her to have stayed over there, immersed in his reading.

"Good evening, Carla," said Solomon, in a slow, calm voice. "I interrupted you as you were saying that the association was doing everything it could to move things along. You tell us the same thing every time you come here. Every one of us could recite by heart the speech you're about to make. The truth is the association isn't doing a thing. We haven't even had our interviews yet! And I'm sure that after the interviews, we'll have to wait for more months. You won't give us the chance to move around, or any prospects. No work, no money, no papers . . . We're stuck here. Like lambs in a pen, a herd of stupid lambs bleating and going around in circles. Night is falling, and the wolf is getting closer, the huge serpent slithering toward us . . . If you were even a little bit observant, you would have noticed that all of us ragazzi are getting more and more sad and aggressive. And it's your fault."

Solomon, who was still walking very slowly toward the two mediators, stopped talking for a moment. No one said anything. He had the floor. Satisfied, he continued.

"You asked us to pose for your calendar . . . We won't do it . . . We won't pose anymore. We're not here to pose while our families are dying of distress. Find us some work instead of making us pose; give us our papers. The longer we wait, the unhappier we'll be. That's dangerous. For us . . . for you . . . All our respect and dignity have been taken from us . . . We're here, waiting, and there's nothing—nothing! And that's dangerous for the spirit. Give us work."

"We're trying, Solomon. We're trying to find work for you. It's hard to find something for all of you. Altino is a little town."

"Then why did you bring us here?"

Carla asked Jogoy if he could translate what she was about to say. She preferred to answer in Italian, to make herself clear.

"In a big city," she said, "it would be even harder. They wouldn't look after you any better. Altino is a small town, but you're safe here, and you have a greater chance of getting your papers, even if it takes longer. You say, Solomon, that I always give you the same speech about how things are going. But what about you? What are you doing? What are any of you doing, here? You say the same things over and over, too: the association isn't doing enough of this, the association isn't doing enough of that . . . I know your speech by heart, too. We're doing our best! Stop dwelling on your frustrations, and start participating in the life of the town. Go to class! Get to know the locals! Lend a hand to the workers, without necessarily expecting money in return!"

Jogoy translated into English. Bemba asked him to repeat it in French or Bambara so he'd understand better. Jogoy repeated Carla's speech in Bambara.

"The time of slavery is over," said Bemba once Jogoy had finished translating. "The time when the Black man was just a pair of hands to be sent to work and exploited, beaten, and killed by the white man."

"But who said anything of the sort?" said Jogoy. "Carla never said that, Bemba."

"She talked about working for free. Or maybe you translated it wrong. Every job deserves a salary."

"What's he saying?" asked Carla.

"Nothing important," said Jogoy, weary.

"We have to stick together," Carla continued, in English this time, her voice broken by fatigue and tension. "We're all in the same situation here . . . "

Solomon gave a derisive laugh.

"We'll never be in the same situation, Carla. And we keep repeating the same thing because repetition is all you have to give us."

"Which would you prefer?" said Carla, overcome by exhaustion. "To be here waiting calmly for your papers, or to be in a big city and run the risk of being crushed there, without even being sure you'll get asylum?"

Solomon had drawn level with them now, and in his terrible little eyes Jogoy immediately saw, before the man even opened his mouth, the intense, brutal gleam that would accompany his response.

"I prefer a million deaths to the life you've given me here. Altino is true death. Waiting here calmly is true death. Your association . . . you're killing us. And we will kill you. Believe me. Believe me: you will soon share our hell."

Upon the deep silence that greeted his words, Solomon walked over to a dark little corridor that led to the bedrooms beyond. But before he reached it, Fantini, who'd remained silent until then, spoke out. His voice was clear, calm, and limpid:

"Then so be it. We'll divide hell up into so many parts, one part for each man. We'll crumble it. We'll tear it up, and then together we'll blow the pieces into the wind. And our great breath will extinguish its great fire as if we were snuffing out the flame of a candle."

He had spoken in Italian, but it felt to everyone as if his words had been addressed directly to their hearts, and no translation was necessary; they all understood. Solomon, taken aback by the poet's sudden voice, stood motionless for a moment; then, without turning back, he disappeared into the darkness of the corridor like a ghost in the mist.

27

Before taking the major cities in the North by storm, Vera and Vincenzo Rivera reserved for Altino the signal honor of the unveiling of *Vanitas Vanitatum*.

The Altino museum was hosting the opening of the exhibition. Francesco Montero and his wife Isabella were there, naturally: the Monteros were close friends of the Riveras. Isabella Montero, a petite woman, always impeccable—pursed lips, perfect blow-dry—was passionate about contemporary art. And whenever she managed to escape the gentle authority of her husband—a man to whom she had pledged absolute devotion and admiration—the timid Isabella would voice knowledgeable opinions on the works exhibited. Alas, this happened only rarely, and her fine sensitivity was often obscured by the burdensome shadow of her husband, who knew almost nothing about art, and spoke therefore all the more volubly about it. And so, most of the time, even when she knew her husband's comments were imprecise or even wrong, Isabella, out of love and admiration, supported him. In short, they constituted one of those couples, far too numerous these days, in which one person admires, believing they are loving, and the other only loves once they know they are admired.

There were also a few of the town's notables, some local residents, a handful of high school students obliged to attend by their teachers, a few members of the Santa Marta Association, and a few ragazzi. Beneath the terrifying gaze of the statue of Athena, Vera and Vincenzo Rivera, with a champagne glass in one hand and a petit four in the other, wandered among their guests demonstrating an exceptionally refined mastery of polite small talk.

In one corner of the exhibition room, Jogoy was trying, together with the few ragazzi who'd agreed to come to the opening, to decrypt one of the paintings hanging under the powerful white lights. In reality, it was less of a painting than it was a simple frame, without a canvas. There was the gilded frame itself, richly decorated with baroque relief, and, in the square space that it defined, the wall, lit by the powerful light. There was neither a canvas nor a painting. A frame and the bare picture rail: this was the completed work as presented to the public gaze. Vera and Vincenzo had entitled it *Off-Frame, Off-Art, Off-Camera*. Jogoy found himself struggling just to translate the title.

Another group was looking at the ragazzi, looking at *Off-Frame, Off-Art, Off-Camera*. This group included Francesco Montero, his wife Isabella, Sabrina, and the Riveras. They were talking in low voices, never taking their eyes off the refugees.

"I wonder what they're saying about that work," said Isabella Montero.

"I suppose they don't get it at all, the poor fellows," said Vera Rivera, her tone maternal.

"It's a necessary stage, Vera," said Vincenzo Rivera. "When confronting a work of art, comprehension begins at the point where non-comprehension begins."

"Perhaps we should go over and speak to them. What do you think?" Vera replied. "Some of them might be seeing a painting for the first time."

"You'd be surprised," said Sabrina, irritation in her voice, "to see how much they know about our culture. They catch on quickly. And I think they're richer than we are from that point of view. They know how we live and they know our art, some of it at least, whereas we know almost nothing about theirs."

"At the same time," said Montero, in the apologetic voice he adopted to remind people of the banality of the obvious, "that work they're looking at is not the hardest one to understand. It even seems to me that of all the works in this powerful cycle, it's the most transparent, despite its spectacular nature . . . "

And he allowed his sentence to trail off, unfinished, filled with a mysterious and sibylline depth that any further explanation would have emptied. The little group meditated for a few seconds on the mayor's ellipsis.

"I agree," said Isabella Montero in her squeaky voice. "This piece certainly is spectacular and provocative, but it repeats a gesture made many times throughout the history of art, above all in the modern era . . . It's an installation and a performance at the same time, the work itself the only actor, the only body. But . . . "

Isabella's gaze had met her husband's, where burning embers of anger were beginning to glow.

"But . . . but I agree with you, darling."

"Actually," the mayor continued, his gaze once again gentle and kindly, "I was struck by the other work, over there."

"Oh, *The Table of Life!*" said Vincenzo.

"Yes, that's it. The human skull and the erect penis separated by a dying candle, all set atop a large hourglass through which you can practically hear the sand trickling . . . Such powerful symbolism!"

"Isn't it just?" gushed Vera.

"And to think you didn't even plan it together!"

"Indeed," Vincenzo purred.

"All this . . . vanity!" said the mayor, unable to contain himself.

(Francesco Montero emphasized the word "vanity" so loudly that the word seemed to be in italics, between quotation marks, and underlined, as it emerged from his lips.)

"All this . . . vanity!" he said again, as no one had reacted.

"That is indeed the theme of the cycle, Francesco, is it not?" asked Sabrina. "*Vanitas vanitatum?*"

A moment of silence ensued.

"But . . . what about the erect penis?" said Sabrina. "Is that also part of the vanity?"

"Not exactly," said Isabella. "I think . . . "

She glanced at her husband, whose eyes were glowing again, but she decided to proceed in spite of everything.

"Because the penis is portrayed so clearly, it's not vanity, strictly speaking, even if the vanity of sexuality has long been discussed and denounced in this type of still life. But I think that in this case, the presence of the erect penis, ready to go wild, like a life impulse, can only be understood in contrast with the rest of the painting, which illustrates, rather, the proximity of death."

"Ah . . . *memento mori!*" exclaimed Montero, proud of his expression, regaining his composure and some color to his face.

"Uh . . . Yes, yes, darling. *Memento mori*, but it's more than that, too. The painting doesn't say just, 'remember that you will die'; it says, 'remember that you will die, but make the most of life.'"

The eyes of Altino's mayor were darting flames. Isabella nevertheless pursued her train of thought, paying no attention to her husband's annoyed expression as he was contradicted yet again: "*Memento mori sed carpe diem*. It's both a reminder of the fear of death and an injunction to pay close attention to the density of the present moment," she said quietly.

"Remember that you will die . . . " Vera began.

" . . . but have a good fuck first," Vincenzo said in conclusion. "Maybe that's what we wanted to say, Isabella."

Vincenzo and Vera Rivera both laughed. Isabella very nearly said something more, to tell the Riveras that they were rushing her conclusion. Were even making a travesty of it. That was not at all what she had meant to say. But their coarse laughter disgusted her and left her disheartened. She decided not to say anything more.

* * *

Francesco Montero was smiling robotically, finding it increasingly difficult to hide his anger. Isabella was sorry she'd stolen his thunder. She kept her lips pursed, every hair in place. The ragazzi gradually lost interest in the paintings. They began talking, rather, about their interview, and their practice sessions with the old priest, Bonianno, which had started the day before. Sister Maria was looking distractedly at one of the works, fiddling with her cross. Sabrina soon went over to her, and they both wondered what they were doing there. The high school students were bored. Fousseyni was trying once again to show some interest in the artwork; he asked naïve questions. Next to him, Lucia laughed and tried to answer him on her scraps of paper. Silent Gianni, in a corner, shot dark looks at them. Jogoy was worried about Carla. She'd been looking particularly down lately, ever since their exchange with Solomon. Vera and Vincenzo were raising their glasses to their future success. They were convinced that *Vanitas Vanitatum* would be a hit: they would soon be holding exhibitions in Rome, Florence, Turin, and Milan, in the social sphere they knew they belonged to—the only one fully deserving of their genius. The statue of Athena looked on, her gaze terrifying.

* * *

The discovery of this major statue, over half a century earlier, had given rise to a bitter dispute among specialists, whose heirs still fought whenever they could by means of articles in major journals (and fists when they met in person). This key dispute centered around the epiclesis[6] to be given to this representation of Zeus's daughter. Two scientific clans were facing off over this formidable and fundamental question in a perfectly theoretical war that was, therefore, tragically deadly: the American clan against the German clan.

The American clan supported the thesis of Professor James H. Hodgson. He had discovered the statue and then advanced the hypothesis that it was undoubtedly a representation of Athena Πρόμαχος / Promakhos, "she who fights in the front line." That is, a warrior Athena. Inversely, the German clan fell in behind Professor Hermann B. Recht, who also discovered the statue (the honorable Professors Hodgson and Recht had been co-directors of research during the excavations) and who held that this was, incontestably, Athena Παλλάς / Pallas, "goddess of Wisdom, guardian of the Arts and Sciences."

The quarrel began in the autumn of 1955, a few weeks after James Hubert Hodgson and Hermann Benedikt Recht had discovered the statue. The two scholars agreed to have it shipped to the United States, as Germany, at that time, was still struggling from the economic aftershocks of the war. Hodgson, therefore, brought the statue back to the United States, and it was put on display in the finest room of a major New York museum. However, before presenting it to the public, it had been necessary to organize an official ceremony where the two professors spoke about their discovery. It was during that very ceremony that the disagreement arose. Everything was set off by an unfortunate comment on the part of the German scholar, just after he'd begun speaking:

"The Altino Athena—it seems to me we can be even more precise by calling it the Altino Athena Pallas—appeared before

---

[6] The epiclesis is the epithet used, in ancient Greece, to qualify a god by emphasizing his or her attributes and functions in a precise circumstance, rite, or place. Thus, a god could have several epiclesises depending on the place and the occasion.

us, that is, myself and my colleague, who is also my friend, James Hodgson, like a miracle—"

"Forgive me for interrupting, my dear Recht, but with all due respect, I believe you meant to say, 'Promakhos.' The Altino Athena Promakhos and not Pallas. My apologies for breaking in, but if we continue to call it 'Pallas,' this would—and I'm sure you'll agree—imply something very different where this marvelous statue is concerned."

"Ach, *nein, nein*, Herr Professor Hodgson, dear friend, *entschuldigung*, but if you don't mind me saying, it is indeed 'Pallas' that I meant, for it is obvious that it is *that* Athena we are discussing here, and in no case is it 'Promakhos,' as you seem to believe."

"Excuse me, Hermann, I'm very sorry, my dear man, but I cannot allow you to say such a thing. It is unthinkable that you might believe even for an instant that this is a Pallas. The moment we managed to uncover her face clearly I saw that she was a Promakhos—I thought you'd seen this, too. Come now! Pallas, Pallas, honestly, Hermann! You cannot be serious. Come on! The very idea!"

"And I say to you, dear James, that it *is* a Pallas! *Mein Gott!* Your supposition is so far off—but I suppose such geographical tropisms come naturally to a man whose country was built on the myth of the Far West—you can't seriously be thinking the statue is a Promakhos! *Unglaublich*! It is a Pallas! I can prove it."

Their exchange went on like that, becoming more and more heated and tense. The words "offense," "fucking disgrace," "incompetence," "*Wissenschaftler von Scheisse*," " amateurism," and "tragic mistake" were thrown in amid angry, irrevocable statements. The only words missing were "Nazi" and "slave trader." Hermann B. Recht stormed out of the room, blustering with angry, emphatic swearwords and refusing to shake the hand of James B. Hodgson, who had not, as it happens, extended it.

Back in Berlin, Recht exerted all his influence to get his government to demand the United States transfer custody of the statue to Germany. The diplomatic battle invited itself to the academic war. Open letters were written in newspapers; people signed their names to arid but erudite articles arguing one side or the other; the scientific world was in an uproar; experts from every discipline rushed to the feet of Athena Promakhos-Pallas to form their own opinion and choose their camp. Those who did not choose were scorned by both enemy trenches. After long months, Germany succeeded in obtaining shared custody of the statue.

Hermann B. Recht and James H. Hodgson both died in 1977, a few days apart. Rumor had it that Hodgson's last words—he died second—were, "I cannot continue to live when Recht might at this very moment be convincing Lucifer that the Athena is a 'Pallas.' I cannot let him. It could be dangerous. I shall go." And he died. The two scholars, despite the impressive intellectual energy they had deployed for twenty years, left this earth without anyone the wiser as to whether the Athena was Pallas or Promakhos.

A few years later, once Italy had taken measures to reclaim the statue, custody was awarded to the little archaeological museum in Altino. That made everyone happy. The Germans were happy that the Americans didn't have it. The Americans were happy the Germans didn't keep it. And the Italians were delighted to have it back. The Altino Athena, after gracing the pedestals of the most prestigious museums in New York and Berlin, had come home, to the land from which she'd been taken. In the little museum, what she lost in prestige she gained in peace. She was, however, still attractive enough for many specialists, art lovers, and tourists of all nationalities to come and admire her. Next to the monument, a plaque showed a black-and-white photograph taken the very day the statue was discovered. The print showed, arm in arm next to the goddess's face, still slightly covered in clay, the eminent and infinitely honorable professors Hodgson and Recht.

28

The interview practice sessions were making good progress. Every day, four or five men would sit opposite the vacant, yet pitiless gaze of Padre Bonianno. Apart from him, only Jogoy and Pietro were allowed to sit in on these work sessions. Jogoy translated when it was necessary; Pietro took notes and almost never intervened. The priest alone conducted the interview. Because he was used to hearing confession, he had learned a certain trade from it, that of souls, and he knew how to oblige them to deliver the bare and sincere confession of their most recent truth. His questions were precise and direct, but they never turned brutal or intimidating. He merely sought to hear something from their heart.

In listening to these practice sessions, Padre Bonianno didn't hear just stories, or adventures, or tales; he was also listening to men, to human voices, through their intonation, hesitation, and silence, where he could distinguish echoes mingled with a multitude of feelings. The point, for him, was not just to hear about their itinerary, their long journey, the people they'd met, their good fortune, the reasons or the purpose that had driven them to leave their country; he also wanted to know what sort of men they had become after so many ordeals.

He listened to the stories they told of their reasons for leaving—their frustration with their native land, no horizons, futures sacrificed, unemployment assured, the death of prospects, the death of hope, the broken dreams, the temptation of a great journey, the moral dilemmas, decisions taken on the verge of the unendurable, and then they fell silent to catch their breath before continuing with the story of their journey, of their fear, of the violence they suffered, of the violence they inflicted, the violence they witnessed, the shame they swallowed, the humiliation they concealed, the hardship, the uncertainty, the despair, the doubt, the hunger, the thirst, the hallucinations, the sun, the dizziness, the fainting, the vomiting, the fever, the sickness, the sunstroke, the desolation, the diarrhea, the naked greed of smugglers tripling their prices, the corruption of policemen turning a blind eye, the inhumanity of guards lashing their flesh, the dozens of exhausted bodies, curled into balls, huddled together, sitting one next to the other, lying one on top of the other in the dust, the piss and shit and blood; then, at that point, as memory revived sorrow, the story would break off, but not for long, never for long, only a few seconds; and then it went on, told in a voice that was sad and hard at the same time, a voice full of pain, but lucid, the story of mingled sweat, of dry saliva, of near-empty water jugs, of endless hours in an endless desert, the story of birds of prey circling in the sky over the desert, the deadly heat of the desert, the biting cold of the desert, the unidentified sounds of the desert, the winds scalping the desert dunes, the howling of drums beating an invisible charge, the whispering of djinns brushing against their bodies, the cannibal voraciousness of evil spirits, the maleficent enclave of divinities, the demons watching out for their wounds and their trespasses, the invisible rustling of shrouds being laid over them, the strips of flesh hanging from human femurs emerging from the sand, the skulls of men scattered along their route like signposts to the beyond, companions collapsing from thirst then abandoned, the smell of rotting human flesh, the unbearable whiteness of fleshless bones; and at this stage in the story, Bonianno, who was, in fact, used to the process, felt like holding his nose and covering his ears, wanted to flee, to gag them, but they'd cornered him, he had to listen, and the story was rushing toward him: a story of finding it impossible to sleep, of wanting to sleep, of being afraid to drop off, wary of water thieves, a story of everyone's mutual suspicion, of an essential solidarity among them all the same, a story of dreams becoming less and less frequent, of nightmares becoming more and more frequent, a story of the memory of departure, a father's last words, an uncle's last blessings, siblings weeping, a mother's dignified sorrow with her silent tears, the friends left behind, the plans left behind, the loves left behind, the sudden return to the reality of the desert, the irremissible solitude, the deep silence rolling into their hearts, the story of their arrival in Libya, of the circle of hell that was Libya, the bottomless pit that was Libya, the careless and deadly bombing of the democratic crusaders, the total lack of safety, the everyday racism, the accepted slavery, the jails that no one could leave, the great human Gehenna, the belittling, the negation, the attempts to cross the sea, the hostile ocean, the ferocious ocean, the voracious ocean, the haunted ocean, the ocean with gloves of iron, the huge jaws of water, of waves as white as fangs, the overloaded ships, stalled inflatables, the never-ending swell, the crashing of breakers as hard as walls of bronze, the deafening thunderstorms, the wandering on the featureless expanse of the sea, the fear, the empty skies, the empty sea, the near-empty hearts, the absent gods, the rescues on the threshold of death, the desperate cries, the upward-rolling eyes of the drowned, sinking into the deep . . .

And where had all of that—those sacrifices, fears, hopeless acts of courage, reckless risks—brought them? Onto this cold chair across from him, telling him about the crossing and how they'd struggled to survive. When he asked them what their plans were, they all remained silent, thinking, and eventually answering, after a while, that their only plan, for the moment, was to obtain asylum. Therein lay the utter absurdity: that after crossing through hell, these men found themselves with their asses on a fucking metal chair as deadly as its electric cousin, facing a commission whose members were in charge of deciding their fate and who would never, ever, have the slightest idea what these men had actually been through.

For the first time since he'd begun working with the association, Padre Bonianno felt powerless to change anything in the situation of the ragazzi.

The one who came in just then looked like a bird of prey. His sharp, thin face, each eye like the eye of a needle, his long arms dangling next to his thin but athletic body. Jogoy cast a gaze full of animosity at Solomon as he took his seat. The memory of the *giro case* was still raw, and he was angry at Solomon for the brutal discourse that had so upset Carla. The priest began the conversation directly in English.

"I've been eager to meet you. So you're Solomon?"

"I am."

"Where are you from?"

"Nigeria."

"How old are you?"

"Thirty-three."

"The age of Christ."

"The age of His death."

"Why did you leave your home?"

"I was living in the north of the country. Boko Haram killed my entire family. So I left."

"You had no other family in Nigeria?"

"I saw my parents and my brothers and sisters die. I have no family left anywhere."

"Tell me about the circumstances of their death."

"I'd prefer not to."

"Fine. What is your story? How did you get here?"

Solomon said nothing for a while. Padre Bonianno's face remained impassive.

"My story," he said eventually, "is that my family was killed.

I have nothing else to say to you. I don't want to tell you about the trip, the crossing, the boat. You already know all that. The main thing is the death of my family."

"As you like. Why are you here?"

Solomon said nothing, and the priest got the impression that it was not so much out of stubbornness as a real inability to come up with the words for his feelings.

"You won't find the strength for your revenge here," said the priest. "Because I know that's what you want. To take revenge. To take revenge for the death of your family. And don't deny it . . . I can hear it in your voice, which paints a picture of both your features and your anger. This is not the place to feed your ang—"

"Yes, it is, Father. It's here. Here in Europe . . . This continent is responsible for everything. It's Europe . . . it's been involved in all the wars that have torn Africa apart. It pretends to be looking on from a distance, that it will come running to save us, but it's in up to its neck in all of it, to the marrow . . . It mustn't go unpunished. I'm here to remind people. I have nothing left to lose."

"I don't know that Europe caused the deaths of your family. It's not Europe that fired the shots, or wielded the machetes. But even if it were, you ought to know that you won't find Europe here. You'll only have the men and women sitting across from you."

"Then they'll pay. This continent must not remain indifferent to the conflicts it's been causing, even indirectly. Conflicts it's still witnessing."

"I still don't know what you want, exactly. But look for peace, my son."

"'Think not that I am come to send peace on earth: I came not to send peace, but a sword.'"

"Matthew 10:34," said Bonianno. "But, in Romans 12:19: 'Dearly beloved, avenge not yourselves, but rather give place unto wrath: for it is written—'"

"'—Vengeance is mine; I will repay,'" Solomon concluded.

They fell silent for a moment.

"I will not judge your cause, Solomon. But it's not with verses from the Bible and the Gospels that you'll win over the members of the commission. And your story of revenge won't help things. They welcome refugees here, not future warlords or frustrated migrants."

"Never mind, then."

"Never mind what? What will you do, if you don't have papers?"

"I'm not that interested in papers. It's mainly my comrades who need them. Their desire to have them is eating away at their souls, haunting them. They can't live anymore because of it. The more they hear about the interview, the more subdued they become. And the association doesn't help anyone. A man in torment is an ugly thing to see, and the association contributes to that torment because it embodies hope, a dangerous hope that kills very slowly. I want my comrades to get asylum. As for me, if I don't get it, I'll know it was my destiny, and I'll go find it somewhere else. In another way. The only thing I know is that nothing will stop me from doing what I have to do."

"Even God?"

"'Thou shalt not be affrighted at them: for the Lord thy God *is* among you, a mighty God and terrible. And the Lord thy God will put out those nations before thee by little and little: thou mayest not consume them at once, lest the beasts of the field increase upon thee. But the Lord thy God shall deliver them unto thee, and shall destroy them with a mighty destruction, until they be destroyed. And he shall deliver their kings into thine hand, and thou shalt destroy their name from under heaven: there shall no man be able to stand before thee, until thou have destroyed them.'"

"Deuteronomy 7:21-24," murmured Pietro.

"You just said it: the sight of a man in torment is ugly. And that's true of you. Your anger will lead to your death," said the priest.

"You, too, will go to your death. In anger or not. Death calls us all. We must reply."

With these words, Solomon stood up and left, in silence.

"There's no point," said the priest after a pause, "in informing Sabrina of his plans, or to try to sanction him or reason with him. It won't change anything. Nothing and no one can make him change his story. That's one story we can be sure is true."

"Do you think he'll say the same thing to the commission?" Jogoy asked.

"He doesn't know how to lie," said Pietro. "He won't change a word."

"That's the proof of his determination," said Bonianno. "He'll have his vengeance, or he'll die trying. In the flesh of his heart, there's a deeply embedded shard. Only death can remove it. His death, or that of his enemies."

"I think," murmured Pietro, "that he doesn't just want revenge on Boko Haram. At least, not only on them. And it's not Europe he has a grudge against; it's humanity as a whole. Having said that, there's still something odd: I get the impression that even as he profoundly hates Europe, he nurtures a sort of fantasy about it, a deep desire. I don't understand how you can hate a continent, criticize it relentlessly, and make it the absolute emblem of decadence in the world, and yet rush to get there at the first opportunity. He's schizophrenic."

"He's not alone, in that case," Jogoy concluded.

29

C alm at last, Salvatore Pessoto was able to smoke a cigarette right to the end. He was proud of his players. On a rival team's pitch, they'd just qualified for the final of the tournament. He was beginning to believe the ultimate victory was possible. The ragazzi continued to amaze him. The joyful rage that had filled them during practice had managed to make him forget their situation.

There were four strong points on his team. The first was "Leone," the captain: Jogoy was able to play just about any position. This year, he'd moved him up to center defense.

The second strong point was Bemba, left wing, who made up for his lack of speed with a powerful, aggressive play, and a fierce determination that made him a warrior on the field. He suffered a lot of blows, but he gave twice as many as he got.

The third pillar of the team was the midfielder. That was Gianni, his assistant. In the beginning, the ragazzi had some trouble accepting him, the little white guy, as one of them. But Gianni had very quickly shown what he was capable of and turned out to be better than any of them, or almost. Like Eminem in American rap music. The ragazzi nicknamed him "Chrono" because he was the timekeeper; his passes always came just in time.

The team's last asset was little Fousseyni Traoré. A fantastic left-footed player. His position was second forward, and his style was all about finesse. He made you think of a ballerina who refused to display any form of rough treatment toward the ball. His smooth technique when receiving the ball enabled him to eliminate one or several opponents and, when making a pass, to destabilize the most solid defense. He was not consistently brilliant, but his blocks were intelligently chosen. Some of his movements reminded Salvatore Pessoto of his idol, Roberto Baggio.

They had won the semifinal, two goals to one. Salvatore Pessoto rejoiced in moderation, but for the first time he'd detected a transmission issue between his two technical leaders: in fact, it seemed to him that Gianni, during the entire match, and in a very odd way, had done everything he could to avoid passing to Fousseyni, opting for less obvious or even stupid solutions. But the main thing, in any case, was the final.

* * *

He got home. No one there. He got out his phone, which he hadn't thought to check during the tension of the match and the euphoria of victory. Thirteen missed calls and one text from Angela: "We're at the hospital in Piazze, in the emergency room. Erica had an asthma attack." Salvatore Pessoto drove at breakneck speed to Piazze, the city closest to Altino, which had a better-equipped hospital. His hair hanging untidily around a pale face, he arrived at the emergency room with his loose plaid shirt open under his coat. This was the first time his little Erica had ever shown signs of asthma. Angela and his son Riccardo were sitting on a bench in the hallway. The moment he saw his father, Riccardo rushed into his arms. He was the one who'd seen his sister struggling to breathe in the living room, eyes rolled upward, foaming at the mouth. Angela didn't get up. She looked at him, and he saw she'd been crying. Pessoto asked her, his voice trembling and panicky, "Where is Erica? How is she?"

His wife's voice was broken; without looking at him, she

murmured, "One minute more, and she would've died; they're looking after her. She'll make it."

He sat down, and a terrible urge to smoke came over him. He made a huge effort to repress it. Riccardo was holding his hand. He looked at his son and gave him the most reassuring smile he could. Next to him, Angela continued to stare ahead of her. Her hands were trembling, and, in profile, he could see her drawn features, the fear and tension not yet dissipated. For a moment, he hesitated between speaking to her and prolonging the silence. He made his choice, the wrong one: he spoke.

"Angela . . . "

"Where were you?" she said, cold anger in her voice as she turned toward him.

Dr. Pessoto lowered his eyes. He felt Riccardo's hand squeeze tighter. Angela continued, "You were at the pitch, weren't you? With those kids, playing football."

"Angela," he ventured, pitifully.

"I tried to call you . . . over a dozen times. You didn't pick up. You didn't pick up because you were with your ragazzi, with Jogoy and all the others, at the pitch. More than a dozen times!"

"Sweetheart . . . "

"No, let me finish. One minute more, and she would have died. Did you hear, one minute, that's what the doctor said. And you, you were off playing football, and you didn't pick up."

"I had my phone on silent."

He'd never been able to find anything to say except the truth, and it was calamitous at moments like these. His slow, apathetic diction was all it took to complete Angela's impression that he didn't give a damn. She shouted, "Our daughter nearly died, and you weren't there to drive her to the hospital or give her first aid; I had to take a taxi with Erica, who could've died in my arms, and you talk to me like this, in such a detached way, about some mode your telephone was in . . . ! What if I hadn't been able to get a taxi! She would've . . . "

Angelo couldn't hold back a loud sob. Riccardo began to cry, too.

" . . . died!" she concluded, no longer screaming, but murmuring faintly.

Sitting between his son and his wife, Salvatore Pessoto resembled a wax statue, pale and frozen.

"I can't put up with this situation anymore, Totò," Angela continued after a few minutes. "I can't take it anymore. You can't go on being out every evening for practice. You're going to have to choose your true family. I can't take it anymore. I don't give a damn whether those practice sessions are the only life raft those men you're coaching have. We are already sinking."

Salvatore Pessoto wanted to explain, to defend himself, to say that he wasn't trying to save anyone, that he was simply trying to slow down the ragazzi's race toward bitter disappointment, and that he was sorry. But he decided, and it was the right choice this time, to keep silent. Ten minutes later, a doctor came out with Erica in his arms.

"She was lucky," he said. "A minute longer . . . "

They thanked the doctor, took their daughter, and went back to Altino in a heavy silence. Erica fell asleep in her mother's arms. Angela hadn't said a word since the hospital. Once she was home, she fed her children, then put Erica to bed. She kissed Riccardo and went to bed herself, without so much as a word or a glance for her husband. He put Riccardo to bed, and, before leaving his son's bedroom, he heard him ask if they'd won the match.

"Yes, we won," he replied. "But I almost lost everything."

He went back into the living room and spent most of the night smoking and drinking. The ragazzi's solitude was too great for him to deal with. He already had enough to worry about with his own. The ambition of saving humanity was a matter for God, and he was merely a man. He had to remember that. People who take themselves for gods often end up trapped between the two, rooming with the devil.

Football wasn't saving the ragazzi. On the contrary, it was their scaffold, and he was one of their executioners, probably the cruelest of all: the one who made them believe that grace was still possible, even though there had never been any question of grace. The purveyor of illusions. All of this had to stop. What did it matter that he was ashamed of not being able to defeat this misery? It was still easier to bear than that other source of shame, the shame of making the ragazzi believe they would be just fine. That shame was reinforced by a despicable lie. And he didn't want to lie anymore.

30

Giuseppe Fantini headed down the central aisle of the nave at a measured pace. Amedeo Bonianno, seated at the big altar table, an open book before him, called out as he approached.

"Ah! At last, there you are! I've been waiting for you for days. But I warn you, I don't have much time; I have to prepare the Christmas mass, it's three days from now."

"Always so original. You tell me you've been eager to see me, then practically dismiss me in the same sentence. What are you reading?"

"The Bible."

"That's less original."

"With age, you know, we become less adventurous, less curious about what's out there, less unfaithful . . . like with women. We always end up remembering or returning to the first one, the faithful one."

"You're becoming a misogynist, Padre Bonianno."

"That, too, is down to age. Anyway . . . How did your *giro case* go?"

"How do you know about the *giro case*?"

"I have eyes everywhere in this town."

"Maybe you should start by having your own."

"Predictable, just as I thought. I lay a trap; you fall in headfirst. Your sense of humor has been eroded, old poet. Right. Enough chatter between childish old men. Tell me."

Bonianno had once again turned serious and grave. Fantini

looked at him for a few seconds. With his pallor, his gaunt face, his dark glasses, and his cassock, the priest, who was seated before the great baroque retable, looked like a guardian from the beyond. Lines from *The Divine Comedy* came back to the poet, which seemed, at that precise moment, to apply as much to Charon, the ferryman of the Acheron, as to the priest of Altino:

"*Ed ecco verso noi venir per nave
un vecchio, bianco per antico pelo,
gridando: 'Guai a voi, anime prave!'*"[7]

"I am sure of only one thing," said the poet after a few seconds. "I am going to write. I'm going to try to get back to it."

"I knew it. I've always been convinced, deep down, that contact with these men would bring you out of retirement."

"Why haven't you insisted, all these years, then, for me to meet them?"

"*Primo*, because you would have refused. You're as stubborn as a mean mule. And, *secondo*, I think you can't rush a poet into writing. I wanted it to come from you, for you to see it all for yourself. When I was first in contact with these young men, the phenomenon had not yet taken on such a dimension. But I knew it could make you write. I sensed there was an energy in these men that could stir the foundations of Europe."

"Not just Europe, Amedeo. It's humanity as a whole that they are calling out to."

"Humanity as a whole, abstract humanity, does not exist, you know. Humanity is always somewhere. In Europe, in our case. That's what I meant. I got the impression that for the first time in a long time, when all notion of the sacred seems to have

---

[7] "And here, advancing toward us, in a boat, / an aged man—his hair was white with years—/ was shouting: 'Woe to you, corrupted souls!' Dante, *The Divine Comedy*, Hell, III, v. 82-84 Trans. by Allen Mandelbaum, Digital Dante, Columbia University.

disappeared, when God is complaining and dying on an old bed of rags and refuse—which, you will agree, is a more terrifying vision than His death—where solitary pleasure is the only horizon, where everything is relative, even human life, where it is almost no longer possible to pray or to meditate in silence, where it's no longer individuals that matter, but their navels, I had the impression, yes, that for the first time in a long time, this continent had a fantastic opportunity to achieve greatness once more. To become great, if not by recovering the meaning of the sacred, at least by recovering the meaning of courage. The human courage to go deep into the heart of a human being once again, and not flee one's own shadow through perpetual entertainment. The courage to go deep inside oneself and confront evil, the shadow, the fear . . . The arrival of these young men was an opportunity for Europeans to pick themselves up and respond as human beings to those who had come, with true energy . . . "

Padre Bonianno said all this in a low voice, and as he spoke, it seemed to Giuseppe Fantini that his friend was becoming more and more somber, more and more disenchanted, almost worryingly so. This man, who was ordinarily animated by a sort of inexhaustible and ferocious positive energy, was yielding for the first time to darkness.

" . . . *non isperate mai veder lo cielo*
I'vegno per menarvi a l'altra riva
Ne le tenebre etterne, in caldo e'n gelo . . . "[8]

However, the priest continued to speak:
" . . . but I've been disappointed. Once again, Europe is weak, not up to the task. This continent isn't ready to welcome these men. On a vital level, it's not ready. It has nothing to offer

[8] "Forget your hope of ever seeing Heaven: / I come to lead you to the other shore, / to the eternal dark, to fire and frost." Idem. 85-87

them that would elevate them in a meaningful way, that is, as human beings. Europe is impoverished, spiritually impoverished, emptied out. We take people in thanks to our wealth. But none of our human attempts—if we even make any—will be retained. Europe cannot take in all the misery of the world, that's true, but I might add: that's because Europe itself is miserable. It can't even grasp the value of human life; it's terrified by it . . . We're always the first to lecture others on morality, to talk about human rights, but look at us! Degenerate humanism. The broken lighthouse of a civilization caught in a storm . . . And the Church . . . even the Holy Church . . . It's got it all wrong. It takes them in for the grace of God, but it should be taking them in for the salvation of mankind . . . For the Church, charity's a dogma; it doesn't come from the heart. And the ragazzi can sense that; they know it. It's killing them. Ever since I started meeting with these men and listening to them, I've been learning what makes them saddest, Giuseppe, and that is the emptiness of our continent. They're disappointed by the living conditions, which are, to be sure, far less brilliant than in their fatal delusions about a continent of economic superpowers. But I can tell that, above all, they're disappointed in the Europeans themselves. This continent is finished; that's what they've taught us."

"I think you're too hard on Europe, Amedeo," Fantini said. "Human grandeur has become weaker all over the world. Maybe it's going faster here, causing more destruction. Or maybe it's just more visible."

"Doubtless. As men, those boys are worth so much more . . . "

"They're neither better nor worse. Don't turn them into saints. That's all they need."

"I'm not turning them into saints. I'm just expressing my despair when it comes to their fate."

"I've never seen you in despair about anything or anybody."

"*Bob*!" The priest made a face.

"One thing you said is true, and for that alone, you have no right to despair: the presence of these ragazzi is an opportunity for more humanity."

"That's the whole problem, Giuseppe," the priest said calmly. His face was now completely drained of light. "I'm not sure I know what humanity is, what defines it. All these words with majestic capital letters on which we hope to build . . . Humanity, courage, freedom, brotherhood, solidarity . . . It's so relative, so uncertain. Illusions."

"You're the one who uses them."

"Nothing but disillusionment, I tell you. I don't believe in them anymore."

"It's because for you they're still mighty, moral words. You have to see them in everyday life, in reality, in actuality. In what is happening, in practical terms. If you no longer believe in humanity, just look at—I won't use a capital letter—human beings."

"They're the worst."

"You can't say that. There are people here who are dedicated to making them feel truly welcome. Look at Carla . . . "

"She's an intelligent, sensitive young woman. But she's still a bit young . . . "

"Jogoy . . . "

"Courageous and a bit lost. A foot in each camp . . . "

"Sabrina . . . "

"A bulldozer when it comes to charity. She's got a fighting spirit and is ruthless in all her admirable efforts. But I don't think she always understands everything . . . "

"Because you think you do?"

"No, far from it. But at least I'm aware of the fact. She isn't. Do you have any other names?"

"Yes: all the other members of the association who are part of the struggle. And all the—numerous—local residents who aren't hostile toward the ragazzi. You're one of them, whatever you may think. However much you may despair about all this, you do act."

"Good lord! I never thought the *giro case* would transform you to such a degree. You've started talking like a good Christian. Like a man of the left. Like . . . a humanist!"

"You won't insult me with such a word, my friend, don't wear yourself out. I speak as a man who wants to fight the way you're fighting. They're little deeds, but they're already a refusal to admit total failure. There are some things that have been botched. Misunderstandings. Frustration on one side and the other. Hatred, anger, violence, resentment, boredom, fear, mistrust. It's tempting to withdraw, to stay among one's own kind, to give up. Yes, there's all of that. But all of that is the hell of any human encounter. You have to live it before you can come out on the other side."

"Or die trying, Giuseppe. Or die trying. We won't make it to the other side . . . If it's hell . . . If it's hell, we're done for. When you're in hell, it means you're already dead. Or that you're about to die. We will all die, every one of us having failed to understand the other, having failed to understand ourselves."

" . . . *Per altra via, per altri porti*
verrai a piaggia . . ."[9]

"Why go on helping those men, if that's what you really think?"

It was a fairly simple question, but to Amedeo Bonianno, it seemed as thorny as the crown of Christ. There was a long pause before he replied:

"Even the Lord despaired briefly of the men he was trying to save."

[9] "Another way and other harbors /—not here—will bring you passage to your shore" Idem, 91-92

After murmuring those words, the priest seemed to melt into the surrounding darkness, to pass through the retable toward the other world, to become shadow himself. Fantini couldn't see him anymore, as if he, in turn, had become blind. Padre Bonianno eventually reappeared. He gave a sigh. Suddenly his eighty years were weighing heavily on his body, like the yoke on the neck of an old bull. Amedeo had not appeared so feeble to Fantini in a very long time.

"I need calm," said the priest in the same tired voice. "This mass will not write itself. But before you go, I'd like to ask you a question, too. You can guess what it is. Time has gone by. You can tell me now."

Fantini didn't answer right away. He'd known a day would come when he would no longer be able to avoid the question. A few seconds passed, and then he began to speak.

"Why I stopped writing fifteen years ago, is that it? It's simple, Amedeo. I stopped writing because I got the impression that everyone was writing. Everyone believed they could write and be worthy of the act of writing. At the events I was invited to, at seminars devoted to my oeuvre, or even in the street, more and more people, men and women of all ages, would tell me that they were writing or had written and were looking for a publisher. They all had a novel, or poetry, or a short story collection, or an essay. They all thought their work would shake the world of art and the wider world to its core. They thought they had something to say. Some sent me their manuscripts. In the beginning, out of politeness, or unhealthy curiosity, I don't know which, I read them. But it quickly became unbearable, not only because most of these texts were bad on every level and reading them was incredibly taxing, but for an even more important reason: I got the feeling, faced with this mass of people claiming to be writers, that my own commitment as a poet had suddenly lost all meaning. I was disgusted. Now that it was accessible to everyone, down to the last imbecile on earth, who, without having read a thing, wanted to 'express himself,' 'tell his life story,' 'compose some simple verses,' 'entertain people,' 'tell a pretty story,' 'share a slice of life,' or 'denounce' who knows what 'injustice,' writing no longer had any raison d'être. I stopped. Under the circumstances, it was the only thing to do. With the unshakable certainty granted by their own stupidity, everyone thinks they can make literature. And I—who'd devoted my life to literature without ever, even once, being sure it was literature I'd created, not even a single line of it—I couldn't go on writing. It was beyond my powers. My entire life had just been dragged through the mud, all at once."

"What you've just said is anything but simple," said the priest. "Your conception of writing could be seen as—"

"Intolerant. Arrogant. Pretentious. Haughty. Scornful. Elitist. Reactionary. Yes, I suppose. And I accept that. There's nothing worse than people who think they're writers when they haven't even stepped off the first step of the stairway that leads deep inside them, all the way down into the absolute darkness where one is alone, but where the truth is possible at last. It's not for everybody."

"That's your opinion. But there's something I don't understand: you're going to start writing again. I don't get the impression, though, that people are writing any less nowadays."

"That's true. I think it's even worse now than fifteen years ago. Writing, unfortunately, has never been more democratic."

"Why do you want to write again, then?" the priest said, without hesitation, his tone shot through with a fierce irony. "You don't care about your life as a poet anymore?"

"If I don't write about what's happening, not only will my life as a poet no longer make any sense, but I will lose more than my life: my honor as a poet."

"Such beautiful, grandiose words. Good for the newspapers and your biographers. Or your epitaph. But let me tell you what I think, Giuseppe, and it's far less glorious."

"Go on, then."

"The ragazzi and the situation they're in have certainly influenced you, but I still think there's more to it. There's something else. That something else is that you couldn't stand the silence anymore. You missed writing. Your encounter with the ragazzi came at the right time: they've given you an opportunity to rescind your farewell for a morally noble reason, a good reason. But the true reason is that you weren't strong enough anymore to put up with the poetic silence. That's It."

"That may be," said Fantini. "I was weak. I didn't have the strength to keep silent for good."

"Fortunately."

"Or unfortunately. I don't know, Amedeo, I don't know."

The priest smiled. Fantini told him he would come for Christmas mass; then he took his leave.

31

Fousseyni Traoré

There's no practice tonight, which is how it's been for several days. Jogoy said there wouldn't be any for the time being because Dr. Pessoto couldn't coach us anymore.

It's a little cold out, but I don't want to stay home by myself. I'm bored, and I keep thinking about my past and life back home. I prefer the cold to all that. Everyone else went out. Bemba is with the Ghanaians and Nigerians. Ismaïla and Kanté will be with the priest all day, practicing for their interviews. Fallaye's spending the afternoon with the other Malians. I wanted to go and say hi to my big brother Jogoy, but I forgot that he helps Padre Bonianno with those practice sessions.

I don't know why Dr. Pessoto canceled our upcoming practice. Maybe it's because of *Natale*, the Christian holiday. It's the birthday of their prophet, Jesus Christ. They'll all go to church tomorrow night to wish him well. Anyway, I hope we'll be able to start training again soon. If we want to win the final, we have to get better.

I'll go for a walk over by the Villa. Hey, there's the Altino Museum. I was there a few days ago. They showed us the paintings of those two crazy artists. I didn't understand a thing about their pictures. There was even one where there was nothing, no picture at all. Lucia told me it was very expensive. What is it that makes it so expensive? That's what I asked her. What's so expensive, since there's no picture there? She laughed a lot. She told me it's the nothing that's expensive. Honestly, only a white person would go and buy nothing, and pay a fortune for it. They want to possess, always possess. And since they already have everything, all that's missing is nothing. So they buy that, too.

* * *

Gianni

She's particularly lovely today. She's always particularly lovely. As if she had a special kind of beauty set aside for each day. She changes her beauty the way she changes her clothes. But I've never dared tell her. Yet I must be the one who spends the most time with her. But instead of talking to her, I stay silent. That's all I know how to do. Of the two of us, the one who's truly mute is me. I'd like to be more talkative, even just to say stupid things. At least it might make her laugh. Instead, there I am, sitting at my desk, pretending to concentrate on my files when, actually, she's all I can see.

Sometimes, when we get to talking, she tells me about her father, who has a little restaurant in the center of town. He's a good, simple man. He tries to keep his business going in spite of the crushing competition from La Tavola di Luca, right nearby. Most times, there's hardly anyone there, but they manage. I go and eat there often. It's Lucia's father who does the cooking and waiting on tables. His food is simple and tasty; it's all local produce. When Lucia is off work or has some free time, she goes to help him at the restaurant. She's all he has.

Four years ago, Lucia's mother committed suicide. It took her father two years to recover. As for Lucia, she was so traumatized that she lost the ability to speak. I was with her when they broke the news about her mother. She let out a horrible scream which seemed to go on forever . . . then she fell silent, and hasn't spoken again since. She was twenty years old then. For twenty years, she spoke. Then nothing: profound silence. The best specialists have tried everything. To no avail: her speech refuses to come back, as if it went so deep inside her, so deep in the labyrinth of her being, that it got lost for good.

But I haven't forgotten it. Haven't forgotten her clear, melodious voice, like that of a bird at dawn. She used to be so talkative. She would talk and laugh and sing all the time. But for four years, silence. And yet she isn't gloomy. Once her grief was behind her, she found the light inside again. Now it's her entire body that speaks, with a new and joyful voice. The tiniest crease that forms at the corner of her eyes when she smiles is a voice. But in spite of that, in spite of all her beauty, I can sometimes sense a sort of infinite sadness in her. As if, for a few seconds, she realized that she feels cramped inside her body without a voice. I would so like to find the words to console her at moments like these. I would so like to tell her she's beautiful, and that I can still hear her voice. But I say nothing. My shyness is a curse. I'd like to be able to speak, to be an explosion of words and sentences, to be able to speak for two . . .

Invite her over. I have to invite her over. It's now or never. The day's almost done. I can see her packing up to go already. I want to spend time with her outside of work. I'm not ready yet to confess my feelings, but I want to at least be closer to her, try to overcome my shyness, try to show her I'm not just this timid Gianni . . .

Two minutes. I'll give myself two minutes. Enough time to take a deep breath and gather my courage, and then I'll do it. Two more minutes, and I'll invite her over.

* * *

Lucia

He's so shy, I was really surprised he invited me to have tea with him. I said yes right away, with pleasure. I was already glad he came to see us. But the fact that he's suggested going to his house on top of it is something quite new. Fousseyni really is exceptionally kind. He told us he went for a walk, and since he was near the medical center, he suddenly thought he'd come say hi and ask us if we wanted to have tea at his place. Gianni declined the invitation. He said he had something to do. I may be wrong, but I think his gaze turned dark, almost hostile, when he saw Fousseyni. And yet they're on the same football team. I don't know what's going on with him. Since this morning, I've been able to tell he's a little tense, as if he had a secret to tell me and couldn't find the right words. It might've relaxed him to come with us, but he preferred to go home. It's a pity. I'm sorry to see him like this, so withdrawn. I'd like to be able to help him . . .

Fousseyni doesn't speak much, either, but I like his company, too. Maybe it's because he gives off an aura of shyness mingled with mystery. I always get the impression when I'm with him that I'm about to come upon a secret. Ever since the very first day, when we talked after the housing placement, this sensation hasn't left me. We didn't say much on the way there. We talked again about the disconcerting art exhibition by the Riveras, those two artists from Altino. We joked and laughed again about the empty frame exhibit. He told me about his football practice, too, how they've stopped for the past few days, since Dr. Pessoto told them he wouldn't be coming anymore, for now; he hasn't been looking all that great lately, either. He seems sad.

We've reached Fousseyni's place. It's a big first-floor apartment. I remember it. I helped Carla set it up one day, before the ragazzi arrived. I haven't been back since. The big room, which they use as a kitchen and living area, hasn't really changed. It's a bit untidy, but the room is clean and well-maintained. There's a particular smell in the air. Fousseyni tells me that it's the smell of mafé, a dish with peanut paste that Ismaïla Camara, one of his flatmates, made. He tells me that next time he'll invite me for some.

I'm sitting at a table, watching him prepare the teapot. There's music coming from his phone, but I don't understand the language. But it's a gentle melody. The voice singing makes you want to dream; it's the voice of a storyteller, deep and enchanting, immediately compelling you to listen. I ask him who it is, and he tells me it's Ali Farka Touré, a great singer from his country. He tells me he's singing about the beauty of his native land. It makes me sad. Tears well in my eyes. I quickly wipe them away. He comes back to the table with the tea tray and pours me a cup.

There's no one in the apartment. I ask him where the others are. He reads my note—as he's made a lot of progress, I write straight in Italian—then replies that Bemba must be with the Nigerians and Ghanaians, that Fallaye went to see the other Malians, and that Ismaïla Camara and Kanté are practicing with Padre Bonianno. I completely forgot to ask him how his interview went. He'd told me a few days beforehand that he was about to have it.

He replied that everything went well. That the priest was very kind. That he just listened. That's a relief. Padre Bonianno is the kindest person I know, but the form his kindness takes can be frightening. Fousseyni is silent for a moment and sips his tea. I do likewise. It's delicious. The song by Ali Farka Touré ends on a sublime note. I look at Fousseyni. Once again I'm touched by his eyes, so beautiful, so sad, so old. I want to know their secret.

32

Scene 1: Lucia and Fousseyni

Fousseyni's apartment, the living room. On the left is a large dining table where Fousseyni and Lucia are seated. In silence, a pen is racing nervously across a sheet of paper. While Lucia is writing, we can hear her voice.

Lucia's Voice
What did Padre Bonianno ask you?

Fousseyni, *once he has read her writing*
To tell him my story. Why I left.

Lucia says nothing, but there's something she's dying to ask. A few seconds go by. Fousseyni says nothing, either. Lucia decides to ask him her question. She wants to know. The pen starts racing across the paper.

Lucia's Voice
Why did you—

Fousseyni, *interrupting her*
I know what you're going to ask. You want to know why I left, too. I'll tell you. It was my mother . . .

Slowly, the room goes dark. Lucia and Fousseyni disappear

into the shadow. A little lamp comes on and lights up the right-hand side of a kitchen. A tall Black woman comes forward, wearing a pagne tied above her bosom. Her beauty is one of great nobility, despite the suffering visible in her features and her voice. This is Fousseyni Traoré's mother.

SCENE 2: Rokia Traoré, Fousseyni's mother

Rokia Traoré

My Fousseyni, I think about you all the time, so I won't vomit. Your uncle has just turned over onto his side of the bed. He's breathing like an old warthog. He stinks of alcohol. He's already snoring. His bestial desire has been satisfied for the moment. Since you left, it's gotten worse. He's insisting. It's as if thorns had grown all along his fat penis. It hurts whenever it's my turn. He tears me open. Your aunts, my sister spouses, tell me it hurts them, too, but they repeat that a woman in this place has to be brave and put up with her husband's violent desire. I've never been able to put up with it, or understand it. As long as you were here, I didn't dare do anything, I was afraid for your sake, I was afraid of him. But now that you've left, I'm not afraid of anything anymore. One day, I'll chop it off, his spiny dick.

He's the opposite of his brother, your father. Who had his faults, but loved me. Wherever you are, my Fousseyni, you have nothing to be ashamed of: you're the child of a true love. That will give you your place among humankind. Your father was a brilliant man. He died young. An extraordinary musician, a really talented guitarist. He was beginning to have a reputation in the region. They invited him everywhere: baptisms, weddings, wrestling events, all the celebrations. He was making a bit of money and helping the family. He was their pride and joy, unlike your uncle, who did fuck-all and still does fuck-all. But your father adored his little brother. He gave him money and spoiled him, let him get away with everything, stood up for him against their parents. Your uncle virtually sponged off us for three whole years. When you were younger and your father was still alive, your uncle played with you a lot; you loved him. I'd even begun to appreciate him, whereas before, for a long time, I'd kept my distance. I thought that, in the end, he was basically a lost man but, deep down, not a bad man. I would catch him looking at me sometimes, but I didn't think it meant anything . . .

I was wrong. I would realize it soon enough, when your father was found dead outside a bar. He died just like that, all of a sudden. We buried him quickly. And because he hadn't left a will, there was nothing for us, nothing for you; traditional law was applied, and everything went to his young brother. Everything. Even you and me. And that's how our life became hell. He wouldn't let us have anything. Not even your father's guitar, which he sold. He said a real man wasn't supposed to sing like some weak woman, but had to look after his family. He married two other women and behaved like a tyrant with all of us. You'd loved him so much, but he began to put the fear of God into you. And me, I knew then that those looks he'd given me in the past were anything but innocent: they were filled with desire. An animal desire that he rushed to satisfy, with violence, without shame, even when your father's body was not yet cold in the ground. The sacredness of my mourning was defiled.

My body has always refused to give him a child. No womb can give birth to something the soul cannot bear. He hated me for that. He hated you for that. Not only were you the child he didn't manage to have with me, but you were his brother's child on top of it, the child who'd inherited the delicate features, the sensitivity, and the intelligence he would never have. He hated you more than ever because you weren't a brute like him. You have always been, and always will be, my revenge over him. His most formidable shame.

But you couldn't stay here. There was nothing for you. Only violence. You had to leave. And I did what it took so you could leave. Don't ask me how I gathered the money you needed to leave. No, you couldn't stay. He would have ended up killing you, and killing me at the same time.

When he found out you'd gone, your uncle went mad with rage. He looked for you everywhere, sent others to look for you. Sent his cousins all the way into the city to hunt for you, because he was sure you were there. Luckily, you were already far away by that morning after you left . . . That night, a boundless rage filled him. He blamed it all on me. He said I'd helped you flee. My whole body starts trembling again when I think about that night . . .

I still remember our parting. Obviously, you didn't want to go, and I had to break down weeping before you understood and agreed to go. You told me you'd die if we were apart, and I replied that it was I, rather, who would die if you stayed. I can still see you, in tears, heading into the night toward the city. It was better for you to leave. There was nothing for you here.

My prayers were answered: now you're far away from this hell, in that little village in Italy, after all your trials. On those rare occasions when you call me, in secret, we don't say much, our emotions are too raw. Every time I ask you how you are, you say that all is well, that you're waiting for an interview to get asylum. You don't tell me anything more precise. I know nothing about the crossing, nothing about how you live there from day to day, nothing about what you've experienced. I hope you'll tell me someday. I'm your mother. I need to know about your suffering and your fears, to be able to take them upon myself.

I can see your face in the ceiling of the room. After all this time without seeing you, I still know what you look like, down to the finest detail. You're so handsome, with those eyes of yours, so sad . . .

*The mother's voice slowly fades away, together with the little
light that was shining on her. For several seconds, the room is
plunged into total darkness. Then gradually it grows light again,
with a faint light. The mother is not there anymore. Lucia and
Fousseyni reappear.*

SCENE 3: Lucia and Fousseyni.

Lucia's Voice, *as she writes*
So it's because of your mother that you left home?

Fousseyni, *after reading her note*
No, Lucia, no. It's for her sake that I left home.

*They are silent. Lucia is trembling. Her eyes are moist with
tears. She stares at Fousseyni. It's a wrenching plea. She wants him
to go on with his story. She wants to hear everything. Fousseyni
understands this but doesn't know if he can continue. He looks
away, stands up, goes to the fridge, opens it, takes nothing out,
and goes back to the table but doesn't sit down. He looks out the
window. Night has already fallen.*

Fousseyni, *his gaze lost outside the window*
I walked all night through the bush, from my village to the
city. I was always afraid out in the bush, because there were a
lot of legends about it. But I was so sad that it wasn't fear that
filled me that night. Leaving my mother had been awful. If I
met a bad djinn, I wouldn't be afraid. In my heart, there was
only space for sadness. And nothing else. I walked for hours
and hours and heard noises and rustling all around me. But I
kept going. Not long before I left the bush to follow the paved
road that led straight to the city, I came upon a snake. It was lying across the path. It was a little snake, about the length of my
arm, and it was very thin. I could step over it, or go around it.

But I knew what it was. It was a djinn. My mother had already told me stories about this little snake that lies on the road. A lot of people have come upon it. She told me that the people who tried to go around it had been swallowed by the bush and lost. Those who tried to step over it were propelled into the sky and then fell back down, heavily, and landed broken and dead. Even cars and trucks that had tried to drive over the snake had been tipped over. My mother told me that when you came across it, you had to sit down and wait as long as it took. Whatever you did, you mustn't try to go past it. So I stayed sitting there by the snake for a whole hour, as motionless as it was. Then it began to move, slowly slithering. And before it disappeared into the bushes, I heard a voice, like a whistling, that said, "You are getting ready for a long journey. Step over with your right foot." Then it disappeared. When I reached the place where the snake had been lying, I saw the trace of its body. I stepped over it with my right foot and continued on my way.

When I reached the city, the sun had only just risen. I went to the neighborhood where the bus station was, the noisiest and busiest in town. It was early, but everyone was already bellowing: men and animals and cars. They were shouting with one voice, the voice of the city. It smelled like diesel oil, it smelled like omelettes, it also smelled like human piss and animal excrement. I didn't know where I was going yet, but first I had to eat. My mother had prepared a lot of food for my trip, but I didn't want to touch it yet. If I'd eaten what my mother had made, I would have turned around at once and gone back to the village. So I went into a *tangana*, a sort of popular greasy spoon we have in my country. There was a fat woman sitting at a big table, surrounded by famished customers who were ordering or already eating. The little café was packed. Everybody was talking at the same time. Try to imagine the atmosphere. I don't know how that woman selling her food managed it all. She stayed calm and saw to everything.

When a spot freed up, I sat down and waited to order. Just then, a man came in. He was short, with a big head. He was wearing a grand boubou. His eyes were lively, shining, clever. He looked around quickly to see what there was to eat. Then he cleared his throat and began to speak, very loudly. We were all obliged to listen. He said . . .

At this moment, a little man wearing a fine three-piece dashiki suit bursts onto the stage, with majestic, somewhat comical theatricality. He begins to speak.

SCENE 4: Fousseyni, Lucia, Adama Kouyaté

Adama Kouyaté, Prince of Poets

Famished people of the night, dawn eaters, morning eaters, I salute you! Hard workers, I salute you; your wives have tired you out this night. Eat! It is proof that the night was beautiful! In the old days, a man's vigor was measured according to his lust in bed and his appetite in the morning. Unfortunately, few women still know how to satisfy a man where either is concerned. Eat, my friends! Greetings to you! What is certain is that you have made the right choice by coming here to Lady Téné Tandjigora. Listen, and I shall tell you of her legend; listen, let me recount her glory.

Yes, Téné, mistress of taste, mistress of our stomachs, mistress of life, I will tell you the honor of your blood! You, daughter of Bintou Tandjigora, granddaughter of Ramata Tandjigora, great-granddaughter of Kadi Tandjigora, and so on, back to Sanou Tandjigora, who belonged to the court of Sogolon Djata, the mother of the Lion, the mother of Kaya-Maghan! She belonged to the women who helped Sogolon prepare the couscous with the leaves of the baobab that her son had uprooted with one hand, to come and plant it in his mother's courtyard. She belonged to the women who boosted the warriors' morale after a tough battle by giving them the most delicious food. No guest was ever hungry on leaving her place. Nor was she ever obliged to lower her brow in shame because a guest had not eaten well. And you, Téné, you are her heir. You are heir to the secrets of her ingredients; you are the queen of the most subtle compositions. Immense is your knowledge. Boundless is your talent. Oh, you, chef to every Man!

Those who doubt, listen again a while. Those who doubt, lend your ears to the story I shall tell, the confrontation between Téné Tandjigora, whom you see here before you, and Sidi Diabaté, the greatest glutton our country has ever known. Who? Sidi Diabaté, I say. Who? The belly of Mali, I say! Its leaking paunch! The absolute stomach! The ogre of the Manding! The terror of every famous lady chef! Remember Sidi Diabaté and his exploits! He traveled to every country, and wherever he went, the lady chefs pushed and shoved to invite him to their table. Because every one of them wanted to challenge him, every one wanted to win the sacred honor of having succeeded, with their fine fare, in making him eat his fill. Diabaté was a test! Diabaté was a competition! Every chef who came upon him knew that if she could assuage his formidable hunger, she would attain eternal glory and preserve forever the title of mistress of the stomach.

For many a year, only two women had ever managed to satisfy the absolute stomach's immense appetite, to calm the voracious cravings of the ogre of the Manding. The first was his own mother, Fanta, who knew how to feed him to satiety, from infancy through to manhood. The second was a witch Sidi Diabaté met during one of his tours: a woman gifted with supernatural powers, who could multiply her meals to infinity. And despite this, even the witch had difficulty: she had to multiply a thousand times before Diabaté would admit to having eaten well. There we have it, that's all: his mother and a witch. They were the only two women who had ever defeated the belly of

Mali. And I can tell you, there were countless lady chefs, among the most famous and talented, who had tried. Countless!

Listen! One day, Sidi Diabaté came to a small town where I just happened to be, by chance. And I saw with my own eyes what he was capable of. He asked where he could find the best restaurant in town. They pointed him in the direction of Ramatou Koné's place, a fabulous lady chef if ever there was one. Diabaté sat down at a table. Ramatou got to work. We watched the battle. And I can swear to you upon my memory and upon my tongue, which are the most precious things I own, that on that day I saw the belly of Mali put away, without effort or interruption, eleven whole broiler chickens, chewing straight through their bones; seven kilos of rice generously topped with mafé sauce; three kilos of thick mashed yams; sixty hard boiled eggs; sixty more eggs cooked into an omelette; seventeen loaves of whole-wheat bread; thirteen pairs of grilled sheep's testicles; three large calabashes full of millet porridge in curdled milk; and let's not forget the lettuces, tomatoes, onions, roast potatoes, boiled potatoes, fried potatoes, cabbages, sweet potatoes, bowlfuls of millet fritters, beans, stuffing, aloko, quarters of meat, haunches of warthog, legs of veal, and roulades of ewe's tripe, all accompanied by marrow, beef shank soups, heavy lakhou bissap, and lakh, and saame, and nanji, and tô, and what about ceré bassé, and laaxu caaxan, cebu goor-jigéen, ndambé, saka-saka, fufu, brains, ndolé, and let's not forget the fresh fish, fried fish, dried fish, manioc, sorghum, gumbo, noodles, watermelons, melons, mangoes—whose pits he nibbled scrupulously till they were dry—and I will spare you the rest!

Do you doubt? *Walay*, don't doubt! Sidi Diabaté was not like us. That day, he ate everything Ramatou Koné was able to offer him! Every thing. When he left, saying he was still a little peckish, Ramatou broke down sobbing, and, the next day, full of despair and humiliated by this failure, she closed up shop.

Thus, Diabaté continued to wreak havoc throughout the

land, in the manner of the army of Soundjata as it conquered and unified the empire of the Manding. Until one day he arrived here, at Téné's place. And I was here, too. Téné was still young, but she already had a great reputation. It was to her establishment that Diabaté of the leaking paunch came when he arrived in this town. The struggle began at dawn. I was there. And despite all my talents, I would be incapable of telling you everything that absolute glutton ate. It might even be preferable that I refrain from telling you. It might seem indecent or deceitful of me. But as I think back on it, I tremble. How could a man, even the absolute stomach, eat so much? I don't know, and prefer not to know, because some human mysteries must remain mysteries. In any event, I was there. Téné then served her most legendary offering. What she made that day was historic. She stood up to him. The confrontation lasted one day and one night. At dawn on the following day, I was still there. And all night long, Diabaté had been eating. All night long, Téné had been cooking. It was only the following day, as noon drew near and Téné was wilting with fatigue, about to give up, that Diabaté, after swallowing an umpteenth meatball, burped.

And that burp! The burp of Sidi Diabaté! A monumental burp, a formidable burp, the effluvia of which are still here, carrying the odor of everything he'd eaten. Oh, grandiose and sublime eructation! Oh, glorious gas! The burp from the stomach of the world. He was full; he had burped a titanic, prodigious, colossal, cosmic burp. And Téné, moved and exhausted, fainted away! She had just, after the mother and the witch, become the third and last woman to claim glory before eternity for satisfying the legendary appetite of Diabaté the Stomach, Diabaté the Belly, Diabaté the Paunch, Diabaté the Appetite!

After that, after this ultimate feast, after that last burp that consecrated a lady chef, Diabaté, happy, got to his feet and went into retirement. Today, he lives on the banks of the river, at home, where he tells of his exploits and pays homage to the three women who left him feeling truly glutted. He doesn't eat much anymore. He says he's eaten enough for a lifetime. Know, therefore, dear morning eaters, that you have the supreme honor of being served by the woman who got the better of Diabaté! Pledge allegiance! Give thanks!

The man goes out, somewhat breathless, accompanied by cheers.

SCENE 5: Lucia and Fousseyni

Fousseyni

After delivering this speech, the man came and sat next to me, while around us people were still applauding. Téné Tandjigora served him. He greeted me and asked me my name. We talked a while. He wanted to travel, too. He told me he knew the way and that we would go together. I trusted him immediately. That's how I met Adama Kouyaté, Kouyaté the prince of poets.

After we'd eaten, we started out. Kouyaté had traveled through a number of African countries. I asked him why he wanted to leave for good. He replied that it was because he felt useless in a society that no longer cared about its memory. He told me the griots have become useless. They're kept on so people think that the past, and myths, and legends, and the dead have not been forgotten. But deep down, they're no longer treated with respect. He told me he was sad: he had no place in society. And while he was telling me this, I thought that he was like me: he was leaving because his present-day life was nothing but humiliation, and his future nonexistent.

Kouyaté was trying to get to Europe for the second time. The first time, he'd made it to Italy. They'd received him in a little village near Palermo. He'd stayed there for over a year, but in the end he didn't get his papers. They sent him back to Mali.

He decided to leave again. But because they'd already taken his fingerprints and put them in the big European database where they kept the fingerprints of all the ragazzi taken in by associations, Kouyaté burned the tips of all ten fingers before departing. The skin on his fingers was black, with wrinkles and tiny strips of flesh. The scars hadn't healed properly. Kouyaté would have liked to shed his skin, like a snake. To have another identity. He wanted to become another man and have another life. All the ragazzi want to be someone else.

Kouyaté knew the way. You had to go through Burkina Faso, then over to Niger. There, you had to stay in the capital, Niamey. Then you would go to Agadez, another town. From there you would go to Libya, crossing the desert. That was the way. I trusted Adama. He protected me. He advised me. He told me stories. He consoled me when I was sad. He became my friend. He was very resourceful at the borders. He knew how to talk, how to bargain, to bribe people. That's how we got all the way to Niamey. We waited there for a few days before the smuggler came to get us.

While we waited, we were all put together in a pretty shady, squalid neighborhood. It stank; it was dirty and poor. Piles of rubbish surrounded by other kinds of detritus, human detritus: us. There were fifty of us, roughly, all of us young, or mostly. Malians, Guineans, Senegalese, Nigerians, Liberians, people from Niger, from Cameroon, Ivorians, too.

In the beginning, we didn't talk to each other. It wasn't out of shyness or wariness. It was due to the fear we might not understand each other. The fear we might not speak the same language. And yet, after a few hours, we knew we spoke the same language: the language of shame. And so we began to speak, to build our fraternity like a hut around our shame. When a Liberian or a Nigerian spoke English, everyone else understood. Why? Because this Nigerian or that Liberian was, above all, a man who was ashamed, speaking to other men who were ashamed. It wasn't the shame of leaving; it was the shame of not having been able to stay, not having been able to find one's place in one's own country. We don't all leave for the same reasons, but each of us has a reason linked to the shame from which society has made us suffer. But we spoke, all the same. And the more we spoke, the more that shame faded away. As if our individual reasons for shame were consoling and comforting one another. So bit by bit, shame gave way to the Dream. Because that, too, brought us together: the Dream.

Yes, we spoke about the Dream. Leaving, fleeing the shame, fulfilling our dream, and then returning to kill the shame. To look it in the eye at last. To look at shame and society in the eye. To return the insult, to spit back at them. We would never be ashamed again; we would be the men who'd managed to turn our dream into reality. Oh, yes, we spoke a lot and for a long time about all that. We were trash, and we were dreaming surrounded by trash, in the middle of the great garbage patch where all the world is floundering. But as we were doing it, we were men like all the others, because everyone on earth does it: they dream, even when all around them are garbage, flies, dirt, and corpses. Everyone else does it. So we had the right to do it, too. You have to dream to get ahead; otherwise you rot. It was Adama who told me that. For nights on end, each of us would talk about our Dream.

Sometimes, someone reminded us that first we had to cross the desert and the sea to get to the Dream. When that happened, we were suddenly jerked awake to reality, amid the trash. Some people told stories: a brother who'd died at sea, a father lost in the desert, a cousin who went mad after the crossing. Everyone had a story. But it never lasted. Our Dream was too strong. Our desire to get away was so great that we were not afraid. We couldn't allow ourselves to be afraid. We had to think about Europe and not about death, even if the path to Europe passed through death, even if the path to Europe was death. Then somebody would tell a joke to ease the atmosphere, and we would laugh and forget about death.

One day the police found us. They came and began shouting at us, to frighten us. Their leader said he was going to send us back to our countries. He also said we should be ashamed for leaving Africa. That we were cowards for fleeing the continent instead of helping to build it. He said, yes, there was poverty, corruption, unemployment, but that if all the children on the continent left, there'd be nobody left to develop it. He spoke to us as if we were children, guilty of misbehaving. He brought us straight back to our shame. We called our smuggler. He came and talked with the policeman off to one side for a few minutes. I saw our smuggler slip banknotes into the policeman's hand. After that, the policeman left with his men without saying a thing. Men with a great deal of integrity, those policemen, ready to develop Africa and fight corruption.

That was when I understood that nobody could judge us anymore. To leave the way we were leaving meant we were men who could not be judged, because we'd already been judged by the toughest tribunal on earth: our own selves. To choose to leave was to accept that we were worthless in our own countries. That we'd become totally worthless, period.

Our smuggler said he'd come back the next day with the cars to go to Agadez. That night, Kouyaté took me to one side and told me that the "cars" were pickup trucks, and we'd have to squeeze together in the back, on the cargo bed. He told me the best spots were the ones at the back of the cargo beds, up against the cabin. On the sides, you were in danger of falling. And falling meant death, because when someone fell in the desert, the vehicle wouldn't stop. He told me you had to do everything you could to get a good spot. But when the three pickup trucks arrived, there was such a scuffle that in the end, Kouyaté asked me to wait. The others had forgotten about camaraderie: everyone was fighting for a spot that would ensure their survival. Every man for himself. So, inevitably, Kouyaté and I got the places on the side, on the edge of the void, our legs dangling.

Kouyaté tried to reassure me, saying that during the trip it was better to keep an eye on death from the edge of the void than to lose sight of it and believe you were safe, and not see it coming to take you by surprise. He wasn't very convincing, but anyway. We climbed on board. The smuggler gave everyone on the side a big stick. You had to wedge it between your legs and against the sides of the vehicle to have a better purchase and not fall when the car started shaking. I clung to my stick. It was my life from that moment on. I squeezed my thighs and my hands around it. We each received a turban, too. You had to wrap it around your head to protect yourself from the dust and the sandstorms in the desert. And so we set off. We stopped briefly in Agadez to fill up our water supply and take on food. I was afraid. Kouyaté noticed, and in front of everybody he recited a poem for me to the glory of my Tarawélé ancestors. Warriors. I don't know if that really reassured me, but it helped me take an interest in something besides my fear.

Then we entered the desert, heading toward Libya, heading toward the great Dream.

Fousseyni talks for a long time, without pausing to catch his breath. He bursts into tears after this effort. Lucia stands up and goes to take him in her arms. She embraces him with great tenderness.

Lucia's Voice

He's been crying silently for a few minutes now. I don't dare interrupt him. I don't think he's ever taken the time to cry, despite everything that's happened to him. He's never had the time to mourn his friend Adama Kouyaté. He's just told me how he died, during the trip.

Adama was telling him the myth about the creation of the desert when a group of armed Touareg slave traders chased after them. The pickup had to accelerate, swerving spectacularly to get away from these cruel hunters of men and corpses. The vehicle shook violently, abruptly. Adama Kouyaté was flung overboard, but tried to cling to the back of the pickup, desperately trying not to fall as the chase forced the driver to go as fast as he could. Adama, with his elbows on the edge of the truck bed, and his lower body thrown outside the vehicle, begged Fousseyni to help him. But Fousseyni was so petrified, so afraid of letting go of his stick, that at first he didn't move to help his friend. In the confusion, the others screamed at the driver to go even faster, begging him to save them from the slave traders . . . The vehicle felt like it would explode from the pressure of the excessive speed. Adama was screaming hysterically; he couldn't hold on much longer. He had no more strength. Already his legs scraped violently against the hot, sandy ground. He called to Fousseyni, he asked him to give him his hand, but Fousseyni told me he was paralyzed and couldn't let go of his stick. Finally, however, his friend's desperate cries revived his courage. He held out one hand to seize Adama's. He managed. But just as he began trying to hoist him back up onto the truck, a jolt more violent than the others yanked them apart. Adama fell. Did he survive his fall? Was he captured by the slave traders? It doesn't matter. In either case, he was lost. That was the story of his death.

Fousseyni's weeping. He's weeping because he lost his friend. But above all, he's weeping because he feels guilty. He's angry with himself for having been so afraid, for having yielded to cowardice. He's angry at himself for not being able to help the friend who was calling to him. He's thinking that if he'd held his hand out to Adama right away instead of clinging to his stick, he might have had a chance to save him. They might have made it out of the desert together.

Now I know why his eyes are so sad. He weeps soundlessly, trying to maintain his dignity. His story is over. He's a hero: not a superman, but someone who's been forced to live with what is darkest inside himself. And who has been broken by it. Broken, but not killed. You have the right to cry. You have the right to think about your mother. You have the right, finally, to mourn your friend Adama Kouyaté. I wish I could console you by telling you that you have nothing to do with his death. Only you know that. You have to confront that memory. But you're not alone. You don't have to carry it alone. I want to get my voice back so I can tell you this.

They are still embracing. The light slowly fades to darkness. Curtain.

The Christmas mass had been underway for two hours, and, like all self-respecting Christmas masses, it was endless. The storm that was brewing outside had not stopped the faithful from coming to take Communion.

Padre Bonianno had led the service with military rigor and precision. He had confronted the rather disorderly effusions of his entranced flock with austere firmness; against the fervent roar of voices, his own stood out, unadorned and devoid of any affect. He had not yielded to the temptation of faith's excessive theatricality. Up he went to the pulpit. A song of praise to the Virgin was finishing. When at last the worshippers fell silent and, outside, even the storm lowered its voice, the priest stood for a long time saying nothing, motionless on the rostrum, facing the flock who awaited his sermon; then, just when people were beginning to wonder if he was still alive, his priestly speech rose in the silence of the church like that of John the Baptist in the desert.

"I will speak again of those we call migrants, for lack of a better word, because I believe that even if their journey is not over, even if they are still migrating, for the moment they are here, among us. I refer to them as migrants, but I could also call them emigrants, immigrants, displaced or exiled persons, refugees . . . Like all of us, I find it hard to name them, and I think, moreover, that this is one of the reasons why there has been such controversy about them. When you have difficulty giving a precise name to a human being, that is where misfortune begins . . . But let us move on. Not long ago, I was in despair regarding their situation. The thought that, here, they must confront the tragedy of ennui and the fear that they might not get their papers, after crossing the sea on the edge of death, was unbearable to me. I saw no future for them here, on this land that has nothing to offer them. I despaired. But I am sorry that I did. My mistake was that I was looking for a culprit. Don't ask yourselves who's guilty; everyone is guilty in this matter. Their countries of origin, for a start. Then our countries. The migrants themselves. And us. History. The system. The smugglers. Geopolitics. Global capitalism. Colonization. All of that has its share of truth and its share of culpability. But the fact remains that whoever the culprit may be, this is how it ends: they are here before us. It's what we must do now that matters. So that we won't just think that, someday, they'll have to fear death simply to have a better life. There is no sea wide or deep enough to contain the determination and impulse for survival of these men. Whatever we do, they'll keep coming. If we build walls, they'll climb over them or knock them down. If we put up electric barbed wire fences, they'll dig tunnels underneath, or come crashing against them and sizzle like flies on a light bulb, until the light bulb itself sizzles and they make it through. If we try to kick them out, they'll come back. If we kill them, they'll be reborn, or their children will come. So, yes, perhaps taking them in is a collective hell, where no one understands anyone. But not to take them in is a solitary hell, where we don't speak to one another and where, therefore, we have no chance of understanding each other. Between these two hells, I prefer the one where we are all together, speaking to each other, even if we don't understand. For it is that hell that offers the greatest hope. The hope that someday a new, shared language will be born. Everyone has their place in paradise. Everyone has their place in hell. That may be the only thing that paradise and hell have in common: one is never alone there. One is never on one's own. There are people everywhere, people one has not chosen, and with whom one must compromise. It's called living."

The priest fell silent. Everyone waited for him to continue speaking. The silence persisted. And it was just then, as the surprised congregation realized the sermon had ended, that Padre Bonianno collapsed at the foot of the pulpit. At the back of the church, those who hadn't seen the priest fall stood up and began solemnly singing a psalm. In the front row, Giuseppe Fantini, who had only come to surprise his old friend, who'd been so sure he wouldn't see him at mass, was the first to rush toward his motionless body. He knelt by him and took his head in his arms. The old priest was still conscious, but his voice already spoke from beyond the grave. People clustered around them. The singing stopped. There was a call for silence, given the gravity of the moment. The storm could be heard again, but it was no longer howling; its weakening breath seemed to harmonize with the dying priest's.

In falling, he had lost his glasses. His eyes, wide open, seemed to have recovered a last light. His many deep wrinkles no longer wove a complex, labyrinthine web on his face; they seemed to find a sort of secret consonance there. His thin lips struggled to part as he murmured in Fantini's arms. And although only the poet heard clearly what he was saying, the entire church listened to the whispering that grew quieter and quieter, more and more inaudible. Everyone heard death embrace his voice.

"Giuseppe . . . is that you, Giuseppe? How was I? . . . Not all that great, was I . . . Yes . . . I've been better . . . Better . . . Anyway, I did what I could. At least the setting for my exit has been grandiose. Christmas mass . . . When you think . . . With such a flourish . . . What I said about the ragazzi . . . Not enough . . . You were right . . . But it's not my business anymore . . . . Promise me you'll help them . . . Promise . . . Yes, that's it . . . . Now, good riddance . . . Back to F* . . . my village, back to the *ngel* . . . And above all, back to her . . . Gnilaan

Juuf . . . Never could forget her . . . But you're weeping, you're weeping . . . A poet mustn't . . . So that's it . . . God . . . God . . . That will be my last word . . . how original . . . God . . . "

He raised his open hand, as if he were trying to take hold of an invisible object, or bless an imaginary worshipper. The sleeve of his cassock slipped up to his shoulder, revealing his thin arm. He said a few more meaningless words. His arm stayed raised for a few seconds; it swayed, hesitated between falling and staying upright, as if between life and death, then eventually fell down again, slowly, onto his chest. Sister Maria, in tears, was the first to cross herself, and everyone present followed suit. Fantini alone did not move. His friend was still in his arms, staring straight ahead. To the poet it seemed that nothing on that smiling, mischievous face had changed. For the first time in over half a century, Giuseppe silently recited a *De Profundis*. Then he closed Amedeo's eyes for good, as his own filled with tears.

* * *

In keeping with his last wishes, as revealed by a will full of fantastical wishes, Amedeo Bonianno was buried several days later in Switzerland, between his father, Giorgio Maria Bonianno, and his mother, Sylvie Morand. Fantini and a few other members of the association saw to all the formalities and accompanied his remains. The poet read the most beautiful funeral oration ever uttered since the one Victor Hugo gave for Balzac. The late priest left half of his fortune to the association to help the ragazzi. As for the other half, he asked that it go to the village of F*, which he had never forgotten. He had stipulated that his annotated Bible should be given to Solomon, the Nigerian he'd met a few days earlier. His great library was divided among a few members of the Santa Marta Association. His very old, magnificent, mother-of-pearl rosary beads, which had been a gift from Pope John Paul II, were bequeathed to Sister Maria. Finally, Amedeo Bonianno left an envelope to his friend Fantini: no one knew what it contained, but he had asked a notary to place "the most precious thing" he had on earth inside it. In his will there was this cryptic remark, addressed to the poet: "Just in case."

Care was also taken to respect his requests regarding the program of his funeral ceremony: "I will not deprive myself of the pleasure of hearing Giuseppe Fantini say something good about me, in his magnificent fashion. So let the poet speak at length. For all the rest, make it brief. The prayers, brief. The sermons, brief. The songs, brief. The weeping, too, if possible. Not too many flowers; I was allergic to almost everything. Put on some music; that will relax me before I go to meet God, or the devil. Schubert's 'Ave Maria,' as sung by Maria Callas. Then you may cry all you like. Not for me, but for the music. Ciao."

He asked that the following epitaph be carved on his tomb: "Less a man of the cloth than a man."

34

11 *:38 P.M.* Between the foie gras and the caviar, Francesco Montero took a few minutes to reflect on the moral dilemma that had been haunting him for several days. Maurizio Mangialepre's deadline was due to expire at midnight. Should he accept his proposal and vote for someone who would refuse asylum to countless refugees, who'd undo everything Francesco had done for them for over twenty years—knowing that in exchange, he would become a senator? Or should he refuse, go on working to welcome the migrants, and run the risk of staying mayor of this little town forever, thus never fulfilling his ambitions? He'd been thinking about it. Morality or power? Honor or glory? Ideals or ambition? He hadn't been able to decide—too weak, too indecisive. He had twenty minutes left.

11:44. He'd sent both his children to bed, but he knew very well that they weren't asleep because they were waiting for the fireworks. Next to him, Vera, Vincenzo, and Isabella were still talking about *Vanitas Vanitatum*. Vera was explaining that a very rich collector in Milan had made an offer to buy *Off-Frame, Off-Art, Off-Camera*, and they could name their price. "He held out a blank check and told us to fill in the amount we wanted," she said. "Which, obviously, we refused to do," added Vincenzo. "This old technique is a trap: there isn't enough room on a check for all the zeros a masterpiece is worth!" They burst out laughing. Francesco, not to seem absent, laughed stupidly. But he still hadn't decided. Isabella served the fish. Vincenzo opened another bottle.

11:49. He thought about his father, Orlando Montero. A good *contadino* who had always chosen dignity and integrity, despite relative poverty. What would his father have done in his shoes? He would certainly have chosen to decline and stay humble. What would his mother have said? She would've said she'd forgive him and love him no matter what he did. The fish was a little dry, but with the wine, it was all right.

11:54. He asks to be excused, leaves the table, and goes to the bathroom. For the first time in at least ten years, his wife's blow-dry is not quite perfect. He detects a naughty, shining gleam deep in her gaze. Vera and Vincenzo are eating their fish with appetite. They're on the verge of being completely drunk.

11:56. He calls Maurizio Mangialepre but hears "the number you are calling is momentarily unavailable." He lets out an oath.

11:57. Francesco calls again. Maurizio picks up.

"I was beginning to have my doubts about your common sense and ambition, Francesco. You know how to make people wait. Do you accept my proposal?"

"Yes," he replies. "I accept. But there's just one more problem. Elena Rossi. She's the one running opposite Sandro Calvino. She's very popular, and more competent than Sandro for the position. She built her career at the UN but also working for important European government bodies. She was at the head of several major humanitarian organizations. She was made to be president of a commission charged with immigrant resettlement. Even if I give my vote to Sandro, there's no guarantee he'll be elected."

"Don't worry about Elena Rossi, Francesco. Just vote for Calvino. I have to go."

"Wait. You haven't forgotten your promise?"

"I haven't. And as I already told you, I always keep my promises. Enjoy your party, and Happy New Year, *caro sindaco.* Sorry, I meant, *caro futuro senatore.*"

He hangs up. Francesco Montero returns to the living room at the very moment the fireworks explode above Altino. He kisses his friends. He feels much lighter now. He empties his glass and takes a second helping of fish. The year is off to a very good start.

35

I t took a few days for Altino's townspeople in general and the association members in particular to feel the full impact of their painful loss of Amedeo Bonianno.

Carla missed him terribly. Whenever she had spoken to him, it seemed to her—and she thought again of that fine passage she'd read in a work by Proust—that Padre Bonianno also belonged "to that magnificent, deplorable family who are the salt of the earth": the Highly-Strung. She got the impression that with the priest's death, she had lost one of the few people who could help her understand their situation, thanks to the intensity he put into living it. She had gone to see him the morning after the altercation with Solomon during the *giro case*. She described what had happened, then asked him, "What are we supposed to do if all our efforts to make them happy only make them frustrated and angry?" Padre Bonianno was silent for a few seconds, then replied that perhaps they shouldn't try to make them happy according to their own idea of happiness; that was a mistake, and had caused considerable human misfortune. He added that he didn't know exactly what they should do, but in any case he would stay vigilant so that indifference wouldn't prevail. "We have to face things, my little Carla. Not resist, because we're not at war, except against our own inner demons, but literally face things—I mean, put on a face. When we look at these faces in distress, we have to be vigilant and focus on showing them a truly human face, an authentic face, because that's where we find what's most noble. The greatest humiliation for anyone is to see nothing on the face they're looking at, or to sit across from a faceless man. So show your face."

The other members of the Santa Marta Association were also very upset by the loss of the priest. It was true that each of them had forged a unique relationship with him and had very specific memories. Sabrina, Sister Maria, Pietro, Gianni . . . They could all point to some unforgettable lesson the priest had given them one day. Pietro, for example, remembered every word of the long and passionate discussions they'd had about psychology; the priest maintained that psychology was at the heart of religion and that the act of confession, for a believer, was not so very different from a visit to a psychologist or psychoanalyst. The only difference, he added, was that he, the priest, was better at offering relief to the human soul, all while being far less well-paid.

Lucia's feelings for the priest were as tender as a grand-daughter's for her grandfather. He had often told her that they were twins, given their respective handicaps: the blind man and the mute girl. But he always reminded her that, just as his blindness didn't stop him from having a gaze, or even vision, her enforced silence shouldn't prevent her from having a voice, or even speech.

As for Jogoy, he recalled all the hours spent in Padre Bonianno's company, translating the ragazzi's words. And he thought of those moments when they had spoken Serer together, and realized that the old priest had been his last concrete tie with his origins.

In this way, a sort of collective memory was formed, nourished by each individual who had personal reminiscences about the late priest. Amedeo Bonianno was subject to that human law that holds that a person's death is the sudden concentration of his life, all at once, into the memory of each individual who knew him, as if the thousands of deeds, decisions, words, promises, loves, gestures, regrets, mistakes, and flashes of brilliance and shadow throughout the deceased's life were now fated to be reduced to a few facts. As if he had, basically, only lived through a dozen or so moments that would remain in the memory of those who'd known him. As if, in the end, living and dying were the two motions of a large accordion: living, where the individual opens and spreads the instrument wide, fit to dislocate his shoulders, and dying, where others squeeze it closed again, thus producing a sound that is sometimes grating, more often harmonious, but which rarely corresponds to what the life of a person has truly been, with its shine and its rough patches, its peaks and plains, its incandescence and boredom, its heights and abysses.

Giuseppe Fantini shut himself away at home. He mourned in silence and solitude. Perhaps, one night, he might even have written a poem in memoriam. Out of everyone on the planet, the man he'd lost was his best friend.

Finally, the ragazzi, when they learned of his death, thought about the advice he'd given them. Padre Bonianno had not had the chance to finish the job he'd begun with them on their stories, but they'd all been able to meet with him at least once, and he'd had the time to offer some notes—the only notes they would receive before the real interviews, which, they were told, would be starting "very soon." The day Jogoy handed him the old priest's annotated Bible, Solomon stayed immersed in it for many hours, and his little eyes sparked as he read the holy text and the comments its former reader had left inside.

36

T he sadness into which the priest's death had plunged the association, compounded with the ongoing interruption in their football practice, accentuated the ragazzi's tragic, enduring sense of ennui. They went on waiting.

They could be seen in small groups, sitting on a bench somewhere, drinking in the air, or standing and staring into space. They talked about the same things every day: family, the money they wanted to send home but were completely unable to earn, vague dreams of departure, their anger with the association's inertia, and so on. Thus, as the days went by, they arranged the world, took it apart, put it back together, unstitched it all, then wove it together again exactly as it had been—they were modern male Penelopes, busy with their endless world-crafting and immersed in a time of waiting and its ever-receding horizon. All between two cups of tea and a few puffs on a shared cigarette butt that went from hand to hand and one mouth to the next. Even the Sicilian women seemed to have abandoned them: very few went near their idle councils now. Their all-too male reaction of making some saucy remarks when a pretty woman walked by, laughing coarsely—even that pleasure was taken from them, denied them. They went on waiting.

The precise dates of the asylum interviews had still not been announced; they seemed to be no more than a distant oasis they despaired of ever reaching. Their inner sea was calm. There were no waves; there was no fear of storms. This sea was empty, and its sun was covered by a gray sky, so low on the water that it looked like its sinister hat. And the ship in which they were sailing was no longer the one that had brought most of them to a Sicilian shore. No, this ship had suffered no storms, and for that reason alone, it was even more awful. They went on waiting.

And the cold became more raw, the days shorter, their moods gloomier, and the silences more bitter. In the evening, the calls to their loved ones back home were filled with gravity. They were questioned about their situation; they were asked how things were going. And the ragazzi, tired of always saying the same thing, would change the subject and ask for news of a distant aunt whom, in reality, they didn't much care about, or they fell silent. For the time being, they didn't have much to tell. Their story had been interrupted in the middle of a long sentence. Cut short. They didn't yet know when they'd be able to resume the telling and finish it. But so what. That's just the way it was: wait. They had to wait. So they waited, their mouths open, facing the wind, like those big reptiles sometimes seen on the banks of a river. And the air tasted of decay, of the kind one discovers on clearing one's throat. They were waiting for something that could equally be asylum or death.

Sometimes during the long hours, they sang sad melodies. One day when they were singing like this, the Calcagno brothers went by and jeered at them. They said singing wouldn't help them avoid idleness, waiting, or violence. How could they possibly understand what drove the ragazzi to sing?

37

Maurizio Mangialepre was exultant, and he had good reason: the situation in Altino had never seemed better for driving out the immigrants. Luck was on his side at last, and he had to seize it. God was finally honoring him with His applause, so he must dance like the devil. In the meantime, he was celebrating. He'd greeted the news of the death of Altino's priest with huge relief, even joy. Because with his passing, those believers who were opposed to welcoming asylum-seekers would face no more awkward barriers to clearly stating their refusal to see their land invaded. In the end, he'd realized that the late priest was the last dike restraining the patriotic tide of some of his followers. He had long searched for a way to breach that dike. The surest way, death, had finally taken care of it for him.

Francesco Montero had also relented, finally. For a while, Maurizio had given up hope that he'd agree to his proposal, so much so that at one point he believed the mayor of Altino was truly honest, a man of integrity. But naturally, this was not the case, and the uncertainty did not last for long. Things went back to normal, and his initial hunch—that Francesco Montero was like the majority of politicians, with unhealthy ambitions and hungry for his own glory—had eventually turned out to be the right one. He was now almost absolutely certain that Sandro Calvino would be elected.

From one angle, on a social level, the religious scruples of more than one Sicilian would disappear now that the blind priest had died; from another, on a political level, a member of his family, who, moreover, had long been in debt to him, was about to be elected. Things were looking good. The ragazzi would be leaving soon.

He was all the more convinced of this when he noticed that the Santa Marta Association was struggling to get back on track after the priest's death. It had been a great blow to their morale. Now it was time for the coup de grâce.

And so in the days that followed, Maurizio Mangialepre ordered his followers to talk tougher and act more and more aggressively, all to the delight of Fabio and Sergio. The priest's death had liberated the two brothers; they no longer lived in fear of blasphemy.

They went at it wholeheartedly. Not a day went by without them provoking, intimidating, or insulting the refugees. Feeling vulnerable and alone since Padre Bonianno's passing had left the association in turmoil, the ragazzi submitted to this bullying with a mixture of fear and faint astonishment. Fabio and Sergio were jubilant whenever they found them sitting on a public bench, huddled together in the cold like freshly hatched chicks, and they showered them with the most mortifying insults without arousing the slightest reaction. Sometimes they used stones instead. Even then, instead of responding, the ragazzi merely got up and left. The twins thought this lack of reaction reflected terror, and it made them feel they were reclaiming their lost honor: once again, their appearance alone aroused in others the most irrational forms of fear. At least that's what they thought. It was enough to soothe their pride, which had felt wounded ever since they'd left the virile fights in the stands. The Calcagnos were back. They were spreading terror and mayhem among the ragazzi. Maurizio was thrilled.

Elsewhere in town, his other friends were also playing their part. Gennaro Orso, the butcher who wanted a radical confrontation, and several other townspeople were gaining in influence.

More and more shopkeepers began refusing to exchange their products for the pocket money vouchers the association gave the refugees for their needs. They used the slow rate of reimbursement in hard cash as a pretext to justify their decision. They accused the association of failing to take their own difficulties into account and of negatively impacting them through this system of fake currency. Some of them began saying that the migrants were stealing from them on a regular basis. As for the shopkeepers who continued to accept the pocket money and treat the ragazzi rather more kindly—despite the fact that this meant going against the general trend—they frequently found their shops vandalized or covered with offensive tags and threats.

Maurizio sensed that the jaws were tightening. And this time, they would close, clack, brutally and ruthlessly, over the association's bared neck. He would have his revenge at last. And no one, not the refugees, not Mayor Montero, and not Matteo Falconi, captain of the carabinieri, could do a thing. All the lights were green. He would finally be avenged for the humiliation—he could hardly breathe just thinking about it—he had suffered ten years earlier.

38

Sitting at La Tavola di Luca, Dr. Pessoto and Jogoy were waiting for the Juventus match to kick off.

"How is Erica?" said Jogoy.

"She's fine. It's as if nothing happened. Yet God knows that business nearly changed everything."

"And Angela?"

"She's still angry. I think she's right to be. I have to spend more time with the children. My family's the most precious thing I have."

"I know, Totò. I think Angela knows it, too."

"Maybe. But the incident opened my eyes."

"About what?"

"You know I'm no great optimist, particularly where the ragazzi are concerned. I think they're heading toward disaster."

"You didn't answer me, Totò. What did the incident with your daughter open your eyes about?"

"An extremely unpleasant reality. It's hard to hear, even for me. Especially for me. But I think I've reached a point—" He paused, then continued, "—I've reached a point where I'm fed up with the ragazzi and their problems. I haven't been able to think of anything else since they arrived. I can't take it anymore."

"And what about them?" said Jogoy, his voice hard. "Do you have any idea what *they're* thinking about? Do you think they even have the option of thinking about something else?"

"Don't get mad, Leone. I'm not angry with them, personally."

"Then who, or what?"

"Everything that's going on around them. All the noise. The hatred directed at them, the pity they inspire. The hateful, xenophobic speech, just as much as the hollow, paternalistic talk about solidarity or living together, or how to welcome them. Everything annoys me. All the fuss about the situation. I'm fed up."

"I can't believe you would say that, Salvatore. I knew you were pessimistic. But not selfish."

"It's not that . . . it's not selfishness. I'm simply telling you that I'm tired. And so are they, I know they are."

"And? What's your conclusion? Are you planning to become one of Mangialepre's militants, alongside his two gorillas?"

"Don't be ridiculous. You're pretending not to understand what I'm telling you."

"I'm not pretending. I don't understand you. At this point, I'm not sure I ever have."

"Any friend but me would think that what you just said is really harsh. But I won't complain. Maybe it's true—maybe we *have* never understood each other. I'm not obsessed like everyone else with understanding whoever's there across from me. I think it's pointless. But I'm digressing. What I'm going to do: I'm going to quit coaching the ragazzi. For good. It's over."

"Just like that, a few days from the final?" said Jogoy. "You would drop us, just like that, Totò?"

Pessoto glanced over at the television. The two teams were coming out onto the pitch. His cigarette tasted of hot crap and cold betrayal. Out of the corner of his eye, he could see Jogoy, who was still staring at him, looking both outraged and vexed.

"Yes," he said eventually, taking on his friend's gaze, sheepishly. "I'm dropping you, yes. There's no point looking for some way to soften the simple truth. There it is."

They stayed silent for a long moment. The match began.

"It's your decision," Jogoy said eventually, his voice hoarse, and he didn't look at the doctor.

"I know you're disappointed. But I want to get away from all that. It's too much of a burden."

"I don't want any more explanations. Let's change the subject."

"I'll come and watch the final," Salvatore Pessoto insisted. "I've told the team everything I had to tell you. All you have to do is go in there, play your match, and not give a damn about anything else. I'm sorry I won't be on the bench, but—"

"Enough, honestly. Change the subject. You don't have to justify yourself. You can do what you want."

Salvatore Pessoto finally caught on that he needed to stop talking about the ragazzi. He lit another cigarette, even though he'd barely smoked the one he'd just crushed in the ashtray.

"Have you had a heart-to-heart with Carla?"

Pessoto immediately regretted his question. This subject was only going to complicate their conversation, which was already tense. He felt stupid, even a bit mean. He'd asked the question without thinking. It had slipped from his lips along with a cloud of smoke. To his great surprise, however, Jogoy answered calmly, although he could hear all the sorrow in his voice.

"To tell her what? She's been in love with Roberto for several years now. She's been seeing me and thinking of me as her big brother, ever since we met. Even her parents treat me that way. I have nothing to say to her. It would be disrespectful. And pointless."

Pessoto very nearly told him that he should open up to her, but in the end he didn't, not to come out with any other cruel remarks. He wasn't good at talking about this sort of thing. His friend's tone had been cold and sad. He was the only one who knew how Jogoy felt about Carla, the feelings he'd had for a long time without being able to confess them to her. Without daring to, anyway.

Dr. Pessoto thought for a moment about his own decision to quit coaching. Maybe it was cowardly, but at least it obeyed his gut feeling. After all, he thought, sometimes at a given moment cowardice is our nature, and when that's the case, it's pointless to repress it in the name of some superficial nobility. He didn't want to pretend to be good, or heroic.

He hadn't lied to Jogoy: he had nothing left to say to the ragazzi—or rather, he no longer knew what to say. He'd exhausted all his reserves—which, frankly, had not been all that full to start with—reserves of kindness, hope, and comforting phrases. He admitted defeat. He was ashamed for yielding to weakness in a difficult situation, but there was one thing that surpassed the deep disgust he inspired in himself at such moments: his knowledge that he could live with the cowardice. Life went on, in spite of everything. He thought about that sentence, worthy of a bad novel or a mediocre early-afternoon soap. People thought it told of hope or some related feeling, something positive. They failed to fully comprehend the extent to which that sentence was precisely the opposite: terrible, absolutely without hope. Life went on, in spite of everything. "Life ought to abstain now and again," he thought. "We shouldn't be able to put up with everything. But actually, we can: we can put up with anything. Or a lot. Really a lot. Others think it's brave. Personally, I think it's the ultimate proof that we're monsters."

He took a sip of beer. It was a lukewarm soup, his own heart liquefied. He swallowed it without grimacing.

Juventus scored in the first fifteen minutes. Salvatore Pessoto could not help making a movement of delight. He was already coming to terms with his self-disgust. Life went on. Jogoy stood up at that moment and left the bar, hardly saying goodbye. This was the first time since they'd known one another that they wouldn't be watching the match together to the end, a match with their favorite team.

CHAPTER V

Yes, Valeria: we all leave because we have to leave.

For me, staying would have been equivalent to dying. Symbolically. Socially. Of shame. Of bitterness. Completely dying. It was to avoid it that one fine day, not saying anything to anyone, I went away. I just left a letter giving the reasons for my departure. Over time, my family has learned to forgive. Maybe even to understand. The money for the trip? I sold my only asset: a brand-new computer I'd received after winning the university's philosophy essay contest.

After I'd been with Mario and Valeria for two weeks, they introduced me to their only daughter, who worked with an association that received refugees. That's how I met Carla. I didn't immediately fall under her spell. Naturally, I thought she was beautiful. But I think she's one of those women who knows how to let you take your time falling in love. It's a form of charm not many women have nowadays. It took me nearly a year to love her. A year during which I saw her only once every two weeks, when she came to see me in Catania.

Carla hadn't been able to bring me to Altino, where, at the time, the Santa Marta Association had just taken in all the ragazzi it could. So she found me a spot with the association in Catania, which was bigger and better equipped. That year in Catania was tough. I didn't know many people, despite the solidarity that brought migrants from the same country together. The Senegalese community was pretty big and characterized by a strong tendency to help one another. And yet, their way of life felt foreign to me. I was looking for something else; I needed something else, and I couldn't find it. The Senegalese in Catania were well organized. They made it possible for all the newcomers to earn a bit of money while still being useful to the community. So I found myself with a whole stock of bric-a-brac. I had to sell it all over town through a clandestine business that wasn't officially authorized by the police in Catania. But they couldn't keep up with all the migrants' movable displays that popped up everywhere in the streets of Catania. Exhausted and overwhelmed by everything they had to do in this mafia-controlled town, the cops generally left us alone, provided we weren't too visible. That's how our little business got going; it was modest but flourishing, even if it wasn't honest. We were migrants in every sense: our distress gave us certain rights, even those of us who broke the law.

The advantage of being an itinerant street peddler was that I could explore the town on foot. I got to know it even better because I had a special guide: Thialky Boy Hawaii. I never found out his real name, just this improbable pseudonym that he nevertheless wore like a second skin, with a natural elegance, even panache. Thialky Boy Hawaii! Try to picture him: forty years old, small, weighing less than fifty kilos all told, thin, but what a cocky sense of humor! What a talker! He was a mixture of Wolof Njaay and Kocc Barma, of Balla Fasséké and Sundiata, of Diogenes and Demosthenes, both a beggar and a proud man, wandering and magnificent, noble and cynical, grotesque and sublime, a smooth talker and orator, swashbuckler and philosopher, buffoon and king, griot and emperor, dangerously outspoken and wise. He told me he learned it all in the streets of Guédiawaye, a seaside town outside Dakar (transformed into Hawaii), where he'd grown up and done every job in the book: carpenter, *coxeur*[10], apprentice, counterfeiter, clandestine taxi driver, itinerant peddler, hairdresser, political party hatchet man, mechanic, butcher, cook, tailor, doorman, photographer, cemetery caretaker, road sweeper, garbage man, football coach, gravedigger, fishmonger, fisherman, cobbler, *bujuman*[11], Koranic master, shoeshine boy, wrestler, dealer, charlatan, weaver, petty thief, public scribe, coalmonger, and healer. The other Senegalese immigrants in Catania had labeled Thialky Boy Hawaii an eccentric. He didn't seem to like them much, either. "All they think about is getting money. They don't know how to enjoy life, my boy . . . They're so fond of flaunting their image of brave migrants fighting to uphold their dignity that

[10] Someone who organizes people waiting at taxi ranks, in bus queues
[11] Someone who recycles waste

they've forgotten how to live . . . It's all
an act . . . Pure theater . . . Bad theater . . . ! Characters! And false ones . . .
They don't know how to live . . . And besides, they go around acting all virtuous,
but I know 'em, I know 'em all . . . The ones
that look the most virtuous will never tell
you what they do to survive. Drugs, prosti-
tution . . . They'll do anything. But I'm
not judging 'em! Have to keep your ass clean
before you go telling others they've got a
piece of shit dangling from theirs . . . and
my ass, I know, isn't all that clean. Every
man for himself, and God for me! And for you,
my boy—and for you!"

I got along well with old Thialky. I hung
around with him a lot. In the boredom and
solitude of that first year in Catania, he and
Carla (when she came to see me), as well as
Mario and Valeria (when I went back to see
them), were among the people who kept me from
going downhill. He had a slight handicap: he
was missing three fingers from his right hand:
his pinky, thumb, and ring finger. The Arab
slave traders who captured him in the Libyan
desert cut them off. They'd asked him for a
ransom in exchange for his liberty, and he
couldn't pay it. They took his fingers to make
him call his family and ask them for money.
Thialky refused. So they left him there in
the desert—which was a punishment worse than
summary execution. But Thialky survived and
managed to continue his journey. He didn't
seem bothered by the loss of his fingers. "The
two I've got left are the most useful in life,
my boy! The index and the middle finger! To

scratch my butt, say no, hold a cigarette, give people the finger, and slip some pleasure to a woman. That's really all I need, kid!" He did see a lot of women. Loads of times, in various neighborhoods while we were selling our trinkets, he'd ask me to wait for him outside a building. He'd go upstairs and stay there for a long time. And every time he came back out of one of those buildings, there'd be a woman there with him, glowing, and she'd say, *"Torna presto, amore!"*, *"Ciao, bel Senegalese,"* *"Grazie, stallone nero!"* At first, I thought he must be prostituting himself, but the great Thialky told me he didn't receive anything in exchange for his services: "*Bilé baneex amul njëgg, sama rakk*!" (Such pleasures have no price, young brother!), he said, with a terribly saucy smile. Sometimes he asked me to go with him up to the apartment where he was expected. Then we would both perform . . .

Of all the places he showed me in Catania, however, the most extraordinary, in my opinion, remains the fish market. It was held every morning, unvaryingly, between six and nine, on a small piazza surrounded by apartment buildings, and to get there you went down a few steps, because the market was slightly lower than the town center, as if it were trying to get away from the nosy cameras of the tourists buzzing around the main streets. Leave the Piazza Duomo, in whose center stands the elephant of Catania, sculpted from black volcanic stone and carrying a huge obelisk on its broad back. Leave behind the worldly, elegant cafés that surround the piazza. Resist your fascination with the monumental baroque façade of the Sant' Agata Cathedral. Close your ears to the call of the neverending Via Etnea, which seems to lead all the way to the volcano. Go farther away and look toward the southwest corner of the great piazza, toward the spot through which the invigorating smell of the sea will reach you. Do you see a peculiar fountain of white stone, in the middle of which sculpted figures strike strange poses in a scene unknown to you? Do you see it? Yes, you see it. Go closer. This fountain marks the entrance to the market, and it's constructed on two levels. On the first basin stands the statue of a beautiful young man, naked, with curly hair. On the second one, two large Tritons are kneeling, each carrying a large jar on his shoulder. Water is falling from the two basins, clear and steady, like a white veil, before it channels into a current that flows beneath it: the fountain is built on a little bridge, and under it, a source is winding its way. A plaque will inform you that this source, called the Amenano, comes from Mount Etna. It was once a powerful river, so furious and destructive that it had to be redirected to save Catania from disaster. The fountain marks the precise spot where the impetuous Amenano, as depicted allegorically by the statue of the young man, was redirected. The Catania market, the beating heart of the old city, is held in the very place where the city was rescued from death. Something immemorial refuses to die here; you can feel it.

Then keep going toward the fish market.

Instead of stepping down into the pit, stay at the top of the stairs. On a sort of little balcony overlooking the rectangular court-yard, a number of people stand with their elbows on the railing, as fascinated as you are by the scene unfurling before their eyes. Find a place, and have a look. Rows of huge tables full of wriggling fish of every shape and size, crabs waving their nippers, sword-fish with their glittering swords. Suddenly a hand plunges vigorously into a basin filled with shrimp, takes a generous handful, bran-dishes it to the sky and shouts something you don't understand, looking in your direction. The voice is addressing you and everyone else at the same time; it is boasting of the catch, the freshness of the products, the fisherman's expertise. Around this man or that woman, other fishermen are doing the same thing—heck-ling, chanting, gesticulating, bellowing, strutting, exaggerating. With their calloused hands, worn by fishing lines, salt, and nets, gloved or bare, they grab their finest fish and raise them triumphantly, as if they were trophies telling the epic story of how they were caught, commanding you to buy them if you don't want to be damned. And these men and women promise a discount, assure you of the succulence of their wares, exaggerate their talent, and reel off their sales patter. The powerful odor of the sea's entrails, the tang of salt, the strong smells of fish that are still alive, pulled this very night from the depths of the sea, rise into the air. At the extraordinary morning market, exhortations in Sicilian mingle with inspired onomatopoeias.

This great, popular, fraternal choir echoes the nearby roar of the Amenano.

I spent many hours there with the great Thialky. He told me it reminded him of back when he was a fishmonger. During these moments, the solitude of exile vanished. I was among men.

After a year in Catania, Carla told me the association was looking for a new cultural mediator for the little town of Altino. I quickly accepted her offer. It meant leaving Thialky, Catania, and the mysteries of the market. But more than that, it meant earning some money and finally being able to help my family. I would have to improve my Italian, of course, but Carla promised there would be an intensive course for me, paid for by the association. I left Catania after a brief but touching farewell with the manly Thialky. He told me he hoped I'd get on all right. A great sadness came over his face when it was time to part. I promised I'd come back to see him. He smiled sweetly, then regained his self-control when he saw I was about to cry: "My boy, don't cry here, that's what women do. Cry where no one can see you. That's how a man does it. Come see me soon, and we'll go back to visit the *belle donne* in their apartments." He winked, then held up two fingers in a salute, and at that point the emotion finished me off. I left for Altino with Carla; in the bus, I couldn't hold back my tears.

A month later, I went back to see him. Couldn't find him. No one could tell me where Thialky Boy Hawaii had got to. Some people said he went back to Senegal. Others told me he'd married a blond German and was living in Munich now. A few believed he'd died a violent death. In any case, he was gone. Home, married to a German, or dead. I went back to the market, to the place where we'd spent many hours in productive idleness. There, I held two fingers up to the sky and shouted, "I salute you, great man, wherever you are: at home or buried, deep inside your Teutonic blonde, or six feet under. I salute you!" My voice mingled with that of the fishermen and the fountain.

My new life in Altino could begin.

39

Of the seventy-two men, almost half rallied to Solomon's call. A few days earlier, he'd gone around to every apartment to inform the ragazzi he would soon be holding a meeting at his place on a subject of the utmost importance, one that concerned them all. Solomon would not elaborate, but his air of mystery, his gravity, his long silences, the determined gleam in his eyes all inspired sufficient respect—or even fear—in his comrades for them to refrain from further questioning. And so a number of them went to his place on the designated evening; there was room for them all in the apartment.

Solomon had insisted that no members of the association be present. It would just be them. And so it was. Jogoy, who had eventually gotten wind of the meeting, did not try to go, although he was nagged by a rather worried curiosity. With the exception of Carla, he didn't tell any of the Santa Marta members. They both agreed to try and find out what was brewing before taking action.

Solomon stood up, everyone fell silent, and he spoke.

"Thank you, everyone, for coming. I wanted to bring you together here to talk about something we have all noticed lately: they're abandoning us. They are all abandoning us. I haven't run into those twins recently, the ones who've been spreading terror and anger among us for several days now, but some of you have. It's obvious what they're up to: they don't just want to frighten us; they want to let us know that they're going to attack us—soon. And they'll do it without anyone lifting a finger in our defense. The association won't protect us. The carabinieri won't protect us. No one will protect us. We're on our own. We've been on our own from the very beginning. We are not and never will be like them . . . Our dreams are different from theirs. They all pretend they want what's best for us, but not one of them would stick their neck out to help us regain our dignity. But at least we won't lose the little we have left.

"Do you remember the welcome they gave us at the entrance to town some months ago? That's what will happen again, but this time, no one will pretend to defend us. This time, they won't burn a doll; they'll burn men. Us. We have to defend ourselves; we are not sacrificial lambs. If they attack us, we'll defend ourselves. We have to be ready. If they want to enter the ring, they'll find us there waiting. We haven't risked our lives just to be humiliated now by these people who are nothing but hatred.

"I've been watching what's happening elsewhere, not just in other cities in Italy, but in Europe more generally. And what's happening is that a lot of Europe doesn't want us here, and they're saying so loud and clear, as violently as possible. They say they can't take in all the misery of the planet, when it's Europe that helped create that misery. Who's more miserable, the man who has nothing or the one who stole everything from him? Who's more miserable, the man who flees war, or the one who keeps it going? Arrogant Europe still believes it's the center of the universe. It will be destroyed. It will be destroyed by its own pretension. Everything they've done, everything they're doing—the slave trade, colonization, neo-imperialism, the unpunished pillage of our riches, the conflicts they've created then washed their hands of, only to come back and claim they're saving us, our economies that they've weakened, the financial slavery they keep us in, and the terms of exchange they exact when they deal with us—all of this will come back to haunt them. They have killed, sold, stolen, pillaged: they will be punished.

"There were attacks in France a few weeks ago. They say the perpetrators arrived there together with the migrants, and therefore all migrants are dangerous. Potential terrorists . . . And here in Italy, you all know what the Northern League has to say. They call us monkeys, subhuman. Like in the time of slavery. They say they don't want us here in their land. Did they ask us for permission, when they came and settled in ours?

"They're afraid. Their natural hatred for anything that is not like them is compounded by their fear. What bothers them about us, what frightens them, is not the notion that we're stealing their jobs or invading their land; no, what frightens them about us is that we're the memory of the Evil they've committed. We're their guilty conscience. Why do you think Santa Marta hasn't done a thing since those twins started provoking us? Why do you think they haven't done anything since some of the townspeople started getting verbally or symbolically violent? It's because, unconsciously, they're sensitive to the general climate in Europe regarding immigration, and that climate is bad. It's a climate of fear, distrust, xenophobia . . .

"We can't let people push us around. The asylum interviews will begin soon. We can't let ourselves be overcome by fear. We have to assert our rights. Since Padre Bonianno died, may God rest his soul, we've had no one to help us prepare for the interviews. Deep down, they don't want us to get asylum. And that's all because there's money to be made at our expense. If we don't get our papers, we'll appeal the decision, you know that. The appeal goes through a lawyer chosen by the association. The lawyer has to be paid. The association has to get money to pay him from the state, depending on the number of appeals. So the more appeals there are, the more money the association will make, and the more they'll profit. We have to refuse to let them treat us like trash, like their bread and butter.

That's what I wanted to tell you: united, we are strong. We have to stay united. That's how we'll be saved, by the grace of God. The next time they attack us, we'll respond. We have to show them that we're here, that we know what's going on. And we won't be pushed around. We have to show them."

When he stopped speaking, the silence was charged with emotion, something uncertain but powerful. Then a murmur: those who hadn't understood everything were asking for explanations about the thrust of the speech. This lasted for a few seconds, until applause rang out, hesitantly. Then two, three, four more pairs of hands, timidly, joined in the concert. Then dozens of hands clapping together. And before long, it was a triumph. Solomon calmly sat down again. His comrades went on applauding. It wasn't so much Solomon they were applauding now, but rather the things that had been said in his speech: so many themes had been covered that were close to their hearts, things they felt without really being able to express them. Their bitterness had just been gratified. No, they would not be pushed around anymore.

Next to Bemba, who was furiously clapping and making little sounds like war cries, Fousseyni Traoré was not applauding. He was afraid of Solomon and hadn't wanted to come to this meeting. But his flatmates had urged him to go with them, because there wasn't much else to do. Of all that Solomon had just said, what he'd retained was that now they had to fight. But Fousseyni didn't want to fight anyone. He simply wanted to survive, to keep learning Italian, to play football again, prepare for his interview, call his mother, go on seeing Lucia and breathing in her scent of oranges.

40

The inhabitants of Altino awoke one morning to the terrible smell of something rotten. Every street stank with a mephitic odor of entrails and organic decay. The stench was so sickening that no one, in those early hours, could, or even dared to, go out. People stayed shut within their four walls, doors and windows closed, masks or pieces of cloth covering their noses, seized with horror, disgust, and nausea. The smell assaulted them even beneath their blankets; it seemed to be emanating from the walls of the town, or from the ground, as if it were Altino's very body that had been savagely eviscerated in the night by a huge blade, then left to rot in the open air, a repulsive carrion with its guts spilling out, full of discharge, morbid miasma, and clouds of thick black flies.

At around noon, unable to take this putrid breeze any longer, a few townspeople went out to look for the source of the evil and try, if not to confront it, at least to see it before it killed them. A little group of hardy souls convened and ventured out into the streets, nearly succumbing with every step to the tainted atmosphere they were breathing.

Although the smell didn't seem to be coming from any precise source, as if it were simply suspended everywhere in the air, the heroic group of residents sensed that the scourge was more potent when they faced a certain direction. When, indeed, they turned toward the southern part of town, they could tell that, there, the smell was more than pestilential; it was reaching them in the form of its pure chemical substance, concentrated and raw, possessed by something else. The scouts knew the scourge was hiding there. The smell from that direction was no simple smell. It was both spirit and matter, becoming flesh; it was alive.

As they approached the place they thought was at the heart of the thing, the residents were gripped by a sort of immense terror that was no longer simply the result of the smell. It was a distant, visceral fear, linked to the thought that here, in the southern part of town, somewhere, something sacred and terrible was waiting for them, something they weren't supposed to see, that could crush them. This thought, mingled with the smell, which, naturally, was getting more and more oppressive, caused several of the townspeople to feel sick, and they had to stop, not because they wanted to, but because their legs refused to take another step.

So the group became smaller and smaller, and by the time they arrived at a little street to the south of Altino, a long, dark, and narrow street at the end of which, it was practically obvious, the thing was lurking, there were only eight of them left. They were Matteo Falconi, captain of the carabinieri, Francesco Montero, the mayor of Altino, Gennaro Orso, the extremist butcher, Vera Rivera, the painter, Jogoy, Sabrina, Carla, and Signora Filippi.

"It's like being in the devil's anus," said Falconi from under his mask.

"And I bet even there it wouldn't smell *this* bad," said Vera Rivera, whose husband had been incapable of leaving their big house.

"Does anyone know what's at the end of this street?" asked Sabrina.

"I've never been down here," said Mayor Montero.

"I'll go," said Carla. "We'll soon find out."

She stepped forward, resolute. Jogoy followed her at once. The others hesitated; then Sabrina made up her mind to join her two employees. Signora Filippi made the sign of the cross and went after them.

"You should . . . You . . . should . . . go there, Captain Falconi," whispered Gennaro Orso, who was panting like a breathless old pachyderm. "You have a gun."

"I was about to go, of course. But the gun is useless here. Bullets can't do anything to stop the smell, other than add the smell of gunpowder."

The captain started down the narrow street, where the other four were already walking. Gennaro Orso, after a last moment of hesitation, set off, too, his step heavy with dread. The mayor and Vera Rivera stayed at the top of the street.

"We'll keep an eye out here, *cara* Vera. Someone will have to go to their rescue or seek help if things turn nasty."

"What is it, do you think? Where is that unbearable smell coming from?"

"Who knows. But we'll soon find out."

They waited just beyond the narrow street, watching from deep shadow as their companions headed down it. The seconds ticked by. The smell was still there, melting into space. The mayor was sweating profusely. Vera finally sat down, right on the cobblestones, almost overcome. The handkerchiefs she held to her mouth were also full of a sticky, warm sweat. After five minutes had gone by, the two watchmen saw figures emerging from the shadow of the long street, becoming clearer as they approached. Gennaro Orso was the first to return. All the others followed. They looked as if they had just left hell behind them. Their eyes were bloodshot, and several of them had turned pale.

"Well?" said the mayor.

"It's . . . it's nothing," said Falconi, trying to catch his breath.

"What do you mean? What about the smell?" said Vera. "Where is it coming from?"

"Actually, at the end of that street," said Sabrina, "is the heart of Altino's sewage mains. The town's huge septic tank is there, I guess. I never knew there was one."

"There's been an incident," Captain Falconi continued, looking at the mayor. "The septic tank has been breached, and the sewage pipes have holes in them. There's a huge leak. It's a real shithole, that's for sure. All the outgoing flow of household and toilet waste has been mixed together and is spilling out into the open air. It's not the devil's anus; it's worse: it's our town's anus. It's our own waste we can smell."

"That's no 'incident,'" said Gennaro Orso, who seemed to have regained his courage. "It's sabotage. You only have to see the shape of the holes in the pipes. They were made with a pick-axe. An expert made them, or my name isn't Orso. My father was a plumber. I know something about all that. Someone methodically destroyed those sewage pipes and opened the septic tank."

"Who would do that? What for?" said Jogoy.

"I don't know what for," said Orso, clearing his throat and spitting. "But the who is obvious. The only people living in this part of Altino are the migrants."

"That doesn't prove anything! You have no right to make such accusations," Sabrina shouted.

"She's right, Orso," said Montero. "That doesn't prove a thing. They may be in the majority around here, but they're not alone. And even if they were, that's no reason to arrest them."

"Whatever the case," said Gennaro Orso, who would not stand corrected, "I've noticed they're not here. Not one of them came out. I'm willing to bet they're sitting calmly at home, and the smell doesn't bother them in the slightest. They're used to it. Only the migrants could do this and stay calm. No one else could put up with destroying the sewage pipes and getting that smell right up their nose. No one. Except them."

"Francesco, I will take you as my witness. If he keeps talking, I will sue him for slander."

"Calm down, calm down, Sabrina. Now that we know where

it's coming from, the most urgent thing is to repair the damage. I'll take the necessary measures. We have to tell people what's going on. Go on home and reassure your loved ones."

"What a pity," said Vera Rivera, walking away. "I was hoping it would be something more exciting. More . . . monstrous."

That afternoon, the sewage pipes were promptly repaired, and the tank was sealed. By nightfall, the smell had almost vanished, although a faint residue of its pestilence still lingered in the air, and in people's hearts.

* * *

By the next day, however, the rumors had begun to spread, as persistent as the smell itself: it was the ragazzi who'd sabotaged the sewers. The number of townspeople who were hostile to their presence grew. Bags of dead fish or rotten meat began to appear outside the migrants' doors.

And neither the goodwill and courage of the Santa Marta Association, nor the kindness of the inhabitants who stood with the refugees could reverse this defiant trend. Those who were feeding it were winning, for a very simple reason: for the human mind, rejecting others is the simplest thing there is. All it takes is switching off the mind, letting the intellect go completely soft. The opposite, trying to understand, always takes too much effort. In this sense, laziness—in the strongest sense of the term, intellectual laziness—is the mother of all deadly sins. The source of hatred is less in the heart than in the mind that abandons its first raison d'être: thinking. Though, of course, that in no way prevents the existence of pure hatred, founded on great systems of intelligence.

The fact remained that in Altino, after the episode of the septic tank, a nasty odor of distrust and anger continued to drift through the air. No one ever found out who had sabotaged the sewers.

41

From then on, the ragazzi were sucked straight into the spiral of mistrust fomented by the Calcagnos, Gennaro Orso, and other inhabitants eager to see the last of them. To be honest, it would be unfair to say that the average townsperson stoked the violence. After some time, the violence became self-perpetuating; it proliferated sui generis; it gave birth to itself, the way the smell from the septic tank had seemed to emerge from the very air of the town. The source of the violence had been lost, and now it was spreading blindly and brutally, vehemently, without God or master. This wasn't, as is often said, a sudden escalation in violence. It wasn't vertical but horizontal, spreading outward rather than upward. Vertical violence, impossible to miss, can always subside, but horizontal violence is like a massive, invisible oil slick. It slides under things, covers creatures, soaks them through to their cells, and there's nothing they can do to stop it. That violence hides in people's gazes, in their behavior, their most private thoughts, everyday gestures, and language. It is expressed not so much in fighting or bluster or hand-to-hand combat as it is in mistrust, distance, and conflicting ideologies. It's the kind of violence that murmurs like an evil spirit into the ear of all that is blackest in the human soul.

It was that violence that began to be felt in Altino. A number of the ragazzi were subjected to it, but they also perpetrated it themselves, sometimes with even greater cruelty. They became rougher, wilder, always looking over their shoulders. Their eyes gleamed with a bitter spark that no longer reflected the Dream, just the desire for survival at any cost. All the bitterness they'd been accumulating, all their dashed hopes, all the anxiety of their endless waiting, all their fears were coalescing into a knot of rancor. Their entire beings burned with a deep and distant anger that they no longer sought to contain. It exploded, a grenade of hatred, of resentment, a ruptured ulcer, but before all that, it gnawed away at the fabric of their inner lives. Before it flowed with blood into the world, their violence bled inside them.

More than ever, the ragazzi went around in groups, glaring viciously at everyone, because everyone was a potential enemy. Even the shopkeepers who'd once smiled and acted kindly were not spared their mistrust. Violence was gaining hearts and territory. Everyone was affected.

42

S abrina left the town hall in a rage, not really knowing what she was going to do. "This isn't over; we won't take this lying down. You'll hear from us!" had been the last words she'd hurled at Francesco Montero, but she had to admit that she had no idea what form their reaction would take.

She headed toward the offices of the association, most likely empty at this late hour. Gradually, as she was walking, a great sadness mingled with her anger. Well, then, Francesco Montero had finally chosen the side of cowardice; he was closing his eyes, yielding to fear, pretending not to notice the tension that had been weighing on the town for the last few days. Resorting to all manner of nitpicking, he'd denied that the ragazzi were being threatened and, as a result, had refused to ask the carabinieri to intervene. No matter how she shouted and called him corrupt and cowardly and irresponsible, there was nothing to be done. She knew now that, one way or the other, behind Francesco's sudden change of heart was Maurizio Mangialepre. Him again. Always him.

For the first time in what was almost ten years that she'd been confronting him, Sabrina felt weary and helpless confronted with this man whose determination to destroy her seemed inexhaustible—because deep down, that was what Maurizio wanted to do.

She was surprised to find the offices open. She went in. Sister Maria was still there at her desk, a pile of documents spread out in front of her. Sabrina, who had wanted to be alone, was happy all the same to find her old friend there.

"You're still here, Maria?"

"Sabrina . . . forgive me, I didn't hear you come in. Yes, I'm still here. With the interviews coming soon, there are a thousand things to do for the ragazzi's files. And since Padre Bonianno died, they've become . . . difficult. The way the Calcagnos provoke them doesn't help matters. It's really tough right now, really. We have to be on top of every detail. May God protect us. Were you able to speak to the mayor? Is he going to do something, finally?"

"I just saw him. He's giving up on the association. He's given up on the ragazzi."

Sister Maria stood up. It was not only in her friend's voice that she could hear her defeat; it had spread to her entire face.

"What's going on?"

Sabrina burst into tears. And while Sister Maria hurried over to take her in her arms, she murmured, between sobs, that it was all her fault.

* * *

They had met nearly twenty years earlier, at the end of university. Both had been brilliant law students; at first just intellectual rivals, they had gradually grown closer. Sabrina was a force of nature—lively, cheerful, quick-tempered, passionate; Maurizio was a meticulous man, poised and thoughtful. They eventually fell in love. They sat their bar exams at the same time, with the same results, and took the oath side-by-side; no one who saw them together that day could help but assume that soon, still side-by-side and in the presence of another person in a robe, they would make a different kind of vow, for life. They were much admired as a couple, brilliant, committed, in love, and they complemented each other. He was a dashing business lawyer; she was a formidable criminal lawyer.

With a few friends, they set up their own law offices. In those days, Sabrina was in great demand to defend undocumented migrants, even though it wasn't her specialty. But she enjoyed it. Those vulnerable individuals gave her reasons to feel committed, and gave meaning to her life. She gradually began to establish a reputation among the associations that handled asylum claims and cases involving undocumented migrants, and they often called on her services. To be sure, she didn't always win, but people knew that if they chose her, the man or woman she was defending would have their best shot at a positive outcome. Her deep empathy for their distress gave her terrific energy, and her talent took care of the rest. Bit by bit, her passion spread to Maurizio, who also began to take on asylum cases. Their combined talent sent off sparks: while Sabrina's passionate pleas touched people's deepest emotions, Maurizio's rational, meticulous arguments, the solidity of his presentations, his maniacal concern for detail, and his rhetorical gifts all hit home with patent clarity. In tandem, they displayed impressive powers of conviction. Never had so many claims been approved and so many immigrants received as when they officiated together. Their law office was staggering under the weight of requests. This lasted for a number of years, and reinforced their love for each other. They promised to set aside more time for themselves—which meant, to think about their wedding—as soon as work allowed it. Maurizio bought a ring, which he hid away for the big day when he would propose.

They ended up leaving their practice to work exclusively for the most important refugee association in Catania, for whom they became the designated counsel. They worked so hard and so efficiently that when the association decided to open a new office in a little town in the middle of the island, everyone thought it was perfectly natural to appoint Maurizio and Sabrina as directors. It was good timing: they'd been hoping to leave the city for a calmer environment. And that was how they ended up in Altino, as co-directors of the new branch that Santa Marta had just opened.

As they had not yet hired a team, Santa Marta initially sent only a few ragazzi to Altino, and Maurizio and Sabrina were able to take charge of them while waiting for the necessary funds to hire deputies. But for nearly a year, it was just the two of them who organized the arrival and reception of ten ragazzi. In the beginning, the town didn't really know how to react to this totally new phenomenon. As time went by, however, Maurizio and Sabrina were able to rally the population to their convictions. They were assisted in this by the new mayor, Francesco Montero, who supported hosting the ragazzi. And so the first ten refugees were eventually accepted, despite some perfectly natural and understandable reticence, given the deeply rural nature of this part of Sicily.

In those days, there was a man by the name of Hampâté among the ragazzi. He was a splendid, strong giant, whose handsome, powerful physique was in complete contrast to his nature, which was very gentle. He was one of those men who are so kind that it would be easy to wonder if they have a shadow side. This deep goodness was compounded by a serious and secret humility, which became obvious through his behavior, self-effacing in all circumstances, even when his physique and his personality quite naturally made him stand out. This paradox, in everyone's opinion, gave him a certain aura of mystery, real or imaginary. The locals liked him, and his fellow refugees respected him. In spite of himself, he became the first face of the association in Altino. Maurizio and Sabrina liked him a great deal. He was the living refutation of all the intolerant clichés immigrants were branded with when people sought excuses not to accept them. Hampâté was their most brilliant success. Maurizio and Sabrina talked it over, then offered him the first post as Santa Marta's cultural mediator in Altino. It was Sabrina who gave him the news. Hampâté, as usual, kept his joy to himself, was very humble, and comported himself with great nobility. Sabrina admired him. One day, when she went with him on a *giro case*, Hampâté, with the touching simplicity that pure souls display when dealing with serious issues, told her that he liked her a great deal and thought about her often. He added that he did not hope for anything in return, but he needed to be open with her in order to put his mind at ease. Sabrina was touched and troubled, but she replied that she was engaged to Maurizio. Hampâté said that he respected her faithfulness.

The weeks went by with no further mention of this confession. And although Sabrina often still felt deeply troubled when thinking of Hampâté's fine, sincere words, not for a moment did she question her love for Maurizio. Maurizio, on the other hand, was beginning to show more and more signs of nervousness. Sabrina hadn't mentioned Hampâté's declaration, but, as if he'd guessed or had some mysterious intuition, as if he'd magically been able to read his fiancée's mind at those moments, ever more frequent, when she thought about Hampâté's words with an absent, enchanted look on her face, Maurizio became wary and possessive. He was seething, his consciousness constantly overheated, and this filled him with a prodigious energy for imagining, over-interpreting, spying, doubting, ferreting, fretting, worrying, harassing, and losing himself in a pitiful, grandiose love for Sabrina that was as tyrannical with her as it was with him. That instant when a jealous man does not yet know he's jealous, when he's drawing near that great black door, still unaware that it will open onto an inner hell, when he's suffering and doesn't yet know that he himself is the cause of that suffering: that was the instant Maurizio was experiencing, day after day.

Sabrina was finding it increasingly difficult to put up with what she'd initially taken for a simple passing crisis. Maurizio was beginning to suffocate her, to crush her with his burdensome anxiety and relentless suspicion. She had tried to reassure him, swearing she loved no one but him. Which, up to a point, was true. But what she failed to see was that while she'd never stopped loving Maurizio, she was often—more often than she cared to admit—living in the sweet memory of Hampâté's words. They had become her natural refuge; she went back to them time and time again, sometimes without even realizing, as if to a restful place, all to herself. The more jealous Maurizio became, the more she thought about Hampâté's words. And the more she thought about Hampâté's words, the more deeply mired in jealousy Maurizio became, seeing that she was no longer there, was no longer listening to him, had withdrawn into herself, into a land to which he would never have access, a land where not only did she seem happy without him, but also seemed happy because he wasn't there. She was getting away from him. He became even more jealous as he tried to hold her back. And Sabrina ran ever faster toward Hampâté's words. Maurizio was filled with rage, and shifted up a gear in his jealousy. Like little lab animals, they ran after each other in a great circle that was neither vicious nor virtuous, that was content just to be a circle, that is, a maze with no possible way out—perfect, therefore, a geometric projection of madness or hell. Without knowing it, they each became a monster to the other, while mutually accusing each other of being one. Whose fault was it? Gradually, all communication broke down. Love died, quietly. Sabrina eventually had the courage to leave. She moved into a little house, and Maurizio stayed alone in the one they'd shared.

In the first days that followed their separation, they nevertheless tried to continue working for the association and for the refugees it hosted. It was difficult, increasingly tense, but their shared commitment to Santa Marta managed to continue for a few more months, for one very simple reason: contrary to what Maurizio had believed, Sabrina had not immediately taken up with another man after their breakup. She took the time to work through the pain of separation. Maurizio even began to realize he'd been wrong, and that his jealousy had been unwarranted.

Unfortunately for him, it was just when he was thinking of apologizing, and was dreaming of having a new chance at their relationship that Sabrina, who had completely recovered from the painful separation, grew closer to Hampâté. The young man had left her the time to mourn. Maurizio lapsed back into unspeakable torments. It would be easy to say that this was when he touched bottom in his suffering, but that would be inaccurate: his sorrow knew no bounds, it was a bottomless pit into which he kept falling. If there was one thing he had learned, it was that pain is never-ending. Those words—pain is never-ending—became a certainty, almost a motto. Maurizio could not stand seeing the woman he loved, with whom he'd had ten years of a shared life, with another man, a man he had once helped. He resigned from Santa Marta, left Altino, and went back to Catania. He threw out the engagement ring.

Sabrina stayed on her own in charge of the association in Altino. A few months went by. Asylum, and documents, were granted to Hampâté. Sabrina went with him to Catania to pick them up. When he came out of the commission offices, his documents in his hands, Hampâté was so intoxicated with joy that he set off—something he almost never did—at a run, mindless and overwhelmed with happiness. He was hit by a car. Awed and honored by his new status, for which he'd risked death and sacrificed so much, he hadn't been paying attention. The driver didn't stop, but fled the scene; he was never found. Hampâté lay dying in the ambulance that took him to the hospital, with one hand held tight in Sabrina's and the other still clutching his documents, the privilege of which he had enjoyed for only a few seconds. They were both weeping. He asked her for a kiss and died as Sabrina's lips left his. His fingers relaxed, and the documents that had led him to his death scattered onto the floor of the ambulance that took him to the morgue.

Sabrina suffered her fair share, too, perhaps even more than Maurizio had. The Santa Marta offices in Altino were closed temporarily, to give her time to recover from this second emotional shock in only a few months. Her strength of soul enabled her to find her way back. She hired Carla during that time and, a few days later, called on Padre Bonianno.

When he heard that the association was going to reopen and go back to helping the ragazzi, Maurizio decided to return to Altino to live. He'd hoped that moving away from the town would cure him. It did no such thing. On the contrary, his hatred had flourished. It burned his heart, inhabited it with a jealousy that refused entry to any other passion. He hated Sabrina as much as he had loved her. He also hated the ragazzi; they all reminded him of Hampâté. The first time he saw Sabrina again, he told her he was glad to hear that Hampâté had died and that—as far as suffering went—she hadn't seen anything yet. He swore to her that he would do everything in his power to ensure that no migrants could ever be welcomed again by that association he'd once co-directed.

Since that day, they'd been engaged in a fight to the death.

* * *

After her confession, Sabrina wept for a long time. Sister Maria held her in her arms with the kind of tenderness only a dear friend can show.

Immigration: CRISIS Has Acquired a New President

Yesterday, the City Hall in Catania hosted the election to decide the new president of the Commission for the Regulation of Immigration in Sicily and Its Surroundings (CRISIS). Given its importance and timeliness, with so much at stake for this administrative body, the vote has been eagerly awaited. It will determine Sicily's policy regarding the asylum question for the next four years. A heavy responsibility, therefore, weighed upon the shoulders of the 24 members of the council.

Contrary to all expectation and all the polls, it was Sandro Calvino who was chosen by a vote of 13 to 11 in the first round of voting. He defeated the woman all the observers had foreseen as the clear favorite in the election, Elena Rossi, who seemed a natural candidate for the post. Her prior posts of responsibility with the United Nations, and even within several successive Italian governments, were major points in her favor. And yet it was the outsider Sandro Calvino, whom she elegantly "congratulated" and "encouraged," who was chosen. Elena Rossi declared that she would do her best to assist the new president-elect of the commission.

Sandro Calvino, 54, will take up his first post of regional importance, after positions as prefect and president of the Municipal Council of Messina. He twice ran for election to the Italian Senate, as well, unsuccessfully. The son of a former apparatchik of the conservative party he has campaigned for virtually since childhood, Sandro Calvino is not very well known to the wider public. But those who follow him recall his sensational declarations on mass immigration, which he has often compared to the "consequences of poor plumbing in need of repair." More recently, as prefect in Messina, he was behind the decree barring immigrants not registered with the European database from access to the town. A clear indication of his open opposition to hosting asylum-seekers.

One of the representatives who voted for him shared this with us: "This is a different position, one that will allow him to show us what he's made of. His great strength is that he knows how to unite people, despite their differences. You'll see; he'll surprise us all." Another representative, still stunned by the result of the election, assured us that, "If the European Union is not vigilant, Calvino will implement disastrous policies and voice opinions that will echo the darkest hours of fascism in our country."

A surprising and controversial election, to say the least, with a divisive winner. Sandro Calvino, however, has called for "resisting hysteria in this debate over such a sensitive issue." He has affirmed that he is working with full transparency "for a dialogue with the European Union, but also with those who will be the first affected, the Sicilians," saying, "It's not for nothing that 'Sicily First' was my campaign slogan." Sandro Calvino will take up office next week. He replaces Riccardo Barzaglio, who has an excellent rapport with Brussels but whose final term was rocked by several financial scandals and increasingly severe criticism of his policies, judged too "lenient" by the right.

The new president of CRISIS has his work cut

out for him, in any case. According to the figures of the European Migration Observatory, 1,132 migrants died in the last three months trying to reach the Sicilian coast, and nearly 1,874 others are currently seeking asylum all over the island. All the while, on a daily basis, many are still arriving on the death boats.

43

C arla gradually pulled herself together. After a few days spent in Noto with her parents, she had regained the strength to confront the ragazzi. Ever since the meeting they'd had at Solomon's place and the episode of the sabotaged septic tank, the men had been openly more aggressive. Fousseyni was one of the few who remained calm, even though Carla sensed he could not totally avoid the toxic atmosphere in town. When they asked him what had been said at the meeting, he replied that the ragazzi had decided to take charge of things on their own. They would no longer expect the association or the carabinieri to protect them from harassment. This had been steadily increasing, and nothing seemed to be stopping it. The police, whom Francesco Montero had under his thumb, were doing nothing, despite outraged appeals from the association. Carla felt it was as if the entire town had locked itself away inside a huge trap.

The final of the football championship might be the opportunity to break out of the spiral of tension. Carla hoped that the game would manage to restore some sense of joy to the ragazzi and, for the duration of a match, dissipate the great cloud hovering over the town. But to win, they had to play. And to play, they had to practice. The team hadn't been practicing. For several weeks now. It seemed to have disintegrated into the mistrust and absence of dialogue of recent days. But Carla refused to be resigned. For once, the team was in the final: they had, if not to win, at least to play, and they needed every bit of luck on their side.

She tried to persuade Dr. Pessoto to start up practice again. In vain. No matter how she tried to remind him of the positive psychological influence football had on the ragazzi, he wouldn't budge, invariably telling her that there was nothing more he could do. Carla knew that the doctor sometimes lapsed into a mood of deep pessimism, but she would never have thought he'd feel that way about anything to do with football. She tried, however, to avoid judging him too severely: his wife Angela was a friend, and Carla suspected, even though she'd hardly discussed it with her, that Salvatore had given up practice to be closer to her and their children. Naturally, she approached Jogoy, but he told her it would be pointless for him to try to re-mobilize the team since all the ragazzi, or almost all, considered him a traitor.

Carla didn't lose heart. She decided to play her last card: to ask for help from the formidable Giuseppe Fantini. She went to his grand house and rang the doorbell. She hadn't seen Fantini since Padre Bonianno's funeral. And yet, despite the fact she didn't think she had much of a chance, she had to try . . . She rang the bell. She heard a dog barking in reply, followed by the sound of footsteps coming down the stairs. A few seconds later, the door opened.

Fantini, looking for all the world as if he'd stepped out of a painting by El Greco, stood before her: his immense fatigue accentuated by his waxen complexion and a stubble that had sprung up like weeds. He removed the large dark glasses that hid his eyes. His empty gaze was that of someone who has just had a visit from death—unless he himself, Fantini, was incarnating death. His lackluster gaze swept the horizon. He didn't seem to see Carla. She was about to emerge from her torpor when he suddenly spoke.

"Amedeo, is that you? Is that you?"

The hoarseness in his voice, its hallucinatory tone, the way he was addressing the dead priest all had a ghastly effect on Carla. She almost turned to flee, feeling perilously faint.

"Signor Fantini?" she said.

Giuseppe Fantini seemed to emerge from a deep night. He fluttered his eyelids.

"Maestro Fantini?" said Carla, her voice slightly more confident.

The poet looked down at Carla, and for a few seconds, it was as if he wondered whether it was a person standing before him or a hallucination. He seemed to be taking forever. Then he returned at last from the unknown place where he had been.

"You? I—I'm in the middle of work. What can I do for you?"

"Maestro, we need you. The ragazzi need you. The football cup final is approaching. Our team is supposed to participate. But . . . but they've lost their coach. The ragazzi are being very difficult at the moment. It would do them a world of good to win this match."

"Yes, I'm sure it would. But I still don't see why you're here."

The poet had returned to speaking in his aloof, brusque tone of voice. Carla stammered, "I was wondering . . . I was wondering if you could, if you could be their . . . their . . . *Mister*. Their coach."

Fantini was silent. After a moment, puzzled, he said, "If this is a joke, I don't think it's funny. I have no idea what's brought you here, Carla. I know nothing about that sport. And even if I did, I wouldn't have time. I am hard at work. Good day."

He was about to shut the door when Carla staked her all: "Padre Bonianno told me a few days before he died that I should come and see you if I ever needed help with the ragazzi. I swear to you that's the truth. I would never dare to sully his memory with a lie. I was afraid of him when he was alive; imagine, now that he's dead . . . ! I know this isn't something you're specialized in, but . . . "

Carla let her words hang in the air. Fantini still didn't say anything. She was about to open her mouth to apologize and give up when the poet interrupted her with a wave of his hand. A long moment went by, then Fantini said he would do it.

"You . . . you agree?" murmured Carla.

"I do. I understand even less about football than about the Riveras' paintings. Which is saying something. The only thing I know about that sport is that all those players would be a lot less tired if each of them had his own ball instead of all running after the same one."

Carla, disconcerted, didn't know whether the great poet— normally so unpleasant—had just made two jokes in the same sentence. Cautious, she didn't laugh and merely replied, soberly, "I'll let the ragazzi know that practice will be starting up again, with you. Oh, thank you, Maestro, thank you."

"Don't thank me. I'm not doing it for you. Or even for the ragazzi."

With those words, the door to the big house closed abruptly.

44

As incredible as it might seem, the facts were there: four days after Carla had asked him to help, Giuseppe Fantini had persuaded a few of the ragazzi to come back to practice. Some had refused, pointing out that they were following Solomon now, and he'd advised them to avoid getting back into football ("It's a tool to make us stupid, to make us forget the appalling conditions they've inflicted on us"). But there were enough players to make up a fine team. Even Bemba, who'd applauded Solomon, came back, because without him, he said, the team would win nothing.

And so in the days that followed, despite unrelenting harassment and escalating violence, they practiced. They agreed to let Jogoy manage the practice sessions. Fantini had not exaggerated: he really didn't know a thing about football. But he always came to practice, watching from a distance, his eyes hidden behind his glasses. From time to time, he wrote something in a little notebook. Complex tactical notes? Poetry? No one knew.

From time to time, Carla came to cheer them on. She didn't know it, but ever since she'd managed to get practice going again, Jogoy's desire for her had become even more ardent—which had nothing to do with football and everything to do with the fact that, to him, she seemed even stronger and more determined.

The final was approaching.

* * *

The referee blew the whistle when regulation time was over; neither team had scored. After ninety minutes, followed by thirty minutes' extra time, there was still no goal, even though the match had been very animated and hard fought. The entire stadium had let out a hoarse, savage sigh when they heard the three blows of the whistle. Excitement had reached that peak of wild pleasure which pure passion alone can induce. In the stands, fired-up louts were swearing that the pleasure of football was even greater than that of fucking.

It had been an epic, grandiose show; the players had been prepared to give their all, drawing from who knows where a strength and determination no one thought they even had anymore, and everyone wondered whether they had enough left to endure the only real tragedy left to mankind: the penalty shootout. Those who'd made bets were panicking. Those with weak hearts cautiously dictated their wills. God Himself condescended, for once, to turn some attention to His turbulent brood.

The shootout began with the first five kicks. Like every good captain, Jogoy went first. He performed an audacious panenka, which chipped the crossbar before it slipped into the net. In the stands, Carla, on her feet next to her fiancé Roberto, shouted Jogoy's name.

Piazze, too, scored. 1-1.

Bemba was next, awkwardly coming forward in a wobbly run, as if he were about to fall over. But his left kick sent the ball into the top corner of the net before the goalkeeper could move a muscle. To the opposition supporters who heckled him, Bemba gave the finger and uttered a few tender words: "*Vaffanculo! Vi ho purgato! Vaffanculo a tutti!*"

But Piazze equalized. Ismaïla Camara, the ragazzi's goalkeeper, had managed to touch the ball. But his hand was not firm enough. Two all.

Musa Ngom, from Gambia, a discreet, not very talented but dutifully hard-working player, stepped up next, and took his kick without any long run-up. The ball went straight down the middle. But fortunately, the goalkeeper dove to his left. Goal. 3-2.

Once again, however, Piazze scored. Three all.

Ismaïla Camara was ready to take his kick. Absolute sang-froid. His aim was very precise, sent toward the side of the net, mid-height. Unstoppable.

But Piazze, their relentless pursuers, scored once again with a little luck—the ball hit both posts before crossing the line—and they equalized. 4-4.

The fans could hardly breathe. There were sighs, people felt faint.

Fousseyni, last up to take his kick, got up. It had to be him. He put the ball down calmly. Took two steps back. Ran forward. But just as he was about to make his kick, a searing contraction went through the back of his left thigh. Thrown off balance by the sudden pain, he couldn't control his momentum. He'd already started his kick, but the result was so feeble that the goalkeeper was able to stop the ball with his foot. Humiliated, seized with cramps, Fousseyni collapsed. Gianni was burning inside with both rage and joy; his gaze sought out Lucia, who was at the edge of the pitch. "You see? He's going to make us lose! You see, he's not the perfect man you thought he was." The Altino supporters remained silent, in shock. The Piazze fans roared with joy. Fousseyni burst into tears. Jogoy went to help him up and comfort him. They hadn't lost yet, after all; there was one kick left to the opposing side.

If the last Piazze player scored, all the glory would be his, and the victory his team's. The silence in the little stadium was crushing. The player came bounding forward, energetically, and sent his kick, hard, toward the right corner. Ismaïla Camara stretched his full length, desperately reaching out with his left hand. The ball hit it. This time his hand stayed firm, but the strike, which was powerful, was only deflected. Back out, past the post. Luck had smiled on the goalkeeper at last. Altino was still in the match. Fantini got up from his bench, saying nothing. Even he, who felt profound scorn for the dense, brute passion of football, seemed to have been caught in its appeal.

It was time for sudden death: each kick was the guillotine. Gianni placed the ball on the grass, with almost no running start. Feeling self-assured. Full of confidence. The referee blew the whistle. Gianni casually, even arrogantly, sent the ball into the net, out of reach of the opposing goalkeeper, who did, at least, dive the right way. 5-4 in favor of Altino. Gianni immediately sought out Lucia's gaze and found it. She, too, was over the moon. She admired him. She loved him. She had to love him. "I scored with my kick, just you wait and see, this will be the decisive penalty kick, because they're going to miss."

The Piazze kicker, a hateful player who'd been committing nasty fouls all throughout the match, came to stand opposite Ismaïla Camara.

"If there is a God and any divine justice, he has to miss," prayed Sister Maria, who'd spent the entire match shouting obscenities at the opposing players and invoking the help of the Lord. "Come on, Padre Bonianno, you're up there now, do something."

It would seem that Amedeo Bonianno had heard Sister Maria's pious plea, because the ball soared toward him, toward the sky, completely out of bounds, very high. Pressure had triumphed over the last kicker, who fell to his knees in tears, broken and alone. Altino had won the match at the end of a heart-stopping encounter.

It took the local fans a few seconds to realize that their team had just won. An incredible explosion of joy filled the stadium, after a moment of incredulous silence.

Everyone who had fellow feeling for the ragazzi poured onto the pitch, which soon turned into a vast theater of hugs. People put their arms around the players, congratulated them, raised them up triumphantly. Sabrina was radiant, overflowing with delight. To her, this victory symbolized the most incredible response the association could have given to all the provocation. To the Calcagnos. To all the xenophobes. To Maurizio. In the intoxication of the moment, she invited everyone for a drink at La Tavola di Luca, to celebrate the victory and the announcement that the interviews were going to be held at last, after all these long months of waiting. Because, yes, the exact dates—at last!—of the interviews had come in a few days earlier; they were due to start in one week's time.

45

F antini was already on his way home. He deemed that he had fulfilled his promise and could now devote himself to his great poem, far from the party that would be held after the match.

It hadn't been so complicated after all, to put the team together again: most of the ragazzi, despite their fear and mistrust, wanted to play football again. He'd sensed this at once, and all he had to do was to push them a little to convince them. There'd been one moment, however, that was more trying than the others: confronting Solomon. He remembered every word of their conversation, which, to the poet's great surprise, had been held in Italian. Solomon had made progress in mastering the language.

"You've succeeded," he said to the poet as soon as Fantini had entered the apartment, "in changing the empty, weak-willed minds of the other men. But don't even bother trying here. No one will go with you. No one will ever go back to playing football."

"I know," Fantini replied, "that no one will listen to me here. But I would simply like to say one thing: the path you are offering them is also a trap. Worse than that: you're falling into the trap of hatred, and you'll take others with you, men who don't feel hatred."

"Hatred is healthy; it's good for us. I'm not afraid of it. Hatred keeps us from going mad. There's violence all around us, so don't ask us not to use it in turn."

"Sooner or later, it will end in tragedy."

"You Europeans, that would be a first for you, wouldn't it? But we are already living in tragedy. You're the ones who created it, and we're the ones subjected to it. Tragedy isn't probable or potential; it's certain. It's our daily bread."

Fantini looked at him for a long time before responding.

"You're right about one thing, Solomon. Tragedy is already here. But the big difference between you and me is that I refuse to feed it with hatred. I'm trying to get away from it; it doesn't fascinate me. I don't waste all my energy trying to find a guilty party. Unlike you. You are calling upon death."

"No, it's death that's calling me."

"Don't answer."

"You don't understand. It's not calling for me alone, but for all of us. I'm not looking for a guilty party. We're all guilty. Some more than others. Think about that, instead of going to play football. Think about that, instead of going to write. You're useless, like all poets. You can't do a thing in the face of this world that's collapsing."

The poet wanted to respond to his last two statements, which were horrific. But in the end, he decided not to, not out of despair or resignation, but because he'd suddenly realized that Solomon no longer saw any difference between living and dying.

* * *

Now he'd come home. Bandino greeted him with his joyful barking as soon as he was through the door. The old man caressed his dog, then apologized, saying he couldn't spend more time with him. With all his being and despite his fatigue, he had to be receptive to his poetry. The great masters were watching him. They were waiting for him at the edge of the dark forest he was preparing to enter.

As he began to write again after an interruption of fifteen long years, he was reminded of what it meant to be a poet. The world was once again something to be translated. For what was a poet if not the ultimate translator of meaning—not meaning that had been lost, for in that case the poet would be useless, but meaning that was always on the verge of being lost. Who is a poet if not the person who, from the edge of the great void he'd like to fall into, retains the possibility of meaning with one hand and, with the other, tries to transmit it to fellow human beings? He should have replied to Solomon's terrible words. It was true: poets could not keep the world from collapsing, but they alone were in a position to depict that world as it collapsed. And, perhaps, to rebuild it where it collapsed first and most heavily: in language and speech.

He looked out the window. It was a very clear night. Mount Etna was wearing a fine scarf of white cloud. Far from being massive, the outline of the volcano looked chiseled, as if freed by a divine sculptor from the heavy brute matter of the world. It seemed more inclined to share secrets with him tonight. The volcano's crater was an immense inkwell. The poet took up his pen, dipped it into the well, and with a hand both steady and fragile at once, began to write.

46

By nine o'clock that evening, La Tavola di Luca was under siege. Ragazzi, members of the Santa Marta Association, ordinary locals: everyone was drinking, eating, celebrating. It was an interlude of joy amid the tension of recent weeks. The ragazzi who had played in the match had taken the time to shower and change before coming. Signora Filippi offered drinks on the house; she was full of cheer, dancing and bursting into song. The victory had put her in an irrepressibly good mood. She'd been supporting Santa Marta for a long time and still actively encouraged hosting as many refugees as possible in little Sicilian towns. Unlike certain others, Signora Filippi didn't believe that mass immigration was the cause of youth unemployment in Italy; on the contrary, she thought it went a long way toward boosting the economy.

As the evening progressed, everyone went on drinking, dancing, and celebrating. Bemba was talking loudly, getting overexcited: "Did you see my penalty kick? How uncle Bemba got it in! In the corner. If the keeper had tried to get it, his head would've split on the post or the crossbar! I told you the team couldn't win without me!" And he laughed and swallowed half of a huge mug of beer all in one go. He seemed not to have any limits on quantity: his big belly could, of course, easily contain a considerable volume of alcohol, but he also continued to line up glass after glass dripping with foam, without ever weakening, as if that big belly had a double bottom, a trap door where all the drink disappeared into a parallel universe. Seeing him drink like this, Fousseyni thought of Diabaté the absolute stomach. A few ragazzi around him, as well as members of Santa Marta, were also drinking, just a bit less than Bemba, which was already a lot. Veronica and Rosa, for once, were laughing hysterically, clapping their hands. Pietro was listening to Sister Maria tell him a slightly intoxicated story about a carnal temptation to which she'd almost succumbed a few years earlier. Off in a corner, Carla was talking with her fiancé Roberto, occasionally casting strange glances at Jogoy that were half-worried, half-angry. It seemed to Carla that Jogoy was avoiding her, preferring to spend his time with one of Signora Filippi's daughters. He was holding a sort of black notebook, which he opened now and again when the Filippi daughter gave him a moment of respite.

Gianni, the "man of the match," was also making the most of the evening. Everyone kept coming up to congratulate him, and before long he could no longer count the number of times someone, usually Bemba, proposed a toast: "To Gianni, our savior!" And the entire room raised their glasses to him. Under normal circumstances, he would have found this amount of attention terribly embarrassing. But this evening was special: this evening he could handle everyone looking at him because he thought he'd seen sweet promises in the eyes that mattered most, Lucia's. At the end of the match, she had thrown her arms around his neck. She'd kissed him on the cheek, and her eyes were full of admiration. Gianni nearly passed out. At last she could see that he loved her. This evening he would seal the deal. He had to. For the umpteenth time since the party started, he looked around for her. Had she come in? She'd told him she had to go home to get changed and see her father, but that she'd be back.

There she was, at last. Between the euphoric guests, the raised glasses, the flowing drinks, and dancing bodies, Gianni watched Lucia as she entered the room. He was not the only one to have his breath taken away when he saw her. Among those present, most of whom already knew her, there were those who were realizing only now that she was more beautiful than they'd thought, and there were those who were seeing her beauty for the first time; they all seemed to stop for a few seconds and gaze at her. What had she done to bloom in this way, like a sudden and unexpected ray of sunlight in the middle of the night? She'd simply let her hair down, worn a tiny bit of eye makeup, and transformed her lips into a ripe red fruit. It was all she needed to produce a marvelous metamorphosis, one worthy of Ovid.

Lucia stopped, hesitating. As if she were looking for a familiar face among the throng of dancers whirling before her like a cloud of starlings. At the back of the room, Gianni raised his hand to wave, but Lucia didn't see him. Instead of going over to the man of the match, she went up to Fousseyni, who was alone at the table that Bemba and a few other ragazzi had left to go and dance. His hand still in the air, stupidly motionless, Gianni felt something horrible welling inside him, with three heads—Sorrow, Jealousy, and Anger—devouring each other, forming a wild, demented Cerberus guarding his inner hell. But he was the hero of the match! He was the one who'd saved the team, he was the one who had guided them. Gianni, and no one else. He couldn't understand why Lucia was going over to Fousseyni and not him.

Unaware of all these inner dramas playing out in the restaurant, the evening continued on its way.

It was eager for songs and for bodies to rub together, thirsty for euphoria and intoxication, heading irreversibly toward pleasure, all restraint unleashed, all buried passion unearthed, as if in that moment the tension of recent weeks was finding an outlet that everyone must fill with energy and rage, liberated at last;

and Sabrina wept as she danced with the ragazzi, who thought she was weeping for joy, but in fact she was thinking of Hampâté, because it was the anniversary of his death;

and Sister Maria confessed to Pietro that in the end she had yielded to the diabolical call of the flesh, and had made confession for days afterwards;

and in one corner, Rosa and Veronica were dancing a flamenco;

and Carla was giving Roberto fiery kisses, watching Jogoy out of the corner of one eye; and Jogoy also glanced over at her as one of Signora Filippi's daughters was kissing him;

and as they moved on the dance floor, the shadows seemed obscene, twitching and rubbing together, more slowly, languorously, as if they wanted to melt together, charging the dance floor with immense desire;

and propositions were whispered about how to end the night;

and Signora Filippi danced behind the counter, her breasts bobbing up and down;

and the party became a fug of alcohol-scented breath, French fries, and sweat;

and the deliciously infernal music roared and filled the entire space, and

Concetta ci fa mangiare
Come le altre non sanno fare
Così vorremmo darle in cambio amore
Più che alle altre, con maggior vigore

bleated Bemba, his Italian accent perfect, while he and Concetta made passionate love against a wall in the rear kitchen;

and Fousseyni was still at his table, so close, so very close to the fruit that smelled more fragrant than ever of oranges, but blood orange, Lucia's lips; and then all of it ceased to matter when she leaned over to him, and he himself was nothing more than a pure blood orange, overwhelmed by sweetness; so this was what it was, a kiss, this was feeling a mouth and lips and the soul of a woman; so this was it, the warmth, the tenderness; yes, this was it, but he would think of it later, dream of it later, when he returned to the world, he'd try to find his mind again later, if he survived this kiss;

the kiss that Gianni would not survive, because he saw them kissing, and he was dying, oh, yes, he was dying, and his heart was exploding, Pain, Jealousy, and Anger killing one another.

And so the party continued to spill forward, rushing, pouring ever faster into the depths of the night, in a great indifferent flow of rapids, equally desire, pain, friendship, jealousy, love, cries of joy, drunken vociferations, floods of alcohol, whirlwinds of neon light, dances of the devil, ballet of shadows, and all the rest, and all the rest.

Tragic Night in Altino

The residents of the small town of Altino made a shocking discovery upon waking this morning. In this charming little Sicilian town, where as a rule nothing ever happens, during the night something truly horrific occurred: lifeless bodies were found on the town's central piazza. They included three brutally disfigured women, two of whom, according to the earliest information we've received, had been raped. All the bodies appear to have been subjected to extreme violence.

For the moment we have very little information regarding the circumstances surrounding this terrible tragedy. The sinister nature of events seems to have left residents and local authorities shocked and speechless. No one wants to speak of the horror; no one seems able to thus far. Or even to believe it. We did, however, manage to reach Captain Matteo Falconi, commandant of the Altino carabinieri, who refused to "comment on this barbarous act, when the bodies [were] not even cold." He did confirm that in 20 years of service in Altino, he had "never seen anything this horrific." To the question as to whether one can already conclude that there has been homicide, Matteo Falconi replied that this would be determined by the first elements of the investigation. "But I fear it is very likely," he added, visibly upset.

The identity of the victims has not yet been established.

Captain Falconi did not wish to say anything about it. But it is only a matter of time before the first statements will be heard. The mayor of Altino, Francesco Montero, whom we tried unsuccessfully to reach for comment, is expected to give an initial press conference in the hours to come. We will keep you informed in our upcoming editions.

The circumstances leading to these terrible deaths still have to be clarified. Without venturing to speculate, we can nevertheless share with our readers the statement that a local resident who lives not far from the central piazza in Altino (and who has asked to remain anonymous) was willing to give us. We would like to point out that this statement has not been verified; for the moment it is still hearsay, and it is up to each reader to evaluate its veracity until the investigation proceeds. We have reproduced it here in its entirety:

"It's awful, what happened. I didn't see anything, and I don't know who killed these people or how . . . Apparently there were rapes, it's terrible; I hope they'll catch the people who did this and that they'll get what they deserve. I didn't see anything, but I heard. There was a lot of noise coming from the restaurant across the street, La Tavola di Luca. But that's nothing new; there's always a lot of noise coming from Signora Filippi's place. But last night was worse than usual. There were more people. They all came to celebrate the victory of the ragazzi from the association over Piazze. It was a great match, with a series of incredible penalty kicks. I was there. Last night, they celebrated. When I went to bed, there was a lot of noise, music, all that. Then in the middle of the night, I woke up because I heard screams. Yes, screams, and also the sound of a fight. Broken bottles. But I wasn't worried, because that, too, happens from time to time at Signora

Filippi's. Rarely, but it does happen all the same, when people drink too much. So I didn't worry, and I tried to go back to sleep. And when I woke up, like everyone else, I heard about the terrible events. Those poor people. May God rest their souls. Particularly those poor women. It's really a disaster; we've never seen anything like it here."

Following a quick investigation, we can confirm at least some of the things this witness said. A party was indeed held last night in honor of the migrants. Because, while nothing unusual tends to happen in Altino, one thing that has happened for a dozen years or more is that refugees have been arriving here. They are the responsibility of the local branch of the Santa Marta Association for hosting refugees. This association organized the celebration party after the migrants won their football final. Unfortunately, we were unable to reach Signora Filippi, the owner of the establishment where the victory was celebrated.

The carabinieri's investigation, in any event, should determine whether there is any connection between the party and the gruesome tragedy that occurred the same night in Altino. If indeed there is, which is "probable," according to Captain Falconi, it would vindicate the many voices who maintain that the migrants are a danger to European values.

THE LANGUAGE OF STONE

47

He heard the ring tone—Pavarotti performing "Nessun Dorma"—and it rescued him from the claws of a nightmare. Still upset because of the dream, Sandro Calvino, the new president of CRISIS, took a few seconds to find his iPhone, lost among the folds of the duvet. The great voice of the Herculean tenor was already coming to the end of the first couplet. Sandro Calvino finally found his phone and answered, his mind still fogged with sleep.

"Hello? Sandro? It's me. I didn't wake you, I hope."

"Maurizio? No, no you didn't wake me . . . Well, actually you did, but I was about to get up. But . . . What can I . . . ?"

"I couldn't resist the urge to call you. I've just had some good news. I haven't heard all of it yet, but it's everything we've ever hoped for. A real stroke of luck, a miracle. Something terrible happened in Altino last night. There was a fight, and people got killed. I don't know the details, I'll check with the authorities as soon as we hang up, but one thing's for sure, Sandro: they're leading themselves to the slaughterhouse of their own accord!"

"Who, they? What are you talking about, exactly?"

"The Blacks, obviously! They're mixed up in this, directly or indirectly, but they're involved no matter what, in what happened last night. For the moment, we haven't got the facts. Everybody's coming out with their own version. But something happened. There are bodies. Men, but also women. A few of them raped. And apparently the migrants have something to do with it. Some of the rumors are even saying that they're the perpetrators. The important thing is that they'll be implicated in this sordid business. We couldn't have found a better pretext to prevent them from appearing before the commission. This is the official justification we've been looking for in vain over the last few days. And it's fallen into our hands like an overripe fruit. To think they were going to start in only a few days! Just think! Providence is smiling on us," said Maurizio excitedly.

"It's better than anything we could have hoped for; you're right," Sandro replied. "If they're implicated, it's all for the best where we're concerned. If there were victims, it will cause a scandal, and no one will be able to go on maintaining that they have a place in our civilization."

"Exactly! I hope with all my heart that they killed someone! What a godsend that would be!"

"Indeed."

"I'll call you right back. In the meantime, get started writing your press release. Announce that after the night of horror in Altino, CRISIS cannot allow the ragazzi to appear before the commission for their asylum hearings. Bring up issues of safety, reasons connected to the investigation, and all the appropriate political jargon. *Puff*! Let's rejoice, *amico mio*!"

Maurizio hung up. Sandro stood motionless for a moment, quite awake now. He felt somewhat relieved, not so much for himself as for Maurizio, who over recent weeks had been channeling all his energy into finding an official justification the commission could use to refuse authorization for the Altino ragazzi to have their asylum claims heard. But this justification had to be reasoned out: that had become Maurizio Mangialepre's obsession. He wanted CRISIS, once it had made its decision, to know in advance what to say to the irreproachable-moral-world. Which would react vehemently to any mass obstruction of the asylum process.

Sandro Calvino knew that appearances mattered to Maurizio Mangialepre. It was out of friendship and respect for an old debt he owed him—a few years earlier, Maurizio had saved his political career by helping him out of a nasty predicament—that Sandro had agreed to take part in this charade. Deep down, he thought the idea of justifying a refusal was fairly ridiculous. The commission he headed was sovereign; it did not have to explain itself to anyone. Not even the all-powerful, irreproachable-moral-world, those bleeding hearts with their tepid humanism cloaked in tolerant charity, who would be indignant if asylum were denied to two-thirds of the ragazzi who sought it. The irreproachable-moral-world, obviously, would call the commission xenophobic, intolerant, and, predictably, fascistic. Some would even dare to call them Nazis. As usual. It no longer bothered him.

Maurizio had assured him that he no longer paid attention, either, to the curses people threw in his face. But if that were true, why was he so eager to come up with a justification? One day he had asked him, and he recalled Maurizio's answer: "Because, *caro* Sandro, the irreproachable world is never blinder than when it becomes indignant. Its indignation functions as action. For that world, that's enough. Those people don't much care about acting if they've voiced their moral condemnation. So let them condemn, and we'll go on acting. The irreproachable world sees itself as a great democracy. And like all democracies, it's dying because of the image it has of itself: the empire of Good."

Sandro Calvino thought again about Maurizio's strange phone call. If Maurizio hadn't insisted on coming up with an official argument, Sandro would have based his refusal on what, to him, seemed the simplest and fairest of reasons: Italy, and Europe in general, could no longer accept such a massive influx of refugees without dooming themselves to disaster. Taking in those people without having the means to look after them was tantamount to dooming everyone: hosts and guests alike. Moreover, not only were the politicians of the irreproachable moral-world irresponsible, but they were also such hypocrites! How he hated them, those authorities who rushed to release funds for the migrants, to find work for them, to construct housing for them, when hundreds of poor, homeless, unemployed people, and beggars, and workers on the edge, had been suffering and barely surviving for years right there before their indifferent gaze. How he hated those leaders who offered their generosity to outsiders while refusing it to the unfortunate among their own people.

He finally got out of bed. He sang "Nessun Dorma"—off key—in the shower, already thinking, per Maurizio's suggestion, about the press release that CRISIS could publish if it turned out that Altino's Blacks were indeed mixed up in this murder business. Who had died, anyway? Who'd been raped? The questions vanished from his mind as quickly as they entered it. Deep down, Sandro didn't care. Whoever they might be, these victims were above all—what was the word Maurizio had used again?—yes, that was it, he remembered: a godsend.

He took a deep breath, then let out the final "*vincerò!*"

48

Captain Matteo Falconi watched as the three ambulances pulled away, taking six bodies to the hospital morgue in Piazze. The nauseating smell of corpses persisted; the smell of disfigured bodies, of broken flesh, the pure exhalation of death, in all its conditions. Matteo Falconi, surrounded by a few of his men, who were as if thunderstruck by the proximity of such horror, could find nothing to say to comfort them. In the middle of the piazza, in the place where the bodies had been only a few minutes earlier, a large brownish-red stain spread across the cobblestones.

Falconi suddenly felt sick and withdrew into a side street to throw up into the first rubbish bin he saw. He vomited until his bowels protested in pain. The smell of the dead, disfigured bodies reached him even there in that narrow street. Flies were already clustering in his vomit, slowly dying.

He didn't know where to begin. As far as tragic news items went, Altino had no antecedents on this scale. Crimes! He knew that until the following day, at least, he would have to manage on his own. Naturally, he'd already contacted his superiors in Catania to inform them of the tragic events and ask them to send a forensics unit, as well as more qualified criminal investigators. But they'd replied that until the following day at best he wouldn't be getting any help. All their teams were already busy investigating some bloody vendetta between mafia families that had been plaguing Catania for several weeks. They made it clear to him that, in comparison, a few murders in his little town could wait for a while. In the meantime, he could start his own investigation.

When, at around six o'clock in the morning, the carabinieri on duty had roused him from sleep, he was convinced they were drunk. They were talking gibberish: six people dead, blood, people injured, faceless victims, a fight, the restaurant ransacked and deserted. It made no sense. He got up in a hurry. When he'd reached the piazza, he saw his two men standing next to the six bodies. It was still dark; the smell of the corpses caught at his throat. He asked his men what had happened. They told him, trembling, that they had no idea: that night, during their patrol, there'd been a lively atmosphere at the restaurant but nothing suspicious. They'd gone on to the other side of town, and it was when they came back that they'd found the six bodies on the piazza and, inside La Tavola di Luca, complete chaos: broken glass, broken chairs, shards of bottles everywhere, and a few more victims, who were unconscious.

Falconi had rushed over to the restaurant. He'd found more victims, nine or ten on the floor, injured, sometimes severely, but alive.

He immediately called Dr. Pessoto, who answered after a few rings, his voice heavy with sleep, but Falconi's news woke him up with a start. Half an hour later, with the help of carabinieri and firefighters, he was in the little Altino infirmary, taking charge of the nine unconscious victims from the restaurant. As for the others, laid out like red rags on the piazza, he didn't even need to confirm that they were dead. You could tell.

The sun rose and, with it, the curtain revealing a very particular scene: that of a town waking up to horror. A sinister ballet. Initially, there was stupefaction, speechlessness, fear, an inability to think. Then, gradually, the first comments and theories, rumors and accusations began to emerge. Words already classifying. Stunned reactions gave way to shamelessness. A moment of quiet contemplation was rushed, spoiled. Standing next to the still-warm bodies of the dead, Falconi could see how the little dignity they had left was being eaten away by the huge, obscene Jaws of the living.

Falconi resolved to leave the little side street where he'd taken refuge to throw up. He knew that just nearby, on the piazza, they were waiting for him. Yes, there, so close, the Jaws of the crowd were gaping wide. They didn't care whether his guts were twisting in pain as he threw up. What they wanted was another sacrifice to society, another candidate for the media to tear apart, another victim for the rumor mill, another body to satisfy the blabbering Jaws. Without that blabbering, the community would have to resign itself to true thinking, instead of yielding to the brutality of easy impulses. It needed scapegoats to prevent the onset of complexity. The community wanted culprits, now, right away, hic et nunc. Falconi knew he could well come first.

He took a handkerchief and wiped the sick from around his lips. Then, making an effort to walk straight, he headed toward the piazza. Six people had just been savagely killed in his town. Nine others were in the infirmary, gravely injured. The Jaws were waiting for sensationalist commentary. The victims' loved ones were calling for truth and justice. And the mayor wanted facts before his press conference. And he, Matteo Falconi, the modest captain of the modest Altino carabinieri station, did not have many facts.

The journalists were waiting feverishly. Before confronting them, he went to speak to the victims' loved ones. He got the impression that anything he could say to them was derisory in the face of their sorrow, but he said it anyway, because he had to: saying nothing would have been worse. After his speech, he asked his deputy, Lieutenant Federico, to look after them. Then he took a deep breath before confronting the journalists. There was a hail of questions the moment he was within earshot.

"Do you know who committed these murders?"

"Do you have any theories?"

"Is it true that Signora Filippi is among the victims? Can you confirm this?"

"Is it true that there were rapes?"

"Is there any connection between what happened and the migrants? Are you going to arrest them?"

"How far are you in the investigation?"

"Will the mayor be speaking?"

He answered as calmly as he could. Several times, they asked him if he thought the ragazzi could be involved. Each time, he replied that at this stage in the investigation, they might be, just like anyone else at the restaurant last night. This answer did not seem to satisfy one small group of journalists, who kept asking the same thing. In the end, tired, tense, harassed, and stressed, to get out of there Falconi had to assert that, given that the ragazzi had been present at the restaurant last night in greater numbers, there was a higher probability that one of them might have killed at least one person. And no matter how often he repeated that this was only a stupid theory, and that he personally did not think so, the two or three journalists who were still there seemed satisfied, let him go, and even—something that was always a bad sign—thanked him. Falconi was cross with himself. He'd just plunged merrily into the Jaws, like the flies into his vomit. But who could truly get away from them?

He gave orders to have the bloodstains removed, then headed toward the mayor's office, where other indefatigable journalists awaited.

49

W ith the help of a few firefighters, Salvatore Pessoto went from one bed to the next, ascertaining with precise, meticulous gestures that the nine victims lying there were still breathing. For the time being, he wasn't trying to understand what had happened last night. The only thing that mattered was life. The unconscious victims lying in a row before him in the main room of the infirmary might be gravely injured, but they hadn't lost their lives—unlike the six whose remains had just been taken to the morgue in Piazze. Confident, controlled gestures, supple yet firm, quick but accurate: Pessoto felt as if there were certain occasions, like this one, when the practice of medicine was no different from that of a martial art.

"There's one over here who seems to be saying something, Doctor," said one of the firemen suddenly, leaning over the patient closest to the entrance.

Salvatore Pessoto hurried over. The man was indeed struggling to open his mouth, murmuring inaudibly, incoherently.

"Leone," said the doctor gently after a few seconds of listening, "it's me, Totò. Leone, can you hear me? Leone . . . "

Jogoy lapsed again into mute unconsciousness. But his eyelids were moving imperceptibly, as if somewhere inside him, in a deep, unknown land where he had no allies, he was struggling to return to the light and to himself. Salvatore Pessoto stood up straight, helpless. He looked at the eight other patients near Jogoy. Among them, at the end of the row of beds, with her head wrapped in a huge bandage that completely hid her hair, was Carla; it was her name that Jogoy—or so Salvatore Pessoto thought—had just murmured. The doctor had also thought he could make out two other words, repeated in the midst of Jogoy's delirious breathing and fever. "Notebook" was the first; of that much Pessoto was certain. As for the second word, he didn't recognize it. It must have been a word in one of the numerous languages that Jogoy spoke. Something like "nut," or "ndût," or "ngut."

"This is like a nightmare," said Pessoto, in a low voice.

"It isn't *like* a nightmare, Salvatore," said Caruso, head of the fire department, who'd heard him. "It doesn't just resemble one. It is a nightmare. I don't know if I'll ever be able to walk on the main piazza again. What I saw there this morning will never leave me. I've never seen anything like it. It's horrible. It's really horrible. Horrible . . . "

Salvatore Pessoto couldn't tell whether Fire Chief Caruso, a man in his fifties with a kind face, wanted to comfort him, or be comforted, or simply say something. Pessoto merely repeated that, yes, it was horrible. He thought that other than the words "it's horrible," they still weren't capable of saying anything else. The horror had restricted the possibilities of language, reducing vocabulary to a few words; it had sucked almost all the other words into a black hole. The horror had left them only a few expressions, like "It's horrible," bleeding scraps of the carnage of language. Scraps that everyone rushed to use, clutching at them like their last chance at survival. Stunned, almost entirely dispossessed of their once vast language, murmuring these few words of terror, pain, communion, and compassion the tragedy had condescended to spare, people had to learn how to speak all over again. Horror was what had stripped them of speech, but it was also what had forced them to give power to the few words they still possessed. A power they'd forgotten with the erosion of language, its collapse into banality and ossification into cliché. It was only at times of disaster, in the very situation that had deprived them of speech in the first place, that humankind, paradoxically, succeeded in re-establishing a form of speech that was whole. The rest of the time, when everything was going well, or just about, they said nothing, or very little. Perhaps because happiness, or anything like it, did not always need to be expressed.

Looking at the victims, Salvatore Pessoto thought he could have been there instead of any one of them, if he'd agreed to attend the ragazzi's victory celebration. For indeed, after the match the previous day, Sabrina had insisted he come and join them. He had declined. The shame he would have felt on finding himself in the presence of those players he had abandoned, and who had nevertheless managed to win without him, had put him off. And, perhaps, saved his life.

His telephone rang.

"Hello, Salvatore . . . ?" his wife murmured on the other end of the line.

"*Si*, Angela, I'm sorry I didn't call earlier. I was going to."

"Don't apologize; I just heard . . . They're already talking about it on the radio. Six dead and nine injured. It's horrible."

"Yes, it's tragic. Looks like news is spreading fast."

"Where are you?"

"At the infirmary. Standing in front of the nine injured victims you mentioned. How are the children?"

"They're asleep. Who is there, where you are? Who died? Who's been hurt? Do you know them?"

"We know them. Altino is a small place."

"Who is it?"

Pessoto remained silent.

"Please, tell me, Salvatore."

Pessoto took a deep breath, as if he were preparing to hold it for a spell; then, mechanically, he began to recite the names of those who lay there before him. It was a macabre roll call.

"Signora Filippi, her daughter Francesca, Veronica the communications person from Santa Marta, Pietro their psychologist, Sister Maria, whom you know, Bemba, one of the ragazzi— he's got a serious knife wound . . . "

His throat was dry. He fell silent.

"That's only six," murmured Angela.

"The last three," said Salvatore Pessoto, swallowing, "are Jogoy, my assistant Lucia, and your friend Carla."

For a moment, Salvatore Pessoto heard nothing but his wife's breathing, until finally it mingled with sobs. She managed to speak all the same.

"How is she? How are they all?"

"Carla is unconscious, like all the others," said Pessoto. "They were all brutally attacked. But I think they'll recover. I'll keep you posted."

Another pause, then Angela asked the fateful question: "And who died?"

50

D o you know who died, Montero?" said Maurizio. "Not yet, Mangialepre," Francesco Montero replied. "But we'll know soon. I'm expecting Captain Falconi any minute now. He's going to give us a first update regarding last night's horrific events. And right after that I'll prepare a press conference."

"But I can't believe that your—*puff!*—teams still haven't been able to provide you with more precise information."

"What happened will affect everybody. Nobody expected a tragedy like this. Everything is a little disorganized. The fact that it happened during the night doesn't help matters. It's overwhelming, to wake up to such a sight. Between the rumors, the theories, the unverified sources, it's difficult—"

"Haven't you been to the crime scene yet?"

"Not yet. I found out rather late. The bodies had already been removed. Besides, I can't stand the sight of blood. But I'll go over there in a little while. That's where I'll make my statement. Just think, we dined together at La Tavola di Luca only a few weeks ago . . . "

"What happened is awful, Montero, but this is not the time to let yourself be overcome by emotion. I hope you see what I mean . . . *Puff! Puff!*"

"What . . . I . . . I'm afraid I don't, Mangialepre."

"I need you to imply that last night's disturbances—"

"Disturbances?" said the mayor, indignantly. "God Almighty, Maurizio! People died! Six brutal deaths, and rapes! Here in Altino! And you call that *disturbances*? It's indecent."

"Fine, but please spare me your political sweet talk and sermons about decency and respect. It's inappropriate, coming from you. But we'll call it a tragedy, if you like. *Puff*! So I'd like you to imply that the tragedy—you can even add 'horrible'—last night was, in part, the work of the migrants."

"Good lord, Mangialepre, you can't ask—"

"*Puff, puff, puff*! Let me finish, please. Last night's tragedy was probably, in part—you can hear all the rhetorical caution I'm exercising—the work of the migrants, and an investigation will soon be underway to assign blame where it's due. That's all I want you to say. To imply that they have something to do with it. And anyway, that's the rumor that's going around. You're a clever enough politician to know that in our profession, you must always keep up with what people are saying, with the rumors. They're what the people want to believe. After the emotional turmoil, which will be over fairly soon—and I think it might already be over—the people will want culprits. Or at least suspects. And the ones who fit the profile are the ragazzi."

"Mangialepre . . . Maurizio . . . I don't believe it . . . This is . . . this is indecent and immoral."

"Now, now, Francesco. Get a grip. I'm simply asking you to imply it. You'll express it better than I could, more skillfully. You'll spin the idea in a different way. But say it. No one will accuse you of being xenophobic—after all you've done for those people. They'll praise your sense of justice—you, who, out of love for your town, are prepared to speak out against the very people you've always defended. You will show yourself to be a knight in shining armor, without a blemish."

"I can't do that," said Francesco Montero, his voice hesitant.

"Yes, you can," insisted Maurizio Mangialepre. "You can

because after all this, you'll be a senator. You won't be dragged into it. All you have to do is introduce the idea. We'll take care of the rest."

"I can't. It's indecent, at such a time, to level accusations against people . . . "

"You're allowing your emotions to get the better of you, *vecchio mio*. Remember, I always keep my promises."

"And I have kept mine; I voted for Calvino. And more. I made sure the carabinieri wouldn't intervene, even though your men have been harassing the ragazzi for several weeks now. I did more than I promised."

"Then you can do even more. Given the general emotional upheaval, no one will notice. Just say that it's likely the ragazzi are involved. Which is—*puff!*—true, objectively."

"Don't you realize? That would be sullying the memory of the dead! I'd never have thought that one day you would let your desire for revenge take you this far."

"Well, I can."

They fell silent. Francesco Montero was breathing heavily. It had been scarcely an hour earlier that he'd heard the news, and he was still numb with shock. He was prepared to do a great deal to be a senator, but what Maurizio was asking him was beyond his ambitions. To sully the memory of the dead with such slander, such a lie . . . he wasn't sure it was worth it.

"Montero?" said Mangialepre impatiently.

"I—I can't do it, Maurizio. I believe in Hell."

"You'll stay in the hell of Altino forever if you don't do what I'm asking. It remains to be seen which one you prefer—hell on earth or the other Hell, the existence of which, incidentally, is still open to debate."

"Don't go adding blasphemy to immorality, Mangialepre. I believe in God."

"You've always been gifted in the art of lapidary pronouncements, Montero."

310 - MOHAMED MBOUGAR SARR

"I have to go. There's someone at the door. I have to prepare my speech."

"I hope you'll make the right choice. I'll be listening to your speech later. I want to hear the words that will make you a future senator, Francesco. A senator!"

51

T his time, Solomon didn't even need to send out a call to the ragazzi. The moment they heard about the previous night's events, they all headed spontaneously to his apartment. The first ones arrived just as day was breaking. The others followed soon thereafter. The news of the events had spread quickly to every apartment. And they were afraid: afraid of what people would say about the night, and what might be said about them. Even though Solomon's apartment was spacious, this time it was packed.

They waited in silence for the first official statements. Solomon stood among them. He told them they had to expect to be accused of all the crimes, and to be taken off to prison. He reminded them that they weren't from here, and if culprits had to be found, then they would serve the purpose. He prophesied repatriation, convinced that after prison they would be loaded onto cargo ships or chartered vessels and be taken home by force. He said that they had to expect the worst. That they would have to fight for their lives. The only echo to his words was his comrades' tense, frightened silence. As for Solomon himself, he had never seemed more alive. His eyes were shining. He was like a general trying to rally his demoralized troops on the eve of a decisive battle.

Fousseyni Traoré was sitting in a corner, hugging his knees to his chest. He seemed completely absent, not just indifferent, but absent, as if his entire soul had withdrawn, leaving only a sad body with no breath. His gaze wandered, incapable of settling on anything; it slid over people and things, went through them as if they had no substance. But in truth, at that moment, he was the one with no substance. He didn't even react to Solomon's fiery speech or to the enthusiastic reception it received at the end from the ragazzi, who emerged from their torpor and gradually regained their composure.

Solomon went over to crouch down at Fousseyni's side, but Fousseyni initially didn't even notice him. He was startled when, after looking at him for a few seconds with unusual tenderness, Solomon began to speak to him in French, with the heavy accent of Anglophone Africans.

"Fousseyni . . . how are you?"

He didn't answer, but his eyes did. The gaze they cast on Solomon was pure distress. Oddly, Fousseyni found Solomon's gaze unexpectedly comforting, almost tender; there was something, in any case, that didn't shy away, that knew how to support a man.

"Don't be afraid, Fousseyni. No one will lay a finger on you. No one will come for you. I'm here to protect you. You're a brave man. You didn't do anything wrong."

Fousseyni lifted his eyes again to Solomon's. He thought about his mother and suddenly burst into tears. He would have given anything at that moment to be with her, to have her hold him. Solomon put his arms around him and murmured words of consolation. Fousseyni wept for a long time, thinking, in succession, of his mother, his father whom he'd hardly known, his uncle, Adama, Jogoy, and, of course, Lucia. Where are you, my blood orange? It seemed like centuries ago now that they had kissed. And yet, the sensation of her lips was still fresh; he could almost feel them, still, through his tears and in spite of Solomon's rough tunic; those lips were infinitely soft. No, he hadn't been dreaming, and their kiss had happened, not in his mind, or centuries ago. They had kissed only yesterday.

"Come," said Solomon, pulling away. "I think the mayor

is about to speak. But whatever he says, we won't be pushed around. You're one of us; no one will lay a finger on you."

He helped him get up, and then both of them wove their way through the crowd of ragazzi in the living room. There was a television, but the radio, too, would be broadcasting Francesco Montero's speech. Those who couldn't see the screen resorted to one of the several radios placed around the room. They didn't immediately recognize the mayor's voice. It seemed changed, not because the radio or the television distorted it, but rather because the mayor gave off an impression of total helplessness, as if what he was about to say would serve no purpose. He began to speak.

52

M*y dear fellow citizens,*
An unbearable emotion has come over me this morn-
ing, filling my heart with pain, as it must surely fill
yours. An unspeakable horror has been committed. Last night,
in a restaurant that is the symbol of a love of life and friendship
in our small town, six people died, brutally murdered, and two
of them, women, are alleged to have been raped. Nine other peo-
ple were severely injured during the night and are, at this very
moment, between life and death at the Altino infirmary. All my
deepest thoughts go to the victims' families and loved ones. I
want to express my most sincere condolences and the solidarity
of the entire town. How could anyone imagine that, in a peaceful
place like Altino, such a tragedy could take place?

"You tell us, Montero!" shouted someone in the crowd.

"We want the names of the victims and of those who did this!" said someone else.

I . . . I ask you, my dear citizens, to show some restraint. I
know the pain you must be feeling; I know you are upset and an-
gry. But I ask you to show restraint out of respect for the memory
of the victims and the grief of their loved ones. Therefore, before
I continue, I'd like us to observe a minute of silence, of prayer and
thoughts for those who died last night.

"We'll all finish in silence," said Solomon, in his home, listening to the speech on the radio.

. . . thank you, dear compatriots. And now,

"Get on with it, Montero," said Maurizio Mangialepre

impatiently, also listening to his radio. "Talk about the migrants!"

. . . some information about the circumstances of this tragedy. For the moment, we have only conjecture. The investigation has already begun and will confirm or dismiss our theories. We know that last night, at La Tavola di Luca, there was a party to celebrate our ragazzi's victory in the final of the football tournament. The party was organized by the Santa Marta Association. We can reasonably confirm that it was at this party that something got out of hand. How or why, the investigation will determine. We do know, however, that not many people were present at the time of the events. Most of those who'd been there at the beginning of the evening had already gone home. We haven't yet compiled a list of eyewitnesses, but several people living in the immediate vicinity of the restaurant are said to have heard, late in the night, near dawn, the sound of a fight. A violent fight. Everything seems to indicate that, in all likelihood, there were still a good number of migrants at the restaurant when the events took place.

"Bravo, Montero! I thought you were going to chicken out!" cried Maurizio Mangialepre, flopping back into his armchair with relief.

"Shit," said Matteo Falconi, who stood not far from the mayor.

"And why haven't they been arrested yet, huh?" cried a voice in the crowd.

"I was sure they were in on it, the bastards! We give them a warm welcome, and this is how they thank us! They're going to pay," said someone else.

. . . dear fellow citizens . . . I understand your fears and your questions. I share them. The investigation will elucidate this point. If any of the refugees are guilty, they will be arrested. But I implore you not to yield to hatred and . . .

"What, we're supposed to turn the other cheek now? How long are we going to keep worshipping those blasted refugees?

First they were stealing our jobs, and now they're killing and raping our women!"

This time, Falconi spotted the man who had spoken. It was Gennaro Orso, one of the town's butchers, notoriously opposed to the migrants' presence.

"We have to root them out of their hole and make them pay!" Orso continued; radio and camera crews swung round in his direction.

"Yes!" voices chanted, here and there.

My dear fellow citizens, please preserve a little decency. You are setting a trap of hatred. There are people in this town who like these men. Who don't demonize them.

"That's true! It's a disgrace to fuel xenophobia!" said a few voices.

. . . we must keep a cool head and a just heart in this matter, dear citizens. I will give Captain Falconi from the carabinieri a free hand to lead the investigation. He will tell us what happened. He will find the perpetrators, I'm sure of that. I refuse, at this time, to single out a guilty party.

"You're a clever one, Signor *Sindaco*! You've just accused us," said Solomon.

"Do you really think it's the migrants who killed them?" said Vincenzo Rivera, who was in the studio with Vera listening to the mayor's speech.

"You know very well that it doesn't matter. Don't stoop to that level, *caro*. What's exciting about this is not to know who killed, but feeling the eternal gesture of death as it strikes. There's something beautiful about it."

"You're right," said Vincenzo. "It's art. Art is death."

"Switch off the television, and let's get to work. *Vanitas Vanitatum* is more important than this. Our only freedom now is in indifference to the misfortunes of humankind. It's on that condition alone that we'll be able to make art in the future. We have to be scandalous."

. . . my dear compatriots, I appeal to you for unity and solidarity. But, above all, I ask you to pray and to stay calm. The memory of the six victims calls for it. Pray for them.

Pray for Concetta Montella, who worked as a cook here, and who was raped. For Serena Filippi, the daughter of Signora Filippi, the owner of the restaurant, whom I will visit at the infirmary later. For Gianni Ferrara, who was a young and promising doctor. For Roberto Rizzoli, a brilliant anthropologist. For Sergio Calcagno, who worked at the funeral home in Altino.

And finally, for someone who did a great deal to make this town a refuge for the migrants: Sabrina Campagnaro. She was director of the Santa Marta Association, and, like the five other names I have just cited, she died last night. She, too, was raped. She was my friend.

"Fucking liar," said Salvatore Pessoto, reaching with a desperate, enraged gesture to switch off the television in the infirmary. "Sabrina told us how you'd changed sides."

Let us pray for all of them. Courage to you all, dear friends. Stay strong and united.

Matteo Falconi decided to leave the crowd just as the journalists, like a cloud of flies over fresh dung, were preparing to hover around Francesco Montero and assail him with questions. He didn't like what the mayor had said, but there was nothing he could do about it. And in any case, he couldn't recall having ever heard a single word from a politician's mouth that he'd liked. Now that Mayor Montero had spoken, he would have to assume the consequences of his words. As Matteo left, he saw Gennaro Orso with a few other townspeople, a sinister air about them as they talked, their voices hushed.

He walked on the piazza for a moment. The police cordon still marked off the crime scene, even though he knew the murders had not been committed there. The bodies had merely been taken and placed on the piazza, then abandoned. The two carabinieri who'd alerted him assured him they hadn't touched anything. When they'd gotten there, the bodies were already perfectly lined up in a row, as if in a cemetery. Why this staging? Who had orchestrated it? The murderer? Murderers? He knew nothing at all. Apart from the identity of the victims, he had nothing to go on. Not an element. Not a clue.

He felt as naked and helpless as a young virgin about to have sex for the first time. No sooner did he think of this than, fleetingly, the memory of his own first time sprang to mind. He saw snapshots of that long-ago afternoon; they sparkled and hurried past in his memory like so many shining suns, one after the other. Him, both petrified and electrified by a feeling that wasn't desire but rather an extreme curiosity, an unbearable tension, as if he was on the verge of discovering the last secret in the universe, or of meeting God in person—and, after all, maybe he was. And her (impossible to remember her name), slightly older, amused at his gaucheness and overplaying her own confidence, which actually was genuine. He saw her again: her little nose, the dimple in her left cheek, the russet brilliance of her hair, the copper tint of her skin, where beauty spots and freckles sketched unfamiliar itineraries, illegible captions, forti- fied cities. She had slipped her dress off with supernatural ease: to this day he could swear she took it off without touching it with her hands, simply by swaying her body. He almost called up as a comparison the image of a snake in the midst of molt- ing, shedding its dead skin with a lively wriggling motion. But he didn't, for two reasons. First of all because he knew nothing about the way a snake molts, and then because to re-use the analogy that woman = snake (and in the context of a woman luring him from the garden of his innocence) would have dis- played a total lack of imagination. The metaphor was already taken. So there they were, naked in the middle of a field, in the heat, among the olive trees and on top of ants. She had kissed him. He had drooled on her, had bitten her tongue; his teeth had bumped against hers. But she put up with his awkward- ness. Obviously, he'd been hard for a long time already. Then *suddenly*—really, he couldn't remember what had happened in the meantime, and maybe nothing had happened—suddenly, therefore, he had found himself between her open legs. He saw himself as he'd been, on all fours, ass in the air and emerging slightly from the young olive trees, confronted with her sex, which was framed by a fine, unpruned tussock of russet hair. A sort of wild, flaming bush. The Burning Bush. He opened his mouth and waited for the voice of God. Dear Lord, speak, he recalled thinking. Tell me what to do. The powerful perfume of turned earth in the field mingled with the equally pungent perfume of sex, and the two smells mingled to make a third, a smell of sea salt, of the sea, a red sea. He stayed like that for several seconds, transfixed, fascinated by the complex subtlety of Creation. "God, speak to me." In response, God was incarnated in his partner's hand (her name really was lost for good), which seized his hair then buried his head more or less delicately in the fiery bush. He immediately understood, then, that unlike the Lord, he did not have the right to lose his tongue. So he did what he could.

A shout roused Matteo Falconi from his memories. He was cross with himself for thinking about all that at such a grave time, when there were murders to be solved. Inwardly, he tried to repent, with sincerity. The crimes were there, senseless and opaque. He hesitated for a moment, not knowing which lead to follow. His idea was to see several people who he thought might be able to enlighten him regarding the night's events. The crowd had not dispersed outside La Tavola di Luca. He imagined the mayor in the middle of it all, subjected to the ruthless assaults of a few journalists. It made him smile and gave him resolve. He would go to the infirmary first.

Dr. Pessoto, whom he knew well, and Fire Chief Caruso were in the lobby of the building. They were talking in low voices with three people: a very tall woman and two men, one with graying hair and little round glasses, the other short and thin with a big nose. Falconi went over to them. As he approached the group, he recognized the two men. The one with the glasses had a little restaurant next to La Tavola di Luca; he recalled having a good meal there. The other man, the little one, actually worked at La Tavola di Luca; he'd seen him there a few times. The woman looked vaguely familiar, but he couldn't place her.

He went up and greeted them.

"I saw you just now, behind the mayor during his speech," Pessoto said, shaking his hand. "You looked despondent."

"Kind of, yes."

"With good cause. He wasn't up to this. But anyway. This is Simone Marconi; he's Lucia Marconi's father, she's among the injured. And this is Rustico, who's a cook at La Tavola di Luca. And finally, Rosa Di Livio, the sister of . . . "

" . . . Veronica, who was also injured," Matteo Falconi said, finishing his sentence.

"Precisely," said the doctor.

"I'm very sorry for your loved ones," said Falconi, looking at the three of them one after the other. "Truly. It's tragic. I hope they'll make a quick recovery. It doesn't seem too serious, if I've understood correctly. I'd like you to know, in any case, that I'm doing everything I can to get to the bottom of this affair."

The two men and Rosa mumbled weary but sincere thanks.

"How are they, in there," he said, addressing Pessoto. "Have any of them regained consciousness?"

"No. We decided not to take any risks, so we gave them morphine. They need rest. More than anything, it's to avoid an onset of fever. They'll come round in a few hours, if all goes well."

"It will all go well," said Falconi.

"May God hear you," said Fire Chief Caruso.

They were silent for a moment, then Falconi asked Rosa, Rustico, and Simone Marconi if they would mind answering a few questions. They looked at one another hesitantly, then murmured no, that wouldn't be a problem. Salvatore Pessoto said nothing, but Falconi noticed his dubious expression, the reproach in his gaze.

"Thank you. I'd just like to know if you were at the party last night."

"I was there, yes," said Rosa. "I was there until midnight, roughly. Then I decided to go home."

"Why?"

"Because I'd drunk too much and then hurt my head falling

off a table where I was dancing flamenco. I was really drunk. I can still feel the little bump I got when I fell; you can see it, just here . . . That's why I went home, to get some sleep. And when I woke up to hear the news . . . I was . . . The dead, the injured. Almost all of them friends, people I knew . . . It's awful."

She burst into tears. Falconi handed her a handkerchief. As Rosa was noisily blowing her nose, Rustico said it had been his day off yesterday and that he'd spent it in a little village not far from there, where his mother still lived.

"What's the name of the village?" asked Falconi.

"I beg your pardon?" said Rustico.

"What's the name of the village?" Falconi repeated.

"Perdicola. It's ten kilometers from here."

"I know it. I was born in Carpolenza."

"Ah, right, it's not far at all. I go to Carpo often; I have friends there. It's a really pretty village. Especially the fields. When the sun is setting, you should see the light on the fields."

"So true. And were you at your mother's all day?"

"Yes. I came back this morning on the first bus. I was on my way to work as usual, but then I saw all the people crowded around the restaurant and realized there was something wrong. I asked one of your colleagues, and he told me what had happened. I was worried about Concetta, and the signora, and her two daughters. I came here straight away since no one could tell me where they were. I found the signora and her daughter Francesca, they're alive . . . but poor Serena . . . and Concetta, especially. Oh, dear God . . . I still can't believe it. She could be a hard taskmaster in the kitchen, but she had a heart of gold. She was my friend. She didn't deserve this. Everyone loved her. I don't understand how someone could have done this to her. I don't understand what they could've had against her . . . It's so awful, so unfair."

He, too, began to sob. Rosa had calmed down in the meantime, but Rustico's tears must have reminded her of her own, and she began crying again. Signor Marconi confirmed that he'd gone home at around ten thirty P.M., after locking up his restaurant and saying goodbye to his daughter.

"Ten thirty? That's early, for a restaurant."

"Mine doesn't get much business. We're just ticking over. We have a faithful little clientele. If we don't see them before nine, I know I won't have many customers. So I stay open an hour more, as a formality, but I know that any other diners will go to La Tavola di Luca."

"And yet your food is just as good as ours, Signor Marconi," said Rustico, drying his tears.

"Thank you," Simone Marconi replied.

"I see," said Falconi. "So it was already busy when you left?"

"Very lively, even. There were a lot of people, and it was really noisy when I left. My daughter . . . "

His voice trembled, but he got hold of himself.

" . . . my daughter, my Lucia, had promised me she'd come give me a kiss before she went to the party."

"Because she wasn't already there?"

"No. After the match, she told me she needed to get changed. She went home to get ready. And then she came to say goodbye before going to La Tavola di Luca. She looked lovely, as always. I'm so glad she's still here. She's all I have left. I already lost her mother, tragically, and I've had trouble getting over it. If I lost Lucia . . . if I . . . "

He broke off; his eyes were bloodshot, his lips trembling.

"And you, Signorina Di Livio? Did you see anything unusual when you left?"

"I don't think so," said Rosa. "It was lively, but nothing unusual. It was a party; everyone was singing and dancing, drinking, flirting . . . "

"Can you tell me who was there?"

"Matteo," interrupted Dr. Pessoto, "the signorina is still in shock. These questions can wait."

"Yes, you're right, sorry."

"No, it's okay," said Rosa. "My sister is hurt, and friends have died or been injured, too. I want you to catch the monsters who did this."

"Then tell me who was there," Falconi continued, abruptly.

"Yes . . . yes," said Rosa. "There were ragazzi. A lot of them. But I refuse to believe they did this, the way that unbearable mayor suggested. It wouldn't make sense. There were some locals from Altino, too."

"Would you be able to identify them?"

"Yes, I think so. At least some of them . . . I don't remember everybody. Like I said, I was drunk when I left."

"I see. Do you remember anything else? Someone starting to argue? Even any unfriendly looks . . . "

"Falconi, you're going too far," said Pessoto.

"No," said Rosa. "When I left, I didn't see anything unusual. There was nothing out of the ordinary. Nothing that looked like it could lead to last night's tragedy."

"Were other people drunk?"

"Falconi, stop it," said Pessoto, raising his voice.

"Yes, people were drunk."

"A lot?"

"Almost everyone," said Rosa.

Falconi looked as if he were about to attack with another question, but he held back. Salvatore Pessoto was getting angry. Falconi apologized, then asked if it would be possible to see the victims who'd been injured.

"I just want a quick look, in case there's some detail about them I've overlooked. I'll leave you alone after that."

Reluctantly, the doctor told him to follow him into the big room. The patients were all still sleeping. Falconi found it very difficult to hide his disappointment. He'd been hoping that, miraculously, one of them would have regained consciousness. The doctor asked him to leave. Falconi made him promise to call as soon one of them was conscious and had enough strength to talk.

"I'd like to question them fairly soon, Salvatore. For the moment, until I find some other leads, they're the only ones who saw what happened last night. Who know. No one else knows."

"I'll call you."

"I have a really bad feeling, Salvatore. There's something not right about this business. The sooner we find out what it is, the better. I'd like to make good progress before the end of the day."

"That's ambitious."

"I know, I know . . . but I get the feeling that if the day goes by and we still don't know anything, it will get complicated. It's a very strange premonition."

"What do you plan to do now?"

"To go and see the men everyone's been talking about since this morning, who have virtually been accused."

"The ragazzi?"

"Don't you think it's strange we haven't seen a single one of them all morning?"

Salvatore Pessoto had been busy since his brutal awakening and hadn't noticed this, but admitted it was strange.

Once he'd thanked Rosa, Rustico, and Signor Marconi, who were still in the lobby with Fire Chief Caruso, Falconi took his leave. He decided to go first to the station to drop off his weapon. He didn't want it on him when he went to see the ragazzi. After seeing him off, Salvatore Pessoto told the three visitors to go home and get some rest; otherwise, they could wait in a little room set aside for that purpose. All three preferred to go to the little waiting room. Fire Chief Caruso said he was going to have a walk around to clear his thoughts. Dr. Pessoto found it strange that, to clear his thoughts, he was now headed toward the town center, toward the very place where the bodies had been found. But he didn't say anything, and went back to the big room to make sure his patients were all right.

He still couldn't believe it was real, what they'd been going through over the last few hours in Altino. Yes, it had been only a few hours since they'd discovered the bodies, but it was as if this sad, heavy atmosphere had been there for several weeks. Pessoto was worn out by all the words, comments, questions, interviews, tears, and images surrounding the tragedy. On the radio they talked of nothing else. The television was the same. During the night, horror, with its long bloody claws, had dug a tomb, a vast bottomless tomb into which the town was sinking in slow motion, as if into quicksand, seeing a nightmare unfurl in broad daylight, its eyes wide open, watching helplessly as the sky receded farther and farther, and it continued its descent into the great gaping hole.

54

He was upset to hear his cousin Sergio's name on the list of victims. But when Francesco Montero read out Sabrina's name, it took away his will to live. He felt as if his armchair were swallowing him. He was nothing but the shadow of a living creature, the ectoplasm of a man. A pile of bones. Sabrina was dead. He never wanted this. His telephone began to ring. Sandro Calvino was calling him. Fabio was calling him. Francesco Montero was calling. All this ringing resounded in his brain, mingled together, all clamoring the same thing: Sabrina is dead. Maurizio Mangialepre sank even further into his armchair, and it continued to swallow him. He resembled a wad of paper being crushed in the palm of a gigantic invisible hand. More calls, thousands of calls. Francesco, Sandro, Fabio, Sandro, Fabio, Francesco, Fabio, Francesco, Sandro, and on and on. The ringing was drowning him in three demented cries, torturing him; it was like fingernails tearing at his flesh. The armchair, swallowing. Sabrina wouldn't be coming back to life. More ringing filled his skull. Without knowing why, or who was calling, Maurizio picked up the receiver.

"Hello? Hello? Maurizio? Hello? Ah, you're there! You're a hard man to get hold of! I can imagine that with everything that's going on over there, that's to be expected. Our wishes—yours, above all—have been granted, like you said this morning. It's tragic, all this death, but hey, no pain, no gain. I wrote the press release, which I'll send right away to Santa Marta and the Altino carabinieri. I wanted to read it to you first, to get your opinion. Listen: *Ladies and gentlemen, it was with immense sadness that we learned this morning of the tragedy that has befallen your town. Rest assured that I speak for all the members of CRISIS in offering you our condolences and support. You are not alone in this horror.* Do you think that sentence is okay? A bit tearful and emphatic, maybe? Well, you'll tell me; let me finish first: *You are not alone in this horror. We can well understand the state of shock you are in; consequently, we have decided to postpone the Altino migrants' interviews, which were initially scheduled to start tomorrow. Rest assured that this was not an easy decision. We know that you, and the migrants, have been waiting for these interviews for months. But the present situation called for a quick, strong decision. We don't think this is the right time to hold the interviews. Last night's tragedy may have unsuspected psychological consequences and disturb these good men's ability to communicate.* I really like that passage . . . but listen to the end: *Moreover—we cannot disregard this possibility, even if we doubt its veracity—it would seem that some of the men were implicated in the events that have afflicted you. We do not want to take any risks. We are keeping a very close eye on events in Altino, and we are convinced that everything will soon be back to normal. In the meantime, please accept our condolences and our renewed friendship during these most trying times.* And then I'll write some obsequious polite sentence, as befits the situation, and I'll sign, 'Commission for the Regulation of Immigration in Sicily and Its Surroundings, as represented by its president, Sandro Calvino.' There! It's a bit long, in the end. And you see? I was very diplomatic. I thought about you. I already informed all the other members of the commission. Everyone agreed with me. Even those who were historically friendly toward ex-President Barzaglio. So, what do you think?"

The armchair was still slowly swallowing him, like a huge snake ingesting its giant prey.

"Hello?? Maurizio, are you still there? You haven't said

anything. You didn't like it, did you? I could maybe change the passage where I say that—"

"Go ahead, either send it or put it up the first ass you find, Sandro. Which, in principle, should be your own. I don't care either way now."

Maurizio Mangialepre hung up, leaving Sandro Calvino no time to react. To prevent any more calls, he flung his telephone into the flames in the fireplace. Increasingly devoured by the Scandinavian count's big armchair, Maurizio was ready to continue suffering, now and for all the centuries to come. Because the pain was truly unending. He wanted to die, too, to be with Sabrina, to love her, to beg her to forgive him for having caused her so much pain, for having suffocated her with his jealousy, for having pursued her with his hatred, for having killed in order to re-conquer her love. Because it was true: the hit-and-run driver who had killed Hampâté in Catania—it was him. It was Maurizio.

Sabrina was dead. He was the only one left, all alone with his useless hatred, all alone with his pointless love.

55

Whorn Salvatore Pessoto went into the big room, at first he thought he was hallucinating: Jogoy was conscious. He was sitting up in bed, motionless.

"Jogoy! Leone! You're awake! But what are you doing? Lie down. I'm here."

He rushed over to Jogoy and made him lie back down. Jogoy complied, silent.

"Leone . . . If you only knew how happy I am to see you. We were so afraid. How do you feel? I knew you were robust, but not to this degree. Do you—"

Salvatore Pessoto broke off. His friend's gaze was strangely empty, empty and deep, as if it were opening onto immense darkness. It was as if Jogoy were questioning him and begging him at the same time. As if he were saying, "Who are you?" and "Get me out of here."

"Leone . . . can you hear me? Do you recognize me?"

Jogoy gave him a strange look. He seemed to be making an immense effort to remember.

"Totò . . . Is it you?" he murmured eventually. "Is it really you? I . . . I feel as if my head's about to explode, but it's better than before, when I was back there . . . "

"Back there? At the restaurant? Last night?"

"No, not at the restaurant. Back there, all the way down, inside me. In my depths."

His voice was still hoarse. Salvatore Pessoto stared at him. The impression of an infinite void in his eyes was gone, but his friend seemed to be having trouble coming back from it altogether. He put his strange words down to shock. He thought Jogoy must be slightly delirious, from the effects of the morphine and the traumatic moments he'd lived through.

"Carla! Where is Carla?" Jogoy asked suddenly, in a panicky voice.

"Calm down, Carla's here," said Salvatore Pessoto, pointing toward the other end of the row of beds. "She's sleeping. She's alive."

"She's alive," said Jogoy; the doctor couldn't tell whether he was asking a question or expressing unhoped-for, incredulous relief.

"Yes," said Pessoto.

"She's alive," said Jogoy again, closing his eyes.

"You need to get a little more rest. You have to go back to sleep. And when you wake up again, you'll feel just fine. Maybe Carla will be awake, too."

Jogoy, who now seemed to have regained all his wits, smiled and told him he wasn't sleepy anymore.

"Are you hungry?" asked the doctor.

"No, I'm thirsty."

He poured him a glass of water from the pitcher on the bedside table. Jogoy rested on his elbows and took long gulps, his thirst avid, ferocious. A little water spilled onto his cheeks, his torso, and the bed. He drank two more glasses this way, then rested his head on the pillow.

"Leone," the doctor began.

"Yes?"

"Do you know what happened last night? Do you remember?"

Jogoy looked at him for a long time. For a brief moment, Salvatore Pessoto thought he could again see the desolate, infinite abyss opening behind his eyes.

"Yes, I remember," he said.

Jogoy fell silent for a few seconds, then continued. "People died. People died, and there were bodies, wounded."

"Do you remember everything?"

"Yes," said Jogoy. "There was nothing I could do. I'm sorry." Two tears fell from his eyes.

"Stay calm, Leone. Stay calm. It's not your fault."

Salvatore Pessoto wondered if he should call Captain Falconi. But the memory of his tactless interrogation of Rosa was enough to dissuade him. Jogoy needed to rest. He would tell his story later.

"Who is here with me?" asked Jogoy, his tears still flowing.

"There is Carla, like I said. And then there's Signora Filippi, her daughter Francesca, Veronica, Pietro, Sister Maria, and Bemba."

"And Fousseyni . . . ? Fousseyni isn't with them?"

"No. He wasn't among the wounded."

"We have to find him."

Jogoy held his face in his hands.

"Forgive me, Leone," said Salvatore Pessoto. "I'm making you talk when you're tired. You'll tell us about all that later on. Captain Falconi will be here. We'll talk about Fousseyni. I'm going to give you a tranquilizer. It's not as strong as morphine, but it will help you sleep a little."

"I don't need it, Totò. I can go back to sleep on my own, don't worry. Can you just give me the black notebook that's in the jacket I was wearing, please? I'd like to write down some details I mustn't forget. They'll be useful to Captain Falconi. I'll go to sleep after that, I promise."

Salvatore Pessoto found the notebook and handed it to him. Then he told Jogoy he'd come back in two hours or so.

"That's about the time the others should be waking up," he added. "I'm glad you're all right, Leone."

"Me, too, Totò. I'm glad we've been able to see each other again. Thank you for taking care of me. Of all of us."

"About last time, at the bar, I'd like you to know . . . "

Pessoto broke off, embarrassed. He couldn't find the right words.

"You're here today; that's all that matters," Jogoy said to him.

He held out his hand. The doctor squeezed it, and they looked at each other with great tenderness. Salvatore Pessoto smiled for the first time that day. Then he went out and left Jogoy who, with an earnest expression, was already bent over his notebook.

56

C aptain Falconi knocked on the door and waited. But as with the three previous apartments he'd gone to, no one came to the door. It looked like none of the ragazzi were at home. For a moment he was filled with doubt, as the crazy thought occurred to him that they might all have fled. But that was impossible. And, what's more, why would they have left? "Maybe because you've all started accusing them—starting with you," said a mean little voice inside his head, which he immediately stifled. He reflected for a moment and concluded that, if you really thought about it, what happened last night, although it was horrific, was not that surprising: everything over the last weeks seemed to have been building up to it.

Sabrina had come to see him on several occasions recently to ask him to protect the refugees. She said they were being threatened and that it could end in violence. He heard very clearly what she was saying, but, every time, he told her that he didn't have enough men to allocate specific protection for all the ragazzi. It was not enough to discourage Sabrina, who often returned to the attack, as fierce as a mother protecting her offspring. One day, she even asked him to go and arrest the Calcagno brothers and Maurizio Mangialepre. "They're the ones provoking the ragazzi, and you know it. They haven't stopped making life impossible for them ever since they got here. You know that. You've seen it. You were with us when they tried to intimidate us a few months ago. The posters: that was them, too. You know all that, and you're not doing a thing!

Arrest them, Matteo! Don't be a coward!" That's what she'd told him; he still remembered it perfectly. Sabrina had never been afraid of pressuring him. She'd never been afraid of pressuring anyone.

But she was right on this point: he had known. He had known but couldn't act. The orders he'd received forbade him from going beyond his usual duties. His superiors had made it clear to him: he must not listen to Sabrina, whom they called hysterical. And he obeyed. He closed his eyes to it all. But that didn't prevent him from seeing and, what was more, from feeling how the atmosphere in town was changing. The ragazzi he occasionally ran into would tense up, as if they were afraid he might pull out his weapon without warning and line them up against a wall to kill them. Lately, he couldn't help but feel his own rising sense of insecurity and unexplained aggression, a feeling of being threatened and a desire to strike out. But threatened by what? And to strike out at who? These two sentiments were connected: what he wanted to strike out at, or kill, was the same thing as whatever he thought was threatening him. And what was that thing? A shapeless, faceless creature, hiding in the shadow. A creature he couldn't describe, he couldn't even see, but whose terrifying presence filled him with a panicky disquiet. There were times when he got the impression that the creature was hiding inside him, was part of him, pressing up against him, mingling with him in the narrow confines of his skin and his conscience, and other times, he could sense it all around him, watching him, lying in wait, toying with his nerves.

The church bells struck noon. He started walking again. He thought he knew where he could find them. At the home of the man who, since the advent of the fear, had apparently become their champion. He began to regret leaving his weapon at the station.

On arriving outside the apartment building, it was immediately clear that they were there. Not because he could sense it, but because Solomon in person, surrounded by a few other ragazzi who must be his personal bodyguard, was waiting for him outside the building. He stopped a few yards away and tried to keep his voice neutral, neither too aggressive nor too affable.

"Hi, guys."

"Hello, Captain. I thought you might come, but I confess I'm surprised to see you alone. And unarmed. Unless your men are hiding nearby, ready to intervene."

"I don't know what you're talking about, Solomon. Is there some reason I would come see you armed, with backup?"

"Now you're playing the fool. Okay, let's play. The question is, rather: is there some reason you're coming just to see us?"

"Right," said Falconi, his features hardening. "Let's get down to it then. You know what happened last night?"

"We all know. And we even know that your mayor didn't hesitate to insinuate that we were the sole reason it happened."

"And is that true?"

"Is it because none of the ragazzi died that we immediately become suspects?"

"Bemba was hurt."

"I know. We decided to leave him there because his wounds were serious, and we were afraid we couldn't care for him properly."

"So you were there last night?"

"Yes, I was there, like a lot of us."

"And the dead?"

"Some of them got what they deserved."

"Who are you thinking of?"

"Sabrina, and the dead Calcagno brother, whatever his name was. The others don't mean a thing to me."

"Did you kill them?"

Solomon smiled, and his eyes narrowed even further, until they were nothing but two slits in his face, drawn by the fine point of a blade. Falconi remained impassive.

"Did I kill them? Let's suppose I did. What would you do?"

"I suppose I would be obliged to call for backup. And they'd be armed. And I would arrest you. Well? Was it you? Was it all of you?"

"You'd really like for it to be us, wouldn't you? Captain, I'm going to tell you the truth. Whether or not we killed those people, we will be accused of it, and we will be mistreated."

"There's no reason to arrest you if you're innocent."

"But that's the problem. We're not innocent. Nobody is, here on earth, that's for sure—but our lot, even less so. Everyone wants to kill us. To kill us in every possible way."

"I don't understand, Solomon. Stop talking philosophy at me. I'm simply looking for murderers."

"And you think you'll find them here?"

"They could be anywhere. And stop saying *vous* to me, it pisses me off."

"Then go look for them anywhere. *You* can," he said, stressing his continued use of *vous*, "*you* can also have a go at coming to look for them here . . . "

He paused for a moment. His expression was demonic.

" . . . but then," he continued, "*you'll* have to assume the consequences."

"You're threatening me, Solomon. You're threatening me, aren't you?"

"You can see it as a threat. But it will only be carried out if you try coming here with particular intentions."

"What you just said could cost you dearly with the commission. Don't forget—for your asylum claims, I have to provide good conduct reports for every one of you. And I can tell you that my opinion counts for something . . . "

This time, Solomon frankly burst out laughing, a laugh of such dry irony that it bordered on brutality. His companions next to him snickered.

"Captain Falconi," said Solomon, his voice still on the edge of laughter, "you must honestly like us a little, or else you're really naïve, or both, to believe that these interviews will still go ahead. After what happened, Sabrina's death, and the natural suspicion that's hanging over us, there won't be a single interview. We're not even expecting it anymore; it's over. I'm convinced they'll announce it officially by the end of the day."

Matteo Falconi clenched his jaw. His bluff had failed. Solomon had got it right: the announcement that the interviews had been canceled had already been made. When he'd gone to drop off his gun at the station, he'd found an email message from the president of CRISIS.

"I'm sure you're right, Solomon. It's unlikely any of you will have your interviews with this shitstorm going on."

"In any case, at the moment we don't really care much. The interviews are just one more ordeal. We'll sort that out later."

"What do you mean?"

"That until you find out who is really guilty, we'll be in danger. And you can be sure of one thing, Captain: we won't be pushed around."

"Who is really guilty?"

Solomon's expression became half-mocking, half-serious: "Don't you find it strange that one of the Calcagno brothers was among the victims, and not the other one? What was he doing there?"

"Having a drink, I suppose."

"If you think the Calcagno brothers could calmly have a drink in a place where they'd be surrounded by ragazzi, then you're even more naïve than I thought."

"The Calcagno brothers? They couldn't have done it just the two of them with so many people at the restaurant. I admit they're strong and muscular, but not to that degree . . . "

"Who said it was just the two of them, Captain?"

Matteo Falconi stayed silent for a moment, then replied.

"I'll be taking my investigation in that direction, Solomon, but whatever the case may be, you're not out of the woods. You are implicated, along with your men, in this business. We'll meet again."

"I'm sure we will, Captain. I look forward to it. And I suppose you'll have your weapon on you next time."

"You suppose right."

Once again, Solomon burst out laughing. And this time, as he walked away, Falconi heard none of its resonance, only a deep cruelty. He headed toward the Calcagnos' apartment.

57

T wo hours earlier, just when Francesco Montero was about to give his speech, a dozen men had gathered at the apartment of Fabio and Sergio Calcagno. The air in the room stank of cigarettes, alcohol, and blood. Sitting on chairs or on the floor, the ten men were bandaging their wounds in silence. Their glum faces were covered with the marks of blows and gashes from fresh wounds. In one corner, a television had been switched on.

"He's dead; I saw him fall during the fight," said one of the men.

"Are you sure about that, Cesare? Are you sure my brother died? Think carefully."

"If Sergio were alive, Fabio, he'd be here with us," said Cesare.

Fabio Calcagno said nothing. It was surely true, what Cesare had said. After a few seconds, Cesare went on: "He died in battle, like a real man. A true warrior."

"He was a true, courageous warrior," said Fabio Calcagno.

"That he was," Cesare echoed.

"For sure, he was," said a third man, whose name was Andrea.

"They got one of us. They made pure blood flow. We'll make them pay. I want to avenge my brother."

"We'll avenge him," said Cesare. "Starting now."

Although he was overcome by profound sorrow, Fabio Calcagno knew he could count on the men around him as if they were his own brothers. He wept a few tears, but he knew they wouldn't be seen as signs of weakness. On the contrary, in the ultra code of honor, weeping at the death of a brother provoked great respect. All the more so if that brother was a true brother, a blood brother.

Cesare, Andrea, and the others came to give him fraternal hugs. Fabio was grateful to them. All of these men who had agreed to join them made him even prouder. For the first time since he moved to Altino, he got the impression that he was exactly where he belonged, among men. He thought how wonderful it would have been if Sergio had been there with them. It was his idea to contact Andrea and Cesare, their old rivals at the head of the Palermo ultras. He called on the nostalgia they felt for their fine, virile rivalry to convince them to lend a hand in Altino, where, he told them, there were some vermin that needed crushing. Andrea and Cesare replied a few short days later that they'd be honored to join them, that they missed them, and that they'd been bored ever since the brothers had left the circuit. "You were way better than anyone since," they said. "Compared to the Calcagnos, the ultras there at the moment are like alcohol diluted with three parts water—liqueur for simpering little women." The Calcagnos were flattered. They returned the compliment. On the ashes of their past rivalry, they built a solid new friendship.

Sergio Calcagno had asked them to come as soon as they could, with a few other men they could trust and who liked brawling. Andrea and Cesare brought their loyal right-hand men. They agreed that they would arrive in Altino the day before the football final, now two days earlier. That evening, they got dead drunk amid bursts of laughter and drink, of swearing and all sorts of vulgarity, malicious slurs against women (with the exception of their mothers), nostalgia for the past, and diatribes against modern football, which had become worthless.

On the day of the match, once they'd barely recovered from

their hangovers, they found their place among the Piazze supporters and tried to rally them to their ultra stance. But they soon had to face facts: no one around them was familiar with the ultra codes or chants. This annoyed them. Those Piazze supporters were weaklings, they realized, who knew nothing about the true value of football. They left the stadium at half-time, wandered around Altino for a while, then went back to the Calcagnos' place. There they got drunk again, but not as much as the night before, and re-watched videos of themselves fighting during the violent confrontations that followed local derbies between Catania and Palermo.

Sergio Calcagno gave a speech with semi-fascist overtones, thanking his brothers for being there, whipping them up. He talked about the migrants who were invading Italy, polluting the purity of its blood, stealing jobs and money from Italians. He said it was time to stop them—it was their duty, as worthy sons of Italy. He mentioned Maurizio Mangialepre, their cousin, who, despite all his good will, had been unable to get rid of the Blacks for good.

Fabio Calcagno remembered every word, every intonation, every effect of that speech. He still got goose-bumps thinking about it. He wept for his brother for a long time. Sergio couldn't be dead. He was strong, he was invincible, he was a dragon whose fiery breath was inextinguishable. He had to reject the idea of his death. And rejecting it meant avenging it.

"Here we go," said Cesare suddenly. "I think they're going to speak at last. Some official is about to say something."

Someone turned up the volume on the television. And the ten men listened to what Francesco Montero had to say as he stood outside La Tavola di Luca with a devastated expression on his face, surrounded by a crowd of political counselors, onlookers, carabinieri, and journalists.

Thus, several minutes later, thanks to Francesco Montero, Fabio Calcagno knew for certain that his brother was dead.

This only increased his thirst for revenge. He stood up among his comrades and said, "We have to continue what we started yesterday. For Sergio."

"For Sergio!" the men cried in chorus.

Fabio then tried several times to call Maurizio Mangialepre to update him on recent events.

But Maurizio Mangialepre was still not taking any of his many calls. Fabio Calcagno, therefore, could not inform him about the circumstances of Sergio's death. He would also have liked to let him know what he and his friends planned to do, no later than that afternoon, to avenge his brother.

Maurizio Mangialepre could no longer reply to Francesco Montero, either; after his speech, Montero tried to call him. He simply wanted to make sure that Maurizio was pleased with what he'd done. To make sure, too, that he would indeed be awarded his seat in the Senate because, after his statements, he thought he more than deserved it. But Maurizio Mangialepre didn't reply. Francesco Montero figured he was too busy celebrating his future victory to take the call, and that in any case he would get through to him later. Francesco Montero, obviously, could not know that, far from partying, from the moment he'd heard Sabrina's name on the list of victims, Maurizio had entered a downward spiral.

Weary, Fabio Calcagno gave up on the idea of going to see his cousin. He'd rather try and get some sleep, the better to prepare his revenge.

* * *

Two hours later, Fabio Calcagno woke his friends. He hadn't been able to sleep. The memory of his brother and the excitement of the coming fight had kept him in a sort of wonderful waking dream, where he crushed the Blacks' skulls with baseball bats alongside his brother, who'd returned from heaven wearing a halo of purity and wielding a sword of flames. Sergio, resuscitated in his brother's hallucination, was like an angel who'd come to drive the migrants out of Sicily, the way the seraphim drove Adam and Eve from the Garden of Eden.

His comrades got up, still tired, but determined to stay with him to the end.

"Don't you want to wait until after they bury Sergio?" Cesare asked.

"That will take too long."

"We should have brought him with us last night," said Andrea.

"Yes," said Fabio. "I'm sorry we didn't. But we didn't have time. The two carabinieri were heading toward us. I thought Sergio was only hurt."

They all fell silent.

"But what's done is done. All that matters now is revenge."

"Did you tell your cousin Maurizio?"

"No. No need, in the end. Knowing him, he'd only tell us to do nothing. And that is out of the question. We're going to fight."

His phone rang just then. He picked up without recognizing the number.

"*Pronto*?"

"Fabio? Fabio Calcagno?"

"Speaking. Who's this?"

"It's me, Gennaro Orso. The butcher. I'm one of your cousin's supporters."

"I remember you, Gennaro. No need to stand on ceremony. I saw you earlier on television. Good for you, for reminding everyone of the truth. Thank you."

"I wanted first of all to express my condolences for your brother's death. It's a great loss. He was a true fighter for the cause. He died for it."

"Thank you, Gennaro. I will avenge him."

"I want to avenge him with you. *We* want to avenge him with you."

"What do you mean?"

"After the mayor's speech, all the partisans got together at my place. Those immigrant savages are raping and killing. If the mayor doesn't want to stick up for us and arrest them, we'll deal with them ourselves. I tried to call Maurizio, but it was impossible to get through to him."

"Maurizio's unavailable. He's handed our combat over to me," Fabio lied.

"Right. So what do we do?"

"How many are you?"

"Almost all our supporters are here. Men and women. Almost two hundred of us."

"Battle ready?"

"We'll die to defend our land if we have to."

"I'm glad to hear it, Gennaro. I was getting ready to go into action with a little team. There are ten of us. With you, we're sure to drive them out."

"When do you plan to act?"

"Now."

Gennaro was silent for a few seconds. Then, in a somber voice, he said, "We're with you."

"Let's meet in an hour on the main piazza in Altino. Today they leave, or we all die."

He hung up. Fabio looked at his friends and then, with a demonic smile on his lips, announced, "Now we're at the head of an army. They're not ultras, but their hatred of the migrants is huge. Together, we'll crush them. For Sergio and the honor of Italy!"

"For Sergio and the honor of Italy!" his companions shouted in chorus.

Matteo Falconi, with his ear against the door of the Calcagnos' apartment, understood. After leaving Solomon and his cruel laughter, he had come to the twins' house. Out of caution, he'd preferred to listen at the door before knocking. He didn't hear everything that was said, but he heard enough to know that something nasty was afoot. He had to get all his men together and prepare for a tense afternoon. Or worse: a bloody one. He hurried to the station.

58

S alvatore Pessoto started awake, his heart racing. He had nodded off in his office. For an hour? Two? More? How long had he been asleep? He got up and went out. The infirmary courtyard was deserted. The firefighters must have gone back to their station, as he'd asked. He went into the waiting room. Rosa, Signor Marconi, Rustico, and Fire Chief Caruso, seated in a row of chairs, were sound asleep. Rustico's mouth was wide open; Signor Marconi was having trouble containing his snoring. Salvatore Pessoto went back out and headed to the room where the wounded patients were. He couldn't help but cry out the moment he went in: "Bemba!"

Bemba, his torso wrapped in a huge bandage, was sitting up in bed. The doctor hurried to his side.

"How do you feel?"

"I'm tough, Coach. I'll recover."

"How long have you been awake?"

"Maybe half an hour. I tried to get up, but I think I'm still a little tired. What happened yesterday . . . "

"You don't have to talk now."

"I know. Tell me, Coach, the girl who used to cook at the La Tavola di Luca, did she die? Her name was Concetta . . . "

"Yes, she died, sadly. Did you know her?"

"We only met yesterday. It was off to a good start, a very good start in fact. It was great. She was made for love. I think we could've . . . "

He gave a sad smile and didn't finish his sentence. At

the same time, as if they'd spread the word to each other, or Bemba's rather loud voice had woken them, the other patients began to stir. One after the other, they opened their eyes. Dr. Pessoto left Bemba and ran to rouse the others sleeping in the waiting room, and they all came back, almost stumbling in their haste. It was heart-wrenching to see them reunited: sisters, father and daughter, and friends. Pessoto went over to Carla. She touched the white bandage covering her head, then closed her eyes. The doctor thought she must be trying, at that moment, to remember the sequence of events, to return to a sense of reality. When she opened her eyes again, her panicked, horrified gaze searched desperately for a voice that would tell her that she was mistaken and that, no, what she'd just remembered had never happened. But her gaze took in Lucia and her father embracing; she saw Bemba with his chest wrapped in white; Pietro with his head in his hands; Sister Maria praying, her cheeks wet with tears; Veronica and Rosa holding each other; Rustico comforting the Filippi mother and daughter. And she understood that her memory was not the memory of a nightmare. Or, rather, it was—the painful, searing memory of a nightmare, a true, pure nightmare of the kind reality alone knew how to create. Carla's gaze wandered, then finally, after emerging from a journey through the void, met the doctor's as he approached her bed. She tried to get up, but her strength betrayed her; she fell back against the pillow, and Salvatore Pessoto stopped her before she could try again.

"Carla," he began.

"Tell me it isn't true," she moaned.

Pessoto didn't reply and turned his head, as if to flee from Carla's devastated expression, but there was nothing but sadness and tears around him. On waking, the patients had to face the horror the town had suffered as they slept. Some were learning, or remembering, the death of loved ones; others simply could not think.

A great weariness came over Salvatore Pessoto. Once again, like when new ragazzi had just arrived and were waking in the huge warehouse, he felt an urge to leave the room. He was experiencing the exact same weakness and immense fatigue in the face of scenes that left him in deep despair. He wanted to be far away, miles from all these suffering people; he could no longer stand the sight of their faces. Let them go suffer and weep elsewhere. Let them—

"Roberto is dead," sobbed Carla, interrupting his black thoughts.

He looked at her without replying. An urge to leave her there to wallow in her pain went through him for a second or two. He struggled with himself, not to let it explode in Carla's face, already so ravaged.

"Roberto is dead," she said again.

"Yes," he said eventually.

He didn't know whether Carla was asking a question or accepting a fact.

"I'm so sorry. His body is in Piazze," he added, trying to cling to the last trace of kindness he thought he might still have inside him.

Carla said nothing, but the doctor saw that her entire body was trembling. She was breathing deeply, as if she were struggling for air and trying not to faint.

"Thank you, Totò," she said after a moment. "Did Sabrina die, too?"

"Yes," Pessoto said coldly.

"And Gianni?"

"Yes."

She closed her eyes, feeling dizzy.

"And who else?" she managed to say after a while, opening her eyes again.

"Concetta, the cook; Serena Filippi; and one of the Calcagno brothers—"

"May he rot in hell, that man," said Carla.

"Is he the one who—" the doctor started to say.

"And Jogoy?" Carla said suddenly, as if she had just remembered him.

"Jogoy's alive. He's here. I spoke to him a little while ago. He went back to sleep. But he should be . . . "

Salvatore Pessoto turned his head in the direction of Jogoy's bed, then broke off, thunderstruck. He went pale, as if the devil had appeared before him.

"Totò . . . ? Are you all right?" said Carla.

Salvatore Pessoto couldn't speak. His voice only came back to him after a long moment. His eyes wild, he just managed to say, "It's Jogoy . . . he's not there. He's not in his bed."

The first bed in the row was indeed empty, and had been carefully made up. How could he have failed to notice that there was no one there anymore? Was it the nap that had muddled his mind? Was it the fact that he had spoken with him two hours earlier that had produced such an inexplicable effect on his unconscious with regard to Jogoy? Was it the emotion of seeing all these faces again, come back to life, that had blinded him? He didn't know. Whatever the case may be, the fact remained: Leone had left the infirmary. Salvatore Pessoto recalled their conversation, from before his nap. It was odd he hadn't remembered it at once, but now it came quickly to mind, that gaze where there was nothing, neither desire, nor love, nor memory. Nor life. Only a short while ago, that gaze had worried him; now it terrified him. Instinctively, he looked toward the coat rack where all the wounded victims' belongings were hanging. Jogoy's things were gone.

"What do you mean, he's not there?" said Carla, trying to sit up.

"I . . . I didn't see him go out," muttered the doctor. "He was there just a while ago. We spoke. Then I told him to sleep. I left him."

Salvatore Pessoto rushed from Carla's bedside to Jogoy's un-occupied bed and inspected it, quite brusquely. What did he hope to find? He himself didn't know, but he went on, in a rage, unmaking the bed. The others watched him. It was only then that Fire Chief Caruso, Signor Marconi, and Rosa saw that one of the patients was no longer there. They hadn't noticed earlier, either, as if Jogoy had left behind a powerful spell to make them forget him.

"Bemba, you were the first one awake, weren't you?" said Pessoto, continuing to pull at the empty bed.

"Yes, Coach."

"Did you see Jogoy?"

"No, Coach. Otherwise, I would have apologized to him. I never really liked him, but he was a good guy. He saved my life last night. Was he there, on that empty bed?"

"Yes."

"It was already like that when I woke up. There was no one."

Overcome with fear, disquiet, and anger, Salvatore desper-ately tore the last sheet from the bed. The black notebook he'd fetched for Jogoy earlier fell at his feet. Trembling, he picked it up. He was about to leaf through it when Lucia's father's voice rang out, "Doctor, my daughter has a question for you. Do you know where a certain Fousseyni Traoré is?"

Pessoto remembered that Jogoy had asked him the same thing. He said no and saw a shadow of fear and disappoint-ment darken Lucia's face. He put the notebook into the pocket of his lab coat and decided to go on tending to the injured, despite his ever-increasing desire to flee. Jogoy was probably still weak, but he didn't want to worry about him; he would surely return. Carla agreed with him. Both of them knew, how-ever, that the Jogoy they had always known would never have behaved like this.

59

Matteo Falconi mobilized all the men he had under his command; thus, forty armed carabinieri went through the town, past curious gazes, heading in formation toward the ragazzi's refuge. They reached the place and stood in a double row outside Solomon's apartment. Their faces were somber. Most of them had only just graduated from police school, but fear veiled their features and made them look older. The guns that were slung over their shoulders gave them a strange, spectral allure; they didn't seem to understand what they were carrying, nor what they were supposed to do with it. Anyone who saw them there like that would see right away that very few of them were prepared to shoot a man, or even shoot into the air—to shoot at all. They were petrified by the notion of a gunshot before it had even resounded.

Matteo Falconi hoped things would not reach that extreme, where they'd have to shoot. But given where they stood already that day, he wasn't holding his breath: more men would die before nightfall.

He turned to look at his men. With the exception of Lieutenant Federico, they still appeared just as pale and frightened. He thought it was pointless to make some fancy speech; when the time came, when they'd have to shoot in order not to die, every one of those men, even the most cowardly, would fire not one bullet, but an entire hail of bullets, at whatever was threatening them—man, beast, or god.

Solomon, still surrounded by his personal bodyguards, came out just as the carabinieri were finishing their maneuver.

"So here you are, as promised, with your men and your weapons."

"As promised," said Falconi.

"We won't let ourselves be arrested or gunned down for something we didn't do."

"I don't know yet who the killers were last night, although I'm beginning to get an idea. And I know it's not you. Or at least, not you alone. I'm not here to arrest you, Solomon, neither you nor the ragazzi. Not yet, in any case."

"Then what are you doing here with all your soldiers?"

"I'm here to maintain order."

"And why is that? What is threatening that order?"

"The Calcagnos. The one who's still alive, I mean. He'll be here soon, at the head of an army. They aim to drive you out."

"Or kill us."

"Or kill you, yes."

"We don't need your help, Captain. We can defend ourselves on our own. We'll kill them."

"I'm not offering you my protection. I'm not trying to defend you; I'm trying to defend my town. I'm just doing my duty."

"And what is that duty?"

"I told you. To keep the peace and maintain order in this damned town. I think there will be a confrontation between you and them. That's what I want to prevent. And I'll use force, if I have to."

"You're a bit late. For months there's been no peace, and anything but order, here in Altino. You've even been complicit. Or do you deny it?"

"I don't deny it. But if there's still something that can be saved—"

"Too late."

Falconi didn't answer. He ordered his men to stand ready

to protect the town. Solomon laughed and whispered to one of his men, who went back inside the apartment building. When he came out a few minutes later, all the ragazzi were with him. Falconi immediately saw that most of them looked like his own men, fear-stricken but determined not to be killed without a fight. They had little in the way of weapons: one man held a bludgeon, another had a knife, and others had big rocks or pitchforks. Some of them were clenching their fists, and Falconi supposed these were the men the others would be entrusting their lives and hopes to in the coming fight. As for Solomon, he was holding a simple wooden stick roughly three feet in length, slightly twisted in the middle, curved at one end into an unusual knob. The weapon, in Solomon's hand, looked like a simple shepherd's crook or an oracle's staff, a humble pilgrim's stick or a royal scepter.

The little piazza where the ragazzi and the carabinieri were waiting was shaped like a large archer's bow. The ragazzi, massed together chaotically, stood in the curve of the bow, and in front of them, in two rows, stood the carabinieri. Both groups faced the bowstring, represented by a row of tall buildings, whose open windows and little balconies hung with laundry indicated that they were residential. A single street bisected the regularity of the bowstring; it was located exactly in the middle, at the very spot where the archer would have placed his arrow if the little piazza had been his weapon. Falconi thought that Calcagno and his men would arrive from this street. His plan was to let them reach the piazza and then to drive them back against the buildings of the bowstring, making them like prisoners with their backs to the wall as a firing squad took aim, ready to gun them down.

The two groups waited like that in utter silence. The afternoon was drawing to a close, and the sky was already getting dark. Half an hour went by; then, from the little street that divided the two long rows of white buildings, the very street

Falconi hoped Calcagno, Gennaro Orso, and their troops would take, came a horde of women and men. For a moment, Falconi thought these were the people he was waiting for. But there was nothing about their attitude that suggested they were coming to attack the ragazzi, even if their faces did express great determination. They were unarmed. A tall man with white hair was in the lead. Falconi recognized Giuseppe Fantini.

"What are you doing here, Maestro?"

"These men and women are here to stand with you. There aren't many of us, but none of us wants Altino to become an open-air cemetery."

"You've come to defend the ragazzi?"

"No, some of them are preparing for violence, too, even want it. We've simply come to defend a certain idea of communal life."

"I see," said Falconi. "That's admirable, but I don't think that such noble ideas will have their place here. There's going to be a terrible fight. There will be deaths. Blood will flow. I can't let you stay."

"Well, maybe not me, since I'm an old man. But you can't stop these men and women from defending their town."

"I'm already here to defend it."

"I think you'll need help. A lot of people are coming to fight, and they're full of rage."

"Did you see them?"

"They're gathering. They'll be here soon."

Falconi stepped aside, and the people behind him came onto the piazza. They were inhabitants of Altino, simple townspeople.

"How did you manage to get them all together?" Falconi asked the poet as the men and women converged onto the piazza.

"I didn't get anyone together. They gathered on their own

and came to ask if I would like to join them. I wasn't aware of what happened last night. They told me about it."

"Well, I warn you: what will happen here in a little while will be the highlight of the show. The bloody cherry on the cake."

"You won't dissuade us."

"You still have time to leave."

Fantini replied that he was not going to leave, and he went over to join the others. Matteo Falconi saw that it was useless to try and make him change his mind.

The poet walked over to the ragazzi, who hadn't moved from their spot. He recognized a few of the players who'd agreed to come back and train with him; they greeted him. Fousseyni was among them, looking like an injured sparrow in the midst of a storm. His eyes, as sad as ever, now voiced infinite distress and a prayer: make all this stop. Fantini recalled the day the men had arrived and he'd watched discreetly as they walked through the streets of Altino. Several months had gone by, but he thought he could read the same emotion on their faces.

"It's you again," Solomon said when he stopped in front of him.

"Me again," said Fantini.

"This time, you won't convince anyone to follow you. Our lives are in danger."

"I didn't come here to convince you," he said loudly, in Italian, so that everyone would hear. "I just want to tell you that you're not alone, and that if you think everyone wants you dead or gone, it's not true."

"That's ridiculous. It's too late, always too late," said Solomon, snickering. "There's nothing left for us but death. And once again, Europe is to blame. That's what your late priest thought."

"You know nothing about Amedeo. Don't sully his memory."

"That's what he wrote, in plain Italian, on a little piece of folded paper he forgot in the Bible he gave me. Deep down, he saw eye to eye with me. It's all your fault, you Europeans: you're arrogant and violent, incapable of openness or real hospitality. It's all your fault."

"You wouldn't be here if Europeans were incapable of hospitality. You'd be dead, or on your own."

"If I'd known what was waiting for me here, I would have preferred to be dead or on my own. I've already told you that."

"You care more about life than you think. And before this story is over, you'll realize it."

Solomon wanted to reply, but a loud clamor prevented him. Fabio Calcagno, Andrea, Cesare, and Gennaro Orso were marching at the head of a mass of individuals coming toward the piazza. The crowd was brandishing pickaxes and pitchforks, bats and broken bottles, bludgeons and knife blades that glittered in the darkening twilight. Some of their rank were holding torches: their menacing flames flickered nervously, letting off large sparks that fluttered for a few seconds in the air like fireflies. In the glow of their deadly light, as they came down the street, the men in the crowd were chanting. The chant was martial, warlike, but the words were garbled, as if their voices were mingling with no concern for harmony, creating a loud buzzing noise. But this confused, guttural rumbling, despite its lack of coherence, resonated with formidable power as they approached the piazza.

Solomon became agitated. His little eyes were like those of a cobra ready to strike. Giuseppe Fantini walked over to join Captain Falconi at the head of his troops. Solomon came up to them a few seconds later. A dozen yards from there, Fabio Calcagno, his ultra friends, and Gennaro Orso ordered their troops to stop chanting.

The piazza soon lapsed into an uneasy silence. From their balconies or windows, inhabitants were watching fearfully. They were terrified by the sight of firearms. One stray bullet could easily find its way to one of them. They didn't know what was going on, but they sensed something terrible might happen.

"Calcagno, you are under arrest for disturbance of the peace and threatening the security of the inhabitants of Altino," said Falconi.

"Come over here and arrest me, then, Captain," Fabio replied, with a snort of laughter.

"We won't hesitate to shoot."

"We're not the only ones who'll die tonight," shouted Fabio. "We have a job to finish! And we will finish it! You should be ashamed of standing there shoulder-to-shoulder with a Black," he continued, looking at Solomon. "I'm here to kill him. We're here to send them back to where they came from!"

The men behind him roared like beasts. Falconi gave up on talking, and the already-slim hope he'd had that the presence of his armed men might dissuade Calcagno's fighters evaporated. The men there before him were spoiling for a fight. He listened to them shouting, and behind that shouting he thought he could hear the fetid sucking sound of the great pit, so near, somewhere in the twilight, opening all around them, ready to swallow them up.

"This is madness," murmured Giuseppe Fantini.

"It's too late to go back now," said Falconi.

"I know. That doesn't stop it being madness. Don't shoot."

"Too late. If they attack, my men have orders to shoot."

"At this distance, it will be absolute carnage."

"Even if we don't shoot, it will be carnage, Maestro."

The two men fell silent. Next to them, Solomon said nothing, either, but his entire being expressed the wild excitement seething inside him.

The string of the bow came to its highest degree of tension. The arrow was vibrating, ready to whistle and slice through the world until it pierced Altino's breathless heart. The silence was calling to death, whose steed whinnied in the distance as it sped toward them, a scraggy, terrifying mount with bloody hooves and steaming nostrils, foaming at the mouth with poison, its coat in flames, black despair riding pillion as it galloped hell for leather through a field where flowers stood, white and rigid: human skulls. And the eye of the sun hung motionless in a darkening sky, watching the men.

Chapter VI

After nearly a year of literary impotence, here's a new chapter for this journal. It will be the last. After this, I won't be able to write anymore. I don't even know where I'll be. I already feel, writing these lines, as if I'm on the edge of the void.

I saw six people die last night. Six too many. They died before my eyes, and I can't find it in me to try to endure this. Everyone has their limits; mine haven't just been reached, they've been surpassed. Yesterday, I felt that I couldn't take it anymore.

It was still dark when they came in, but daybreak was imminent. There were ten of them, maybe a few more. The only ones I recognized were the Calcagno brothers. A lot of us had stayed on at the restaurant. Quite a few association members: Sabrina, Sister Maria, Lucia, Gianni, Pietro, and Veronica. And Carla, of course. She and I hadn't stopped eyeing each other all evening. It was obvious that we were attracted to each other, but we preferred to play stupid and go on hurting one another. She knows I love her. Every time she kissed Roberto, I pulled Serena Filippi closer to me. I was cruel. That poor, beautiful girl didn't deserve to be used just so I could hurt Carla, and hurt myself at the

same time. I hope that she'll forgive me from
up there. A lot of ragazzi were still at the
restaurant, too.

Calcagno and several other men strode in,
shouting. I don't know why, but as they
shouted, each one of them exhibited his penis for a few seconds. They were armed with
long baseball bats. Drunk. I didn't have
time to yell a warning before one of the
Calcagnos was already hitting Francesca
Filippi; her head smashed against the bar
counter before she fell, inert. Her mother
had no time to cry out: another man in the
group punched her in the temple and sent her
flying. Screams rang out, glasses were
smashed, shards of broken bottles glittered.
Meanwhile, the Calcagnos were wreaking havoc
with their baseball bats, which they would
spin in the air then bring down almost at
random on heads, bodies, tables. Figures
collapsed and stopped moving. Others managed
to get up and rush out of the restaurant. I
yelled to everyone who was still standing to
move to the back of the restaurant and arm
themselves with anything that could be used
for self-defense. In the general wave of
panic, I saw Sabrina going the wrong way,
toward our assailants. She was yelling, "He
sent you, didn't he? It's Maurizio again!
The coward! He can't even come in person and
take responsibility! The coward! On the anniversary of Hampâté's death—it's disgust-
ing." I don't know who Hampâté is. I don't
know what she was hoping to do. I think she
hadn't realized how violent these men were.
One of the Calcagnos grabbed her and hurled

her against a wall, as if she were no more than a feather pillow. Then, as she was regaining her wits with difficulty, he went over to her and began to undo his fly. On the floor, Sabrina was powerless: she tried to resist, to scratch, to bite. The man was too strong. He pinned her to the floor and, before our eyes, began to tear off her clothes. The other aggressors formed a barrier, as the Calcagno brother laughed and Sabrina screamed. I went on the attack, armed with a chair. All the others—Pietro, Sister Maria, Carla, Veronica, Lucia, Fousseyni, Roberto, Concetta, Bemba, Serena, Gianni, and a few ragazzi—followed my desperate, impulsive example, and the fight turned nasty. We slightly outnumbered the attackers, but we were less well armed and less battle-ready, unlike the assailants who, clearly, were well acquainted with violence. Sabrina was still screaming, and then we stopped hearing her voice. As we tried to get through the barrier—of baseball bats, knives, and knuckledusters—keeping us from her, as we were driven back again and again, all we could see was the rapist, hunched over Sabrina, pummeling her with punches that made a nauseating sound as they landed on her motionless body. When the rapist stood up, his fists were red. This fueled our rage, and we managed to open a little breach in the human wall by knocking two of their men to the floor. Sister Maria slipped through first, screaming. But before she could reach Sabrina's bleeding body, she was stopped by the fierce blow of a baseball bat. Her veil was torn away; her blonde hair,

which I'd never seen, fanned out in the air
in a streak of gold, and then she fell.
Pietro and two of the ragazzi who were right
behind him met the same fate. Pietro didn't
immediately pass out; he tried to get up,
but a powerful kick almost broke his jaw,
and he lost consciousness. The ragazzi who
were with him took a beating, too, and passed
out. Ranks were broken, and little groups
formed and went on fighting. I lost sight of
so many—Serena, who'd been behind me, wasn't
there anymore. I didn't know where Veronica
was. Maybe behind the bar. Maybe in the
kitchen. Concetta, too, was nowhere to be
seen. In one corner Lucia, Gianni, and
Fousseyni were grappling with two men; next
to them, Carla and Roberto, armed with broken bottles, were confronting two other aggressors; Bemba was getting the better of an
adversary, thrashing him. One of the Calcagno
brothers rushed toward me, his bat in the
air, ready to break my skull. I dodged instinctively, so quickly it surprised me, and
I gave him a left jab with all my might,
which sent him into a pile of overturned tables and chairs. I grabbed his weapon and
ran to help Bemba, who had almost knocked
out his adversary when another one surprised
him from behind: the new aggressor slashed
at him with a knife, lacerating his chest,
then broke a wine bottle over his head. I got
there just in time to stop the man from
planting the broken bottle into Bemba's neck.
I walloped him in his stomach with the bat,
and he began screaming and writhing in pain.
I thought I heard Bemba, on the verge of

losing consciousness, murmur thank you, but
I was already rushing toward the back courtyard, where Carla was screaming in terror.
When I got there, I saw two men had driven
her into a corner. There was a big spot of
blood staining her blonde hair. Roberto was
at her feet, face down in a pool of blood. I
hurried over to her and managed to hit the
first attacker with my bat, not hard enough
to knock him out, but enough to make his brow
spout blood. Swearing, he fled toward the
main room. The other man came at me, and we
rolled onto the ground. Carla was still
screaming, with Roberto's motionless body
next to her. The man who'd come after me was
quicker to get back on his feet and ran after
his comrade, toward the main room. Before
following him, I looked over at Carla. Our
gazes met, she opened her mouth to say something, but before she could, I saw her—surely
because of her wound—collapse on top of
Roberto. I wanted to stay with her but
couldn't: there was still fighting in the
main room. Everything was chaos, smelling of
alcohol and blood. I saw Veronica lying inert next to the bar. Was she dead or unconscious? Next to her, the other Calcagno
brother, the one I'd nearly knocked out when
I punched him, lay on top of Serena; helpless, she was screaming frantically. I was
about to go and help her, but two men—the
Calcagno brother who'd raped Sabrina, and
another man—were blocking the way. I moved
back. Serena was screaming, fighting. I saw
the hideous face of the bestial man on top
of her, smiling, drooling. Desperate, I

rushed over. They pushed me back, and with
the shock, I dropped the baseball bat. When
they saw that, the two men fell on me, beating me senseless. I couldn't hear Serena's
cries anymore. Just when I thought it was
nearly over for me and that I was going to
die (I was on the floor, at the mercy of knife
jabs and blows from the baseball bat), I saw
Solomon come in with several other ragazzi.
Someone must have alerted them. Their arrival evened out the fighting. My torturers
had to leave me to confront the newcomers,
who, this time, were armed. Solomon was a
formidable warrior. I was about to pass out,
but I saw him, armed with a simple stick,
teaching the aggressors a lesson with the
help of his fellow ragazzi: they fell, cried
out, retreated. Drawing on my last resources,
I managed to crawl through the fight that was
still raging and the nameless bodies that
were scattered over the bloodstained floor.
Crawling through human blood, the blood of
one's dead or injured friends, must be one
of the worst things there is. Humiliating,
sordid, and macabre all at once. Suddenly,
as I painfully made my way toward the back-
yard, where I hoped to reach Carla, Fousseyni
came crashing down not far from me. I looked
over at him and saw that the man who'd pushed
him, one of the Calcagno brothers, was now
standing across from Gianni. Gianni, visibly
exhausted, his face bloodied, was trying to
protect Lucia. He attacked, but he didn't
stand a chance: the colossus easily warded
off his blows, and without a moment's hesitation, with a gesture both brutal and

precise, he drove a huge knife blade into
Gianni's abdomen. Gianni, impaled on the
blade, began spitting blood; his eyes rolled
upwards. Calcagno didn't pull the blade out;
he twisted it for a long time in Gianni's
guts, like a fork in a plate of spaghetti,
then left it there. Gianni fell to the floor.
Calcagno kicked him out of his way. Now Lucia
was his. I saw him unbuckle his belt. With a
superhuman effort, I crawled over to Fousseyni
and began shaking him. He came around almost
at once. Still dazed, he immediately looked
over to where Lucia was, as if, during those
few seconds of unconsciousness, he had only
been thinking of her. Calcagno was already
spreading her on the floor as she struggled.
Elsewhere in the room, Solomon and his men
were getting the better of our attackers,
but there were too few of them to come over
to the corner where we were. I groped around,
looking for any object that Fousseyni might
use to stop Calcagno from committing his
second rape that evening. My hand came upon
a knife that one of the fighters must have
dropped. I grabbed it and gave it to Fousseyni,
who got to his feet. Calcagno had lowered
his trousers and was tearing at Lucia's
clothes; her silent screams were even more
horrifying than Serena's had been. "Kill
him," I said to Fousseyni. "Kill the swine."
We stared at each other for a moment. I'll
never forget the look in his eyes: his gaze,
ready to lose all innocence, no longer simply observing the ugliness of the world but
about to take part in it, about to become
another wound among all the wounds poisoning

the great stinking body of human carrion with its gangrene. His gaze pleading. "Kill the bastard," I repeated. He turned his head away, closed his eyes, and rushed toward Calcagno, who was now trying to penetrate the young woman as she struggled pathetically, scratching at his face. Fousseyni drove the knife between the man's shoulder blades. Blood squirted, splashing Fousseyni's face. Calcagno screamed and tried to turn around to grab his opponent, but Fousseyni left him no time: he was already raising the knife again. He plunged it into the eye of the huge bald monster, then into his neck, his chest, his mouth, his other eye, and wherever he could in the upper part of his body, striking blindly, striking with rage, with pain, striking, striking as if possessed, striking like a maniac, striking despite the spasmodic squirts of blood that blinded him as he wept, and his shouts were mingled with the bellowing of the man he was killing, the man he was bleeding dry, striking and striking with an inhuman savagery—or a savagery that was all too human. And all the while, I was on the floor, watching him kill, and smiling with pleasure and horror and lunacy, certain in that moment that not only could nothing on earth ever be saved, but also that nothing deserved it. Nor could anything, in all that is inhuman, ever be alien to us again. Calcagno collapsed, awash in his own blood, as if torn to pieces, as if a pack of werewolves had fought over the flesh of his face. Fousseyni dropped the knife and turned to me, out of breath. He had just made the greatest physical effort of his life. He looked at me. The gaze of a man through whom, fleetingly and painfully, the most extreme degree of violence had just passed. A gaze of fear, of absolute disgust with himself and with the world. I saw him there, on his feet, while all around him others were fighting, and all around him there were dead bodies. He looked at Gianni, and I got the impression he was wondering how a human body could contain so much blood. Lucia had lost consciousness, but I think she'd had time to see Fousseyni kill her aggressor. Fousseyni looked at her for a long time. Then, unable to bear what was happening around him, he slid to the floor. I didn't have the strength to crawl over to him. I heard someone shout, "Sergio is down, Sergio is down, and the carabinieri will be here any second; let's get out of here." A few seconds later, it was Solomon's voice: "Let's take our people and go. I think they're all alive. They'll come around. We'll leave Bemba here; he's already lost a lot of blood, and we don't have the means to look after him. They'll take care of him better than we could. Hurry."

"What should we do with Jogoy?" said a voice that sounded like Appiah Mohamad, Solomon's right-hand man.

"He's not one of ours," said Solomon. "We'll leave him here. Take all the dead."

"Why?" said Appiah Mohamad.

"We'll leave them on the piazza. I want them to see death at the heart of their town."

His comrades took the bodies and dragged

them outside. Then I saw Solomon go over to Fousseyni, pick him up, and sling him over his shoulder. That's the last image I had of the battlefield. I wanted to crawl, but none of my limbs would obey me. A great black hole opened up, and I slid into it.

That's it. I've told my story. Maybe it makes sense to have written it down. Maybe it doesn't. But because I believe I was the last person still conscious last night, I thought I'd better tell it.

Totò, I know that you will find this notebook. I'm leaving it for you. This is all I have to say. Let Carla read it if she wants to; let her know what I couldn't tell her. Quite simply, that I love her. I've written it clearly because I'm afraid I won't be able to tell her after this. I would also like to say thank you to her parents, Mario and Valeria, who were like parents to me. God knows what would have become of me without their help and their kindness. As for you, my dear Totò, I want you to know you are my friend. A great friend. And that whatever you may think, you're a man who's fundamentally good. I hope all the horror of the world won't convince you of the contrary. I'm very grateful to you.

That's it.

I'm tired, I'm on the edge of the void. Very close. I want to go home. I want to see my family. I don't know if I'll have the time before I fall into the void forever. But if there's not enough time, and I have to stay here, if I don't have time because the void has swallowed me, I hope someone will find me and carry me home. Carry me back to my loved ones. Carry me back, among the songs and circles and choirs of the *ndût*, the only place where a soul can be healed, the only place where loneliness doesn't exist, where people know what they're talking about, where people still know how to bow down before the world, where words are never lost but continue to flow in the veins of the world, of which they are the sap and the blood. I hope I will be placed among the learners, that I will be beaten, will be spoken to, that they will dance for me by the fire. Because I was born of the *ndût*, and to the *ndût* I shall return.

* * *

Salvatore Pessoto was trembling, the notebook open on his desk. What he had just read upset him greatly. The final paragraphs brought tears to his eyes. He didn't know where Jogoy was. He didn't know where to look for him. If he even *should* look for him. Distraught, he went back into the main room. The injured patients, still with their loved ones, were trying to recover. Carla was lying flat on her bed. Salvatore Pessoto headed over to her.

"Carla," he said gently, rousing her from a dark reverie.

She gave a start, and took a few seconds to return to them.

"Ah . . . Forgive me, Totò . . . Yes? And? You've read the notebook then . . . Do you know where he is?"

"I've read it, yes, but I don't know where he is."

"What's in it? What did he write?"

"A lot of things. Everything he is. Everything he's been through. You have to read it."

He handed her the notebook.

Fire Chief Caruso came into the room suddenly, breathless.

"There's a slaughter about to take place in town . . . The carabinieri are there, ragazzi, locals . . . I don't know who wants to fight who, or why, but people will die if they do. A lot of people. As if we haven't already seen enough death . . . "

"Death is never sated. It's always eager for more live flesh; that's its nature," said Pietro, the disillusionment clear in his voice.

60

F abio Calcagno was about to give the order to attack, and Matteo Falconi the order to fire, when a furious roar resounded in the air. It was a shout of rage that lasted long seconds, like the anger of a flouted deity on the path of vengeance. Then a first flow of molten lava burst from the crater like a blinding blade pulled abruptly from its sheath after centuries of sleep. Red and black smoke belched from the mouth of the volcano and gathered in the sky. On the piazza of the archer's bow, the men preparing to fight stood stunned, terrified by the threatening roar they'd just heard.

"*Che diavolo* . . . What the hell was that?" said Falconi, breaking the anxious silence.

"That, Captain," said Giuseppe Fantini, "is Mount Etna. And I can tell you that I've seen it erupt dozens of times in my life, but never has it begun with such a roar—that was almost human."

"And what does it mean?" asked Falconi.

"That the town will probably be affected," the old poet replied. "We have to get ready to evacuate Altino."

"Bullshit!" shouted Fabio Calcagno, who'd overheard them.

"There's only one way to find out if it's bullshit, you vile, overgrown gorilla," said the poet. "Just stay put and wait patiently for the toxic clouds to suffocate you."

Fabio didn't respond. He began to look slightly doubtful.

"Listen to me, all of you," Fantini continued, raising his voice. "What you just heard is Mount Etna starting to erupt.

And I think this eruption will be powerful enough to reach our town."

No sooner had he stopped speaking than the wail of a siren pierced the air. It was the alarm telling the townspeople that a great danger was threatening the town and that they had to seek cover, or leave. The howl of the siren was unbearable. A lot of the men on the piazza blocked their ears to muffle it; it lasted for a full two minutes before fading away.

"That siren . . . It hasn't gone off once in my entire life," said Falconi.

"I've only heard it twice," said Fantini. "That was a long time ago, and only for a drill, each time. This is the first time since World War II that it's sounded for real. You have to leave!" he shouted. "Get out of here! Save your families! In half an hour, the cloud will be on top of us!"

"It's true!" one of the locals shouted from a window overlooking the piazza. "They just said on the radio that the volcano's erupting. They think it could be the worst eruption this century. They don't know why it suddenly woke up; there's been no sign of activity. We have to get out of here!"

From the windows came cries of panic. On the piazza, the men stood motionless, incredulous, not knowing what to do.

"For Christ's sake," shouted Fantini, "do you think it's a—"

The end of his sentence was drowned out by another terrible roar from the volcano. The earth trembled for a few seconds. This time, panic overcame the piazza. The good townspeople who had come with the poet were the first to run wildly through the streets, shouting, everyone trying to get home to find their families and children, and prepare to flee. Gennaro Orso hesitated for a few seconds, but fear finally got the better of his original plan, and with a cry of terror, he ran from the piazza, tossing aside the butcher's knife he'd been holding. Fabio Calcagno tried to restrain him, but Gennaro Orso, like a threatened boar, sent him packing, then disappeared.

The entire horde he'd brought with him followed suit, amid a clamor of fright.

"Break ranks!" Falconi ordered his men. "Go help evacuate the town! Be a credit to your uniform! Don't leave as long as a single inhabitant remains!"

The carabinieri dispersed toward various neighborhoods in a clatter of boots. All the while, the sky was being splattered with huge jets of fire. Lava poured down the slopes, deadly flows of gold which an alchemist, the devil himself, had melted in an evil athanor. It was no longer teardrops that flowed, but furious torrents. At regular intervals, Etna roared. In its language of stone, a language that was thousands of centuries old, unknown or forgotten by humankind, it bellowed its fateful curses.

In town, the screams continued, and from the piazza, men could be seen helplessly racing about, women stumbling as they tried to save their children, the first cars being loaded for evacuation. The only people still on the piazza were Falconi, the ragazzi, Fabio Calcagno and the handful of ultras who'd been with him, and Giuseppe Fantini. Now the poet turned to the ragazzi and said, "Go back to your apartments, take what you need, and meet on the main piazza in town. We have to leave this place."

"Stay here with me!" said Solomon.

"If you stay here, you'll die!" said Fantini.

"And if you leave, you'll die!" Solomon replied. "Wherever you go, you'll find nothing but death and hatred."

"Then leave, and die later. That's still better than dying now."

Two or three ragazzi went off at a run. Others followed. Solomon stammered threats that were swallowed by the roar of the volcano. In the end, he was alone with his bodyguards and Fousseyni. Still looking lost, Fousseyni had not moved.

"Aren't you leaving, Fousseyni?" asked Fantini.

Fousseyni was astonished that he remembered his name, and now he looked at him and said that he wanted to die. Solomon gave a snort of laughter and took him by the shoulder. Fantini looked at him with infinite tenderness and told him he would always remember the way he'd recited his poems, that it was something he'd never forget. A flash of gratitude appeared in the boy's eyes, then vanished behind the dull glare that seemed to possess them.

"Captain," said the poet, "go find the mayor and tell him not to abandon his citizens. Tell him to help with the evacuation."

"What do we do with this lot?" said Falconi, pointing to the ragazzi and the ultras who were still there.

"We can't do anything for them."

"And you?" said Falconi.

"I have to go home and get my dog first."

"Let's meet on the main piazza in ten minutes. I won't leave without you. My mother would never forgive me. She's asked to be buried with one of your books."

"I'll be there," said Fantini.

Then the poet headed quickly toward the labyrinth of little streets leading to his house.

"And now you can kill one another, if that's what you want," said Falconi, also taking his leave.

The ragazzi who'd stayed loyal to Solomon stood facing Fabio Calcagno and his mates on the piazza. Apart from them—maybe twenty people in all—the piazza was deserted, as if already doomed to destruction. Next to Solomon, Fousseyni Traoré was thinking about the blood that had splattered his face as he killed Sergio Calcagno. He still saw himself holding the knife, stabbing the man's eyes, tearing at his chest, driving the red blade into his mouth, slicing his tongue. Images of horror danced before his eyes. Gianni, losing all his blood. Lucia, with her torn clothing, unable to cry out as they tried to put her through hell. Jogoy, covered in blood, crawling through blood, telling him to kill. And Adama in the desert, falling, begging him to save him. It was to prevent another person who was dear to him from dying that Fousseyni had killed Sergio Calcagno. Last night, at the restaurant, when Sergio was about to hurt Lucia, the image of Adama losing his grip came back to haunt him.

Last night—was it a nightmare or some supernatural reality?—he'd heard his mother's voice, saying, "Fousseyni, my darling Fousseyni, it's done, I did it at last; I cut off your uncle's spiny dick. There he is, he's writhing in pain, he's dying, he's screaming like a madman with a voice torturing him in his head! I did it!" His dreams were filled with blood. His mind was nothing but blood. And the red of blood had covered over the red of Lucia's mouth, and the sensation of blood on his lips replaced that of the kiss. The oranges no longer smelled of anything but blood. Blood oranges, thirsting for blood . . . He had to die. Once again, he found himself standing before the djinn-snake. And this time, he would step over it; he wouldn't wait for it to slither back into the bush. He would step over it, and the offended god would strike him to the ground with unbelievable strength, and his neck would break.

The two groups looked at each other in silence, Solomon and Fabio Calcagno defiantly, with the same thirst for death.

Mount Etna continued to roar with curses in its ancient, untranslatable language of stone. It was too late to appease it.

61

S word-like, the eruption continued to tear open the sky: all its innards poured out in a vast red and black cloud shot through with lightning. An inexorable stream of blood, the cloud was headed toward Altino. People cried out, the volcano roared, the pit in the center of town continued to beckon, to produce its ignoble sucking noise. It was all a symphony without a conductor, setting off at full tilt toward an uncontrolled finale.

Matteo Falconi hurried to the town hall, not really hoping to find Francesco Montero. And yet there he was, outside the building, his sleeves rolled up, trying to advise inhabitants who were running in every direction with their belongings.

"Falconi, there you are; I tried to call you."

"Shocking, under the circumstances, that you didn't reach me. Have you been told about the carnage that was about to—"

"Yes. I was on my way there when we heard the volcano. Where are the ragazzi?"

"They're gathering on the piazza. Almost all of them, that is."

"I've requisitioned as many buses as I could. They're already there. I want everyone who hasn't got a vehicle to board a bus. We're leaving."

"But where will we go?"

"It doesn't matter. We have to leave. The radio just announced that in twenty minutes, the cloud you can see there will be above the town, and anyone who is below it or near it will die of asphyxiation. Not to mention the possibility of a shower of flames."

"And the town?"

"It will be destroyed. But we'll come back, and we'll rebuild, if there's anything *to* rebuild. We'll be brave."

"And the investigation? The murders?"

"We'll deal with that when the time comes. Justice will be served. It's a question of human rights, and it's important to me. I've left instructions for the bodies of the victims to be put in a safe place. My counterpart in Piazze is busy with the evacuation of his own town, but he found the time to take care of what we needed. Now, I want you personally to see to the evacuation of the injured patients who are still at the infirmary."

"And your family?"

"They've just left. I'll join them later. The captain is the last to leave his ship. Get going, Falconi! No time to waste chatting. Altino needs us."

Matteo Falconi thought there was something very theatrical about the mayor's diction and body language, but nevertheless he stood there gaping while Montero, with a worried frown, tried to help a woman who'd lost her child in the press of the crowd. Falconi turned around and went off toward the infirmary, thinking that, in the end, maybe not all hope was lost when it came to politicians, that sometimes they actually could demonstrate some courage. He hadn't noticed the man a short distance from the mayor who was holding a little camera and filming him. Nor had he seen the tiny microphone poking out of Francesco Montero's shirt. He'd completely failed to see how Montero had staged the whole production.

Night would soon be falling over Altino, a red night, covered in dust, surreal. Falconi, hurrying to the infirmary, glanced over at Mount Etna and saw that its fury had not abated. Right to the end, he knew, they'd have to fight against the dark energy that was encircling the town like a noose around a hanged man's neck. Etna was saying something, but its words had been muddled by anger. Falconi reached the infirmary and found a great deal of agitation. Salvatore Pessoto was already organizing the evacuation. Two ambulances from Piazze had come back, and the casualties had already been placed inside them. Carla had insisted on helping with the evacuation. In spite of her injuries and the grief caused by Roberto's death, she was showing exceptional courage.

Salvatore Pessoto charged Falconi and Fire Chief Caruso with finishing the evacuation. He had to fetch his family. He'd called Angela the moment he heard the volcano roar. He told her to prepare what was strictly necessary and to wait for him, promising he'd come and get them as soon as possible. Falconi, Caruso, and a few firefighters took over from him, and he went out, with Carla on his heels.

"Totò! I think I know where he is . . . "

"Who? Jogoy?"

"Yes. I think I know . . . I'm going to have a look. You see to your family. If I don't find Jogoy, I'll come back to the piazza."

"Let's meet on the piazza in fifteen minutes. Don't waste time, Carla. It will be here soon," said Pessoto, looking at the cloud.

Carla was about to leave when Pessoto asked her one last question.

"Did you read his journal?"

"Yes," she replied.

"So you know."

He didn't give Carla time to answer, but went off to help his loved ones. Carla headed down the street, where she passed faces filled with terror going the opposite direction.

* * *

Seen from the Villa, the flaming cloud seemed to be advancing more quickly. It was coming closer; it obscured, destroyed, banished, ravaged. Mount Etna, at the edge of the horizon, was watching its troops lay waste to everything in their path. From the Villa, it was no longer possible to contemplate the peacefulness of nature; the only option now was to bow to its fury.

That was where Carla found Jogoy. Standing on the balustrade, facing the void, stripped bare; his clothes had been rolled up and placed on the ground. The wind was blowing in sudden, furious gusts that struck his naked body. It was the sirocco, the wind that drove men mad, but this sirocco was charged with heat. Carla went up to him, slowly. She stopped only a few yards away.

"Jogoy . . . "

He didn't turn around. He didn't seem to hear her.

"Jogoy, it's me, Carla."

This time he heard her and turned toward her. Carla saw right away that his gaze had changed, not because it was expressing his emotion differently but because it expressed no emotion at all. It was an icy steppe across which one could ride to exhaustion looking for a feeling, a vast, arid plain where nothing grew. He seemed absent from himself.

"Jogoy . . . We have to leave. We don't have much time."

Jogoy didn't answer, and looked back out at the void.

"Jogoy . . . "

Etna growled again. A massive bolt of lightning lit up the heart of the cloud. Then a strange silence reigned, and in that moment the world was as if petrified, caught in the gap between two tremors. Jogoy, his gaze still turned toward the void, murmured, "*A mossa.*"

Carla didn't understand the language, but she didn't care. All that she wanted was for Jogoy to come down.

"Jogoy . . . I read your journal. I know. I know everything."

On hearing those words, Jogoy finally looked at her, and a smile of infinite tenderness lit his face that had been so closed to all emotion. He opened his mouth, perhaps to voice out loud the love he felt for her, but the words didn't come. Two huge tears rolled down his cheeks. It was all he could say.

The sirocco swept over the Villa. Jogoy closed his eyes. Carla didn't even have the strength to cry out when she saw him topple over into the void.

62

A hellish heat began to bear down on Altino, announcing the terrible cloud and the long flames that would come with it. It was nearly there. It was knocking at the gates of the town, licking them with tongues of fire and sulfur and ash. At regular intervals, the earth threatened to split open. People had already taken to the roads, like a routed army, forming a long column of black beetles, their cars following one behind the other as they fled the town.

One solitary pick-up truck, however, went on driving through Altino's trembling streets.

Simone Marconi, Lucia's father, couldn't refuse his daughter's request, but he did tell her that if they didn't find Fousseyni Traoré in this neighborhood, they would have to leave. Simone Marconi could already feel the effects of the cloud on his lungs. The air was getting thicker and thicker, hard to breathe, and the heat blurred his vision. But Lucia insisted on looking in this last neighborhood for the young refugee she loved. Marconi drove as fast as he could through the absent, ghostly town, devoid now of all human substance. It was terrifying. He didn't recognize Altino; it was nothing but a heap of ruins that the eruption was about to reduce to nothingness. The town, like human beings, was about to return to dust. He stopped abruptly when, at the end of one little street, they came upon a courtyard where he could see bodies laid out in a row. He saw them as if through the veil of a nightmare. He wondered if it wasn't a hallucination, yet another evil spell cast by the volcano to keep them there, to lose them there, to make them go around in circles until exhaustion and death ensued. Yes, that's what he wondered. Maybe he should have followed the convoy, whose last vehicles had left a quarter of an hour ago with Francesco Montero on board. But his daughter had begged him to go look for Fousseyni. He couldn't refuse.

They climbed out of the truck. The bodies were scattered on the ground. Simone Marconi got the impression that they'd killed one another down to the last man, like sailors shipwrecked on a desert island eventually devouring one another. The piazza was clouded in dust; he could hardly see anything now. The toxic cloud was entering the empty town, like a victor easily taking a province abandoned by its soldiers.

The dead men, shrouded by the first particles of ash, illuminated by the peculiar light the apocalypse projects onto the worlds it reveals even as it destroys them, appeared yet more ghostly to him now, and as he looked at them, he was reminded of a painting by Goya he particularly liked. In it, two men hit each other with sticks in a beautiful crepuscular light, and with each blow they sink deeper into the swamp where they are fighting. Is that how they died, killing each other as the cloud that was about to cause their death unfolded over them, urging them to make its task easier, to spare it the trouble of killing them? Marconi looked up. He could see nothing now, and he was having difficulty breathing. They had to leave. He turned around but could not see Lucia. He'd thought she was right behind him.

He was seized with panic, his voice breaking, his heart bursting, his vocal chords fraying, and he couldn't cry out. In that moment, as his voice refused to obey him, he understood the degree of pain his daughter had felt, mute for four long years. He imagined the worst: that they would die without seeing each other, without hearing each other, lost in darkness, lost in the dust, asphyxiated probably only a few yards apart, separated by these corpses that had killed each other. The smoke was getting thicker. Only a few more minutes, and the cloud would kill them. Panicked, still reduced to speechlessness, he turned around and around in utter despair, like a bull in the ring where it will die.

* * *

All at once, Lucia saw him. It was him. It was Fousseyni, lying there, a few yards away. Her emotion was so great that she forgot to signal her father, who was walking ahead of her. She ran to the body, knelt beside it, and, despite the blood that covered his torso and hands and neck, she quickly felt for his pulse. It was beating. Weak, to be sure. But beating. Lucia raised her head, and only then did she realize that her father was not there.

She couldn't see anything. Beyond just a yard or two, the dust cloud covered the world and obscured her gaze. The heat was overwhelming, slowly tightening its grip on her throat. Fousseyni lay unconscious on the ground among the other bodies, which all seemed dead. She waited. She waited for her father to come or at least to call out so she could find her way to him from the sound of his voice, could reach him. But no human voice pierced the powerful breath of the wind, regularly punctuated by the rumbling of the volcano. She was on the verge of suffocation. Slowly, gently, she began to lapse into unconsciousness, crushed by heat and asphyxia.

A loud cry roused her from the mortal drowsiness threatening her. A powerful, terrible cry, torn from the very heart of her. It took her a few seconds to realize it was coming from inside her, from her own body, that the cry was her cry and the voice her voice. It was as if this cry, four years later, after the long silence, was the prolongation of the cry she had given when she learned of her mother's suicide. That scream, after which she lapsed into muteness, was the same scream with which her voice was now returning to life, to save herself and to save Fousseyni. She didn't stop screaming. Before long, even as she was about to collapse for lack of air, a figure stood out against the dark haze of dust. Her father, breathless, helped her carry Fousseyni's body to the car, whose headlamps were still on. As Simone Marconi turned the key in the ignition, they failed to hear a voice pleading, a man who'd fallen not far from there, a tall thin man with eyes as narrow as thread, wearing a loose black garment. Solomon.

He whispered faintly, "Don't leave me here; I don't want to die, not like this." They didn't hear him. Next to him, a long curved stick, stained with blood, lay next to a tall bald man who no longer had a face: Fabio Calcagno.

The first flames of the volcanic storm were reaching Altino when the pickup truck, driving at breakneck speed, left the town. Fousseyni Traoré, his bleeding head on Lucia's lap, had just opened his eyes. He thought he was in hell but, once again, as when he first awoke in Altino, it was the smell of oranges that intoxicated him. Lucia's tears fell on his face as she kissed him. He had the strength to ask where he was. Lucia replied that he was in her arms.

He was returning to paradise, to love, to Lucia's face, which was the light of the sun and of all the other stars. He heard her voice for the first time, and for the first time, amid the physical pain and the taste of his own blood, he knew what love was. Lucia, and no one else, was the redemption of shame; she was there with him, and all the rest—the voyage, the shame, the desert, and the sea—now seemed both far away and inconsequential.

63

Imperturbable silence, as if timeless.

Giuseppe Fantini put down his pen. The great poem was finished. In any case, he didn't think he had to add anything more. He'd written the final verses facing the enraged volcano and the black cloud as it approached. Bandino lay at his side, as calm as always. But in the dog's eyes there was something changed. Something like an intuition, the imminent end of a long journey. The old poet stood up and, strangely, felt no pain in his joints. He stood by the window for a moment. Cruel, fierce, and superbly proud, Mount Etna refused to calm down. Fantini liked it all the more. He wished he could get very close, the way he had in the old days. To be there by the mouth of the volcano. He suddenly realized that until now he'd misunderstood Empedocles' final gesture. He'd always thought it was sublime, the ultimate philosophical act, a sort of moral testament. He'd been wrong. Or at least, that was not all it was. Empedocles, at the mouth of the volcano, the crater of red lips, had done no more than embrace it. His act was a gesture of love. Erotic. His heart letting go, the call of the body.

Fantini went back to his desk, where the thick manuscript lay. Five hundred pages of poetry. He'd never written this much. He who'd always rejected the disorderly effusions of bad romanticism, who'd always found in the aridity of language the place of its poetic precision, knew all the same that the length of his last collection had been imposed on him by a necessity inherent in the work itself. It was the work that had required, and dictated, its form; the poet had merely obeyed orders. It was a unique, great poem that had sprung all at once from a single impulse. And in it, Fantini had tried to rediscover a dimension that poets had neglected, or forgotten, for far too long: story. That which relates and connects.

Ragazzi. The title had come quite naturally. He knew that there was a novel by Pasolini with the same title, but that didn't bother him. He had a great deal of respect and admiration for Pasolini; they had even corresponded for a time, not long before his murder.

He had nothing more to say now. All that was left was to revert to silence and to show poetry something more than just decency: the loyalty of remaining quiet. He looked at the manuscript. All that was missing was the dedication. He picked up his pen, and on the second page he wrote, with a steady, supple hand: "*To Amedeo Bonianno, scout of light in the darkness.*"

"We'll be there soon, my friend," he said.

He turned another page. It was the beginning of the poem. Giuseppe Fantini called to Bandino. The dog knew the time had come and stood up with a joy and agility he'd not displayed since his younger years. The poet stroked the dog tenderly, for a long while; then both of them, like old friends, entered into the work and disappeared into the opening verses of the great poem, as if those verses were a passage into another world. The poem welcomed them. It was the proof that it was a great work of art: it was possible to enter it and live there.

Mount Etna roared again; then the black cloud covered the town in a whirlwind that was as silent and deadly as a hitman.

64

There, in the distance, in the middle of one of the numerous hairpin turns on the mountain road they'd taken to flee, and from which they could see the entire valley, some of the residents of Altino stopped for a few seconds to gaze at their town. The cloud was about to descend on it. Every one of them wondered if they might one day be able to go home, or whether they'd be obliged to make their life elsewhere. A tragic question which, when they were leaving home and could see only distant lights or a darkened skyline, the handful of ragazzi who were now at their side must have asked themselves, too.

Salvatore Pessoto, with his family and Carla, still couldn't understand what had happened to Jogoy. Carla's words had been confused. He thought she'd said, "Villa," "naked," and "fall," all mixed up, incoherently, as she spoke. He wanted to question her again about his friend, but his wife Angela stopped him. Carla, in tears, was in no state to talk. When he saw her come back to the piazza by the town hall without Jogoy, Pessoto initially wanted to go himself to look for his friend, but there had been no time. Reluctantly, he'd had to leave in a terrible rush, still no wiser as to the fate of his friend. Angela was pressuring him to hurry: the cloud of sulfur would threaten Erica with a sudden asthma attack. They had to get her away from the volcano's toxic fumes as quickly as possible.

Vera and Vincenzo Rivera, in their little red convertible, which didn't have the space for them to take much with them, were weeping in concert: they'd had to leave their *Vanitas*

Vanitatum behind—although, through her tears and snot, Vera said several times over that Art was destruction and that you couldn't be a true artist until you'd seen your work go up in flames at least once.

Matteo Falconi was thinking about Giuseppe Fantini. The poet hadn't shown up as planned. Counter to Francesco Montero's directives urging him to get on a bus and go, Falconi went to look for the poet at his home. But no one answered at the great house. He forced the front door open. Once inside, he called out as loudly as he could, in vain. So he decided to inspect all the rooms, but to no avail: the poet wasn't there. In one of the rooms on the second floor, he'd found a thick stack of pages on the desk. He hesitated, wondering if he should take them, but something about the sight of the manuscript made him feel mysteriously certain that he must leave it there, that this was its place, and that it could only have meaning in this place, on this desk. In the end, he left without touching it. He hoped Fantini had managed to get away. As for the little bow-shaped piazza, he didn't go back there. He was in no doubt as to the fate of the men he'd left there.

Sister Maria was still praying, her hands joined around her little gold cross. The thought of Sabrina's death was unbearable, and her prayers were said as much for the peace of her friend's soul as to ask God to preserve her, Maria, from the anger that was stalking her in the face of the injustice and impunity of that crime.

Gennaro Orso had no regrets. As he watched the death of his town, he thought of how he'd defended it to the very end, and how his cause was just.

Francesco Montero grandiloquently asserted that reconstruction was a question of will and solidarity. "Our love of the town will serve as both cement and trowel; it is with our hearts that we'll rebuild," he said. On his phone, he received a message from Sandro Calvino: "Is Maurizio with you? I haven't been able to reach him." "No, he's not with me. He'll be in a safe place; he must have found refuge somewhere," Montero replied. Somewhere, yes, somewhere where no one would find him, not even the raging volcano and its cruel emissary: the belly of his armchair, which had completely swallowed him up and torn him from this ruthless world, where Sabrina, so hated and so beloved, was no more. And anyway, thought Montero, wherever he is, I don't care now. After the documentary on my leadership during the eruption, I'll be more than a senator. I'll be a national hero.

And, strategically ignoring the little camera, he adopted an expression that was both tragic and determined as he shot a penetrating gaze at the place where Altino was.

The ragazzi stayed silent. They were used to all this. Their second life had just gone up in smoke. They set their course for the third one, then, and the fourth, and the sixty-eighth, the one-thousand-eleventh, what difference did it make; a course for life, for the next life, whatever it held in store, fulfillment or death; a course for the vast earth, for happiness, for the worst; a course for the coming struggle, the eternal struggle to deserve to be a human being.

Then the convoy of exiles set off again along the mountain road's tight twists and turns. The outline of Altino, swallowed by the black cloud, had just disappeared before their eyes, as if forever. From time to time, they looked back in hopes of seeing their little town again. But all they could see, in the distance, were the last fires. People had spoken out, their voices mingling, chaotic but together, to express some of what they felt. Then they all fell silent again, one after the other, tired and torn. The last song did not belong to them. It was Mount Etna's. The volcano had begun to sing it alone. Then the choir of Altino had fallen silent.

The substance of the town would belong from now on to the poetry of ruins. All that remained intact of the old town was memory. The allegory of it, at least: the statue of Athena did not fall. This land where she had lain for many centuries had spared her. On purpose.

Because, hours later, amid the desolation and silence, the statue became memory incarnate: it was no longer an object of academic argument but the subject of divine energy; its stone came to life; the cold whiteness of marble that imprisoned her became the opaline rose of flesh gorged with life; the goddess stepped down off her pedestal, then walked toward the only person who had stayed behind in Altino, and who had survived.

The little woods below the Villa had protected one miraculous survivor, the way the forest where he'd received his initiation had once protected him; a naked individual lying among the tall trees as if in the center of a stage, a man who'd gone mad to save himself from the madness of his peers. Athena was there to transmit the memory of place to him. After that, it would be up to him to tell the story of Altino's ragazzi.

Acknowledgements

I would like to express all my gratitude to the Fondation Facim in Savoie, where I was invited for a literary residency in 2016. My stay at the wonderful Château des Allues, in Saint-Pierre d'Albigny, as well as all the fine friendships forged in those places, nurtured the writing of this book.

My heartfelt thanks also go to all those who reread, encouraged, corrected, critiqued, or simply accompanied this book through the power of their thoughts: all my family (Papa, Maman, all the Cro-Magnon men, and more), my Mellie, Elgas, Reynald, Laurent, Lyncx, Marc, Emma, Aram, Anne, my steadfast Bango pals, and last but not least, the entire team of Présence Africaine Editions.

M. M. S.

Mohamed Mbougar Sarr was born in Dakar in 1990. He studied literature and philosophy at the École des Hautes Études en Sciences Sociales in Paris. *Brotherhood*, his first novel to appear in English (Europa, 2021), won the Grand Prix du Roman Métis, the Prix Ahmadou Kourouma, and the French Voices Grand Prize. In 2018, he became the youngest writer to receive the World Literature Prize, for his second novel, *Silence of the Choir*. His third novel, *The Most Secret Memory of Men*, won the 2021 Goncourt Prize and was long-listed for the 2023 National Book Award.